Ashraf El-Ashmawi is an Egyptian author, judge, and legal scholar who is a regular contributor to newspapers and online publications, writing about crime prevention and social issues. The author of nine critically received novels in Arabic, in 2013 he was longlisted for the International Prize for Arabic Fiction (the Arabic "Booker") for his novel *Toya*, in 2014 he won best novel at the Cairo International Book Fair for *Barman*, and in 2019 he won best novel at the Bahrain Cultural Forum for *Sheepdogs*. His books have been translated into French, German, Japanese, Italian, among other languages. He lives in Cairo, Egypt.

Peter Daniel, a long-term resident of Egypt, has worked as a teacher of Arabic as a foreign language and an Arabic-to-English translator for many years.

T0346359

The Lady of Zamalek

Ashraf El-Ashmawi

Translated by
Peter Daniel

hoopoe
AN IMPRINT OF AUC PRESS

First published in 2021 by
Hoopoe
113 Sharia Kasr el Aini, Cairo, Egypt
One Rockefeller Plaza, 10th Floor, New York, NY 10020
www.hoopoefiction.com

Hoopoe is an imprint of The American University in Cairo Press
www.aucpress.com

ISBN 978 1 649 03076 4

Library of Congress Cataloging-in-Publication Data

Names: 'Ashmāwī, Ashraf author. | Daniel, Peter, (Translator) translator
Title: The Lady of Zamalek / Ashraf El-Ashmawi ; translated by Peter
    Daniel
Other titles: Sayyidat al-Zamālik. English
Identifiers: LCCN 2020043844 (print) | LCCN 2020043845 (ebook) | ISBN
    9781649030764 (paperback) | ISBN 9781649030788 (adobe pdf) | ISBN
    9781649030771 (epub)
Subjects: LCSH: Cicurel, Solomon, 1881-1927--Fiction. |
    Murder--Egypt--Cairo--Fiction. | Burglars--Egypt--Cairo--Fiction. |
    Egypt--Politics and government--20th century--Fiction. | Historical
    fiction gsafd | GSAFD: Mystery fiction. | Biographical fiction
Classification: LCC PJ7914.S475 S2913 2021 (print) | LCC PJ7914.S475
    (ebook) | DDC 892.7/37--dc23

1 2 3 4 5   25 24 23 22 21

Designed by Adam el-Sehemy
Printed in the United Kingdom

1

"WHY DID LOVE COURSE THROUGH my veins and restore me to life only to stab me in the heart?"—Nadia

I tiptoed toward the basement, looking behind me for the third time to make sure everyone was asleep, especially that new servant with her prying eyes. I crept down the wooden stairs, eased the key into the lock, opened the door, and slipped inside. I inched my way forward in near darkness to avoid colliding into the junk and bric-a-brac piled here and there with no rhyme or reason. I'd bruised my legs quite a bit down here when I was a child. I passed wooden crates labeled in various European languages. The letters had faded and altered in shape over time. There were building tools, garden implements, cans of paint as old as the place itself, and metal frames and wooden posts of strange shapes and sizes. I spotted an old brass trumpet with corroded buttons and a rust-covered Belgian bicycle that had once been white. Its front wheel had gone missing—heaven knows where—so the bike leaned forward, propped on its front fork, mourning its loss. I nearly bumped into the ancient gilded bed. As always, I stopped to stare at it in awe. It was over three yards wide and pitched slightly to one side since it had only three of its original legs. A stout column of bricks stood in for the fourth. I smiled and felt my face flush with embarrassment when I recalled how he'd tried to coax me to that bed yesterday. Hundreds of old medicine containers were stacked near the wall and covered in a layer of dust thick enough to warp their shapes. I stroked my father's antique wooden desk on which were stacked thick files and folders, with the contents spilling out of some, all covered with dust. I could make out some yellowed envelopes bearing the emblem of a green palm tree and the name Solomon Cicurel in an ornate script. My father had discarded countless other objects down here over the years with no care for order. They seemed poised to ambush all who strayed into this treacherous landscape and force them to retrace their steps.

I whispered his name once, then once again, peering anxiously into the darkness. He blinked his tiny flashlight on and off to help me locate him. He had changed his hiding place. He looked rather haggard this morning and some blood had seeped through the bandaging I had affixed over his wound. He'd probably gotten out of bed and moved around in the middle of the night in order to alleviate his boredom.

He seemed different today. He still had the mischievous gleam in his eyes that I'd noticed the night I hid him down here. He was as attractive and beguiling as ever. His urges radiated from him. Taking care not to move too much, he made slight feints with his torso, thrust his head forward to steal a kiss, flung out an arm to reach for my waist. I deftly parried his movements, trying not to laugh at the contortions of his face, which at one moment spoke of spasms of pain from the wound, and at another of a deep yearning that bedeviled his mind and fired his lust. Yet something in his eyes seemed lost and confused, as though tormented by thoughts that had kept him awake all night.

He grabbed hold of my arm and yanked me toward that expansive bed. Something in his eyes made me resist. They weren't looking at me, but through me to the need that had preceded us to the mattress and held out its arms to both of us. When I wrenched my arm free, my hand struck his wound. I quickly gathered my wits and cast about for the items to stanch the bleeding. He was strangely resistant to my attempt to treat him. He reproached me for reopening his wound, as though I had done it on purpose, and he backed away as though I meant to hurt him again. I persisted, smiling to reassure him as I drew closer. At last he yielded, reluctantly, when he realized he had backed up into a wall. He remained still for a few minutes, a cunning smile playing on his lips, while I tended to the injury. Fortunately, the flesh had begun to pull together over the past few days. He didn't make it easy for me to concentrate. I had to jerk my head away a couple of times when his lips made stabs toward my cheek. At last they managed to hit their mark and plant a kiss while I was busy fixing the bandage in place on his shoulder. I pretended to be on guard in case he tried again, though I had no intention of evading him if he did. In fact, I hoped my perfume and my proximity would entice him. I longed to melt into his embrace as I had done when we were much younger. His warm, panting breaths brushed my cheeks and whispered his manly arousal. My heart pounded and my body trembled. Both were ready to receive him warmly and passionately as I dipped my cup into the well of the distant past and tasted its still-fresh waters.

Yet he had changed, though I couldn't put my finger on how exactly. I sensed that he was feigning something. Perhaps his feelings for me had died, and instinct alone was driving him. I tried to push that dismal thought from my mind. Or maybe he had an open wound in his heart like the wound from the bullet that had almost killed him. He came here that night, several days ago, panting, blood oozing from his shoulder, whispering my name as though in harmony with an exquisite melody, laying his life on the altar of his first love, and certainly his last. I was intoxicated by his arrival. Yes, his mere appearance at my door moved me in a way I could never have anticipated. There was no need for him to say more after he told me he still loved me. It was sufficient that he chose me again over all others. I was the only woman in this world

3

whom he trusted enough to place his life in her hands. I was the roots from which sprouted the blossoms of his love. He returned to me. It was my love that made him live, my feelings that made him breathe.

I stared with yearning at his lips and sighed. A faint tremor passed through my lips and coursed slowly through my body, nudging it toward his broad chest. I stepped closer. We closed our eyes as though succumbing to a delicious stupor induced by a heady wine. Our rapid breathing betrayed our burning passion. Moving simultaneously, we thrust out our arms to clasp each other and locked in a secret vow of eternal love. Suddenly we heard a knocking, faint but harsh and rhythmic, like military footsteps. The sound wrenched me from my euphoria and rendered our kiss forever incomplete.

I listened more intently. I heard a cane rapping on the floor and approaching from afar. I held my breath until my ribs ached. The chill of fear set my limbs on edge. The knocking persisted, but it slowed as it approached the door, which was at the opposite end of the basement from where we stood. A few beads of sweat formed between the strands of my hair. I felt them roll in quick succession down my forehead, as though on a reconnaissance mission to let others know it was safe to follow as the heat soared in my head, which was about to explode. I exchanged a quick glance with him, to reassure him. To my amazement, he already seemed assured—too much so. I signaled him to remain silent, to stop breathing if he could. Then I turned my attention back to the rapping cane.

2

"I WAS SHACKLED BY MY ambitions, like a statue in the middle of a deserted square with the sun drumming on its head every morning."—Abbas Mahalawi

The boat lurched and pitched, and I awoke. One of the other kids must have gone ashore. I looked at the space between the five remaining boys to figure out who had skipped off at this early hour. I turned toward the wharf. There was no one on it as far as I could see. A few fishermen on some boats were preparing to set sail. It was six in the morning and still dark, despite some streaks of light. The cold stung my cheeks. I wrapped myself in my blanket and tried to go back to sleep. I tried for three hours and failed. With a long yawn, I got up from my sleeping spot in the hull and stretched my limbs. Then I leaned over the side and splashed some seawater in my face. That perked me up. Grabbing my wooden vendor's case, I hopped ashore and hurried into the streets around the Dekheila port. I paused at a long row of King Fuad posters someone had hastily pasted across the walls in the middle of the night. Someone else must have followed to slap on crude stripes of black paint to blot out the eyes. Smirking, I continued on my way. I went from coffeehouse to coffeehouse to sell cigarettes, but mostly to hunt for a new job. I was hoping to come across Fuad Iskandrani, a frequent subject of gossip, but rarely seen.

Some months before coming to Alexandria, I'd managed to graduate from secondary school in my native village in the Tanta governorate. Since my grades weren't good enough to get into university, I decided to come here with my elder uncle and enroll in Don Bosco, a vocational training school run by Italians. That was another experience I didn't like to recall, which hadn't stopped it from forcing itself on my memory from time to time. I skipped school so often I was expelled after my first year. Still, I'd learned a smattering of French and a lot of Italian, which I picked up easily. I didn't tell my uncle that I had been expelled for fear he'd cut off my allowance or, worse, send me back to the village.

Don Bosco was a boarding school. So, once a month, I'd drop by my uncle's place to let him know I was still alive and pick up my allowance. He lived in the Manshiya neighborhood, not far from the Dekheila port, though I let him continue to think that I was still at school, which was in another part of town altogether, and slogging away at my studies. But school bored me to death, while skipping classes and peddling cigarettes was a good way to look for a lucrative job to compensate for my academic failure.

I'd heard about Fuad Iskandrani so often that I felt drawn to him. I'd been doing the rounds of the coffeehouses and bars near the port for over a month, and at last I found him in one of them. He was in a dapper white suit, with a white hat and white shoes to match. He was playing odds or evens with an itinerant pistachio vendor and winning round after round. He'd reach his large hand into the vendor's box, scoop out a fistful of nuts, and toss them onto his table, shouting something to encourage Lady Luck. Everyone's attention was riveted on him. Each time he bet that the nuts would come out odds and each time he won his bet. Yet, in the end, he tipped the pistachio vendor a whole pound note. I gasped louder than the vendor.

When Iskandrani turned toward me, I instantly felt a magnetic pull. His eyes fixed on me and, from time to time, the corners of his mouth curved up in a brief flicker of a smile. Catching what I believed was a wink with his left eye, I smiled back. When he invited me to his table, I accepted willingly. I spoke to him about myself and my ambition to find a job where I could make lots of money. He appraised me with an avid stare and gave my leg an affectionate pat. I started work with him that very day.

As I had told him that I had no home and slept on an old boat in Dekheila, he promised me accommodation. He took me to a large house in the middle of some fields and immediately led me to the backyard and dozens of ditches dug randomly here and there. They were the length of an adult male, wide enough for two people to lie side by side comfortably, and cushioned with a bedding of sand and dirt. Flabby naked women as old as my mother lay in those pits on old sheets that had turned gray and had dark stains in the middle. The women covered their private parts with scraps of old rags as they waited for their next customer: the second-class sort who was always in a hurry, or sex-starved students. This is where I had my first assignment in the Iskandrani establishment.

Of course, I realized immediately that this was a *kerhane*, the type of bordello where women service one john after the other, where half-men in striped *gallabiya*s furtively slip in and out, where lights in the halls and rooms are dim, where even a blind man can tell where he is by the way the women speak and laugh. As I would soon learn, the younger whores were quartered inside the house, into which only the more "respectable" clients were admitted. There were maybe ten rooms for them. But my job was to take care of the pits, and my duties were straightforward.

Once the women's shift ended, they'd climb out using a short wooden ladder, hair matted with dirt, body drained of strength after servicing sometimes up to five johns an hour. They assembled in a ragged line in order to receive from me two bunches of green onions, a piece of cheese, and three pieces of bread. I was the rations manager. I jotted down everything I dispensed to them in a large ledger.

I was given boarding on the same premises, which was located among some farms in the Mandara Qibliya district, on the outskirts of the city. Seven of us slept in a single room that was separate from the main house. A look in the eyes of one my roommates made me sleep with my backside facing the wall.

We weren't allowed to live in Alexandria proper, or even to roam the streets there. A police officer only had to take one look our ID cards to know that we were Fuad Iskandrani's pimps and panders, and send us packing, after some gruff questioning about what business we had in town. Fuad had insisted on getting me an ID card that stated my occupation. I tried to wriggle out of it, but to no avail. When he handed it to me, he deliberately raised his voice for all the officers in the Laban police station to hear: "This is so people will see you're one of Iskandrani's men and you'll get respect."

I didn't like my job with Iskandrani. But I couldn't say I hated it either. I was promoted quickly: from rations officer to procurer in only a few weeks. He gave me a big tip that soon doubled for every girl I brought him. After two months in his employ, "Uncle Fuad," as we called him, summoned me to his office. I was nervous and baffled as I made my way upstairs. The only reason he ever summoned a staff member was to give him a dressing down. I found him on the terrace, where he liked to spend the late afternoon, smoking a water pipe and going over the accounts with the whorehouse madam. Suddenly the noise of an angry scuffle wafted up from below. Iskandrani grinned. He stood up, leaned over the railing, and watched his staff teaching a lesson to a pimp who, as I would learn, had threatened to strike out on his own. I peered down from behind Uncle Fuad's back. The men were punching and kicking the life out of the kid. Before long, he toppled into one of the pits in the backyard. After casting a last look down on him, bleeding, groaning, and half unconscious, they pulled up the wooden ladder and started to shovel dirt onto him. My insides froze, but I managed to keep my face under control.

Fuad returned to his seat, took a puff from his water pipe, and blew the smoke in my face. "That punk thought he was going to get away with setting up a business of his own. The ingrate! After we trained him, honed his skills, and turned him into the best pander in the whole of Alexandria!"

He took a puff from his pipe, then asked, "So, tell me, what do you like most about women?" He leaned forward to study my reactions. I answered in a word or two. He leaned back in his chair and told me to convince him about the charms of one of the girls at the *kerhane*. He chose the skinniest and least attractive of them all. After I gave him an explicit description, he turned to the madam and said, "That kid's going to be our new pander, starting tomorrow. What good are the girls he brings us if they don't have customers!"

My new assignment was to work the bars, coffeehouses, and streets to lure clients to the bordello. A piece of cake compared to procuring. Men are child's play when you play on their lust, whereas it takes time to breach the ramparts of a woman's mind to convince her to spread her legs for money. My job relied primarily on my powers of persuasion and imagination. I'd concoct a story about a raunchy night I had with a bevy of sexy dames, adding plenty of juicy details about their velvety thighs as white as marble, breasts like pomegranates, and luscious backsides the likes of which were hard to find in any other brothel. I was quite successful. But despite how often Fuad and his men said they appreciated my work, I couldn't shake my fear of them. There was always someone watching me and trailing me. It was enough to make even the shadow of a daydream of escape to take flight.

They were as merciless with the girls as they were with my mutinous predecessor. Some of them had been abducted and forced into prostitution. Others were beaten frequently for refusing to service certain clientele. The more defiant they were, the greater the risk of having their faces slashed with a jackknife or marred with nitric acid.

One form of punishment was one of Uncle Fuad's occasional sources of entertainment. He'd turn the backyard into a kind of wrestling ring. When he gave the signal, a group of the girls would close in on a wayward girl, blocking all avenues of escape. Then they'd shove her into one of the pits and keep her pinned down until the madam arrived. After climbing down into the pit, the madam would tear off the girl's panties and apply chili pepper to her " bread and butter," as the girls here called it. Fuad roared with laughter as he watched from his terrace above. His laughs were drowned out by the screams of the girl writhing and clawing at the walls of the pit like a slaughtered duck. She'd repent for good after that.

Salvation came at last following Fuad Iskandrani's arrest for inflicting bodily injury on some of the girls, one of whom he'd blinded. As one girl after another plucked up the courage to report him to the police, the affair blew up into a sensational scandal. He was tried and sentenced to five years in prison, of which he could endure only one. He died a year later. Afterward, we learned from his prison mates that he was a homosexual. That would probably explain his instant admiration for me and the eyes he had always given me, though he'd never made advances. Afterward, I tried to guess which of the men he did it with, but never could figure it out. They were all real men—though I did have my doubts about that one who looked at me in a way the others didn't.

Following Iskandrani's arrest, the police searched his house and confiscated bags of money in bills and coins. In the storeroom, they found tons of green onions, dozens of wheels of old cheese, and, to my surprise, sacks full of coarse salt. They destroyed the food we fed the girls year in, year out. The girls themselves never grumbled or griped, even though their health was always ailing due to the poor diet and lack of hygiene, and they would often die after only a few years of service. But then, Fuad could replace them easily thanks to his procurers, such as I had been at one point.

My first plan of action was to marry the madam so I could inherit Fuad's position, and his land and assets. I came within an inch or two of winning her heart and soul. But suddenly she pushed me away. I plotted theft, but she surrounded herself with more thugs. Eventually, as the police harassment and raids increased, especially after they discovered his hidden fortune, I abandoned all plans to acquire that establishment.

The madam, who now ran the place alone, was more generous with the food and pay, if only to keep the police from accusing us of maltreating the prostitutes. But she didn't have Uncle Fuad's business acumen and his strictness. So, what with the confiscations and dwindling revenues, she was soon forced to let in "street trade": your ordinary freelance pimp with a street girl and some johns in tow. Eventually, due to poor management and growing laxness, our girls stopped staying at the *kerhane*, and instead took up quarters with guys who'd rent them by the month. The madam had to summon the girls when clients turned up, and in some cases the girls refused to come.

The moment I'd been waiting for came two months later when the madam had to renew the girls' permits. All officially registered prostitutes had to have a physical checkup every three months at al-Hod al-Marsoud Hospital in Cairo. If not, they'd face a fine, which generally had to be paid by their pimp or madam mistress. We took them down by train, then proceeded in a long convoy of carriages flanked by police to protect us from hecklers and rowdies. As soon as our procession came to a halt near the hospital entrance, squads of thugs and toughs formed a protective ring around the walls. Once the physicals were over, each pimp resumed charge of his particular group of whores. Some of the poor girls, especially the older ones who were diagnosed with a disease, emerged from the ordeal wailing bitterly, both because of the maltreatment they'd experienced in the hospital and because of the loss of their livelihood.

While I was waiting with the other pimps for the girls to finish their physicals, angry shouting erupted nearby. A brawl was brewing between the pimps and gawkers. At first there were some stones and curses. Then some kids plucked up the nerve to rush forward, stick their tongues out, and put their fingers to their foreheads in the shape of horns. To our toughs, the old cuckold gesture was like red to a bull. They charged, the two sides clashed, the police moved in to break them apart, and I seized the opportunity of the distraction. "I'm just going to buy some cigarettes at the kiosk," I told the madam's boy servant, who acted as her vigilant eye outside the hospital wall. He'd been clinging to me like a shadow because I was carrying the money for the doctors' fees and travel expenses. The prostitutes' permits would be issued to me on the basis of a power of attorney the madam had given me so I could sign on her behalf.

As soon as I slipped around the corner, I broke into a run, bounded across an empty lot to the main street, and flagged down a hansom cab to the central train station. I found the train bound for Tanta and hopped aboard. I was going back to my village. As I stood near the door, panting, I counted my winnings. Thirty pounds plus a handful of silver riyals—not bad after three years of pimping. I could now purchase a cabriolet and an English horse to drive it, a dozen new Italian shirts, three woolen suits, and two pairs of lace-up shoes from the Sednaouis department store, and I'd still have ten pounds left over. No . . . no need to squander. I could spend a little, put aside two-thirds of the money, and still live in comfort for the next year without having to lift a finger.

The whistle screeched, the iron wheels rumbled on the tracks, and the train began to pick up speed. I looked behind to see the madam's boy, the tail of his *gallabiya* clenched between his teeth to free his legs, racing like the wind in order to hop on the last car. I grabbed a few of the silver coins from my pocket and aimed them at the boy's head. One of them hit the mark. He slowed down as his eyes widened at the coins rolling zig-zags around him and his ears eagerly picked up their metallic ring. My train moved farther and farther away, and the boy grew smaller and smaller as he bent over to collect the coins, until he shrank to a distant dot that soon vanished.

The night of "the incident" would change my entire life. In fact, I would say that it was then that I was really born. Not much was worth remembering beforehand. My present was fretful and unsettled. My past was a mess. When I rummaged through the attic of childhood memories to feed on, I saw only our cramped and stifling house. Exit from the back door and you walked through an animal pen to a field. Exit from the front door and you hit the main road. Since keeping it open exposed our private lives to passersby, my father ordered it closed during the day.

Images of my sisters when we were young flickered before me. The eldest was a year younger than me, and I was three and a half years older than youngest of the bunch. Through the haze of my memory, I saw them bustling around the house in my mother's wake, like her duck's ducklings. They felt woozy from the humidity, but they obeyed my mother's every order. Except for Zeinab, the youngest. She grumbled, but never stepped beyond that line.

We lived in a village called Fuadiya, on the fringes of the Mahalla Marhoum district, which was near Tanta, the capital of the Tanta governorate. There was nothing to distinguish it from other villages in the Delta: an odd mixture of farmers and effendis, huddles of houses, and endless fields that ran right up to the walls, encircled the buildings, and sometimes snuck between them in narrow snakelike strips.

As my memory moved forward to when I was a bit older, I recalled the one *gallabiya* to my name. It was an exact copy of my father's and I hated it. My socks were full of holes, the smallest large enough for my big toe to peek through. My shirt, which my mother had picked up at the used-clothes market next to Sayyid al-Badawi mosque in Tanta, had faded over the years. I still wore it and had to wait for it to dry after washing. My shoes had come apart at the soles from kicking pebbles as I walked. It was pointless for me to complain because I wouldn't get another pair for another two years. So decreed my father.

At the time of the incident, I was a few months short of twenty. That was according to my mother's reckoning. My ID card disagreed. My father disagreed with both. He called me a useless donkey, as always, and insisted I was the same age as his donkey Hasawi. We were born within a month of each other, putting me at just over twenty-five at the time of the incident, which was after I made my escape from him and before he absconded from Mahalla Marhoum. I'm speaking of my father here, not the donkey, fortunately. Hasawi was useful. People tended to believe my father about my age, because they thought me much older than I really was. That was probably because of my height, build, and fair complexion. My mustache also played a part.

Once, as a child, I asked my father why I was the only white-skinned child in the family. "Go ask your mother. Maybe a British soldier knocked her up," he snarled, reeling from drink.

When I repeated the question, he whacked me in the face, grabbed the closest thing in reach, and hurled it at me. I never asked again. In fact, I lost interest in the reason for my complexion and my true age.

The second time I boarded a train for Cairo, I was on my own and had no responsibilities. Before setting off, I borrowed two and a half pounds from my mother, promising to pay her back twofold. Some months previously, I'd seen her tuck away a tidy sum she'd earned from the sale of the yield of two small fields she owned and that my father farmed along with some other fields he had co-inherited with his brothers. That would be after he got out of jail. According to the village gossip, my father was a thief. My mother swore that he was arrested and jailed by the British for taking part in the protests in support of Saad Zaghloul and national independence. I never believed her version.

It was my parents' daily squabbling after my father took a dancer as a second wife that drove me to escape the village and settle in Cairo. The city "ate me alive," as they say. It crushed my bones between the jaws of poverty and alienation. But at last I found a respectable job in the Naguib Rihani theater. I was just an extra with a single line of dialogue in the last act. The pay wasn't bad. But I soon got bored with standing on the stage every day for more than an hour just to say, "We all lie, my dear," after which I turned my back to the audience, which never applauded for me.

I knew it wouldn't be easy to find another job. I decided to avoid the whorehouses in Wish al-Baraka and Darb Tayab, despite my expertise in that field. I was beginning to wonder if I'd inherited Fuad Iskandrani's complex. I started to imagine that all women were whores. I was wary of the way they darted their eyes at me from behind their yashmaks. I suspected that every veil concealed a brazen smirk, a clandestine encounter, an amorous adventure that, even if only for one passing occasion, ended in bed. I'd suddenly be taunted by that silly question: did my mother really sleep with a British soldier like my father said? I never dared ask him about my origin again, of course. But the tone of his voice and the way he scrutinized my face when he said it suggested that there was some truth in it, even though he was a habitual liar.

Time passed slowly during the daytime. After roaming the streets around Ataba until my feet gave out, I would head to the "Commerce Café" on Mohamed Ali Street, where I'd spend the rest of the day smoking a water pipe and people watching until it was time to go to the theater.

One day, I noticed a couple of men who'd been watching me from the moment I entered the coffeehouse. One of them came up to my table and politely introduced himself as the impresario for the Hasaballah music troupe. To my raised eyebrows he responded in the same calm and friendly tone: "Do you want to wear a music costume?" He whisked over a chair, sat down, and slid himself close enough for me to feel his breath. "There's a big demand for our troupe, and musicians are hard to come by these days. You look like a respectable gentleman. All you have to do is wear a musician's uniform and hold a trumpet. But don't blow into it! It's just for show, not for playing. So, what do you say?"

I contemplated him with a different kind of surprise now. What was this strange job he was offering me? I smiled to myself as I thought of the irony: I wanted to quit my nighttime job as an extra because it was so boring. Now the role was following me into daytime.

"Your pay is a shilling per night plus dinner."

"Agreed."

I quit the Rihani theater and joined the Hasaballah troupe. I lasted for eight performances. These included a circumcision celebration, a joyful bridal procession, and the wedding of a woman who had nearly missed the marriage train —she must have been almost thirty. Then there was a graduation party for an eldest son and a more sedate ceremony in honor of a senior government official who had been granted the rank of bey. My "musician's costume" resembled a British military uniform and was topped by large red beret. With my lips pressed to the mouthpiece and cheeks puffed out, I'd point the trumpet to the sky then lower it toward the ground while swaying rhythmically from side to side. When I took a brief rest, I'd distribute smiles evenly among all members of the audience.

Then came the funeral procession for a government dignitary. We marched solemnly down the main thoroughfare of Shubra, playing the mournful "Return" that military bands play at sunsets and funerals. The music was slow and monotonous. At one point I became so involved in my performance that I accidentally blew into the trumpet. The sound came out like a squawk but I liked it. So I repeated it. A couple of my fellow performers chuckled. I repeated it again. The chuckles multiplied and spread to some bystanders. Suddenly, one of the drummers gave several sharp raps on his tabla. Whether that was a declaration of solidarity or a warning remains a mystery, but a frenzy of madness swept through us like a sandstorm until every member of the troupe joined in the riot of noise. The deceased's family were furious. They accused the impresario of conning them. The impresario cursed us. The troupe members cursed back and exposed the scam of the fake musicians. Some women watching from nearby balconies pelted us with overripe tomatoes because of our disrespect for the dead. My uniform acquired quite a few dark red stains. Then a brawl erupted. I had no idea how it started or who was fighting who. All I remember is that I had to abandon half my uniform. I wriggled out of my jacket, leaving it in the grips of the kid who was tugging at it violently and stubbornly while his father tried to slap me. I fled in my undershirt, still holding my trumpet, which had saved my life when I used it to fend off my attackers.

A week later, I found another job at the Rixos bar. By that time, my savings had just about run out and I had to leave my small room at a boarding house because they jacked up the price by a whole piaster in one go. I'd been hired to replace a bouncer who had lost his eye in a bar brawl. My employers had seen promise in my physique. My duties were to restrain rowdy customers and discipline those who refused to pay their bills. I'm no fan of roughhousing. When it comes to getting rid of bothersome people, I've always preferred to make it quick and quiet.

My sense of self-preservation would convince me to change my line of work again after my first night. A flying bottle neck struck the right side of my face, leaving me with a permanent scar that spanned the upper and lower lids of my right eye. The doctors couldn't restore the flesh there to normal. Having narrowly escaped my predecessor's fate, I managed with some difficulty to persuade the club owner to hire me as a waiter on the night shift. It was part-time and the pay was poor, but I pinned my hopes on generous tips from the clientele. From then on, staff and regulars knew me as "One-Eyed Abbas," even though I could see perfectly well out of my right eye.

During the daytime, I continued the hunt for a better-paying job. I was also on the lookout for a small room to rent because I'd grown tired of sleeping at the bar. After the accident, they let me stay there out of pity and out of appreciation for my magnanimity. I'd told them I wouldn't file a complaint with the police out of consideration for the establishment's reputation. Of course, there was nothing charitable about my motive. I was afraid the police would discover I was an ex-pimp if I went to file a complaint.

The narrow space behind the bar became my sleeping quarters. It gave me a backache but it had an advantage: I could help myself to small amounts of money from the till every night. I'd cover myself by fiddling with the tabs before the bookkeeper reported to work in the morning. With this improvement in my financial circumstances, I stopped the search for another job.

After an uneventful month, fate decided to amuse me by throwing in my path a Greek called Ernesti and a Jewish lad about my age called Jonah. They met in the bar every night and were eventually joined by a third guy: a tan-complexioned, remarkably obese, and taciturn Egyptian who wore baggy trousers held up by wide, blazing-red suspenders. I could tell they were plotting something. They had such a furtive air as they huddled over a sheet of paper on which they were drawing something and making notes. I positioned myself closer for a better look. They were so absorbed in their work that they didn't notice me lurking nearby. By the time I brought them their third round of drinks, which I'd made extra stiff, they were speaking loudly enough for me to catch snatches of their conversation. Fortunately, much of what they said was in Italian, so I could follow them easily, aided by what I could make out on that piece of paper.

The obese Egyptian stopped coming after three nights. Ernesti and Jonah were then joined by two other men. One had ears as large as a soup ladles and was dressed like the informants at the Ezbekiya police station. The other could have been a peasant from my own village judging by his features and complexion. But neither of them spoke Arabic. I later learned that they were Italians from Naples who'd been living in Egypt for a long time.

I made the newcomers uneasy and they let me know it. Whenever I approached their table to remove empty glasses or to set down small dishes of appetizers, they shot me a glare that warned me to back off. Their eyes emitted evil sparks and their clenched fists were ready to strike in a flash. But they were too late. I had already heard enough to blackmail them all. From the snatches of conversation I'd overheard, I'd pieced together the whole script except for the finale.

Ernesti worked as a chauffeur for Solomon Cicurel, the owner of the famous Cicurel department store chain. One of the two Neapolitans worked as a butler and the other as a gardener twice a week at the Cicurel villa. The Jewish guy, according to our long-serving elderly barman, was none other than Jonah Dario, the notorious safecracker who had managed to dodge numerous prison sentences. He rarely showed up at the bar before midnight, and generally stayed until dawn.

From my eavesdropping, I had learned that the fat man was the ringleader and that the Greek chauffeur had once lived in the villa's basement. The plan was for the gardener to leave the main gate ajar. Then the butler would guide the thieves from the basement to the safe so they could pick it, strip it of its jewels, cash, and other valuables, and get out as fast as possible. When I told them what I had overheard, I asked for fifty pounds in exchange for my silence. They refused, because it was too large a sum. But they did not refuse to make me a partner, which put me in a predicament.

I'd learned that they had set the heist for a Friday night. Fridays were the doorman's day off, which he spent with his family, and he wouldn't return until Saturday afternoon. But the men put off the plan at the last moment. Either they were afraid I would give them away even if they paid me what I asked for or they decided I needed more testing. Evidently, the gardener and the butler, whose names I'd learned were Marco and Eduardo, had put a bug in Ernesti's and Dario's ears about me. I knew too much and had to be eliminated. Their suggested method was to tie me up, attach a heavy stone to my feet, and toss my body into the Nile. This I would learn from Ernesti one night after the others had left. He was in his cups and decided to allay my suspicions. He didn't; he heightened my alarm. I did all I could to reassure them, but no matter what I said or promised I could tell they didn't believe me. Maybe because I really did intend to betray them, or at least those nasty Neapolitans.

Meanwhile, the idea of joining was brewing in my brain. As it matured, I decided to go with it, consequences be damned. So, after a week of offering every pledge and reassurance I could think of, I found myself together with them at their table after all the other customers had left and dawn was approaching. Ernesti, the eldest, finally agreed to count me in after conceding to Jonah's argument that the best guarantee for my silence was to make me a primary accomplice. Eduardo and Marco grumbled their assent. Ernesti actually seemed like a decent guy. Or at least he didn't seem like an avaricious sort, even though he was the one who had come up with the scheme. I later learned that he felt death approaching because of a lung disease and that he'd been fired from his job some months ago for having regularly pilfered money from his employer. Now his greatest hope was to leave a sizeable fortune for his children to spare them from need after he was gone. Petty thievery is only good for making ends meet from one day to the next.

We agreed to meet half an hour after midnight the follow-ing day at a corner near the Cicurel villa in Zamalek. This was an elegant neighborhood that was quiet at all times of day and night. On the night of the incident there was no one in the street apart from us. I was the only one of us who had never seen the villa from the inside. Even the Jew, Dario, had visited it before as a friend of Ernesti's. I was awed by the stately vil-las and palaces, by the tranquility that enveloped the area in collaboration with the weave of foliage overhead, by the dense yet orderly hedges that lined the streets we passed through. We reached a massive wrought-iron gate. On the wall next to it was an elegant wooden plaque on which was inscribed in Arabic "The Heart of Palm" and in French "Villa Coeur de Palmier." I was seized with a longing to live there forever. It occurred to me to run off and report them, then enter into Cicurel's employ and replace them all. As it so happened, events that night took a turn that we had never anticipated despite all our planning.

3

"THE WORLD OF OPPORTUNITY IS like a wave: if you don't ride it, all you get is mouthful of sea salt."—Zeinab Mahalawi

Ever since I can remember, I've felt closer to my brother, Abbas, than to either of my sisters. He was the only one who'd stand up for me against the whacks from my father's heavy hand and my mother's tongue-lashings before she grabbed the thing closest to hand and hurled it at me. She hated my desire to learn to read and write. She hated it more when I stood for hours before our splintered mirror, singing and dancing like Aziza Amir in the first movie I saw with Abbas after his return from Alexandria. It was a silent film, but easy to follow. I could replay most of the scenes to myself. I can still feel the sting from the smack my father gave me when he caught me imitating Aziza's belly-dance moves!

Abbas wasn't spared my father's temper either. He called my brother a pansy when he found out that he'd had taken me to the movies with two of his friends. One of them had felt up my thigh in the dark, but I held my tongue for fear of Abbas and the scandal. My father spat other insults at him until, at one point, Abbas had enough. He curled his lips, muttered some angry remark, then threw up his hands and turned to leave. My father must have thought Abbas had sworn at him because he charged at my brother from behind. My father was a big man, and strong as an ox. He had no difficulty in pinning my brother's arms behind his back, hauling him outside, and tying him up to a pole in the pen. Then he snatched up an old piece of hose and whipped Abbas until his whole body was covered with welts and his face swelled up like a pumpkin. Abbas never uttered one word of apology.

My father left him tied up and without food for three days. He just set a pot of water at his feet large enough to fit his face into if he wanted to drink. My sisters were too cowardly to do anything, but I snuck out to the pen that night and fed Abbas some food. Then I used a moistened cloth to clean his face and ease the swelling. I spent the rest of the night by his side. I didn't untie him for fear I'd be tied up in his place if my father found out. Even so, my face wasn't spared the flat of my mother's hand the following morning after she got up for dawn prayers and didn't see me on my bedding. She didn't want to confront me outside, in front of Abbas, so she waited for me inside the back door, which leads out to the pen. I didn't have the slightest doubt that she watched me refill the pot for my brother and give him some more water to drink. She had such a soft spot for her only son. But she was too afraid of my father's tyranny to do it herself. As soon as I crossed the threshold, my mother pounced, thrashing me with her hands, spurred on by my father from behind, as though he was the one who'd unleashed her on me.

It was like bellows fanning the hellfire that had been burning in our house for years on end. I wrenched myself loose from my mother's grasp, dodged the long wooden cane with a pointed tip that my father was waving around like a crazy man, and started bolting here and there like a beheaded chicken until I stumbled over some earthenware bowls and bricks. I landed with my full weight on my foot, violently twisting my ankle. By dusk, my leg had puffed up like bread dough on its second proofing. The ointments applied by the village doctor didn't take the swelling down. The pain grew so agonizing that I couldn't visit Abbas for two days in a row. Afterward, I developed a limp that became as much a part of me as breathing because the doctor had set the bones wrong.

I took revenge against my mother by throttling two of her hens and a male duck. That would stop her beating me and making my life miserable, I thought. But her hatred for me only grew worse. I told her to her face that I was the one who'd slaughtered her birds. I screamed it while shielding myself behind Abbas. Having Abbas beside me made me feel stronger and helped me pluck up my courage, but there would come times when I felt that he was the weaker one.

The other village women called my mother "the mayoress." "Mayoress Hamida," they'd say, pulling their black head coverings over their mouths to smother their giggles. She sold fowls in front of our house. She'd set up some reed cages in which she displayed a few chickens, a couple of ducks, and maybe a goose squeezed in between, after binding their legs together to set them clucking and squawking loudly to attract customers. She never tired of haggling. "It's a wrangle on the outside, a happy medium the inside," she'd always say. She'd sell off the items on her makeshift stand in less than hour. Afterward, the neighbor women came over to chat, sometimes joined by a few customers who hung around to hear her advice. She had an amazing ability to solve most of the village women's problems. She taught them how to manage household expenses; how to save time, which fluctuates like sea waves; and how to stay seductive for their husbands to the oldest age possible. She'd perch herself on a reed bench, legs folded beneath her, while the other women gathered around her in a circle, fixing her with wide-eyed stares and craning their necks to catch her every word. Their narrow minds struggled to stretch around the mysteries she'd reveal and their hearts thrilled at the clever way she put things, even though she was illiterate. I'd inch closer, keeping my back to the oven wall in order to keep out of sight. The heat whipped against my cheeks but I paid it no mind as I cocked my ears to catch every word, especially when the conversation turned to the marital problems the village women came to her about. My mother always gave me what for when she caught me eavesdropping, which I thought was unfair, because she'd allow my sister Kawthar to stay.

We had this sweet young neighbor who kept coming to my mother to complain about her husband who'd lost interest in her despite her firm, plump body. I had to clasp my hand over my mouth to keep from laughing out loud as my mother spelled out instructions and secret recipes in vivid detail. Then one day, my mother grew fed up with having to repeat the same advice over and over, and snapped, "Put more salt in his food, dummy!" The woman looked at my mother with surprise. My mother, flashing a secret wink to the other women, explained, "If there's a lot of salt in his food, he'll get heartburn and he'll have to get up in the middle of the night to drink some water. That's when you turn over on your tummy and lift your nightie. Afterward, you'll sing my praises to the Lord!"

The other women hooted with laughter, but my mother kept a straight face. Still fixing her glare on our young neighbor, she picked up a half a length of sugarcane and used it to poke the woman's side as she began to dole out advice to the other women. I couldn't understand most of it. She'd smell their breath. Forbid them from eating onions after sundown. Inspect their legs and advise them to add rosewater when making the *halawa* wax, plus a squeeze of lemon. She'd tell them to remove their long undies at night and to keep a safe distance from their Coptic and Jewish neighbors, who were jinxes and brought the evil eye. She'd go on and on, hopping from this subject to that. But I'd have to sneak away before too long to avoid the cussing and smacks I'd get if she caught me.

I'd always wanted to marry a man who looked like Abbas, with his height, his broad chest, and his dress sense. He was always so dapper, like a gentleman: white shirt with sleeves rolled up to the middle of his muscular arms, dark trousers with pleats. The more I used Abbas as the model for the husband of my dreams, the more attached to him I grew and the more I wondered whether it would be better to remain single. I cried when my father agreed to send him off to Alexandria with my elder uncle, but Abbas was adamant about going. He studied carpentry at a school called Don Bosco—it took me months to get my tongue around that funny name. After graduating three years later, he came home and started work with one of my uncle's business partners who ran a workshop in Tanta. Abbas said the job was a breeze. He told us that he'd picked up a lot of Italian and a smattering of French at school. He'd prattle away in Italian in a way that made us double over with laughter even though we couldn't understand a word. My mother called him "the *khawaga*" because of his ability to speak that foreign tongue and because his complexion was so light he could have been European. But he was so impatient to get ahead that he grew rebellious. My mother begged him to remain patient and prayed he would own his own workshop one day. Then one day, he had a falling out with his boss. Not long afterward, the workshop burned to the ground with the boss inside.

My mother was devastated, mostly for Abbas, who'd lost his job. She offered to help him open a new workshop of his own, but he refused. He said he belonged in Cairo, far away from Mahalla Marhoum. He dreamed of being the richest man in Egypt. Sometimes he'd tell me about that dream: he'd build huge palaces on the seashore, he'd own a vast plantation with fields that stretched beyond the horizon, he'd own at least a hundred horses, and he'd have three carriages at his service day and night. I'd smile and tell him I hoped it all came true. But I knew it was all castles in the air.

Then one morning we awoke to find him gone. It turned out that my mother knew beforehand, but that didn't lighten my sorrow at losing my knight and champion. Some months later, he returned just as suddenly as he'd vanished, and that was in order to sweep me off on his steed and take me with him to Cairo, the "Mother of the World!"

I'd been dying to get out of that village. I was sick and tired of mother's prison bars and my father's whip. There was also the memory of an excruciating experience I wanted to put behind me as quickly as I could. It had to do with this friend of my brother who I'd let feel my body all over and to whom I nearly sacrificed my virginity. It was just that one time. We snuck off together into a field. I lay on the ground and let him lie on top of me. I'd heard my mother speak so often about what married people do, and the way she lowered her voice and filled it with innuendos gave me such a thrill that I just had to discover that mystery for myself. Of course, I didn't let the boy go all the way. I insisted he had to marry me first. I thought he loved me, but he disappeared afterward. There's this saying that goes, "If you want peace of mind, close the door that lets in the wind." But I was stupid. I left my door ajar, like my mother advised the married women in the village, and the wind nearly blew it off its hinges.

I was so overwhelmed as Abbas took me through the streets of Cairo that I just couldn't walk in a straight line. I kept stopping and spinning around. I was like one of those drunks in the bars that Abbas showed me. I had never imagined that the world had all these different kinds of people in it. And what strange clothes they wore! Then there were the cars, the buildings, and all those places people went just to relax and amuse themselves. Abbas took me to many of them, but I'll never forget the Café Égyptien in the heart of downtown Cairo. It was so elegant. It served wine to its clientele in broad daylight and nobody showed the slightest embarrassment. Later, after dinner, Sitt Badia Masabni came on the stage to present her dancing girls. I'd watch my brother's reactions with a mixture of concern and awe. He had an amazing ability to bolt down one drink after another. The veins in his forehead popped out, his face reddened, and sometimes his breathing grew heavier. He'd light one cigarette after another and inhale the smoke greedily. Usually after his second drink, he'd settle into a good mood and enjoy himself. The Café Égyptien was unique in that all its staff were beautiful slender women. Naturally, I tried to imitate them as soon as we got home: the way they walked, the way they set food and drink down on the table. Abbas smiled approvingly and encouraged me to go on. There was this foreign singer who Abbas admired. I couldn't understand a word of the lyrics, but Abbas loved her songs and the way she performed them. When the show was over, he'd toss a whole shilling into her black hat, which was big enough to hide a rabbit.

The greatest attraction, and what customers always waited for, was the arrival of the royal arms bearer in his wide wooden carriage. It was small and looked like the workmen had forgotten to add the final parts at the rear. It was driven by a single horse and the royal arms bearer stood holding its reins "like a British army commander," as Abbas put it.

"It's a cabriolet, Zeinab. Cab-ri-o-let," my brother told me, repeating it twice and splitting it up into syllables like he did whenever he wanted to teach me a new word and help me commit it to memory.

The arms bearer—a huge Circassian—always drove that wooden chariot himself. He'd come crashing into the room, roaring with laughter, a train of brawny attendants sprinting in his wake. Some were Italians who knew Abbas, and they'd stop to shake hands with him in a friendly way. But most were Moroccan or Sudanese slaves. Suddenly, the arms bearer would open his eyes wide, feigning total shock as though somehow he'd lost control of his horse. If the manager or any of the staff complained, his attendants lit into them until he told them to stop. The whole room would fall silent as he paid for the damages, turned to a large painting of King Fuad, and bowed as though apologizing to His Royal Highness. Then he'd leave with as much commotion as when he entered.

Abbas was like a train. He never stopped at stations long. He was far too methodical for me. Everything had to come at its own prearranged time. But he never felt he had to tell me what he had planned in his head. You'd think that if I were going to board a train I should know which way it was headed and where my next station was. But not with Abbas. He pushed me aboard, settled me into a seat reserved in advance, which was always next to the window, so I could see only one side of the road. Then he pulled down the blinds if he thought the light was too bright and might reveal something he didn't want me to see. He was the one who set our course, and my role was but to obey.

One day, Abbas introduced me to a Cairo I hadn't seen before: the terrace of the Shepheard's Hotel for tea every afternoon at five. Despite the pomp that gave the place an elegant veneer, I wasn't very taken by it. I preferred the casinos of Ezbekiya and the downtown cafés. The customers here were different. Even Abbas was different when he came here. He took on the airs of one of those upper-class beys and pashas you come across at Les Grands Magasins Cicurel. He chatted with the waitresses in French and smiled and nodded to other customers and exchanged pleasantries in French. This was not the same person I'd just been with in Ezbekiya, let alone in Mahalla Marhoum before that.

"Zeinab! Sit properly and don't slurp your tea."

I quickly brought my feet down to the floor. I had folded my legs beneath me in my plush leather chair as I stared into space picturing my mother back home in the village and wondering how she was making do. What a shock she must have had that day when she found both me and Abbas gone, and with no news from us since. Despite the way she treated me, I missed her.

I winced as I set my cup aside and shrank into my seat, feeling my face grow redder under his scowl. Then he scolded me for eavesdropping on the people at the next table. I couldn't help it. I burst into a loud laugh that turned everyone's heads in our direction. "If only! You think I can understand a word they say? While they're all blabbering away, I've been worrying about our mother back home in the village!"

Abbas was like a chameleon, changing to suit the place we went. And wherever we went, he tried to make me see the place through his eyes as much as possible so that it would stay embedded in my memory for as long as possible. One day he got it in mind to take me to the opera. This would be a new station for me on the Abbas train. It would be the first and last time I would visit that stop on this journey, which still seemed a long way from its destination. I felt I could barely breathe in that place that night. There were some fat women on the stage bawling ohs and ahs as they bowed in a slow and funny way in front of the men who wore embroidered women's gowns and did nothing but bellow back. After about a quarter of an hour of that, Abbas leaned toward my ear and whispered, "So, what do you think?"

I said exactly what I thought: "That fat lady's howling and squirming like she's got a bad case of colic!" I burst into a loud laugh.

Abbas didn't even crack a smile, though we were in a little balcony box by ourselves. His face had turned beet red and he clenched his jaw as though to steel himself against those glares that shot arrows at us from some seats below. A dignified and grave-looking man wearing white gloves approached from behind. He leaned politely toward Abbas's ear and whispered a few brief words. We left immediately, escorted by the same angry glares. I still couldn't control my laughter.

The whole way home I couldn't manage to pry a word out of Abbas. But the moment we entered the apartment, he pointed to a large suitcase and snarled, "Pack your things. You're going back to Mahalla Marhoum in the morning."

4

"FOOLS GAMBLE WITH THINGS THEY don't own, even though the first thing they'll lose is their life."—Abbas Mahalawi

The gardener had left the gate ajar as planned. We entered one after the other like house cats familiar with their home. Then we sped through the garden like ghosts. Ernesti pulled some large socks out of his bag and signaled for us to slip them over our shoes to silence our footsteps. Eduardo, the Italian butler, assured us that he had drugged the large guard dogs, as well as Cicurel and his wife. He had slipped a barbiturate into the dinner he had served them and had seen them eat it. They'd be sleeping like the dead now and wouldn't awake before noon, he said. After dinner, when he took his leave, he'd made as though heading out the front gate. Then he ducked into the little hut where they kept the guard dogs and waited for us. Ernesti bent down to pick up a small key hidden under a doormat in front of the back door to the basement and opened the door. We slipped inside and scurried through a corridor leading to another door. On the other side, we crept up a flight of stairs and entered the villa proper.

I found myself in a reception room as vast as Cairo central train station. The ceiling soared at least eight yards above our heads. From it hung a chandelier the size of a camel. The soft gleam of polished surfaces and contrasting shades of plush upholstery created a splendid harmony. The old walls were completely covered with large paintings— so many that I could barely make out the color of the walls behind them. Everywhere you turned there were dozens of bronzes, gilded antiques, and items of pottery in subtle bluish glazes. There were oriental rugs of all sizes, the smallest large enough to carpet our entire house in Mahalla Marhoum with enough left over for the animal pen. Yet, despite all this luxury, the place felt gloomy. Almost like a graveyard. Thin cracks zigzagged up and down the columns like field snakes.

I was the only one turning around in circles and gaping at the ceiling. The others were focused on our destination: the safe in the master bedroom. Why it occurred to me right then and there to ask about that obese man with the red suspenders whom I'd seen with them in the nightclub is beyond me. Maybe I'd imagined he'd meet us there or that it was he who had left the key under the doormat. Whatever the case, they were taken aback by my question and exchanged nervous glances.

"Did you know him before that?" Ernesti asked.

"No. No, of course not," I stammered.

Ernesti grabbed my shirt, flashed a blade, and pushed his face into mine. "He was going to do the dirty on us, so we did what we had to do."

The way he spat out those words made my blood run cold. He released his grip, keeping his suspicious eyes glued on mine. Then he turned and followed the others to Cicurel's bedroom, where the Jewish safecracker had begun to work on the lock, using an implement shaped like a car crank. I heard Ernesti's hacking cough. Soon afterward, I heard a muffled cry for help, then some scuffling. An agitated man began to shout in a language I knew very well from my days at Don Bosco. He cursed and threatened. Soon he started to plead and beg. Then came a bloodcurdling cry, a soft thump, and silence.

I was still outside the bedroom. I'd been hoping to pocket something light, but the antiques were all too bulky and heavy.

I rushed into the room and saw an elderly man in light blue silk pajamas lying on his back on the floor. A dark stream of blood flowed from a slash in his neck and had drenched his chest. He'd been stabbed several times. Blood was gushing out of wounds in his side and belly. His eyes bulged in abject terror, as though frozen on that final vision of the knife that had slaughtered him.

The men stood in a half circle looking down at Cicurel's corpse with stunned stares. He was of sturdy build despite his age. The knife lay nearby on the floor, seemingly ownerless, covered with the old man's blood. Jonah stood stock still, holding that large crank-like instrument. Cicurel's wife was still sound asleep. Her beautiful, delicate face was serene, absorbed in a dream far away from this bloody scene. Yet, for a moment there, I thought I saw her move.

As to which of them killed the old man, I puzzled over this as I observed them from my place near the door. But there was no time to linger. Ernesti ordered me to be quick and collect as many items as I could carry from the safe, including papers. As I set to work, he and the safecracker began to bicker. From their mutual reproaches, I gathered that Jonah had used too much force while cracking the safe. Since Cicurel had been drugged, he hadn't felt the need to be quiet. According to Ernesti, it was the noise of the lock breaking that woke Cicurel up. Maybe the old man hadn't eaten enough of the drug-laced food or he had fed it to his wife. Dario refused to take the blame. He shot back that it was the Greek driver's fault because of that asthmatic coughing fit that echoed through to the farthest corner of the villa. Whatever the cause, Cicurel had slept lightly enough to wake to his worst imaginable nightmare and die at the hands of some of the closest people around him.

Eduardo and Marco were busy grabbing whatever they laid their eyes on. They worked so quickly and recklessly that jewels and coins slipped through their fingers, as though they were scooping water from the sea.

We stripped the safe of its contents. It was large, but not as large as we'd expected. Some of the shelves were empty. Others held documents or stacks of bills that looked like thousands but turned out to be several hundreds. There were some items of jewelry that belonged to the dead man's wife. I managed to help myself to some items without the others seeing: a small ring with a blue stone set in diamonds and a small bundle of ten-pound bills. Below those lay a white envelope with a green palm tree embossed on its upper right corner. The envelope bulged with what I thought must be more cash. All these items I concealed in my ample pockets and inside my shirt while the others were fretting over what to do with Cicurel's body. Eventually they decided to lay it out on his enormous gilded bed. Then we hightailed it out of there, with Ernesti pausing only to place the key under the doormat where he'd found it.

Zamalek was as tranquil as when we had arrived. Its residents were still asleep, unaware of what had just befallen their famous neighbor and oblivious to the five phantoms that streaked out of that wealthy neighborhood, weaving this way and that between the dense trees and shrubbery, making rustling sounds like bats stirred from their nests.

The others wanted to meet at the bar the following day at midnight so we could divvy up the spoils away from prying eyes. I objected. I told them I planned to quit the bar job and leave Cairo until things cooled down, so I wanted my share right away. They refused. After huddling for a whispered conversation, they decided we should meet up somewhere safer. They chose Dario's apartment in Shubra and gave me the address and phone number. Then they scurried off, each in a separate direction. It took me half an hour to flag down a passing taxi on Zamalek's main street at that early hour. I told the driver to take me to the train station.

I spent several hours in the station cafeteria musing on the fortune concealed in the folds of my clothes. I pulled out the white envelope. Instead of money, it contained some papers. A quick flick through them had me immediately intrigued. I must have read them at least three times with growing astonishment. Then I smiled, and that smile expanded until I almost laughed out loud at those useless partners of mine. How stupid they all were! Right now they were probably plotting how to kill me the following night. I felt the gall rise in my throat and spat on the floor next to the table. I signaled the waiter and ordered a cup of strong tea and lit a cigarette. I pictured the body of the Jewish business magnate and the blood-drenched bed where they laid his body. Then I homed in on the smooth, ivory face of his wife and pictured how it would contort in horror when she awoke to find her husband lying next to her in that state. I shook my head to dispel that tragic image and began to order my thoughts and make my calculations.

I took the first train to Tanta at seven a.m. But a couple of minutes before that I phoned the police from a public phone booth. I told them about the murder, supplied some details, and gave them Jonah Dario's address in Shubra and his phone number. I took the occasion to remind them he was the famous safecracker, wanted by the police for years. Then I slammed down the receiver. I was dripping with sweat from the fear that the officer would insist I identify myself.

I ran to the platform, hopped aboard the train, and began another trip back to Mahalla Marhoum. I watched the large factory at the edge of town give way to palm trees and fields. I yawned, closed my eyes, and settled back in my seat for a short nap, but not before folding my arms tightly over my belly in order to guard my newly discovered source of wealth which, as of that day, was waiting just for me.

Life had changed back home in the village. As soon as I stepped through the door, I learned that my father had absconded with his second wife, the dancer. He followed her to the *mulid*s, weddings, and celebrations she performed at in neighboring villages. Then they vanished altogether. Some months later, the village mayor informed us that they had set-tled somewhere in the Buheira district but we never were able to find them. I bought five small plots of land from different farmers in the area—about a quarter of an acre in all. Then I built a large house next to our old one, and which I turned over to our animals though, sadly, poor Hasawi, my father's old donkey, had died.

Every morning I would take a trip to the main town nearby in order to buy the newspapers. I mostly followed *al-Lataif*'s reports because that newspaper covered the case more thor-oughly and it published larger pictures of the accomplices. I learned all their full names for the first time. Ernesti turned out to be Anesthi Christo and the two Neapolitans who had wanted to dispose of me in the Nile were Eduardo Grimaldi and Marco Dagaro. I felt that their biographies, as related in the crime pages, couldn't possibly be true. The reports cer-tainly exaggerated the amount of stolen goods. They said that the stolen jewelry alone was worth six thousand Egyptian pounds! My tiny share was carefully hidden at the bottom of the long chest I used as the base for my mattress at home, and which was secured by a large lock. *Al-Ahram* related the shock and horror of Cicurel's neighbors in that tranquil western neighborhood of Zamalek. The newspaper also lauded the efforts of the police, who were able to apprehend the crimi-nals less than twenty-four hours after the incident, and while they were still in possession of the stolen goods.

One paragraph made my blood freeze. It spoke of a fifth suspect called "One-Eyed Abbas," who was still at large. I couldn't sleep for days. I frantically followed the news of the police's efforts to apprehend that "culprit," whom the four sus-pects claimed had committed the theft and murder all on his own. They protested their innocence. All they did was to buy stolen goods from him when he sought them out in Shubra.

At last, after a fretful week, I could relax again and chuckle at their naivety. When police failed to track down "One-Eyed

Abbas," they marched the four of them into the defendants' dock. They had grasped at a straw to save themselves from the hangman's noose, which had been dangling before them like a pendulum ticking off the final moments of their lives, and it had slipped through their fingers. I roared with laughter as I folded the newspaper, lit a corner with a match, and watched the flame grow and spread until it consumed their photos.

Their trial passed quickly in a large courtroom in the National Criminal Court in Bab al-Khalq. There would never be a fifth defendant, not even in absentia. I became the "anonymous other," as the public prosecutor referred to me, since the police were never able to identify me. I did find it strange that the defendants never revealed the existence of their sixth accomplice, the obese Egyptian with red suspenders. It would have been pointless in any case. The beautiful, delicately featured widow surprised everyone in the courtroom: she had been awake all the time, just as I had suspected for a second. She testified that, in fact, there were five intruders. She had identified the four defendants after their arrest. The police put them not just in one, but in three lineups with dozens of similar-looking people and had them change their clothes each time. Each time, she singled them out with ease. You might have thought that she had personally interviewed them for the heist. What came as an even greater surprise was that Cicurel had a daughter called Nadia. All the while, that night, she'd been sleeping in a room in the western wing, on the other side of the villa. I'd had no idea she even existed. She hadn't dined with her parents that night so she hadn't had a bit of the drugged food. Yet she never awoke despite all the commotion. I scoured the newspapers to learn more about her, but to no avail.

According to the news reports, the Jew, Jonah Dario, who had dual Egyptian and Italian nationality, was one of the two men who had stabbed Solomon Cicurel. He stabbed him first with a knife and then with the pointed end of that crank-like drill. Ernesti (or "Anesthi") the Greek had finished him off.

I kept two clippings with photos of the villa from the out-side, one taken from the street corner where it was located in Zamalek, next to the Nile. I folded them and tucked them into my wallet as souvenirs.

Six months later I came across a news item that reported that the defendants had been executed after the court of cas-sation had rejected their appeal. That was the day I decided to take my sister Zeinab back with me to Cairo. She was the one person who could bring me within reach of Solomon Cicurel's real fortune. We had been nowhere near it that night. There were also his stores, his villa, his cars, his cash . . . and maybe even his wife.

Zeinab was the youngest of my three sisters. She was the only one who hadn't married yet, even though, at the time, she was a year above marriage age in our village. Tongues had begun to wag about her husbandless state, which worried and pained my mother, and added to the troubles she'd had since my father ran off. Zeinab's marital prospects weren't great. Some might even have put them at zero, even though she had a nice "rinsed-out brown" complexion, as they say in our vil-lage, and was short and on the plump side, with ample thighs and full breasts. Yet there wasn't a trace of beauty in her face, with its wide pug nose. But God did not leave that head with-out strengths. He blessed it with a sharp, intuitive mind that constantly amazed everyone, not least of all me. She was bold and resourceful. On the downside, she was too tenacious—she would never give up until she got what she felt was her due. Still, she'd been putty in my hands ever since she was a child.

After graduating from the local *kuttab* and then elemen-tary school, she begged our mother to persuade our father to enroll her in the Sultan Hussein preparatory school, which was near the village. My mother whacked her in the face, pelted her with curses, and snatched up a piece of dough she'd been kneading and flung it at her head. Then she collapsed in her chair and started to wail and slap at her own face as though she were at a funeral. That was when she decided she had to get Zeinab married off as soon as possible—"Even if the mayor's mule or the neighbor's donkey asks for her hand!" as she once said in a fit of rage. She was afraid Zeinab's morals would go to the dogs if she continued with her schooling.

Being the only other person in the family who knew how to read and write, Zeinab was the only one who never swallowed my story about how I worked as a porter at the port in Alexandria and raked in a fortune selling smuggled goods to the British after the war. She tried to work out how I came into my sudden fortune, but her imagination at the time could take her no further than that I must have married some rich old dame who died on our wedding night, making me her heir. Once, she actually summoned the courage to test that theory of hers. I gave her an enigmatic smile and an answer that neither affirmed nor denied her question, leaving her scratching her head more than before.

I'll never forget her reaction when I asked her to come to Cairo with me. Her eyes glistened with pent-up tears that she couldn't keep from trickling down her cheeks. She flung her arms around me and hugged me as though I'd just returned from an expedition to a far-off land. The following day she started to waver. I could tell because she didn't pester me for details about when we'd leave and how. She was desperate to break free of her mother, her sisters, and the whole of Mahalla Marhoum; she was like the eternal prisoner waiting for a miracle then when the opportunity to escape comes he needs someone to carry him. Fear had shackled her for so long, even though life at home was better since our father had absconded and I'd made us landowners. too!

It took me three nights to sway her mind. By the time we crept out of the house at dawn, her last reservations had been conquered. So, when she noticed that questioning look in my eyes that asked, "Where's your bag?" she gave me a playful smile and whispered, "Surely you're going to buy me a set of city clothes. You won't want me traipsing around Cairo in this old *gallabiya*!"

I left behind enough money, plus the deed to some fields, to ensure a decent life for our mother and two other sisters, even though they were married. Nor did I forget to leave an extra five-pound note in my mother's purse, fulfilling the promise I'd made her the last time I left. With the first ray of sunrise, we silently shut the door behind us. I, at least, had no intention of returning.

After some careful apartment hunting, we settled in Imbaba on the west bank of the Nile. We could see Zamalek clearly from our small rooftop apartment. It didn't look far away, but it was hundreds of miles out of reach at that point. We spent our first days strolling through the streets of Cairo. I made sure our feet led us nowhere near Emad Eddin Street and my former place of employment, the Rixos bar. But we did pay several visits to "Les Grands Magasins Cicurel," which was not that far away. I bought Zeinab enough clothes to last her a year. What a change they made! Were it not for that slight limp of hers, which sort of spoiled the image, she could have really gone places. As she modeled a dress I had chosen for her in Cicurel's dressing room, I had her remove her head covering. I contemplated her for a moment, then nodded and muttered, "Superb!"

Only her hair ruined the image I had in my head. It was too short and curly. I picked out a colorful silk scarf and, together with a white leather handbag and shoes to match, she was transformed into Zeinab the Cairene. Anyone who saw her for the first time would never imagine she had ever set foot in a dirt-poor rural village, let alone been brought up in one. On one condition, though: that she spoke as little as possible, as her etiquette teacher, M. Edmond, advised me. I was satisfied with the work he was doing with her. My main concern now was how to get back into that basement.

"We're going to the opera tonight. You're going to have the most amazing experience of your life," I said as I lit a cigarette and contemplated the strange way she walked in her new shoes.

"But we got to go to the Friday market, Abbas."

"Why?" I asked with some surprise.

"To buy a couple of hens and a pair of rabbits to raise on our rooftop!"

5

"It's a hard climb up the backstairs, but reaching the top has a flavor all its own."—Zeinab Mahalawi

"Are you happy now, Zeinab?"

I clapped like a child even though I was almost twenty. I kissed his hand. I was so grateful I could have cried. He wasn't going to send me back to Mahalla Marhoum after all. He'd forgiven me and allowed me to stay in Cairo, but on the condition I swore to obey him blindly, no questions asked. I lifted my eyes toward his, but I was too afraid to ask "Now what?" I didn't want to risk another expulsion from paradise. As far as I knew, Abbas had no job or form of steady income that would keep us in this lap of luxury for much longer. What would happen when his savings—wherever they came from—ran out? He stared at me with a stony face, waiting for me to speak. Then his mouth cracked into a grin, as though he had read my worries on the surface of my eyes. "Come on, ask," he said, adding a gentle nudge.

"What are we going to live on after the money runs out, Abbas?"

He gave me a confident smile and said, "It's never going to run out. In fact, it's going to grow and multiply . . . like rabbits!"

He roared with laughter, but I kept my face serious as I folded my leg beneath my bum, propped my elbow on my knee and my chin on the palm of my hand, and gave him a look that said, "Go on." His eyes narrowed at the way I sat, like the women back in the village. He snatched up a cigarette and lit it, and said nothing. I felt my stomach knot. Now he really is going to send me back to the village, I thought. I snapped my foot down to the floor and sat primly, the way he'd taught me. It was Eve who got Adam expelled from Paradise, but with Abbas it was the opposite. He would boot me out if I committed the same offenses again. He had tried to call my attention to them gently at first, but there must have come a point where he felt he had to threaten to send me back to the village if I couldn't adjust to the ways of the city. He'd only made that threat one time, but Abbas only threatens once. After that, he carries out his threat and worse.

My mind flashed back to an incident back in the village. I'll never forget it. One day he learned that his partner at the carpentry shop had harassed our middle sister, Afaf, on her way to the fields. Abbas warned the guy that if he ever did that again he'd throw him into the irrigation canal. So the guy did it again just to defy my brother. Abbas had a dark scowl on his face when he came home that day. I watched from behind the oven as he coiled up a long cord and hid it beneath his shirt. Then I followed him out to the northern field and ducked down among the crops. He hid behind a large tree and waited. Before long, the guy came trotting along on his sturdy mule, cracking a short cane on its back whenever it tried to bolt, and reaching up to adjust his skullcap. Abbas let the guy pass. Then he pounced from behind, threw the guy to the ground, and tied him up with the cord. From between the plant stalks I could see my brother using a length of the cord to affix a large rock to the young man's back. Then he dumped him into the canal next to the field and walked away as cool as a cucumber. I shot up and ran all the way home. My whole body trembled until the next morning. I couldn't sleep for days. Not long afterward, my mother told us they found the young man's bloated body floating in the canal: "Abbas was there with a bunch of other villagers when they pulled the body out and read the Fatiha over his soul. He took part in the funeral procession, too." She fell silent for a moment, then said, "Poor Abbas. He's had rotten luck his whole life. Whenever he partners up with somebody for some business or other, disaster strikes or the guy dies."

I jumped despite myself when I felt Abbas's hand on mine. He gave it a gentle tug to pull me to my feet. I stared nervously into his eyes as I wrestled with that old puzzle: what really made him so angry back then? Was it the arguments he had with that dead partner or was it the offense to our sister's honor and mine? He gave me a pat on the head, as though to brush away my concerns, and pointed to my bedroom.

"Go get changed. We're going to Monsieur Edmond."

Given the threat of expulsion hanging over my head, I followed M. Edmond's instructions to the letter. His establishment was in Zamalek, in an elegant ground-floor apartment in a large new building that was five stories tall. The door was open when we arrived. We passed one room after another. All the doors had been removed so I could catch glimpses inside. In one I saw women dancing in front of other women, who watched them closely while a limp-wristed man swayed back and forth to the rhythm, calling out words in a foreign language. In another, I caught sight of some men bowing stiffly and strutting like roosters in front of other men who remained seated. Some of those imitated women so well I nearly gasped out loud. I was so amazed by everything I couldn't even blink. Suddenly I found a very tall and elegant man in front of me. He made a deep and respectful bow and said, "Mademoiselle Zizi, come this way please."

The name "Zizi" had a ring to it that brought a smile to my face. I followed the man, encouraged by a wink from Abbas, who lit a cigarette and stepped back into a corner, while keeping his eye on one of the dancers. He must have known

M. Edmond for a long time. M. Edmond turned me over to a young man about my age who spoke Arabic in a way that made me want double over with laughter and who flapped his arms and swung his hips like Badia Masabni's dancing girls. He taught me how to walk, how to sit, what to say and when to say it, and when to keep my mouth shut. He also taught me how to eat with a knife and fork, which I just couldn't manage to hold in the right way.

"Mademoiselle Zizi! Please do not speak with your mouth full!"

That was M. Edmond, who wagged his long finger at me and shot a reproachful look at my teacher as he removed the knife from my right hand.

I still had no idea what mission Abbas had in mind for me. He always told me to be prepared, but he never told me for what. Still, I was happy to be learning a lot of words in French, which Abbas said was important. He always threw in soundalike words from Italian, as if that would help. When M. Edmond asked me to "*répétez*" after him, I would *répétez* with the greatest confidence. But Edmond had his own views on my progress. After ten lessons he told Abbas that there was no need for me to speak French in public. Then he leaned closer to Abbas's ear and said, "Actually, it would be better if she spoke as little as possible, in general."

I heard that, despite his lowered voice, and I hated him from then on. Actually, I hadn't taken to him from the start. His voice made my skin crawl. It was as greasy as a lump of raw fat floating in cold soup. Of course, I kept such thoughts to myself.

The moment Abbas had been waiting for came on a warm winter day. I'd been lazing on the couch in our Imbaba apartment when he came prancing into the room in a full three-piece suit and a white broad-rimmed hat, and holding a fat cigar. I sprang to a sitting position. He looked so different. He'd sprouted a small pointed goatee and had darkened his hair with henna, but dyed the hair at his temples to make it look like he'd grayed prematurely. He gave me a wink, then put on a large pair of sunglasses that hid his eyes completely and went off to Cicurel's department store downtown to discuss "a matter of extreme importance" with the director.

When he got back, I listened spellbound as he related what happened. After he was ushered into the director's office and offered a seat, he explained his business. Looking the director straight in the face, he extracted several bills from his wallet and said, "Please take this. It's a hundred pounds—the down payment M. Cicurel paid me. But first, sir, I would be grateful if you could give me the original work order."

I clamped my hand over my mouth to keep from laughing out loud—which Abbas disapproved of—as I pictured the reactions of the department store director. We were out on the balcony of our top-floor apartment overlooking the Nile in Imbaba. Abbas put his fat cigar in his breast pocket and took a Cortelli from his slender silver cigarette case and lit it. He took out another and handed it to me.

"You have to learn to smoke without your eyes watering."

"But I can't, Abbas."

"All you got to do is hold it between your fingers. Take a puff or two at most and then toss it away."

Abbas continued his story over a couple of cups of coffee, smoke wafting around us. The director was reluctant to accept the hundred pounds from Abbas because he'd been unable to find the original work order. He phoned Mme Paula Cicurel to explain that, shortly before his death, her husband had engaged a construction contractor called Abbas Mahalawi to renovate the villa in Zamalek, and had given him a sizeable down payment for the work. He told her, "Monsieur Mahalawi is with me here in the office at this moment. He wants to return the down payment after having learned of the tragic incident that befell your late husband. But he needs the document he'd signed in order to do that."

Abbas placed one leg over the other and flicked his cigarette over the ledge while staring absently in the direction of Zamalek.

"Madame Paula, God bless her, must have rifled through her husband's papers seven times over looking for that work order."

"Did you get it?"

He laughed aloud and said, "Of course not!"

I clasped my hand over my heart and asked, "Are you going to give her the money back?"

"Of course not!"

My mouth dropped open, then shut again. I just couldn't make head nor tails of this.

"But how the hell are you going to sort out this muck-up?" I said as I slapped my cheeks, lamenting whatever fix he was in over that huge sum of money.

He winced and shook his head sadly, and scolded me for speaking with my hands and in such a crude way.

"You're hopeless. From now on, zip your lips. I don't want to hear a peep out of you apart from 'Yes, sir,' or 'As you wish.' Got it?"

I nodded, too afraid to speak.

"I said, 'Got it?'"

"Yes, sir," I answered, barely above a whisper. "But tell me, please. What do you plan to do?"

His face relaxed into a smile as he swung his arm proudly in the direction of the opposite bank and said, "Ta-dah!" He pointed toward a large villa that stood out from the others with its tall palm tree in the middle of its garden. Then he carefully took a folded piece of paper from his wallet and flourished it like a magician with the ace of spades.

"This paper here is our key into that villa over there!"

The next day he went to Zamalek to call on Mme Paula, Solomon Cicurel's widow. I know no more than what he told me afterward, which wasn't much. Basically, she asked him to carry out the contract between him and her late husband, which involved painting the interior from top to bottom, restoring some items of furniture, and renovating the facade. She also got him to throw in, free of charge, refurbishing the large main gallery of the downtown department store. At one point she suggested that the down payment her husband had paid Abbas seemed rather excessive for the work required. As Abbas related, he played the simple, kindhearted man ever willing to oblige.

"I would never ask for a piaster more, Madame Paula. Monsieur Cicurel—may God rest his soul—was always so generous with us."

The widow seemed surprised at this. "Did you know my husband well?"

"He practically raised me since I was a kid. My dad and my granddad used to help him in the warehouses in Tanta. He did so much for us."

And so Abbas managed to get his first foothold in the Cicurel villa. For many weeks, he oversaw a team of workers he hired from a part of Imbaba called Ezbet al-Saayada. It wasn't too far from where we lived. Abbas told me it got its name because so many Upper Egyptians—"Saayada"—settled there after finding jobs as construction workers in Zamalek, which was booming at the time. Then, a couple of months later, he decided to take me to Zamalek with him. Not that he gave me any advance notice, as always.

He had a hansom cab waiting for us in front of our building. We headed north and crossed the Imbaba bridge, then drove south along the east bank of the Nile until we reached the Abulela bridge. After crossing into Zamalek, we turned right and kept going until Abbas suddenly signaled the driver to stop. The horse-and-buggy ride had been so soothing that my anxieties evaporated, which was probably what my brother had planned. We stopped in front of a large, stately building in the middle of a large garden. There was a sign next to the gateway that I couldn't make out because it was written in a foreign language. I asked Abbas whether this was a museum like the Egyptian Museum we passed so often in Ismailiya Square. He smiled and pointed to the sign in Arabic written on the other post of the gateway: "Villa of Mahmoud Amr Pasha." The gate was slightly ajar. An elegant lady was getting out of a large white car. She was in a pistachio-colored dress and a hat to match. I stood there admiring her for a second and then started toward the villa. Abbas gently took me by the elbow to hold me back, and smiled.

"Not this one, Zeinab. Hold your horses. We're almost there."

Why did Abbas stop the carriage so soon and make us walk the rest of the way? Maybe he didn't want the driver to know where we were going. He never trusted anyone.

I was struck breathless by Cicurel's widow when I first saw her. She had to be at least twenty years older than I was. I don't think I was mistaken, because my mother had taught me how to read a woman's age by the circles in her lower neck. Each circle stands for another ten years after twenty. But amazingly, Mme Paula was slender, her face was fresh and youthful, her shoulder-length hair was as smooth as silk, and her face, with its soft ivory complexion, was radiant. The heels of her feet were smooth, without a single crack, and she had shapely legs, which she must have been conscious of because her dress was cut quite a bit above her knees. Her eyes were as blue as the sky. I suddenly found myself wishing I had a daughter as beautiful as her.

Mme Paula welcomed Abbas fondly. The affection between them would have been obvious to a blind man. She greeted me with a simple nod, while she let her hand rest in Abbas's for longer than necessary for a handshake. He was smooth and charming, his voice intimate and pitched deeper than usual, and he sat at the edge of his chair, leaning his whole body in her direction. They left me standing next to a column

52

in the middle of the large reception room until my feet began to ache in my new shoes. I propped my back against the column and kept myself entertained by watching the scene from there. Paula looked completely taken by Abbas, especially when he sprinkled in some Italian. Her wide eyes seemed to devour him like a widow whose bed had grown cold. And why not? A young handsome man many years her junior—surely she wouldn't let this opportunity slip through her fingers. But suddenly she turned to business. They spoke about her late husband and her ideas for modernizing the store. As they went on and on, I had to take off my shoes, flex my toes, move my feet in circles a few times. I cleared my throat to attract Abbas's attention. He whispered something to her, in French this time. I picked up the word "*femme*," having heard it so many times at M. Edmond's etiquette school. She turned toward me and gave me a long scrutinizing look, the way a woman inspects herself and her clothes in front of a mirror. She picked up a little brass bell and rang it. A Nubian servant appeared wearing a red caftan with broad golden stripes, and a short crimson tarboosh on his head. Mme Paula told him to take me to the "office" and offer me some tea and sweets.

I tucked my shoes under my arm, ignoring the glare I got from Abbas—my feet just couldn't bear it anymore—and trudged after the servant, though not without some curiosity to see the rest of the villa. The "office" turned out to be a large room with a table, a few chairs, a big refrigerator, and a large sink. The servant told me it was an "antechamber" to the kitchen, which was reserved for cooking only. Two blond girls came over to introduce themselves. One was called Helga. I forget the name of the other one. I stood up to greet them, thinking they were Mme Paula's daughters. I'd started to sweat so much that my dress clung to my back. The servant told me they were maids, one Swiss, the other Greek. I stared after them as they went to tend to their business and nearly wept as I compared them, with their grace and beauty, to me.

For the next hour and a half or so, I did nothing but chat with Bashir, as the servant was called. He was a sullen sort, but he made me a cup of fancy tea that had a fragrance unlike any I'd ever smelled before. He served it to me with a large slice of cake. Somehow the fool had gotten it into his head that I was going to enter into service in that house. He started to go on about Mme Paula's nature and her daily routine, wagging a warning finger at me from time to time as he explained her waking and sleeping times, the kinds of food she preferred or did not, the types of society people she entertained, and so on. I fought my anger at his presumption and feigned interest. All these secret tidbits might be of use to Abbas in his battle to conquer the heart of the beautiful widow. Still, I couldn't suppress the urge to upbraid that guy. When he set the teapot before me, I pointed my finger at him, arched my eyebrows coolly, and said, "Fetch me some milk."

As I sipped my tea, I pondered my brother's predicament. Poor Abbas. How could he bring himself to marry a woman almost as old as his mother, even if she were rich and beautiful?

"Would you like a brief tour of the villa?" I looked up to find Bashir waiting for me to set down my cup and stand up. We climbed a flight of stairs to see the eight rooms on the second story. There was one that Bashir passed quickly without opening the door. When curiosity got the better of me and I tried the door handle, his face tensed and grew more sullen. "That's Monsieur Cicurel's bedroom. After he died, Madame Paula locked it up and moved to another bedroom."

"Why? Is this where he died?"

"It's where he was murdered . . . may God rest his soul."

I snatched my hand from the door handle and muttered a prayer to ward off the devil. There's something spooky about this villa, I thought, and a queasy feeling crept into my stomach. Just before this, we'd passed a large portrait of M. Cicurel in the corridor. I pictured that face, with its round wire-rimmed glasses and the straight black hair combed back from the forehead, lying dead on the floor, blood oozing out of a big gash in his head after it had been smashed in with an axe. I hastened to catch up with Bashir, who had started down the stairs to the ground floor.

From there, Bashir steered me toward another stairway, which we descended. We came to a halt in front of a door, but he merely pointed at it and said that it was the door to the basement, which he would clean himself. Again propelled by my curiosity, my hand reached to the handle, which turned smoothly. I slipped inside, leaving the servant staring with his mouth open at my audacity. By the time he caught up with me, I'd gone at least two yards into a space as big as a cotton field. Right in the middle of the place there was a large wooden desk, and behind that stood an obese man wearing bright red suspenders on top of a white shirt. He had a tan complexion, frizzy hair, and an ugly face in the center of which was a wide, bulbous nose. He was holding a pile of files in both hands and had frozen midway between transferring them from the desk to a nearby bookshelf as he turned to me with a bewildered stare. The servant started to upbraid me, but the man held up his hand, then dismissed him with a nod toward the door. After carefully arranging the files on the shelves, he turned back to me with a questioning look. I was too confused to speak or even move. He began to circle around me with a faint smile on his face. He looked about my age, but projected a presence that made him seem much older. Perhaps the reason I was afraid to speak was that I thought he was Mme Paula's new husband and I was picturing how Abbas, who was in love with her, would be taken by surprise by this big bear of a man. What would happen if that man discovered Abbas's real reason for being here? There'd be blood for sure. The two of them would fight to the death like the two cocks in my mother's cage back in Mahalla Marhoum.

"Who are you? What do you want?"

It was easy enough to pick up from the way he looked at my legs and waist, and the huskiness that had crept into his voice, that he was interested in me as a woman. But before I could summon the courage to speak, Mme Paula and Abbas came in. The servant must have told them about my impudence. I looked down in order to avoid my brother's reproachful glare. However, contrary to my expectations, his voice sounded friendly, which encouraged me to look up. He smiled as Mme Paula introduced the man.

"Hassanein al-Masri, our financial director. He was very close to Monsieur Cicurel. He helps me with everything. He's been abroad and just returned two days ago."

It was obvious the two men had never met before. My brother shook his hand warmly, despite the fat man's scowl, and kept his broad smile glued to his face as Paula introduced him.

"And this is Monsieur Abbas Mahalawi, a building contractor and a friend of our dear Solomon. My husband had engaged him to do some renovations to the villa. He started the work three months ago. I'd like the two of you to coordinate with each other, Hassanein."

"But we never found the work order, Madame." Hassanein kept his resentful gaze fixed on Abbas's face. "And it's quite a sum of money. Also, the villa doesn't need all that—"

"I've given my assent, Hassanein. The work's already begun, and Monsieur Abbas isn't going to ask for more money."

I could sense my brother's triumph, maybe less because of what Paula said than how she said it. With such enthusiasm and affection. Hassanein looked down in total submission. I started to relax, but I remained still, hands folded in front of me expectantly. It was Abbas's turn to introduce me to Mme Paula and that fat man who'd had his eyes glued on me until she came in—glued on my legs, to be exact. I was afraid to walk, which would reveal my limp, but the corners of my mouth were preparing to smile. I'd already begun to feel enough bashfulness to make my cheeks flush and set my body tingling. This was the first time I'd experienced the admiring gaze of a man in Cairo, even if it came from one as ugly as Hassanein.

I caught Abbas's eye, but he ignored me and continued to discuss business matters with Hassanein. At first I thought that he could have put that stuff off in order to introduce me. But then I realized he was trying to draw the guy out. He'd ask Hassanein questions about the layout of the basement. But Hassanein seemed set on excluding this part of the house from the renovation work. Pointing to the shelves he'd been arranging when I burst in on him, he said, "We can't move out all these files and papers right now." Abbas had moved to a basement wall to inspect it. He bent his ear toward it and hit it a few times with the palm of his hand, then said, "I'm afraid groundwater's begun to seep into the foundations. We'll have to have this checked out." Hassanein gave Paula a long and meaningful look, though I couldn't make out what the meaning was. Suddenly, Paula came over to me, patted me on the shoulder, and told him, "Let me introduce you to Zeinab. She's a gift from Monsieur Abbas, and it couldn't have come at a better time. He made a special trip to Tanta to fetch her when he learned that I needed an Egyptian girl to help me around the house and keep me company!"

I wished that the ground would open and swallow me up right then and there. My blood rushed to my head so fast that the room began to spin. To this day I can't recall how I left the villa and made it back to Imbaba. But I do know that I was determined never to set foot in Zamalek again, and to take the first train back to Mahalla Marhoum.

6

"JUST CROSSING THE BRIDGE FROM Zamalek to Imbaba takes you back through time to poverty, degradation, and grief."—Zeinab Mahalawi

"*Femme de compagnie*, Zeinab. Nobody said you'd be a housemaid."

He said that over and over, calmly and reassuringly, on our way back to Imbaba and after we got home. But I couldn't stop crying. Nothing he said could make me accept what he'd done to me. Did I mean so little to him? I'd never imagined that he could dump me like that. What was strange, though, was how gentle he was as he tried to explain why. He said my job would be different from those foreign servant girls. In fact, I wouldn't be a servant at all. That French term Mme Paula used was a combination of household manager and companion of the lady of the house. That position would make me closer to Paula than anyone else. I'd live with her in the villa and tend to her needs. I'd accompany her to the seamstress, help her with her weekly purchases, and entertain her in the evenings. I'd be the companion of an elegant, high-class lady who occasionally gets bored now that she lost her husband. Even that snooty servant would be at my service.

"Or would you rather just drop it all and go back to the village?"

"Why are you going to all this trouble to get me a job in that villa? What's in it for you?"

I caught a glimmer in his eye, but he didn't answer. We were sitting on the balcony. The tears on my cheeks slowly dried as I compared the pros and cons of the Cicurel villa and our home in Mahalla Marhoum. I was forced to conclude that life back in the village would be easier to bear than the humiliation of working as a maid in a villa. But then I gave more thought to what Abbas said about being a "*femme de compagnie.*" If what he said was true, maybe I really would become the woman who actually controlled that palace with all its servants.

Abbas was giving me a penetrating look, willing me to agree, and my fear of his anger was willing me to yield. He probably wanted me close to Mme Paula's year in order to persuade her to marry him. I also figured he must be feeling ashamed of the way he'd treated me. I held on to that thought, which encouraged me to say, "Okay, I'll do it." But under that gaze of his, my words came out a bare whisper and he didn't hear them. So I nodded my head a few times to signal my agreement.

Lowering his voice, even though there was nobody around to overhear, he said, "With time, you'll be in complete charge of that whole villa. Everyone in it will be at your command, Lady Zeinab." The title brought a smile to my face. "But first you have to either win Hassanein to our side or keep him out of our way."

Hassanein? What did that fat man have to do with Abbas marrying Paula?

"Win him over how? Keep him away from what?"

"You're a smart cookie, Mademoiselle Zizi. You'll figure it out. But for now, just keep him away from the basement."

He smiled and didn't add another word. Did he think that what I didn't know wouldn't hurt me?

The morning of my return to Zamalek would remain crystal clear in my memory for years to come. Despite his reassurances, I was very nervous. After I packed my suitcase and had breakfast with Abbas, I tied my new scarf around my ahead and headed to the door. But just as I reached for the handle, my brother gently took hold of my hand and led me back into the apartment.

"Not right now, Zeinab. We'll leave in an hour because I have some important guests coming and I need you to help out with the tea and coffee."

The guests turned out to be Hajj Abdel-Naim, the well-known construction contractor from Qena, and his sons Fahim and Asran. As Abbas told me later, Abdel-Naim was the first contractor to get into the informal construction business in Zamalek, building modest homes near the Nile opposite Imbaba. He then won the Prince Mohamed Ali Tawfiq tender to develop Zamalek, which earned him an official permit that had to be renewed every three years at the palace. He built more than eighty villas in no time, and now he wanted to build twice that amount. He'd brought with him hundreds of workers from his village near Qena, way down south in Upper Egypt. They were staying near a large stretch of farmland in Imbaba that was now called Ezbet Abdel-Naim, after him. I served them tea and slices of an orange pound cake that Abbas had fetched from Simonds patisserie in Zamalek. He'd first tasted it at Paula's and fell in love with it, he said. It cost an arm and a leg, but I'd planned to throw out the remains because it was so bland. I make a much better cake, and at only a fraction of the cost. But to my surprise, our guests wolfed down the whole thing.

Abdel-Naim might have looked rough, but he was sweet and considerate. Despite how long he'd been in Cairo, he never abandoned his wide-sleeved southern *gallabiya*, turban, and heavy cane. He never stopped twiddling the ends of his mustache either. His elder son, Fahim, was sullen and stand-offish. He wore a *gallabiya* too, but on top of that he wore a jacket of the same color and a tall tarboosh on his head, which he kept adjusting every two minutes even though it didn't look like it was about to slide off. He'd interrupt his father and Abbas every now and then to complain about how much it would cost them to renovate the outside of the villa. Abbas had already begun to strip off the paint, but Fahim ignored that. He'd add up costs and profits in a little notebook he had with him, and whenever Abbas made an objection, Fahim would turn it around and hold it open in front of my brother's nose.

The younger son, Asran, caught my attention. He kept sneaking glances at me. He was a silent type: bashful, modest, maybe a bit on the lazy side. He held a string of green prayer beads that he clicked through his fingers at a steady rhythm like cogs in a machine. He sat with his head bowed, never uttered a word, and only looked up and smiled twice: once when I brought them tea and once when I took the tray away. I was out of sight in the kitchen when they got up to leave and I heard the sound of their footsteps and of Abdel-Naim's heavy cane as they moved toward the door. When I took a peep from behind the kitchen door, Asran's shy eyes met mine and his face lit up. He looked down quickly with a smile that was even more idiotic than the first two he'd given me. My eyes shifted to Fahim, whose face grew sterner as he muttered in a deep, gravelly voice, "*Ya rabb, ya satir*! Heaven help us!"

After carrying my suitcase downstairs, Abbas hailed a taxi to Zamalek this time, instead of a carriage. On the way, he explained the deal he'd made with Abdel-Naim and Fahim. He said he had to forego some of the profit and that the work would start the next day and take a whole year.

"What about Asran? Isn't he included? He didn't say a word the whole time."

"He's a student at al-Azhar. They brought him along as a kind of a good-luck charm. Fahim's got his feet on the ground and he's on the ball. He's also a civil servant. In the mornings he works at the Foreign-owned Properties Registrar at the Notary Public Authority. But don't you worry. I'll be there in the villa with you every day because we've got a lot of work ahead of us."

"If you gave me a better idea about the work it might make things easier for both of us."

He gave my shoulder a squeeze to reassure me, but said nothing—as usual. I wasn't afraid. I was just wondering what my new life in Zamalek would be like. Even then, though, I had this strange premonition that it would fork off in another direction as soon I crossed the threshold into the Cicurel villa. But which of the two would be standing at the fork in the road: the cocky Hassanein al-Masri or the bashful Asran Abdel-Naim?

"Do you need anything else, Miss Zeinab?"

Bashir's servile tones were as soothing as being cradled in a large felucca gently rocking on the Nile at sunset. A magic door had opened, leading me into a new, exciting, enchanted, wonderful world. I was asleep, a blissful smile on my face, afloat in a velvety dream that I prayed would never end. Mme Paula never once made me feel like a servant. It was exactly as Abbas had said: I was the manager of a villa and a lady's companion. My word reigned supreme. Only rarely could anyone alter my decisions except for Mme Paula, and that only happened in the first few months. Then Abbas taught me how to set my sail according to the flow of her mood so as to reach my destination in a way that kept her pleased with me. As a result, she grew more and more attached to me.

Months went by without a single day off. I remained at her side until bedtime, and the moment she awoke, she reached for a little bell, which I could hear from my room nearby. If she overslept, I was the only one allowed to enter her room at nine sharp to wake her up. She took breakfast in the garden, with me sitting beside her reading out some excerpts from the newspapers. I never ate in her presence, naturally. After breakfast, she took her coffee near the dock behind the villa. That was where she would discuss what was to be served for lunch and dinner. If we were expecting guests, the routine would differ. I'd let her take her daily bath while I supervised the Swiss and Greek maids as they tended to their daily cleaning chores. I kept a sharp eye out for fine layers of dust that I could easily detect with a swipe of a finger over a surface as I made my morning rounds of the villa. To me it was "clean dust that nobody can see," as my mother always said, but Paula insisted it had to be removed every day. Bashir, the sullen Nubian servant, followed me on my rounds, and behind him trailed the two maids. I was the one who checked the stocks in the pantry to make sure the chef didn't pilfer. I was responsible for all domestic expenses.

Bashir addressed me as "Miss Zeinab." I'd hoped for better, like "ma'am." He would never dare address me as "Madame," let alone "Lady." There was only one "Lady" in this house and that was how it would stay. So, if he entered the room when I was in Paula's presence, I was content with a brief nod in my direction after he greeted "Lady Paula," even though the rest of us used "Madame Paula."

In short, almost everything in the villa was ideal. The only things that bothered me were Paula's huge dogs. So I gave orders for these not to be let off their leash until after I went to bed.

It was here, in Zamalek, that I rode in a Cadillac for the first time. Paula turned it in every two years for the latest model in the same color: black. It had two wide, cushy seats, plus a foldout seat behind the driver's seat. The trunk was big enough to hold four grown men lying down, with space between them. The door was so heavy I couldn't close it by myself. I sat in front of Mme Paula on the foldout seat—the "magic seat," as the driver called it—attached to the back of the driver's seat. If she had a friend with her, I'd move up front next to the driver and we'd close the glass partition so we wouldn't disturb them or overhear them, try as we might.

Despite her beauty and feminine charms, even for someone of her age, Mme Paula struck me as somewhat frigid. If only my mother could meet her, she'd give her some good tips that would facilitate Abbas's plans to marry her. I once confided in him my concerns in this regard, but he shrugged them off as though he'd lost all interest in her. I found that hard to believe, which left me mulling again over that puzzle called Abbas. I just couldn't make out what was going on his head. I kept my eyes open and picked up every stray detail. But I always felt I was missing something.

Over time, I could communicate with the servants using fewer words. Often, just a glance would let the servants know what I wanted or what I was dissatisfied with. At the same time, Paula taught me how to pronounce French better than I had learned at M. Edmond's school for etiquette. I still had a problem when it came to softening some letters and pronouncing others with the right ring. I always overdid it, forcing Paula to correct me constantly. I just could not get over that hurdle, which annoyed me so much that I came to hate French and the people who spoke it even more. During those first months with Mme Paula, only one incident occurred that would continue to rankle long afterward. It was when we went to the Gezira Club the first time. One morning, Paula fished around in a small drawer, pulled out a little red card, and said, "Here Zeinab, take this carnet. You'll have to keep it with you whenever we go to the club."

I was over the moon when I took hold of my Gezira Club membership card. But my smile vanished as soon as my eyes fell on the gold embossed words: "Nursemaid's Carnet." Inside I found my picture and Paula's name and membership number written in a large font above my name. I folded the carnet and thanked her in a low voice. A couple of weeks before that, I'd been mystified when she insisted on taking me to a photographer to have my picture taken. Now I understood why.

I stared in awe out the window of the black Cadillac as it glided into that amazing club in the very belly of Zamalek, with its large expanses of green lawns, colorful flowerbeds, and innumerable tall palms. I'd never seen so many foreigners all together. I felt as though the car had suddenly transported us to that place called "Europe" people kept talking about. Paula had arranged to meet some of her friends in the club's tea garden. Just as I pulled up a chair to sit next to her at the customary distance, she looked at me and said calmly, but with an edge in her voice I hadn't heard before, "Farther away, Zeinab. Over there, please." She pointed to a long wooden table some distance away, near a low stone wall, and repeated more firmly, "Over there."

There were a number of foreign and Egyptian nannies seated on small wooden chairs. A few of them held children's toys or cradled small suitcases on their laps. Some were perched on the edge of their chairs as though ready to receive instructions at any moment; others sat as still as statues. I turned to head in that direction, but my steps faltered when I caught sight of Mme Maysa watching me. She was Mme Paula's aristocratic neighbor and close friend. With her was her brother, Ambassador Mahmoud Amr Pasha, who wore a permanent scowl. He probably thought I was dawdling—he wouldn't have been able to understand why I was so flustered—so that scowl darkened as he jerked his cane in the direction I was supposed to go.

I always felt that Mme Maysa regarded me with contempt and that the smile she put on to greet me hid a sneer. Not that she ever said an unkind word to me. She was always cheerful and chatty, and she dressed too young for her age, as though she was determined to enjoy every moment of her life. Still, she made me feel uncomfortable. I was also afraid of her huge dogs, which she took for a walk around sunset every day. If they caught sight of me near the gate, they'd make a lunge for me, barking loudly, which caused Mme Paula's dogs to leap at their fence and bark back. Mme Maysa would rein in her dogs on their leashes and say something in French to calm them down. But if I moved, they'd start barking again, and if I bent over to pick up a stone to throw at them, Mme Maysa would tell me not to frighten her dogs and to move away so as not to upset them.

"It's the dogs that are upsetting me, you bitch!" I'd fume to myself as I scurried back indoors.

The main streets were hung with decorations. Banners fluttered and strings of colored lights danced in the summer breeze. King Faruq I peered out from posters with doleful eyes. The broadcaster kept up a running commentary on the royal procession as it passed through the streets. "The king has emerged from the royal coach. Cheers ring out from the crowds and from the balconies on both sides of the street. He is dressed in a white field marshal's uniform."

"What's a field marshal?"

Mme Paula, her ear bent toward the radio, put her finger to her lips, signaling me to remain silent. The king was about to begin the speech from the throne. He called himself "the first servant of the nation," and said the that the poor were not to blame for their poverty and should receive what was rightfully theirs without having to ask. A poor man has the right to find the medicine that cures him of disease and the right to access the education that frees him from ignorance, he said.

There was no way to compare Imbaba to sedate Zamalek. In Imbaba, the thrill at the young king's investiture was visible and the celebrations more boisterous. Not even the tiniest back alleyway lacked pictures of King Faruq and strings of colored lights. Glasses of tea or sweet beverages were doled out for free in coffeehouses and to passersby in the streets. Abbas and I were back in our rooftop apartment, in the living room. I turned to him, after hanging up a picture of King Faruq I'd snatched from a string of decorations on our way back from Zamalek, and said, "I swear, he looks like a decent and humble sort. I bet you he'll be better than his father."

"So you've started talking politics, huh?"

"No. It's just that looking at Faruq lifts your spirits, whereas Fuad's grumpy old face ruined your appetite, like Madame Paula always said."

Abbas was casually leafing through the Muqattam newspaper, tsk-tsking from time to time. Suddenly he said, "The government's changed the names of twenty villages across the country in honor of the new king. Guess what? Our village is one of them. It's now called Faruqiya." He smiled as he folded the newspaper. "The king is dead. Long live the king!"

"Zeinab, hurry up and get ready! We have an appointment with Madame Balock in an hour," Paula said as she finished dressing.

My heart skipped a beat. Had Abbas asked her to marry him? Why hadn't he prepared me for this? If he married her, how would it affect my status here? Would he tell her I was really his sister or would he continue to pretend I was his cousin and force me to live by myself in Imbaba? How could she even think of marriage at this point, after being diagnosed with a heart condition that robbed her of her energy, aged her beyond her years, and forced her to keep a doctor close at hand? The questions rushed into my head so fast I felt it would explode. But I had no one to turn to who could answer them.

Mme Balock, whom I'd visited twice before with Mme Paula, owned a huge apartment that took up an entire floor in an elegant building opposite the Yacoubian building downtown. She was a famous beautician, who ordered all her creams and powders specially from Europe. What beautiful colorful jars and boxes they came in! She was Cairo's foremost expert in making up girls for engagement ceremonies and weddings. Her skillful touches totally transformed her clients' faces, making them look fresher and softer. True, she could work magic, but she couldn't hold a candle to my mother. "Mayoress Hamida" was a true magician. She could work a spindle using an ass's leg, as they say, which is why she became the most famous hairdresser not just in Mahalla Marhoum but in the whole of Tanta. If she had the facilities that Mme Balock had, people here would be calling her Mme Hamida or even Mme Didi. I smiled inwardly, despite my worries. Even the ugliest girls could set their own conditions for marriage after my mother was through with them.

My mind returned to my personal disaster, which I'd discovered a few days earlier. Now, as if that wasn't enough, I had to worry about my position here if Abbas married Mme Paula. I coughed a few times in succession, then told Mme Paula I'd come down with a cold and needed to rest a bit, and that I didn't want her to catch it. She took Helga with her instead. Even as her health declined and the wrinkles crept into her face, she cared for her appearance right up to the end, even before I let in people to visit her in her sickbed.

I went out to the back garden, where Abbas was having coffee while overseeing the workmen who were repainting the outer walls for what must have been the third time. He kept drilling into the walls here and there for no reason that I could see other than to delay the workmen and keep himself in the villa as long as possible. I went up to him, unloaded my concerns about his marriage and how it would affect my position, and plopped down on the chair next to him. He lifted his feet and set them on the reed chair in front of him, lit a cigarette, and exhaled coolly before dropping another bombshell.

"Mme Paula's health is getting worse. There's no hope for a cure, and marriage is the last thing on her mind. But what matters now is that you start planning for a new job very soon." His face broke into a crafty grin, which made me more worried and perplexed.

"Why? Is she getting somebody to replace me? Like a live-in nurse, for example?"

"No. You'll stay with her, of course. But only in the mornings."

"And in the afternoons?"

"You'll be looking after your new home and your husband, Madame!"

No sooner had I recovered from the shock than my fears surged inside me. Had he detected my secret and decided to marry me off as soon as possible? He gave no indication to confirm or deny this. But that was Abbas for you: unreadable. You never could tell what was going on inside that head of his.

He stood up and went over to greet Abdel-Naim and Asran as they approached. I stayed seated, staring out into space. But then Asran stepped into view, with his head slightly bowed and that bashful smile on his face. I smiled in spite of myself. It was probably a feeble smile, because inside I was trembling and praying to die before I couldn't hide my secret anymore.

7

"GREED MIGHT DRAW YOU TO the gambling table, but it's the game of wits that keeps you there."—Abbas Mahalawi

Now that Zeinab's place in the villa was secure, I could put my mind to rest about her at least. She'd managed to get exactly where I wanted her most of the time: right next to Paula. That enabled me to focus on what I'd come here to do in the first place.

My sister adjusted so quickly you might have thought that she'd been brought up in this society. I've always been impressed by her instinctive intelligence. I'd staked my money on a mare, and so far I was winning. After Paula bought her a small camera as a gift, Zeinab had me photograph her in the garden, near the dock, in the reception room—at least twenty-four photos of her per month in different spots and poses. Then I had enough. When I asked her why she was so fond of photography, her eyes lit up as she told me about Mme Paula's and M. Cicurel's photo albums documenting different periods of their life. She wanted to preserve the memories of herself here in case she was ever forced to leave it. Once she learned how to use it, you'd rarely see her without that camera around her neck.

Handling Hassanein turned out to be a piece of cake. I kept his attention diverted by distributing Abdel-Naim's work crews across different parts of the villa. I also hoped that would kill two birds with one stone, because I felt one of the crews would stumble across what I was searching for. After a while, however, my enthusiasm began to flag. I was so set on catching the train of fortune that I staked my remaining money from the Cicurel heist on Abdel-Naim and his construction business. I was the one who needed Abdel-Naim, but it was he who took the first step. He found it hard to communicate with the foreigners in Zamalek, whereas I could speak with them easily.

"You look so much like a *khawaga*, you could be one of them," he said.

I laughed.

Looking me straight in the eye, he said, "Come work with us. We'll pay you well."

I was surprised when he agreed to take me on as a partner for a thousand pounds. It was a huge sum, even if it wasn't that much to Abdel-Naim at that time. I sighed, looking back on those beautiful days when we built all those houses and villas together. How the times have changed since then.

I stamped out what must have been my fourth cigarette in an hour and entered my apartment. I was weighed down with worries and physically exhausted. After caving in to Zeinab's nagging that morning, I spent the day plodding from shop to shop in search of a gallon of kerosene and a cleaning needle for the Primus stove she'd bought recently. Like so many other goods and commodities at the time, they were impossible to find. My poor feet! If only I'd spoken with Abdel-Naim's elder son first. When I did, he told me he could get them on the black market, albeit at twice the price. There was no beating Fahim. He could always find a backdoor to get what we needed.

The war was still raging and there was still no end in sight even four years after it started. The face of Cairo had changed so much you could barely recognize it. It looked bedraggled, as though it hadn't gotten enough sleep after partying all night.

The British were everywhere. Their khaki helmets bobbed up and down on streets and sidewalks where you once saw only streams of tarbooshes and skullcaps. The streets were perpetually crowded. Clouds of car exhaust mingled in the air with the odors of sweaty horses pulling carriages. Clanging tramways edged forward among tired, scrawny donkeys struggling with overladen carts, whose rusty frames made ear-piercing squeals, and ancient buses whose grumbling gears and groaning motors announced their approaching end of service. Fiats and Austins, mostly driven by foreigners, growled and honked to insist on their right of way. The constables at the intersections seemed to slouch. They had probably lost their enthusiasm, because whenever they nabbed a Brit for an infraction, the Brit would get off without a fine.

I flopped down on the couch and stared up at the ceiling until I nodded off. I was awoken by the phone some hours later. I looked at my watch. It was nearly ten in the evening. I yawned as I lethargically reached for the receiver and was greeted by Abdel-Naim's excited voice: "How about a royal night on the town?"

I left my car at his place and climbed into the back seat of his, next to him. He had a driver now. He sped us through the streets to the Auberge des Pyramides. Until about a year ago, there had been nothing special about the place. It was a nightclub like any other where people went to drink and dance. But since it becoming King Faruq's favorite nightspot, it was harder for two people to find a table in there than a place in heaven.

"Do you have a reservation?" I asked.

He dismissed my question with a click of the tongue and resumed twiddling his mustache.

My smile broadened. "So, Hajji, since when did you start hanging out at nightclubs?"

I didn't miss the wince of embarrassment. He lowered his voice so the driver couldn't hear.

"It's the law of the jungle. Might makes right. Anyway, you'll find out in a minute. . . . Making a living's a rat race. When you need a favor from a dog, what do you tell it?"

I laughed and patted his knee. "Yes, master!"

The lights and music transport you to another world, like a vision out of the *Thousand and One Nights*. A gurgling waterfall greets you when you enter. We passed through a long corridor to find ourselves before a huge swimming pool surrounded by dozens of chaises longues, large white armchairs, and tall green umbrellas that had been so tightly folded that they seemed to have coiled inward after the strain of a long hot day under the sun. We passed through the winter dance hall, which was dark and deserted, deepening the shadows cast by the strange jagged triangles protruding from murals I couldn't understand. After crossing a small narrow path near the outer wall, we found ourselves in a large room that opened out onto the garden.

The Auberge was a world away from Cairo. From there you'd never know the country was reeling under economic straits. Champagne bottles clinked, corks popped, the bubbly liquid frothed from their mouths into the glasses of ecstatic revelers. There were more than two hundred people with black masks over their eyes and brightly colored hats on their heads. They barely picked at the huge trays of food set before them, leaving the rest untouched. "There's enough food here to feed the whole of Imbaba!" Abdel-Naim exclaimed. If you didn't know this kindhearted Upper Egyptian villager, you'd think he was fresh off the farm. If I were the manager of this place, I'd take those barely untouched trays from one table, rearrange the contents, and set them on the next table. None of these drunkards would be the wiser, and I'd double my profits.

Abdel-Naim jerked to a stop—as did I, a step behind him—at the left side of the dance floor. He looked left and right over the crowd, then he took a step forward to have a closer look. A dignified man in his fifties with an imposing stature and a red face approached. He was obviously the maître d' and he looked personally offended by our presence. His nose wrinkled as he eyed Abdel-Naim from head to toe without making the slightest effort to conceal his distaste. "What are you looking for?" he asked in heavily accented Arabic. Abdel-Naim bent toward his ear and whispered a name I couldn't catch. The man's expression changed immediately and he seemed to snap to attention, as though he'd just heard a password. He took a small notebook from his breast pocket, flicked through it quickly, gave us a courteous bow, and, changing his expression for a third time, offered us the bright smile a maître d' reserves for longtime customers. He turned to signal to someone across the room, then rested his fist on his chest until a young man in a smart white jacket came up and held out a tray of colorful party hats and small black masks. Abdel-Naim looked at the young man and then at me in confusion.

"Pardon, messieurs. This is a *bal masqué*," the maître d' explained, which only increased my friend's confusion. Fearing a flare-up of his Upper Egyptian temper, I leaned toward his ear and said, "It's a masquerade party, Hajji. We have to wear a mask and hat like everyone else."

"What the hell is this, Abbas? I came here for work, not to make a fool of myself. I'll be damned if I'm going to put one of those things on me!"

I took the elbow of the maître d' and he followed me readily. I explained gently, "The hajji believes that this kind of thing goes against nature as God intended, and that it could be contagious. But I'll gladly wear a mask for the sake of your *bal masqué*. In any case, we'll be leaving in an hour. Agreed?"

"*D'accord, monsieur.*"

I set a mask over my eyes as Abdel-Naim and I followed the maître d' to a round table off to one side, near the exit to the back garden. It was large enough to accommodate three people and looked like it had been hastily set. There were some balloons and more colored hats on it, which Abdel-Naim swept aside with a grumble. Without asking what we'd like to eat or drink, a waiter came over and set out an array of small dishes containing appetizers. They lived up to their name. Just looking at them made you ravenous. Then the waiter set two champagne flutes before us and popped the cork on a large bottle of champagne, causing the people at the table next to us to turn to us with silly grins. Abdel-Naim slid his glass aside toward the empty place for a third party and, without the slightest self-consciousness about his gruff Upper Egyptian accent, he told the waiter, "Get me a soft drink, son. Or better, make that a lemonade, but double the sugar, please."

The place was so packed you couldn't find a place to set your feet. Yet there was a large table to the left of the dance floor, big enough to accommodate at least ten, and it was still empty. Posted next to it was a dignified-looking man in white gloves and a coat with tails down to his knees. The table, which was elevated above the rest, had been meticulously set and looked ready to receive distinguished guests. Even the chairs were different from the ones we sat on. They were bigger and plusher, and had taller backs. Just as I leaned toward Abdel-Naim's ear to ask him about that table, a sudden commotion made everyone's heads turn and crane their necks toward the main entrance. A tall, robust, and imposing figure entered, followed by a retinue of at least eight people. The music quickly faded. Then the orchestra struck up a famous symphony, the name of which escapes me. As he advanced into the room, everyone he passed bowed respectfully at the waist, and it suddenly dawned on me why: it was His Royal Highness King Faruq.

The elevation and angle of his seat at that large banquet table afforded him a splendid panorama over us all. For a second, I thought our eyes met, which sent a nervous shiver down my back. I lowered my eyes and started up an idle conversation with Abdel-Naim. I wanted to avoid eye contact with the king until an opportunity arose to exchange glances again when Abdel-Naim wasn't looking. He continued to scowl as he scanned the place for the person he'd come to meet. Suddenly his face relaxed and he waved to catch someone's attention. Following his eyes, I noticed a man nodding in our direction. I was shocked by how much he resembled me. We could have been brothers, though he was a bit shorter and slenderer than I, and at least ten years older. Out of curiosity, I snuck a peek at the king to find that he had been watching me with a smile on his face. The man whispered a few words to His Royal Highness, who laughed and then turned to converse with some of his guests. As he spoke, he lit a huge cigar, then set it in the ashtray in front of him and left it there.

The man came over and shook Abdel-Naim's hand warmly. Abdel-Naim introduced me as his business partner, but without mentioning my name at first. He then turned to me and said proudly, "Abbas Effendi, this is Pouli Pasha."

I smiled and shook the man's hand. As he set his little masquerade mask on the table and pulled out a chair to take a seat, he brought up our resemblance. I mumbled something about how flattered and honored I was. He smiled, then attacked the champagne as a man stranded for days in the desert would attack a bottle of fresh water.

"Actually, it was His Highness who noticed the resemblance," Pouli said. "He said that you should work as my stand-in so that I'd be available to him every day, twenty-four hours a day!" He burst out laughing and downed another glass of bubbly.

Abdel-Naim and I looked at each other, then back at Pouli, and laughed louder than he. Then Abdel-Naim turned serious and leaned toward him. "I'm ready and waiting," he said. "All we need is the go-ahead."

Pouli shifted his eyes back and forth between me and Abdel-Naim and said nothing.

"Abbas here is my partner and my right-hand man. He gets half," Abdel-Naim said.

"Don't worry, Naim. I'm a man of my word. Or should I call you Naim Bey already?"

"I'll settle for Abdel-Naim, sir. That's *Abdel-Naim*, not just Naim."

Pouli roared with laughter again, and Abdel-Naim and I roared in return. If my laugh was exaggerated, it was in part to hide my confusion. I hadn't the faintest idea what they were talking about.

Pouli made ready to leave, but before he stood up he told Abdel-Naim, "I'll send one of my guys over to your table before you go. In a day or two, the new permit will be ready!"

He took a last swig from his glass and added, "As for the title, congratulations in advance, Abdel-Naim Bey." Then, as nimbly as a lizard, he slid away from our table and was swallowed by the raucous crowd.

Abdel-Naim explained that business was getting complicated. A lot of people wanted a piece of the same pie and if they got their way we'd only be left with crumbs. So he resorted to Pouli Pasha to secure his slice and to renew his construction permit in Zamalek. Just to get to Pouli was a feat in itself, Abdel-Naim told me. It cost him a thousand pounds in bribes plus three dinners in the Shepheard Hotel just to make contact.

"What's so important about this Pouli Pasha?" I was as annoyed at the sum of money that Abdel-Naim had forked out to meet him as if it had come from my own pocket.

He heaved a sigh and said, "The guy started out as an electrician. Now he's one of the most trusted members of the royal court. I was told that he has the king's ear every day and that the king listens. But I bet he's a con artist whose palms need a lot of greasing."

At a preset time, Abdel-Naim's driver appeared at our table with a briefcase containing five thousand pounds. Shortly afterward, a young Italian swaggered over to receive it. He had a beret on his head, tilted to the left, and a short, unlit cigarillo dangling from the corner of his mouth. After distributing a smug smile evenly between us, he picked up the briefcase and put our existence behind him the moment he turned to leave. This was probably all in a day's work for him. Afterward, Abdel-Naim ordered the bill—seven and a half pounds! On top of that, he left fifty piasters as a tip. We left unobtrusively from the rear exit.

That "two days" that Pouli had spoken of turned into a week and then more than a month. By the end of the second month, Abdel-Naim was tearing his hair out. Pouli never answered his calls, he was never in his office, he was always busy at the palace with His Royal Highness. It was beginning to look like my business partner would never become a "Bey." Maybe they felt that title "Hajji" suited him better after all. But what mattered more to him than any rank or title, even one as high as "Pasha," was his construction permit. His current one would expire in a few months and there was no news about the renewal. We tried a few times to go back to the Auberge to meet Pouli, but we never made it beyond "Regretfully, messieurs, we have no free table for two this evening."

In a new three-piece suit, hat on head, I headed to the villa of Ambassador Amr Pasha. I owned this opportunity to Paula, who had interceded with her friend and neighbor Mme Maysa, Amr Pasha's sister. A servant in a bright-red caftan opened the door, bowed politely, and led me to a small antechamber off the reception room. A few minutes passed quickly as I contemplated the lush surroundings. Then I looked up to see the pasha, who uttered a curt greeting. I stood and held out my hand, but he ignored it. He took the seat opposite me, placed one leg over the other, and reached for a cigar from the breast pocket of a silk robe de chambre, which he wore over a shirt and necktie. He lit it calmly, then nodded, indicating that I should speak. As I spoke, laying the groundwork for my request, his eyebrows knitted with mounting irritation, which he vented with a thick gust of smoke. I got straight to the point: I hoped he would help get me an introduction to Pouli Pasha so that I could help Abdel-Naim renew his construction permit. Amr Pasha settled back in his chair with a scowl darker than the one he'd entered with.

"Firstly, Pouli is not a pasha," he said. "Secondly, I'm not some middleman who'll introduce you to a palace employee in exchange for that wily smile of yours, which you expect me to take as though it were down payment for a commission. I'm an ambassador and I have a reputation to uphold. I can't mediate in the business of construction licenses and demolishing villas. Thank you for your visit, Abbas Effendi. Goodbye."

He ended the meeting so abruptly that it took me a moment to realize what had happened. Then I was kept waiting for a long time before the butler appeared to show me out. But I refused to give up. I asked Paula to use the connections she had through her women friends at the Gezira Club who were wives of ministers and ambassadors. Eventually, with great difficulty, I wangled an appointment at the palace. It cost me a thousand pounds, which had to be conveyed to "other parties," as the people I paid put it.

Pouli greeted me warmly when I was ushered into his office. We had a long and friendly meeting in which we exchanged business cards and he assured me that all would be well. He introduced me to his assistants and to some of the pashas who passed by his office. I felt closer to Pouli and his entourage than to Abdel-Naim. "This is the man for me," I thought. "He's the one who'll take me the rest of the way up, and by the elevator, not by the staircase I've been trudging up for so long, clinging to Abdel-Naim's *gallabiya*."

"Count me in with twenty pounds."

Hassanein's eyebrows shot up, as did everyone else's at the table. But his expression quickly shifted to a smile as he exchanged a quick glance with Salem, telling him to make room for me. During the following slow, fraught minutes, cards were dealt and breaths were held. From certain signals from Hassanein to Salem, I knew the cards he held in his hand and I won.

Ever since Abdel-Naim's business went downhill, my main pastime was to watch Hassanein play poker, which he did almost every night in his apartment in Zamalek. I passed by his place frequently, since we'd become neighbors—next-door neighbors, as a matter fact. So next-door that I could hear him speaking in his bedroom. I'd drop by for a glass of whiskey or two and amuse myself watching them gamble. Eventually, I felt I'd learned all the rules of the game. They sat around a table covered with green baize, which Hassanein had bought especially so that he could indulge in his favorite hobby. It had inset grooves in front of each player for their cards and rounded hollows for whiskey glasses and ashtrays. Also, it could be folded into a normal dining table if necessary, in case of a police raid, I supposed.

I enjoyed watching his guests' faces grow more and more despondent as he emptied their pockets and then began playing for their wristwatches, rings, and other belongings. After he stripped them of these, he'd accept wagers in the form of promissory notes. To my surprise, they kept coming back for more of the same on subsequent nights. At first, I was as mystified by this as I was by his ability to win nonstop. It was amazing how his face became an expressionless mask as he picked up a hand dealt to him, fanned it open, and scanned the cards. I was so impressed by how cool, cautious, and patient he was as the betting proceeded and new hands were dealt. What a skill he had! Or so I thought, until I realized he cheated. And brilliantly! He had such a flair for sleight of hand that he could easily draw all four aces, if needed, in order to rake it in at the table. But he was clever. He'd deliberately lose the first few rounds in order to hook in his customers. Then his "luck" would change and, as one round led to the next, he'd raise the stakes until, by the end of the evening, his guests would leave broke, their heads bowed and shoulders slumped. He had a deterrent against a possible fit of rage or treachery: the large pistol in a leather shoulder holster, its wooden grip visible to anyone who might get it into his head to make a grab for Hassanein or his winnings.

Recently, a guy called Salem had become a regular at Hassanein's poker nights. He had a half-cocked smile that seemed permanently etched on his face, and he never spoke. I tried to draw him out a couple of times, but he'd only respond with noncommittal nods or shakes of the head. I figured out he must be a mute. For about three months, Salem would win at least two nights a week. Hassanein would rage, curse, and threaten, then eventually calm down. I could understand his anger: those were not small sums he was losing to Salem. Then one night, I left early. Around dawn, I heard the two of them, voices raised, on the other side of my apartment wall. I put my ear to the wall to hear better. To my surprise, Salem was Hassanein's brother-in-law, he could speak, and the two of them were in cahoots. They had a prearranged set of signals—a scratching of the nose, a tweak of the earlobe, a hand running through the hair, and even the number of times it took to strike a match to light a cigarette—each with a specific meaning, as I understood from the dressing-down that Hassanein gave his brother-in-law for not having paid proper attention to his signals. He reiterated them, and had Salem repeat them over and over like a slow student. From then on, the pair of them became my favorite part of my nighttime entertainment, especially after I learned that this silent Salem got 10 percent of the winnings when he played, even though it was Hassanein's money he was playing with.

Hassanein looked like he was about to have stroke when I won. Salem's jaw practically fell to the floor. Pearls of sweat stuck to his forehead as though the shock had frozen them in place. Hassanein challenged me to another round and doubled the stakes. I accepted and I won again. Three rounds later he caught on. He called me to one side to discuss "something to do with the villa." He offered me a cigarette and poured me a drink and spoke about this and that. It didn't take long. By the time we returned, Salem had taken Hassanein's place and, to my surprise, Hassanein decided to play too, instead of sitting out the rounds that Salem played. I did a quick calculation. I had 140 pounds. I could play with half of that and still come out even. After losing three rounds in a row, I grew nervous. I doubled the stakes for no reason. I tried to concentrate, but I couldn't figure it out their new game. Salem was on my left, back to the bar, cards held high so I couldn't follow his facial gestures. They were quicker than I. Whenever I pretended to be uncomfortable and fidgeted in my seat in order to see Salem's face, I realized that either I'd missed the signal or their signals had changed. As my money dwindled, my hands trembled and I began to feel lightheaded. Before long, I was down to my last 20 pounds, which was what I'd staked at the beginning of the evening. That was when I made up my mind to call it quits, but not to stop gambling. I bent toward Hassanein's ear until my mouth almost touched it and whispered, "I know you and Salem cheat using certain signals. Either I get 10 percent or we play with an open hand."

It took Hassanein exactly ten seconds to decide. In a loud and firm voice he said, "That's enough for tonight, folks. I'm beat and so's my good friend here. So let's call it a night, okay?"

It was close to dawn. I'd become obsessed again with the problem of the treasure. Despite all the years I'd been hunting for it in vain, I now felt closer than ever to solving the riddle. Some hours ago, I'd returned to the apartment after a long day at work with Abdel-Naim. That morning, he told me about a huge safe he'd found buried in the foundations of a villa that had once belonged to a Jewish family and that he'd demolished some months back in order to make way for an apartment block. His construction permit was still valid until the end of the year and he was doing as much work as he could. I went with him to the site and looked at the spot where he said he'd found the safe behind a wall. My mind flashed back to the night of Cicurel's murder and that piece of paper I'd found in his safe and had kept tucked in a secure place all these years.

I unfolded the paper for at least the fifth time and studied the strange design. I picked up a short pencil and began to imagine lines that, if I extended them, would lead me to his stash of hidden wealth. He must have hidden it somewhere behind one of those basement walls, which is what all Jews do, apparently. But no matter what alternatives I tried, I always drew a blank.

I'd been wrestling with this enigma off and on ever since Cicurel died and his brothers and Paula inherited his estate. I must have crept down to the basement and turned it inside out at least twenty times over the years. I'd have Zeinab lure Hassanein away from the house on some pretext or other so that I'd have more time. I'd imagine myself in Cicurel's place as I explored every possible nook and cranny and came up empty-handed. Often I abandoned the hunt out of despair and even managed to put that basement out of my mind for a while. Then something would happen to remind me of the Cicurel treasure, like a mischievous ghost emerging from out of the woodwork to stick out its tongue at me.

I jumped at an alarming thought. What was Hassanein still doing in the villa after all these years? I was the one who had snitched on the others, not him. Did he know where Cicurel had stashed his real fortune? If he did, surely he'd have pocketed it and be long gone by now. Or did he have his sights set on the villa itself? Was he scheming to marry Paula in order to get his hands on it? I shook my head to stop it from chasing these thoughts down blind alleyways, and took yet another look at that piece of paper. Its most salient feature was a geometric design that looked like a slender tree topped with a spray of branches. In fact, it more or less resembled the palm tree that was etched on every floor and wall tile in the cellar. In the center of the tree was a circle with some wavy lines in the background. From this emanated an arrow with its tip pointing down, and another which forked into two tips, one pointing right and the other left. Below them was the number "5."

I glanced at my watch. It was four thirty a.m. I jumped at the ringing of the phone. It was Zeinab. In a voice barely above a whisper, she said, "Get over here as quick as you can. It's important." She said no more apart from that it had to do with "the madame." Then she hung up abruptly, as though someone nearby might overhear her. I stared into space for a moment. The only explanation was that Paula was about to die. Or maybe she already had.

8

"I NURTURED A STRAY SEED alone until it sprouted, only for its fruit to be plucked behind my back."—Zeinab Mahalawi

After weeks of experiencing what it was like to be a desirable woman, I was plunged into a black pit from which I could see no escape but suicide. What could I tell Abbas? How could I look people in the face after what had happened to me and because of me? Would this make my brother lose everything just when it was nearly in his grasp? Question after question pounded the walls of my head, robbing me of sleep, keeping me dazed, dismal, and lost. My life was unraveling before my eyes because of a moment of weakness born in a space between reality and desire, a moment in which instinct won over reason. It was the faintest blip in the arch of time, but it threw me off balance. Now I was left with a remorse that gnawed at me during all my waking hours and sank its claws so deeply into my brain that it became the living flesh of my nightmares.

When my brother told me that Abdel-Naim's younger son wanted to marry me, I leapt at the offer. Abbas took my eagerness as a sign that I'd fallen for Asran when I first met him. I put on a shy smile. It was weak, I'm sure, but it served the purpose and Abbas bought it.

What would have happened if Asran hadn't asked to marry me? I'd been worried out of my mind for two months over my predicament, which would soon be my death sentence. My belly was beginning to round. In a couple of months it would swell, announcing to all and sundry that I got pregnant in sin. God must have sent me that young, bashful Azhar student to cover up that looming scandal, and just in time. Though I have to admit, a part of me was a little proud of myself. I had not seduced a married man in order to get him to leave his wife and marry me. I had not been driven solely by lust. I had given rein to my femininity and experienced genuine love for the first time. That was my right.

I hadn't lived until I met Sandro, a man who showed me my value with his eyes, his feelings, the attention he devoted to me. I saw my beauty in the way he lusted after me. I felt the heat of his affection when I placed my hands in his and let him devour them with lingering kisses. He began with my palms and moved to my fingers, kissing each one of them slowly, sucking some of them hungrily. I loved the way he made love. It intoxicated me and made me want more. My heart throbbed again, but this time it was real. At last there was a man in this wide world who desired me and was ready to marry me.

Me! Not some short, lame, ugly witch with a temper, which was how people back in the village saw me and talked about me behind my back. Here was a man who saw the beauty of his woman with his heart. He didn't care about her pedigree or kin, or her money and estates, as the women in Paula's circles imagined. He was an important, dignified, educated, and wealthy man, twenty years older than me, who came from some distant land to fall in love with me and kneel at my feet.

It was about three months ago that Sandro, Paula's Italian physician, started to visit the villa regularly to treat a weak cardiac muscle. He'd been recommended by Cicurel's brothers. I could tell he was interested in me from the outset by the way his eyes shone and the way they kept turning to me when I was in the room. He destroyed my weak defenses in no time.

I'd had no experience to draw on to resist him. He played me like a magician, touching feelings I'd forgotten or that I never knew I had. Before long, he'd awakened my femininity from a long slumber. When he sensed the quick success of his raid on my heart, he escalated to outright seduction.

To my surprise, Sandro spoke Arabic as though he were born and raised in Cairo, even though he was from Naples. He'd been commissioned to serve at the royal court for a set period of time and to tend to the patients at some charity hospitals free of charge. He told me that he'd studied medicine in Cairo many years ago. He lived in the Munira district at the time. I loved the way he spoke the Egyptian dialect. How he made me laugh! He knew the crudest swear words and could spout a stream of them as fluently as the street kids in Imbaba. I kept a safe distance between us at first, though I didn't want to put him off. That distance shrank with every passing day as he continued his advance. It shrank even more when I took a step or two in his direction. At night, in my room, I'd stand before the mirror and replay his words of admiration for the curves of my body. I'd touch the places he'd described, close my eyes, and imagine him holding me tightly, and I'd feel a delicious tremor course through every inch of my body. I knew I still had the power to stop him, even if I felt I was on a spit turning slowly over the coals of a desire more intense than his. But one night I surrendered of my own free will, and I savored my refusal to resist. Other nights followed and I looked forward to each more than the last. He'd quench my thirst and I'd quench his. He'd hold me in his arms and embrace me, sheltering me from narrowed eyes, watching me stealthily from afar.

I'll never forget that first night. With the excited eyes and thrill-filled whisper of an adolescent discovering new territory, he told me he'd given Paula a strong sedative that would ease her pain and help her to sleep soundly to the morning. I needn't worry about her waking up and calling for me in the middle of the night. That put paid to my last feeble excuse. I led him slowly and silently to the west wing and took him into a room with a window that overlooked the Nile at a sharp angle. This was the very room where Cicurel was murdered. Maybe my intent was to erase a gruesome evil with precious eternal memories from my love story. We climbed into Cicurel's bed and I melted into his arms. I liked the way he described sex: feelings lovers share when they make love. What a far cry it was from the "mounting" my mother described to the women back in the village. Sandro transported me to a magical world that held me spellbound as he kissed my feet, sucked my fingers, and drove me to a frenzy each time as though it were my first. I'd claw his back with my fingernails as he consumed me and brought me to ecstasy time and again. Afterward, when we were both spent, he'd hold me in his arms and we'd talk and laugh and roll around in the bed naked, making me desire him even more. Those few months were the most beautiful times of my life. Then he vanished. He just evaporated into thin air, like a mirage.

The last time I saw him, I told him I was worried because my period was late. He hugged me, said something to reassure me, and performed a quick checkup. He never made love to me again, and I fell. I tumbled from the skies of certainty to the jagged rocks of doubt. Something inside me broke at that point, but I stifled my pain. Sandro was shaken and confused. Even the half smile he tried to keep on his face was too heavy for him. I spent the night in his arms, but it was a cold embrace, like leaning on a rickety fence that could collapse any minute. When I awoke the next morning, he'd gone.

Why did he tell me I was like Cleopatra? Why did he ask me what the procedures were at al-Azhar in order to convert to Islam? Surely that was no state secret. What made him say "No woman turns me on like you do" if he didn't love me and plan to marry me?

One day, I suddenly felt queasy. Everything around me started to dance before my eyes, the ground began to spin, a blackness descended, and the contents of my stomach spewed out. That happened three days in a row. On the fourth I fainted in the middle of the reception room. Paula insisted I take a holiday. I went by myself to a doctor downtown who I knew of because I'd accompanied Helga there once. He said, "Congratulations. Our new arrival is due in about seven months."

So, when Abbas told me Asran had proposed, I pretended to be excited and asked him to make the marriage as soon as possible. But I was so nervous and confused, I was barely able to keep the tears out of my eyes. Abbas's eyes flashed and he started to circle around me, pinning his piercing gaze on my face without saying a word. I began to tremble. I knew the glint beneath those narrowed eyelids. I knew he smelled my fear. I'd already begun to whimper before he slapped me so hard my lips bled and I howled in pain. He didn't ask me the cause of my fear. He didn't have to.

"Who's the son of a bitch, Zeinab?"

Tears streamed down my cheeks. "Sandro. The doctor who's been treating Madame Paula. He left for Alexandria a week ago!"

He sat brooding without saying a word for half an hour while I trembled. When he broke his silence, it was to ask, "What do you know about the permit he applied for to start up a pharmaceutical company in Cairo?"

"Nothing!"

I was so surprised by the question I couldn't manage to say more. Ignoring the question in my eyes, he left for a meeting with Asran and his father in Imbaba. He returned very late that evening. I'd been waiting up for him, desperate for some reassurance, but he left me to spend the night alone with my fears howling at me. As soon as I saw him the following morning, he picked up the phone and dialed a number slowly and deliberately, while keeping his cold eyes fixed on me. Then his mouth widened into a broad, hollow smile, though I could see his eyes twitch as he spoke in a loud and jovial voice. "Asran?

Congratulations! Yes, she's agreed to be your bride. Look forward to a week from now!"

After replacing the receiver, he closed his eyes for a moment. Then he turned to me with a stony expression and told me that he'd had to make big concessions on the dowry, apartment, and other conditions. He also said that I'd been married before back in the village and that I was now a widow, but we'd had to keep that a secret.

"Got that? Or do I have to repeat it?"

I looked down and nodded, silently thanking God for protecting me so far. I was too afraid to ask him about this late first husband of mine, but he volunteered the answer as he prepared to leave: "Tell them he was your cousin, so our stories match."

Seven months and one week later, I gave birth to a beautiful, plump, fair-skinned baby girl. Asran wasn't happy because he'd wanted a son. That was when he started to lose interest in me and grow distant. Two days later his family dropped in and treated me the same way. You'd think I had something contagious.

Some days after that, while cooing at the baby, he suddenly said, "You know, she doesn't look like us at all."

My heart skipped a beat, even though he'd said this in an ordinary, matter-of-fact voice. Fortunately, Abbas was quick on his feet.

"Well my goodness! How the Lord works wonders. She's the spitting image of my mother, may God rest her soul."

Asran gave him an ingratiating smile and said, "Kin speaks through seven generations. So let's name her Hamida, after your mother, sir, and get her blessing. Hamida Asran Abdel-Naim."

"No!" I cried, although my voice came out weak. "I want to call my daughter Lady. That way when she's grown up, people will have to address her as Lady despite themselves."

Asran smiled. He liked the idea. He looked at Abbas as though to ask permission. Abbas gave a smile and a nod that meant, "It's up to you." Then he asked after Abdel-Naim's health.

"Old age is setting in. But tomorrow he's going up to Alexandria with Fahim. We got him an appointment with this doctor Sandro. He's a famous Italian doctor at the Muwasat Hospital."

I gasped. I quickly bent over my baby, pretending a sudden concern. Abbas's eyes flashed and his body tensed. He asked Asran why they had chosen that doctor in particular.

"He was the royal physician, and as you know Abdel-Naim has his connections—surely you know him. He was Madame Paula's doctor. He was practically living at the villa. Right, Zeinab?"

Was Asran hinting at something? I doubted he had suspicions about me. But there was a needling tone in his voice that worried me. I didn't answer. Abbas also remained silent. I felt that he was even more nervous than I. Only after Asran left to register my baby did he speak: "Forget about Madame Paula. Your home and your daughter are more important as of today. Another scandal and I'll kill you."

"Do you forgive me, Abbas?"

He ignored the question. Instead he grumbled, "Why do we make things so hard on ourselves, when the Lord tries to make things easy and shows us a shortcut? To hell with the villa and everything in it!"

Barely a week after Lady was born, Abbas disappeared for over a month. At first I thought he'd returned to the village, as he said he would in a moment of frustration. But why would he leave me in Cairo by myself?

Abbas had grown more and more distant in recent months. He'd become a stranger on the opposite bank of the Nile, strutting in front of the Zamalek villas in his trademark white fedora while I sat here on the balcony of my small cramped apartment in Imbaba waiting for a signal from him.

Then I learned that he had not returned to the village at all. According to Asran, my brother had gone up to Alexandria with Fahim and a couple of other people in order to take care of some business or other. While there, Abbas and Fahim took Abdel-Naim to an appointment with Dr. Sandro.

"But why did your father pick Dr. Sandro out of all the hundreds of doctors to choose from?" I asked, hoping to pry out more information.

"He's your brother's partner in that pharmaceutical factory," he answered coldly. "Do you think my eyes are screwed shut?"

"Pharmaceutical factory?"

"Yes. Your brother went up to finalize the deal. The factory's going to begin operations soon. Now quit playing dumb."

What kind of game was Abbas up to? He'd taken advantage of my condition, but how? What made Sandro agree to his terms? Abbas must have threatened him. It wasn't difficult to imagine how.

One day, Abbas called me up from Alexandria to ask after my health. When I asked him how his business was going, he hung up. When he returned to Cairo some weeks later, his face was as hard to read as stone. The more I tried to pry information about Sandro out of him, the more evasive he got. Finally, I decided to confront him directly. I told him I was disturbed by his partnership with the Italian doctor.

He let a silence hang in the air before answering, "Your secret's buried and Sandro isn't my partner. The factory belongs to me and the land it's on belongs to me. You might say he's just an employee. An ex-employee, because we fired him."

"*Fired?* Who's 'we'?"

"Me and my friend Pouli Pasha, my partner in the pharmaceutical company."

"And what do you mean by my secret's buried?"

He dismissed the question with a flick of his hand and warned me never to bring up the subject again.

He'd killed Sandro. I was absolutely certain of it.

Abbas destroyed what affection he had for me and burned the bridge between us. He was looking out for no one but himself now. For the first time since I came to Cairo I felt torn. I was a tangle of shredded fabrics from different women with no connection between them. I'd become a "monstrosity," as Mme Maysa described anything she didn't like.

Once when I was still a child, I watched my mother uproot some grass in the middle of the fields. When I asked her why, she said, "This here's devil grass. It looks innocent, but it's hungry, thirsty, and harmful. The clever farmer knows it for what it is and pulls it out before it can run riot."

Abbas had become "devil grass."

I was on my way back to Imbaba from Zamalek again. My mind was blank. I was crouched so far back in the seat beneath the bonnet of the carriage that I saw nothing as I crossed the iron bridge. The cracks of the driver's crop pierced my ears as if he were whipping me with every thrash. The horse's hoof-beats picked up pace as though it were about to trample me any moment. I squeezed my eyes shut as I cradled Lady, who kept me busy twenty-four hours a day. Asran had so little time for her. He wasn't nearly as attached to her as I was.

I'd had to stop seeing Paula for a long time. I'd lost count of the number of times she sent for me through Bashir, whose attitude toward me had mellowed since I'd left the villa. My brother's refusals grew more adamant each time. The villa had become the forbidden fruit for me, even though Abbas was the one who'd tempted me to take the first bite. Then, shortly before the end of my first year after my exile from the Zamalek paradise, I learned that Paula had had a relapse and desperately wanted me to return. After obtaining permission from my husband, in keeping with religious strictures, I did. But I kept it a secret from Abbas. To be precise, I didn't feel a need to tell him. At the same time, while I was a hundred percent sure he was aware of my visits, I sensed he chose not to confront me. That was when I began to feel my power, and when he started to feel it too. Still, I kept my visits down to once a week at first and tried to be as inconspicuous as possible about them so as not to provoke him. He could still unnerve me when I looked up to find him studying my face without saying a word.

I'd keep Paula company, entertain her, and cheer her up as I used to do in her healthier days. But now we were confined to the villa. Whenever I was there, my guilty secret seemed to taunt me from that room in the west wing that bore witness to the sowing of the seed whose fruit was now growing daily before my eyes. I'd also begun to see strange shadows and hear footsteps slowly approach then fade away. I recited Quranic verses to ward off evil, lit incense, and even sacrificed a rabbit. The mysterious hidden visitor never disappeared, though he never made himself visible either.

At one point, I had to add a second day per week because of Paula's many visits from her friends and neighbors. There were times when she was too feeble to come out to greet them, even in her wheelchair. Her incapacitation completely changed my position. I could now sit and speak with her friends up close, and if I got bored with their chitter-chatter, I could terminate the meeting. My pretext was right there before their eyes and there was no way they could object.

"I'm afraid Madame Paula needs to go upstairs and rest now," I'd say. "Please excuse us."

It worked like a charm whenever I felt I couldn't bear any more of the guests' snootiness. I used it a lot with Mme Maysa, Paula's most frequent visitor, being her best friend and neighbor. Now I really was lady of the manor.

As the years passed and Lady grew, I began to take her with me to the villa. Paula doted on my daughter, and what a thrill it was to hear her call her "Lady."

It also pleased me no end to see how my child refused to respond to Mme Maysa's attempt to be nice to her. "What's her name?" she asked.

"Lady. Call her Lady and she'll like you and come to you."

Maysa did not accept the name as easily as Paula.

"That's a heavy and inappropriate name for a child," she said in that frigid way of hers. "It will cause her problems when she grows up and begins to understand. Pardon me, Zeinab, but that's my opinion."

Fate also had an opinion of its own. After my love for Lady had taken root in every corner of my heart and soul, it snatched her away from me in the cruelest way imaginable. But not without arranging a feast for me first.

I hadn't brought Lady with me to Paula's that day because we were preparing for a dinner banquet that night. Asran left her alone at home when he went off to work. Lady was outside, playing with the neighborhood kids in front of our building, when one of them, some thirteen- or fourteen-year-old, suggested they all go for a felucca ride. The children were thrilled at the idea and set off toward the Nile, laughing, skipping, and cavorting as they pictured the fun they were about to have on their Nile adventure. They weren't watching where they were going. A tram rammed into her as they crossed the main street. It crushed her slowly beneath its wheels. It pulverized her bones, smashed into her beautiful face, ripped open her belly.

I didn't have the strength to wash her—what was left of her, the face marred beyond recognition. Abbas barely managed to lead me out of the room. I had to cling to his arm to keep from falling. The image of her murdered father, Sandro, hovered before my eyes. Fate must have decided to erase my sin before reclaiming the deposit.

I fainted during the burial. I howled and clawed at my face, and then my head began to spin and darkness descended. I locked myself up at home for a year. My eyes started to

97

bulge for no reason and I gained weight even though I could barely stand the sight of food. Whenever I caught sight of myself in a mirror, I pursed my lips at what I'd become. A few months after my child died, Asran, whom I'd taken for such a shy type, took a second wife, who bore him his first child. I didn't ask for a divorce. In fact, I didn't give a damn about that marriage, even though he'd kept it secret from me until his new wife got pregnant. He wished for a son and she gave him one. Afterward, the distance between us grew greater than before.

Abbas helped me through those dreadful months. He made sure I was never alone. When he learned that Asran had taken a second wife, he insisted I leave my husband's house. It was as though he were atoning for a grave sin. But before I agreed to move in with him, I asked him how he'd heard about my daughter's accident. Neither Asran nor I were at home at the time. Abbas was the one who notified us. This was the third time I'd asked him that question, and once again he told a different story. Suspicion burned inside me like a furnace and consumed the last shreds of trust in him.

The images of Lady, Sandro, and Hamdan, the guy Abbas had drowned in a canal for having harassed my elder sister, danced in front of my eyes like slaughtered chickens and awoke me every night with a jolt. I'd lie awake and wonder, "Whose turn will come first, Abbas, yours or mine?"

I moved into the small apartment my brother had taken in Zamalek, next door to Hassanein al-Masri. It was a ground-floor apartment in an old building that made me feel trapped, especially because of the fire raging inside me. It was Paula, whom I visited every evening, who helped me start to turn my life around. She bought me some nice readymade out-fits at the Sednaouis department store and suggested I take a morning job to keep myself busy and take my mind off my sorrows. She even found me work as a telephone operator at the Gezira Club. All I had to do was jot down the phone number I was given and point the caller to the right booth. It was easy and took up only four hours a day. The pay wasn't great, but it kept me occupied and I got to know the majority of the club's members. They tipped generously, especially around the holidays, but more importantly, Paula was right: the job did take my mind off my troubles a bit. After work, I'd go to Paula's and stay with her until nine every night. The only person I couldn't bear to see again was that old witch, Maysa. I couldn't help feeling she'd cast an evil eye on my child because of her "heavy name." I ignored her whenever I saw her. Even when she came to pay her condolences, I turned away and left without shaking her hand.

Mme Paula's health steadily worsened. She grew thinner, sallower, frailer. Her memory deteriorated and she wasn't always fully aware of what was happening around her. Maybe that was why she'd kept sending Bashir around to Imbaba to ask me to come back to the villa on a permanent basis. She wanted me at her side until she left our world. That was the feeling I got from the look in her eyes and even the final signals she seemed to make with her fingers whenever she succumbed to a brief coma.

The servants got used to my permanent presence in the villa again. I made sure they disturbed Paula as little as possible and kept visitors to a bare minimum. I made no allowances for Hassanein. I had him report to work and leave at set times, and restricted his presence to the office in the basement. I told him it was for the sake of Mme Paula's health, but I'd noticed he'd started sniffing into various nooks and crannies around the villa again, like he used to do many years ago. Also, he'd lock the doors to the basement whenever he was down there. He'd concoct phony excuses when I caught him in the basement after hours or, sometimes, behind the villa near the dock, holding a strange gadget that looked like a cane that buzzed. He always had this puzzled look on his face when I came across him. When I told Abbas about Hassanein's strange behavior, his eyes took on a strange glow. He told me to leave my job at the club so that I could stay at the villa with Paula longer. He urged me to steal that gadget. He even told me to ease up on my restrictions so Hassanein would feel free to nose around the house. "But don't let him out of your sight if he finds anything!" he warned.

"Finds anything like what? You know, you'd make things a lot easier for me if you told me what you two have been searching for all these years."

"A box, a safe, documents, money . . . anything hidden. The important thing, Zeinab, is to keep your eyes on him."

He fell silent for a moment as he searched my astonished face, then added, "And while we're at it, why don't you root around inside Paula's wardrobe and knock on the walls behind it."

Since I was there to keep Paula company and since she was always semi-comatose, I had plenty of time to do that. I searched through every item in the closet, to no avail, and my only reward from thumping the walls was a sore hand. I continued my search until one day, after making sure she was asleep, I took a peek into her jewelry chest. In one compartment, I found a soft velvet bag with some carefully folded papers inside. I gently opened them and felt a bolt of electricity run through me as soon as I scanned the first lines. Despite the late hour, I rushed to the phone to call Abbas. This couldn't wait. It was what he'd been looking for for years and it had fallen right into my hands.

Finally, Abbas came sauntering into the house as though he had all the time in the world. He stopped abruptly and looked around, surprised at finding no stretcher or wailing or anything out of the ordinary. In answer to his questioning look, I handed him the documents and watched his face change as he read them. After he'd finished, he frowned and stared into space for so long that I began to think he'd forgotten I was even there.

I even had to repeat my question a couple of times before he heard it: "Abbas . . . Abbas . . . what are we going to do about Nadia?"

Still deep in thought, he muttered some words to reassure me. Suddenly he exclaimed, "You did it, Zeinab!" and sped back out the door. I hastened after him, but by the time I reached the foot of the front stairs, he had been swallowed up by the night. I shook my head and turned to go back inside, only to find someone blocking my way and pointing a huge gun at my face. Our talk didn't last long, the gun having loosened my tongue. After I told him what he wanted to hear, he bound my hands and feet, covered my mouth with a wide strip of duct tape, and dragged me to the little shed near the dock. When he locked the door behind him, I was plunged into darkness as black as a grave.

9

"SOMETIMES THE SOLUTION IS RIGHT beneath your nose, but you don't see it because you're too busy looking for it."— Abbas Mahalawi

"Abbas . . . Abbas . . . what are we going to do about Nadia?"

Zeinab's question kept ringing in my ears. Of course! Reports of the Cicurel murder mentioned he'd had a daughter called Nadia from his first wife. She'd been in another wing of the house, sleeping like a babe through the whole ugly thing. I hadn't even known she'd existed. But the others did and they'd forgotten about her. As I would later learn from Paula, a few months after the incident Nadia moved abroad to live with her uncle and that was the last anyone heard of her. But now, Zeinab had just found a handwritten will bearing Cicurel's signature and a second document itemizing the estate that would go to Nadia. The documents were in both Arabic and Italian, and bore the official seals of the Mixed Courts, the notary public in Napoli, and the Foreign-owned Properties Registrar in Cairo. There were also dozens of official signatures, countersignatures, and oval, round, and triangular stamps. "Estate" meant everything: stores, shares, land, cars, and, last but not least, the villa, the Heart of Palm in Zamalek, the site of my long hunt for Cicurel's hidden treasure.

Where was Nadia now? Why hadn't she ever resurfaced to claim her inheritance? Nearly all his property had gone to his brothers. Not that Paula was left penniless. Who stood to benefit most from concealing this will? It required little thought. It could only be Paula, of course. There was nothing left for Nadia to inherit now but the Heart of Palm and a few thousand pounds.

Returning to my surroundings, I felt a sudden surge of hopelessness. I contemplated the stately pillars, the high ceilings, the plush furniture, and for a moment I saw the villa shrink into the distance and nearly fade from of view. Then out of Zeinab's mouth popped the question: "Now why on earth would Cicurel call it that? Hearts of palm are small and hollow. What a strange man!"

I stood stock still, staring at her face, which bore an almost indignant expression. Then I nearly jumped for joy. "I found it!" I barely managed to keep from shouting. I looked around to make sure we were alone, then gave her a bear hug and said, "You did it, Zeinab!"

"I did what?"

"I'll tell you later."

"But what are we going to do about Nadia, Abbas?"

"She brought us luck!"

I left my sister with her mouth agape as I rushed out of the house and around to the side door to the basement. Using a lantern so as not to alert anyone to my presence in there, I crept forward on tiptoe and made my way to the office. I unfolded the map on the desk, turned in the direction of the arrows, and began to look for the little tile that had a hollow palm heart, Zeinab's unwitting revelation. All the floor tiles had the same design: a small palm tree with a finely drawn green heart in the middle of the trunk. This was what had confused me before. Now I realized there must be one exception. The map said as much, but of course I couldn't see it because I couldn't think the way Zeinab did. And I was sure she was right.

I searched for over an hour beneath the light of the lantern, tapping the tiles with a fingernail, testing to see whether one would budge. Nothing. I returned to the desk and stared at those crazy fronds and two sets of arrows. Suddenly it clicked. One of them pointed to about a yard above the floor. I swiveled around. I could have kicked myself again for my stupidity! The tile I was looking for had to be behind the tall bookcase against the righthand wall. That piece of furniture wouldn't have been here at the time the map was drawn. I tried to shift it but it wouldn't budge. It was affixed to the wall, which struck me as odd. I took a step back. Then I noticed some large old box files in the middle of the second shelf from the bottom. I lifted them out with some difficulty, as they were bulky and awkward to hold. Behind them were tiles similar to the ones on the floor. I resumed the search with the aid of the lantern, my heart racing. I was very close. I couldn't see it, but I could feel it.

Then I nearly cried out for joy. There it was, right before my eyes: a lone tile different from the rest. The palm heart in the design was white, not green like the others. My hand trembled with excitement as I touched it. It wobbled slightly. When I pushed it gently, it slid into a hollow space behind it. I held up my lantern and saw the metallic gleam of a handle. I quickly began to remove the rest of the tiles around it. The work was easy, but I was pouring with sweat because of my excitement and my anxiety. At last the safe stood before me in its full glory. My God! How in the world did that crafty foreigner conceive of this hiding place? And why? The safe was relatively small. What did he keep in it? Surely he wouldn't have gone to all this trouble just to conceal some more documents.

I jiggled the handle. Locked. This safe had a dial lock with both letters and numbers. I knew the combination had to have five digits. That much was clear from the map. I dialed the number "5" five times, alternating between clockwise and counterclockwise. That didn't work. I tried the numbers one through five. No luck there. I was getting more nervous. I needed to finish this quickly and cover up my tracks. My breathing grew louder as my mind raced.

I couldn't say what time it was exactly, but all of a sudden I felt a hand clamp down on my left shoulder. I jumped, but before I could turn around I felt the cold mouth of a gun barrel on my neck. Then came the command, in a hard voice barely above a whisper: "Dial the letters N-A-D-I-A."

I heard the faint clicks as I dialed, clockwise and counterclockwise in turn. At the fifth click, I took hold of the handle with trembling fingers. It turned. When I pulled the door open, my eyes came to rest on a diamond that was truly the size of a heart of palm, if not larger. It sparkled majestically on a dark green velvet cushion, radiating an inner gleam, yet it was so transparent you could see what was behind it. I was breathless. For a moment I felt lifted off the ground to some space on the border between reality and fantasy. I had never seen anything so splendid in my life. Next to it lay many small ingots of gold, carefully stacked on top of each other. But they seemed to shrink from embarrassment at being compared with that magnificent diamond. There was also an assortment of other diamonds of different sizes, mostly small. When I was a child, I sat spellbound at the tales my grandmother told me about a boy who'd discovered a hidden treasure chest. I was that boy. The fairytale had come true at last. Better late than never.

I'd heard Hassanein gasp when I opened the safe and felt the pressure of his gun against my neck slacken. But I made no move to fight him. I was too enthralled by the vision before me. Its spell was more powerful than the weapon that threatened my life. But then the spell was broken when his big fat hand reached in front of my face, took hold of the diamond, and stuffed it into his pocket, making a large bulge. Using his gun, he signaled for me to take several steps back. Calmly and methodically, he laid the gold ingots side by side inside a canvas carryall, which was large enough that it didn't bulge and divulge its contents. Then he reached back into the safe to scoop up the small diamonds, which he slipped into a velvet pouch. After setting this on top of the ingots, he wagged his gun at me again and said, "Just walk in front of me and don't do anything foolish. I'm sure your life is worth much more to you."

He probably thought he spoke an incontrovertible truth. In fact, I'd decided to risk everything, including my life. I could smell the fear oozing from his pores despite the gun. I may have even detected a faint tremor in his hand. He was using the gun to transfer his fear to me. He probably had doubts about his ability to kill me and wasn't even sure what to do next. I took a seat on the nearest chair and lit a cigarette. I inhaled the smoke deep into my lungs and with it I filled with confidence. I crossed my legs to appear calm.

"Go ahead and kill me. Because if I get out of here, I'm going to turn you over to the police."

"What are you going to tell the police? That I caught you burgling the villa?"

I answered in the same sarcastic tone, "No. I'll tell them you were the fifth culprit in the Cicurel case. You were at the Rixos bar plotting with Ernesti and Jonah. I recognized you the moment I first saw you here. I was sure you'd started hunting for this safe before me. It was you who put them up to the burglary because you wanted them to do your dirty work for you. But you came out empty-handed. I'm the one who pocketed the map that day."

As I spoke I watched his face turn from smug to shocked, and then to awed. Then we both turned at the sound of a cane rapping on the parquet floor upstairs. It was remote but clearly audible. Hassanein hushed me with a finger over his mouth and moved closer to where I was. Our bodies nearly touched as we focused our ears. The knocking was rhythmic but still distant, as though the person were standing in place and knocking his cane on the floor to frighten us.

"Maybe it's Zeinab trying to warn us," I whispered.

Hassanein shook his head. Instinctively, we inched backward until we found our backs against the bookshelf. Hassanein turned around, put the carryall in the safe, and silently closed the door, leaving it slightly ajar. Then the sound stopped. We remained frozen in place for a full five minutes. Finally, he breathed a sigh of relief and stepped away from me.

"I was sure it was you who stole the map. But I couldn't figure out how you did it and when. Madame Paula and I suspected you from day one, but we pretended to accept your pitiful offer to renovate the villa in the hope that you'd lead us to the diamonds and gold. It took you long enough, that's for sure. I kept my eye on you whenever you came down here. I've watched and waited for years for this moment. When I visited Ernesti in prison, he told me how you gave them the slip and ratted on them. That's why I never trusted you for a moment."

"You mean Ernesti who you left the key to the basement door beneath the doormat? Don't take me for a fool, Hassanein."

He thumped his forehead with his the heel of his hand. I too felt I'd given too much away. Our cards were on the table now. From now on, this would be a battle of strength, not wits or luck. Drops of sweat rolled down my back. I needed to keep my tongue in check. My mind turned to Paula. So she'd been Hassanein's partner in the hunt for the diamonds all along. She was a far better actor than he was.

Now that I was sure that Hassanein's fear blinded him to mine, I could relax a bit. His main worry now was to save his neck from the same noose that had taken his accomplices all those years ago. He wasn't going to risk pulling the trigger. He wouldn't want a homicide labeled "Abbas" added to his charge sheet. Our silence was broken by another knocking sound, muffled and distant, but coming from outside the villa this time. I tensed, but Hassanein seemed calm, and gave me a cold smile. He climbed onto an old crate and shoved his head through a small window overlooking the rear garden. When he stepped back down, he told me that Zeinab had tried to block his way when he was heading toward the cellar. She'd picked a quarrel with him for no reason, which made him suspicious. So he tied her up, taped her mouth shut, and locked her up in the shed next to the dock.

We fell silent again. Our silence was so intense we could hear each other's breathing. At last Hassanein spoke, calmly, but with a hint of defeat in his voice, or so I imagined. "All right. We'll go halves."

I smiled inwardly. He'd begun to give in. He wanted to get this over with, and with the least possible loss. But before I could speak, he dredged up some of his dwindling courage and added, "Don't think too much. It's my only offer."

"What guarantee are you going to give me that I get my share?"

"You have my word. That's my guarantee. I'll dispose of the goods in a day, two at the outside. After I pay you, you clear out of Zamalek for good. Go back to your village."

This was a bargaining opportunity. I wagged my finger and clicked my tongue as I approached him slowly. He seemed to shrink, as if possessed by a djinni, and turned passive and pliable, ready for me to mold him. Pausing a moment to gird myself, I lowered the gun in his hand. I could feel his breath on my face.

"Madame Paula should get a share," I said. "Meaning the money's got to be split three ways, not two. And don't even think of ratting on me. Zeinab knows all about you. She'll turn you in and denounce you to the police if anything happens to me. By the way, she deserves a share too. Meaning you get a fourth." Holding up a hand before he could speak, I said, "And after you get it, you're the one who's going to leave Zamalek. In fact, you're going to leave the country."

Hassanein, tired from our circling each other, plopped into a chair and swayed, seeming on the verge of collapse. I continued to pile on the pressure, but he merely stared into space. He remained that way for so long that when he finally started to speak, I wondered whether he was fully aware of what he was saying. There was an echo in his voice, as though he were reading out of an old book he'd dug up in the attic.

"It was by pure accident that I learned about that map Cicurel drew up shortly before his death. Paula let it slip out. He planned to leave everything to Nadia, his daughter from his first wife. He didn't want his brothers or his second wife to inherit anything."

Afterward, he'd worked out a deal with Ernesti to rob the upstairs safe, but he never intended for anyone to get murdered.

"So Ernesti knew about the map too?" I asked.

"No, of course not. He just wanted the money. The agreement was for him to bring me any papers he found and he could keep the rest. But then you stole the map!"

"So Madame Paula knew about the heist in advance?"

"You might say that she was taken by surprise, then chose to remain silent. After the incident, all I cared about was the map. As for Paula, she doesn't have long to live, so remove her from your calculations." He took a deep breath, then continued. "You know the rest from the time you guys broke in and killed Cicurel. One day, Paula caught me hunting around in the basement and figured out what I was doing. From then on, we both started looking for the hidden gold and diamonds until you showed up. I smelled something fishy about you, but she recognized you right away, despite the hat, the glasses, and the phony beard, which you only removed after you thought you'd conned us. It was because she recognized you that she agreed to let you renovate the villa even though it had been recently repainted. She even agreed to take on Zeinab, even though she suspected she was really your sister. She played along with all your tricks, because the sooner you located the treasure, the sooner we could get rid of you. But as the years went by, she gave up hope and, at the same time, she grew attached to Zeinab. Eventually she forgot about it, and then her illness started to eat away at her. But I never ever forgot, not for a moment."

"I'm not the one who killed Cicurel. I took the map and made my getaway. Now this here is my right. I sweated blood looking for this safe. I'm not going to let you take it from me. Not over my dead body!"

He leaned back in his chair and put his feet on top of the desk, with the soles of his shoes facing me.

"No wonder you hid the fact that Zeinab was your sister," he sneered. "You wanted to marry Paula, you scumbag."

My jaws clenched. But I refused to let him provoke me. I was about to repeat my threat, but he cut me off. "Here's my final offer. We'll sell the stuff off and then we'll talk. You can be sure you'll get your share because we'll dispose of the goods together. If you don't like it, I'll report you to the police. Paula—or Nadia, if she's still alive—will get the safe and its contents, and you and I will lose everything. Now think. Paula's dying and Nadia, wherever she is, knows nothing about the will. But you and I still have our whole lives ahead of us."

"And if Nadia returns?"

"She could have stayed and demanded her rights after her father died. But she left to Switzerland with an uncle of hers and hasn't been heard from since. She's not going to come back. Paula isn't her mother and she's got nothing to bring her back here. So, just put Nadia out of your mind."

We were back at square one. He brought his feet back down to the ground and started to wave his gun around again. He was getting fidgety. I suggested splitting the large diamond in half and dividing the rest of the stuff between us. He laughed out loud.

"You're a real peasant from the Delta. Still as green as grass. Paula was right, there's no making something decent out of you." He stood up suddenly and walked toward me, looking straight into my eyes. "You can't cut a diamond just like that. It takes another diamond to cut a diamond. And you need a special machine and an expert who knows what he's doing. Otherwise you'll ruin the whole thing." He backed me into a chair as he continued to lecture me as though I were a dimwitted apprentice, telling me how Cicurel only kept breadcrumbs in the bank, just for the essential liquidity—the cash he needed to run his business with his brothers and for domestic purposes. The rest of his profits he invested over time in the diamond and gold trade. In other words, he converted all his money into diamonds and gold ingots. Despite his obesity, he pivoted with the grace of a ballet dancer, reached into the safe, and pulled out a sheaf of receipts, and flung them into my lap.

"Stop being greedy, Abbas. Take a look at their real value. We can be millionaires in a month at the outside. We're almost there!"

As I turned this over in my mind, he added that he knew Jacob Zananiri, a well-known diamond merchant whom Cicurel dealt with. "Zananiri will be our next stop. He'll buy the diamonds from us, have them cut up, and sell them in Belgium. We'll make a tidy sum—a quarter of a million pounds at least, for each of us. So stop being an ass!"

I gasped. I had no idea the diamonds could be worth so much. I hadn't dreamed of a tenth of that amount, which I wouldn't make even if Abdel-Naim and I were contracted to build every new building in Zamalek.

Hassanein prepared to leave. He lifted the gun again and pointed it at me as he reached into the safe to grab the carryall. He shut the safe, spun the combination dial to make sure it was locked, and replaced the tiles in a slapdash way. Then he flicked the muzzle again to tell me to get moving. I was sure he was now working out how to kill me. As I walked in front of him, my mind scrambled to figure out my next move. As he himself always said, no serious poker player throws in the towel easily.

We went down to the dock and untied Zeinab. She'd fallen into a stupor inside that dark, stuffy shed. She followed us silently up to the house, where we left her. Before going inside, she held me in her gaze as though expecting an explanation, but I had none to offer since I hadn't made up my mind what my next step was. Hassanein warned her against saying a word to Paula or to the police, or he'd kill her and kill me too. I didn't doubt he was serious. I signaled to her to assent.

Hassanein and I climbed into my small Fiat and headed to our building at the north end of the island. On the way, he asked me to stop at the grocer's so he could pick up some food. I told him to plan for me, because I'd be spending the night at his place. "I'm going to stick to you like a shadow until we dispose of that big diamond tomorrow and I collect Zeinab's and my share," I said. He gave me a curt smile and said nothing. We made another stop on the way at a pharmacy because he needed some cough medicine. I waited for him in the car. After a while, it occurred to me he might slip out the back door. I rushed into the pharmacy and saw no one. Then the curtain to a back room swept aside and he appeared carrying a small bag and adjusting his belt.

"Sorry it took so long. I needed a shot," he said. The pharmacist appeared behind him.

Once inside his apartment, he set the carryall on the poker table where it would remain visible. I pointed to his trouser pocket. He took out the large diamond and set it inside the bag. Then I phoned Zeinab to tell her I was going to spend a night or two in Alexandria because of work. She was worried and started to ask questions. I cut her off and, raising my voice, told her to call the police if Hassanein came over to the villa by himself the next day. I replaced the receiver.

"In case you didn't hear that, I told Zeinab to call the police if anything happens to me," I said as I returned to my seat and tried to focus.

He calmly picked up his gun, flicked it open, emptied the six bullets from their chambers, and put them in his pocket. That was meant to reassure me, but I was still nervous. He opened the bag, took out the gold bars and diamonds, and divided them equally. He slid my share across the green baize table, extending an open palm and a greasy smile to offer it.

I began to breathe a little easier. I asked him about his wife. He told me she'd gone to Alexandria to stay with her family until she gave birth to their first child. He yawned, then smiled and said, "How about a bite to eat? Then we'll have broken bread together."

He went to the kitchen to prepare a light meal. I hurried after him to keep watch as he prepared it. His fingers were as quick and nimble at making sandwiches as they were at shuffling and stacking decks of cards. I made sure that he took the first bite, just in case he'd managed to slip some poison into the food. Then I waited a good five minutes before taking my first bite. He prepared a couple of glasses of very strong tea to keep us awake until it was time to go to the diamond merchant in the morning. Neither of us could trust the other enough to be able to close his eyes for a second.

"How about we play a round for the villa and its contents?" he said as he reached for a deck of cards and began to shuffle them with speed and dexterity.

I watched as he riffled and cascaded the deck several times, until my eyes began to blur. I yawned, then laughed, and said, "Who gave you permission to stake something that doesn't belong to you?"

"Well it doesn't belong to you either. So you won't lose anything when you lose it. Anyway, isn't this better than prison, Mr. One-Eyed Abbas?"

Despite the threat, I waved away the invitation to a game.

"Oh, okay. Then you call the shots. It's your right. After all, I haven't forgotten how you earned yourself a 10 percent cut from this table the night you exposed our game because of Salem's stupidity. By the way, whose money were you playing with then?"

I ignored him. He started to talk about this and that: from King Faruq's decision to divorce Queen Farida to the famous traffic accident on Qasr al-Nil Bridge that killed Ahmed Hassanein Pasha a couple of years earlier—"The British were behind that one," he said. I shrugged. What did I care about palace gossip and the political intrigues people were rabbiting on about? He turned to the king's friendship with Pouli. They played cards together at the Automobile Club, he said, and he started to describe how Pouli cheated the king in baccarat. I tried to tune him out. After a while, I jerked my head up. He was still jabbering, but now he was strutting back and forth in front of me in an undershirt and a pair of blue-striped pajamas. He cursed the heat and humidity, and removed the undershirt. Plopping himself down in front of the radio, he started to roll the dial back and forth, causing an infernal racket of squeals and squawks that went on and on.

10

"Our childhood is engraved on our memory like stone. It is an indelible part of our minds."—Nadia

I was about five and a half years old when I learned that King Faruq had sailed out of Alexandria on his royal yacht, the *Mahrousa*. We were gathered around the small wooden table in our beach cabin at Sidi Bishr. Every now and then I glanced out to check on my sandcastles. They were still standing strong against the fringes of broken waves rushing up the beach. I caught a glimpse of the snack vendor in the distance. Then I heard his musical call: "Freska! Freska! Cocoa, hazelnut-filled freska!" I climbed up on the couch to get a better view and saw him clearly. He was headed in our direction, his glass case with its decorative wooden trimming strapped over his shoulders. I pointed at him excitedly. Then I saw Fahim Effendi, my father's secretary, coming from the same direction. You couldn't miss him in his distinctive *gallabiya* and red tarboosh—he never dressed any other way his whole life. He was waving a newspaper as he rushed into the room to give us the news about the king's abdication.

"It says here that he asked for permission to leave the country and they agreed," he said, still catching his breath.

"And where does that useless king want to go?" asked my father.

"Some people say Naples!" Fahim's booming voice drowned out my cry for a freska, which infuriated me.

My father asked excitedly about some guy called "Pouli," if I recall correctly. Then he snatched the newspaper out of Fahim's hand. I was very young, so much of what they were talking about was over my head and my memory of their conversation is rather vague. But I do recall that my attention was caught by the word "Naples" and the picture in the newspaper of the fat king in a sailor's outfit. I asked my Auntie Zeinab about that word, but she ignored me. She looked angry about something and took impatient puffs from her cigarette. I turned to my father, who picked me up, hugged me, and kissed my forehead. He told me it was a city nearby in a place called Italy. Then, holding me gently in one arm, he stretched out the other to its fullest length and pointed toward the sea. "It's over there." I looked hard, but I couldn't see it. Then he said, almost in a whisper, he said, "That's where Paula, your mommy, comes from."

I left my lunch and went outside with my elderly nanny, Helga. I stared silently out to sea for a while, then played on the beach until it was time to leave. When they called out to me to get ready, I ignored them because I was busy sprinkling my sandcastle with my little watering can. But when Fahim, my father, and my aunt started gathering up the wooden beach chairs and towels, they knocked it down with their big feet. As my aunt led me up the stairs to the main street in order to flag down a taxi, I kept looking back at the remnants of my castle until it disappeared from sight.

The reason I recall that day clearly is because, after we got home, my father told me how my mother died. He said she'd been ill for many years and suffered an awful lot. But she loved me more than anyone else in the world. He put up with my repeated questions for a little while, and then pointed his finger upward and said, "She's with our Lord." That perplexed me. I went out to the balcony and stared up at the sky for a long time. I called out her name three times, but received no answer. Then Auntie Zeinab came, took a firm hold of my hand, and pulled me inside. I slept soundly that night, holding a picture of my beautiful mother in the large, white, broad-rimmed hat she wore in the few pictures we had of her. What I didn't realize was that, the following day, I would be saying goodbye to our villa in Alexandria forever.

The king's departure on the *Mahrousa* brought an early end to our summer holiday that year and our return to Cairo at the beginning of August. My father seemed unusually nervous. I sat silently the whole way home along that boring road where all you see for miles and miles is yellow sand on both sides. We were on that narrow winding black strip for hours. I always liked to sit on the "magic" fold-out chair behind the driver in our black Cadillac so I could watch the road in reverse. I'd made a head covering for my doll out of an old piece of cloth, which I'd fashioned to make it look like my mother's hat. My doll rested in my arms to keep me company along the way. The only things I found annoying were my aunt's loud, rhythmic snoring when she slept and her shrill voice when she spoke. At one point I dozed off and slept the rest of the way to our house, which was called the Heart of Palm.

This was where I opened my eyes to the world. It was where I had lived my whole life in Zamalek. When I turned ten, Mme Maysa started to give me piano lessons at the school every day after classes. But Auntie Zeinab objected because I came home too late. So I reduced the lessons to once a week, until eventually I gave up. Then, my aunt insisted on teaching me knitting and embroidery. Worse, she'd keep me with her in the kitchen for hours on end.

"You dummy," she said when I complained. "Piano will drive away suitors when you grow up, whereas food will make them love you. Just take a look at that Maysa, who fills your head with nonsense. Now there's an old maid left fallow!"

This was one of those times when I just couldn't understand what she was talking about. She had such a strange way of putting things. None of the mothers of my girlfriends at school talked like that. My aunt constantly surprised them with her strange vocabulary and homespun sayings, which often made them giggle. I could tell my aunt didn't like my girlfriends' mothers. She never received them with the warmth she showed her own friends.

I first became acquainted with my small world outside the Heart of Palm in the company of my Swiss nanny, Helga. When the weather was nice, she'd take me for walks through Zamalek, from our house at the end of Shagaret al-Durr Street to the Officers' Club on Fuad Street. We often caught sight of the officers going in or coming out of the club, trim and agile in khaki uniforms and tall red tarbooshes. They looked so serious as they strode back and forth on the paths paved with gold and reddish sands. Sometimes we'd hear the bugler announcing the arrival or departure of a commander and we'd watch the soldiers snap to attention and raise their guns in a salute. It was so exciting to see them close up. They stood strong and erect, unlike my father, who was always hunched over files, ledgers, and paperwork. They looked like heroes out of the fairytales my aunt would tell me.

From the Officers' Club, we'd continue on our way to the Gezira Club. We'd pass by stately villas on either side of the road until we reached the back entrance near the horse-racing track. We scurried through the gate because children and their nannies weren't allowed in this area, which made it all the more exciting. We could hear shouted cries and commentaries, but were too far away to make out the words. We saw hats fly into the air out of anger, men holding binoculars jumping with joy, old men fretting and fuming as they lit a fresh cigarette while grinding the butt of another into the dirt. We'd hurry on our way to the children's playground, where we'd spend the whole day until sunset. Being children, our days always ended early.

In order to catch the bus to school in the mornings, I had to wait on the sidewalk near the villa of my mother's friend, Mme Maysa. She was a refined, erudite lady who taught French at our school. I'd see her every morning in her car on her way to school. I would have loved to go with her instead of taking the bus.

During my school years, my aunt asked her countless times to give me a lift to school so I wouldn't have to get up so early. Mme Maysa always responded with a brusque refusal, even though she was always kind and friendly toward me.

On the way to school, the bus would make a stop at the house of my classmate Sara Youssef Mizar. My aunt told me to stay away from her because she was Jewish. But I liked her. Her mother made the most delicious cookies in the world, in my opinion, and she often gave us boxes of them as gifts. But my aunt said they were "hexed" and she crumbled them up and fed them to her rabbits. She called Mme Mary, a friend of Maysa's, a jinx as well because she was a Copt. This troubled and confused me, because most of my schoolmates were Copts.

One day, our driver drove me and Helga to visit Sara at her home because she'd been absent from school for a long time. Sara and her mother weren't at home, and the doorman wouldn't tell me where they'd gone or when they'd come back. I came home shocked and sad. I continued to ask after her, until one day my father took me on his lap and gave me a long explanation, though it was a bit over my head. He said that people didn't control their own fate and that sometimes things happened in the world that robbed us of our friends and families and people we loved. He looked at me with wide, watery eyes and told me how much he missed his Jewish friend who'd died in an airplane accident many years ago. He looked so sad it brought tears to my eyes.

Some time afterward, I learned that Sara and her family moved out of Zamalek after Sara's mother went up to the Lord just like my own mother had. I could understand how

Sara felt. I thought maybe Sara was even sadder than I was. I had never seen my mother, whereas Sara had lived with her mother for more than ten years before losing her. Then she left with her father and her brother to their country, which was far away. Yes, she must have suffered more than me. Thank God I never saw my mother and didn't have to feel the pain that Sara did.

When I was younger, I used to think my Auntie Zeinab was my mother because there were so many pictures of her around the house, plus that life-size oil painting of her in the main hall. Also, she looked after me like a mother. When I grew a little older, I learned that she had moved in with us after her divorce. Then my father explained that my mother gave birth to me at a late age and that the pregnancy had been so difficult for her that she left us only a few months after I came into the world. Ever since then, Auntie Zeinab brought me up. Why it took them so long to tell me all this was beyond me. I also learned that my aunt had had a daughter who died very young, and that was what made her grow as attached to me as if I were her daughter.

"When God loves somebody, He calls them to Him before others. So just praise God and stop asking so many questions."

Auntie Zeinab's stern voice cut into my thoughts. She stood there expecting some sign of submission, as usual.

"Does that mean I have to die young for God to love me? What about you and Papa? Does God dislike you two because you've lived so long?"

Rather than answer my questions, she gave me a scolding. Still, despite how harsh and strict and nitpicky she was about everything, I loved her, and I couldn't imagine our home, or even life, without her.

My childhood and adolescence were probably the most beautiful days in my life. Everything was so easy. My father would always tell the servants, and even his secretary, Fahim

Effendi, "If Nadia asks for sparrow's milk, then you get her sparrow's milk!"

The only person exempt from that command was my aunt. If I asked for something she disapproved of, she'd purse her lips, shake her head, and click her tongue. Then she'd have me do some task that she'd think up on the spur of the moment. She was the only one who ever slapped me when I was young. Once she cut off one of my braids to punish me for being sassy. More often, she'd grab the nearest thing and throw it at me. For example, if I unpinned my hair and let it cascade down to my shoulders, while looking straight at her short, kinky hair and trying not to laugh, her face would suddenly contort and she'd turn into a wild woman, spewing a stream of shrill, guttural curses. Then she'd disappear into her room and reemerge a while later, her face having regained its normal composure. My father totally evaporated at such moments. He'd resurface only after the storm had passed, punishment had been served, and I'd been left to cry and lick my wounds. I'd run to his arms to complain and receive a dose of tenderness, which he administered better than anyone else. He had amazing powers of persuasion. He could sweet talk anybody into anything. Except for Auntie Zeinab.

Tarek and I were sitting beneath the large palm tree in our garden. "Madame Paula was a really beautiful woman, by the way," he said. I wondered where and when he'd seen her. I envied him, of course, even if it was a lie. He had to be lying, because he would have been very young when my mother left this world. But even if he'd never seen her, at least he was trying to flatter me.

Tarek Hassanein al-Masri was a quiet, gentle child who would grow into a handsome, if introverted, young man. He was the son of my father's business manager who had suddenly migrated to some distant land, abandoning his wife and his only son. Tarek had become my playmate when his mother started to bring him along after she began working for my aunt. She was a simple and decent woman, and we certainly didn't see her as a servant. Auntie Zeinab called her a "*femme de compagnie*." She'd tend to my aunt, keep her entertained, and help her manage the affairs of our home. Tarek and his mother lived not too far away, in a ground-floor apartment in the northern part of Zamalek, on the side of the island facing Imbaba.

I always had a feeling that my father hated Tarek. He treated the child coldly and tried to keep me from playing with him. He called the boy a "bad seed," but this didn't stop him from feeling sorry for the child's mother. I sometimes wondered whether that meek, gentle boy reciprocated my father's feelings. I sensed that he did, but I could never be sure. If he did, he never let it show, despite the hostile vibes my father sent his way whenever his mother brought him over.

Tarek was unlike all other boys, and unlike the other young men who appeared in my life as I grew up, whether in school, at the Gezira Club, or, later, at university. As shy and awkward as he was, he had a devilish streak. There was a deep sadness in his eyes despite the guileless smile that lit up his face whenever he spoke. At times his mood would suddenly turn dark and he'd fly into a fit of temper. His face flushed, his eyes gave off sparks, and he lashed out at everything around him. Then he'd stomp off, only to reappear unexpectedly, looking timid and nervous for no reason.

As I grew older yet, he was practically living at our place. I'd see him at his favorite spot in the garden, near the entrance to the basement, where he sat strumming some songs on a guitar that he had made at school. He used an old shoebox for the body. At first he had trouble working out the strings, but he was clever and persistent. He could make or repair anything. He tried some wire and nylon strings at first, but they didn't give him the sound he was looking for. One day, I reached up and removed three thin brown rubber bands from my hair and handed them to him. He attached them to the cardboard body and played his first tune using the handle of an old silver spoon as a pick. I can still hear that tune whenever I recall that day. He told me that it was the latest Umm Kulthum song. I hadn't heard it yet at the time. When I did hear it, sometime later, I discovered he'd played for me "Who can I turn to?"

I seized the first opportunity I could to surprise him. When Mme Maysa asked me what I wanted for my birthday, I told her, "A guitar." She agreed more quickly than I would have imagined. If she had been my aunt, she would have besieged me with suspicious questions and insinuations until I loathed the guitar and everything to do with music. Mme Maysa took me to a music store downtown. When I saw a real guitar, I was shocked by how big it was. It was almost as long as Tarek was tall. And how was I going to hide it from my aunt when it was taller than I was?

Noticing my hesitation, Mme Maysa pointed to a small violin. It was a fine, delicate instrument, though it didn't make much noise when I picked it up and plucked the strings. Still, I thought it would serve the purpose and Tarek would like it. I hid it in my room until I managed to sneak it to Tarek in the garden without anyone noticing, especially my aunt. From then on, Tarek's music would greet me in the afternoons when I returned from school. His music shaped so many of my memories, permeating them like a splendid melodious soundtrack, until the day it came to an abrupt stop.

"By the way, my father owned the Heart of Palm, but he lost it in a game of poker."

Tarek said this quite often as we grew up. He told me he learned it from the stories his mother and his uncle Salem told him. The subject would set this normally sweet-tempered boy into damning the father he'd never known for having skipped the country after frittering away all his money on gambling and abandoning his mother to misery and poverty. A strange gleam would come into his eyes, a blend of anger, tears, and remorse that faded to a cold blankness. He harbored such a deep hatred and anger that it made him want to destroy the nearest thing in reach. I knew of only one way to calm him down when he flew into a temper like that. I would approach him slowly and ask him to play his music for me. He didn't acquiesce easily. He'd back away, clutching his violin to this chest to keep me from touching it, then turn and run off to hide behind the shed out back near the dock. That was where my aunt kept her rabbits, which she'd started to raise after she had my mother's dogs put down because "dogs are foul and defiling." After some time, Tarek would come back, looking meek and nervous. I'd stare into his eyes and we'd stand for a moment without speaking. Eventually, he'd stick the violin under his chin, rub the bow between his legs to clean off any particles that might be clinging to it from when he was tending to the rabbits, and set it on the strings. As he began to play, he'd relax and the innocent child inside him would reemerge. But there came a time when I lost the power to soothe his anger and he smashed the violin into so many pieces that it was impossible for me to collect all the scattered fragments and broken strings.

My aunt's slaps on the face or the cutting of my braid were nothing compared to other types of pain she could inflict, like she did after I begged her to buy me a little puppy like all my girlfriends had. She wouldn't hear of it. She swore at me just for mentioning it and flung one of her sandals at me as I ran out of the room in tears, and muttering bitterly. She missed. The next day, Mme Maysa asked me why my eyes were swollen and why I couldn't concentrate during class. When I explained, she smiled and said, "Don't you worry. I'll see what I can do."

She worked a miracle. Some days later, she told me to drop by her house on my way home after school. When I arrived, she invited me in with a big smile. Then she gave me a tiny puppy barely bigger than a mouse. I don't know what breed it was, but it was so sweet. It had a ruff of thick fur with yellow tints around its head, and it looked at me with doleful eyes. It was frisky and playful. Maysa, still smiling, opened my schoolbag, put the puppy inside, and closed it loosely. He wriggled around in there a bit, then peered out through the flap and barked. She fed him a piece of peeled almond to shut him up and then filled my palm with a lot more almonds to help me sneak him into my room safely. I turned to leave, eager to get home and play with him in my room. As I was about to open the door to leave, I laughed and turned to her to ask, "What's his name?"

"Fendi," she said with a smile. "And it's not *his* name, it's *her* name."

Fendi lived with me a full five months before my aunt discovered her. The only one at home who was in on the secret was Helga, because she hid her for me while I was at school. With much pampering and large quantities of peeled almonds, we managed to keep her quiet for most of the time. On those occasions when she barked too loud, my aunt thought it came from the Cicurel villa or from Maysa's dogs. Once I told my aunt that a street dog in the neighborhood had given birth, and her litter kept yelping all night long. Then came the day I went for a felucca ride on the Nile with my friends—without asking my aunt's permission, because I knew she'd refuse. I did ask permission from my father, though. He nodded. Taking that plus his smile as assent, I went upstairs to collect Fendi and left. The brother of a friend of mine was in charge. He was several years older than us and he rented a small felucca. We were too excited to sit down. We raced around the boat, jumping up and down, until the boat tipped and we toppled overboard. I returned home drenched, even though I'd spent two hours on the bank waiting in vain for my clothes to dry. Because I was so late getting home, I found my aunt waiting for me in the front garden. Behind her stood Tarek's mother, and the three servants behind them. They looked like a regiment awaiting the order to attack. I didn't think I'd ever seen such a thunderous look in my aunt's eyes.

"I got caught in the rain, Auntie. It was pouring down and my clothes got soaked!"

She walked slowly and deliberately toward me, took a whiff of my clothes, and whacked my face with the flat of her hand. Just then, Fendi leapt out of my little bag and started snapping and nipping at my aunt's feet. The surprise made her stumble backward, and she would have fallen if Tarek's mother hadn't caught her just in time. I seized the opportunity to save my hide. As Fendi warded off further aggression, yapping and growling at my aunt, I raced through the back door into the basement to take refuge with my father in his office. She stormed into the room with her hand raised to strike again. I think this was the first time he openly took my side against my aunt. She lowered her arm when faced with my father's threatening glare. Then she stormed out to the veranda and shouted, "Get hold of that bitch and tie it up out back. Or else I'll have you all tied up instead, you sons of bitches!"

Fendi howled all night. I stood at my window, powerless to free her, until her barking stopped and I fell asleep. In the morning, before catching the bus to school, I went to the backyard to check up on her and give her some food. She wasn't there. I panicked. I ran to ask my nanny, but she just stood there crying. I turned to Bashir. He looked away and said, "We have to do what the lady of the house says. It's the rule of the strong, dear. There's nothing we can do."

I don't recall exactly, but I think I fainted right there in the garden.

My aunt forbade Mme Maysa from visiting me, and I cried for nearly a week. Then Bashir came to me, carrying my little puppy, which was now a corpse. He told me my aunt had put poison in its food. We buried it at the far end of the backyard, near the dock. The only person I told this to was Tarek. His eyes shimmered, but I wasn't sure it was from tears. Three days later, he brought a wooden plaque, which he placed on my dog's grave. The verse he carved on it touched me so deeply that I recall every word of it to this day, long after my aunt uprooted the plaque and destroyed it. Tarek wrote:

Dear Fendi,
Farewell, my gentle friend.
Beautiful days left with you
to your sad journey's end.
My sorrow remains, a river of tears
flowing through my veins and to my heart,
stoking a longing that will never part,
for in my blood and in my veins, you sail.

—Nadia

I still recall our first kiss. I can still feel the tingle from the first time his hand touched my fingertips. He gave two of them a gentle squeeze, then gathered the other three and lifted my hand toward his lips as his eyes stayed fixed on mine. He placed a long and tender kiss on the palm of my hand, brought my hand up to his cheek, and let it rest there. Time seemed to stand still, as though freezing us in a picture frame. I prayed for the hands of the clock to stop even though my heart was pounding many beats faster than the second hand. Tarek embraced me beneath a large tree near the western wall of the grounds. Its branches rustled and sprinkled a few leaves on our heads, perhaps to congratulate us for our innocent act and to encourage us further. They seemed to speak, prodding us to repeat after it, "Choose with your hearts. Say that you love each other. Cry it out as loud as you can." But we were young and as green as some of the tree's tender sprouting twigs, unaware of what fate held in store for us. If only we could have remained children.

Our bodies drew together for the first time. A jolt ran through me. I rested my back against the tree trunk, clinging to his arms, longing to lose myself in a long kiss with him. I summoned to mind all the romantic kissing scenes from the films

I'd seen. I closed my eyes and let my body relax, despite the violent pounding inside me. He gave me a single, fleeting kiss on my lips. It wasn't enough. I wanted more. He took hold of my head, rested it on his shoulder, and stroked my long hair. Then he murmured softly in my ear in his beautiful mellow voice, "I love you." I have never forgotten the taste of that kiss.

Tarek was a year ahead of me in school even though he was a year younger than I was. His school was at the end of our street. When I returned home at four in the afternoon, I'd find him waiting for me by the garden doorway to the basement where Fahim Effendi, my father's secretary, had his office. The moment he saw me, he'd rest his violin on his shoulder and play "The Blue Danube" to welcome me. I'd embrace my schoolbag and do a waltz for him, but not without first sneaking a glance to the upper balcony outside of Aunt Zeinab's bedroom to make sure she wasn't looking. She'd hear the music soon enough, and appear behind the glass of her window. She was an imposing and frightening figure from that height as she stared daggers down at Tarek. Moments later his mother, fired up by my aunt, would come hurtling out. She'd rebuke him and raise her arm to strike him. He'd dodge her and scamper off with her at his heels, trying to chase him out of the yard. But before passing through the gate, he'd always turn back to look at me and smile. A smile that seemed as bitter as it was wide.

I was fifteen that day when he revealed his love for me that first time. Often, we'd take long walks through the streets of Zamalek near the Nile. We'd meet in front of Maison Thomas. We'd sit inside for a while, but its glass façade, which exposed us to passersby on Zamalek's main street, made us a bit nervous. So we'd leave the restaurant and head down the corniche nearby. Sometimes he'd insist we return to Maison Thomas to have a meal. He loved the Italian pizzas they made there. He thought pizza was mankind's best invention for sating hunger. My aunt called it "day-old dough tarted up by a useless crow." I'd repeat this to him as we ate and we'd laugh.

Only twice did I get him to come with me to the club, and then only after much wheedling. He preferred the Fish Garden in Zamalek or the zoo in Giza. My friends ridiculed me for going to those places, which they thought too "common." They said Tarek wanted to steal a kiss in the garden like Abdel-Halim Hafez did with Zubeida Tharwat in *A Day of My Life*, and they giggled. That became a staple of their wisecracks whenever they saw me with him. Some of my schoolmates from Le Collège de la Mère de Dieu poked fun at his clothes, his posture, his thick glasses, and his bashfulness. He hated the Gezira Club.

On one of these two occasions, we were in the Lido next to the swimming pool. He was particularly tense that day. He called the place a "cesspool of dissolution." I wasn't really sure what he meant, but he remained angry afterward. I was beginning to feel he was becoming temperamental, or maybe too introverted. I decided to keep this relationship separate from my friends, but I held on to it. His gentleness, kindness, and sensitivity continued to enthrall me, despite his incomprehensible mood swings.

Then I started university. After some weeks, I found myself wanting to put some distance between us. He was so different from my new circle of friends. I began to invent lies to avoid meeting him. Suddenly he'd pop up out of nowhere, coming from the Faculty of Commerce, as though fate conspired to insert him into our midst and expose my lie. But rather than confront me and get angry, he'd forgive me. Eventually he began to admonish me, albeit gently, for my behavior and letting my male colleagues encroach into what he called my personal space. Was it jealousy? Was this possessiveness instead of love? I'd begun to suspect he was growing reactionary. By the end of my first year at the Faculty of Arts, I felt he'd lost his allure and that I no longer missed him. After that last visit I made to his apartment in Zamalek, I decided we'd reached a fork in the road where it was time to part ways. As I proceeded down the separate path, I kept looking back to make sure that he had stopped following. Was that really how I felt? Or did a part of me wish to find him still there, trying to catch up?

The signs of boredom and detachment had begun some months before that visit. But on that day I was strangely irritated, and as I descended the few steps to his front door, I felt a tightness in my throat, as though I couldn't breathe. From the sitting room, where they offered me a seat, I could only see the shoes and calves of passersby, car wheels, some napping cats, and a stray dog sniffing the road. I felt stuck in a large, poverty-stricken tomb where I'd be forced to await an eventual death and be buried where I stood.

Tarek's mother had just died. That was the reason I was there. I wandered into his bedroom, their kitchen, and the bathroom, and was struck by how vast the gap between us was in every respect. Tarek dissolved into the cracks and crevices of that gap. I was so desperate to get out of there that I barely managed to do the minimum required to give my condolences.

Although I would be able to forget him for years, there remained a place deep within me that continued to long for his music and his gentle smile. If his name was mentioned, even if only in passing, it would set off an inexplicable flutter. Was I still in love with him? Or did I just miss his charms without having to think about his flaws? Did I say love? Could this have been the one true love of my life?

Of course I felt some remorse afterward. My heart continued to sway slowly, gently, like when the late-afternoon breeze plays with an old rusty swing. The creaks grow louder and faster, then they slacken and fade, and eventually we grow bored listening to them.

One day, a couple of years later, I bumped into him near our villa. Was it truly a coincidence? Was he hanging around my neighborhood or was this his normal way home? He hadn't graduated from university yet, because he'd failed some exams and had to repeat a year. He was so agitated he could barely speak. So I took the initiative: "Come on, let's go to Maison Thomas and talk there."

He brushed the offer aside. He seemed eager to get on his way. His feet fidgeted while I held him in place with my questions, finding it as hard to draw words from his mouth as water from stone. I was looking at a person I barely knew. His face had grown hard; you might even say harsh. It was now rimmed by a long, scraggly beard. His humility and meek smile had gone, ushered to their graves by that grimness. He'd lost his last glow of affection for me and I'd lost my effect on him, I thought that day. Yet something in his honey-brown eyes still beckoned me from afar. A thread as thin as a hair still bound us, or so I imagined. It whispered longingly to emotions deep in my soul, coaxing them, but softly and without insistence, as though fearful they might suddenly froth over. Yet his lack of persistence was what always made it easy for me to avoid allowing my eyes to voice the emotions that my lips were never able to say. It was Tarek's turn to take a fork in the road. He left me standing in the middle of the street and followed another calling from within. It would steer him to the far right. But the thread hadn't broken yet.

I watched him recede into the distance until he shrank to a black speck at the far end of the road. Something had gone, taking with it quantities of feelings and light, perhaps forever. No, I had no regrets. But I was confused. If time took me back to the moment of separation, I'd probably just slow the hands of the clock a little so I could linger there longer.

Some months after that meeting, my life was turned topsy-turvy. A man appeared who would make me forget everything: Tarek, music, my friends. I even forgot the tremor from that first kiss for a while—until deep needs and yearnings locked horns inside me as others did battle over me.

11

"IF YOUR DOG SLIPS THE leash, set dogs like it after it. They'll sniff him out."—Abbas Mahalawi

"As they say in Qena, 'Keep your eyes on your enemy even if he's an ant.' It turns out your friend Hassanein's a jackal and he's laughing!"

Abdel-Naim's words stung, but I couldn't argue. He was the only one who stood by me. Our business had brought us closer together, to the degree that he had some papers drawn up to put some of his properties in my name in order to dodge the tax authorities and some greedy relatives. He trusted me, and I returned his trust when I told him about Hassanein's treachery. Abdel-Naim now knew my secrets, just as I knew his. Not only did he sympathize, he never even asked for a cut. He said, "You've always been straight with us, Abbas. You never grew greedy or tried to screw us, even when Asran took a second wife. We're family, and we'll support you to the Day of Judgment."

While I'd suspected that Hassanein had bought a strong sedative from the pharmacy, I didn't think he'd be able to slip it into my tea without my noticing. I was standing right next to him, watching him like a hawk. When I came to, he'd gone, together with the carryall. I searched all his haunts and everywhere else I could think of. He'd melted into thin air.

Abdel-Naim was certain that Hassanein would try to bump me off. "He's got to. You know too much about him. He'll hire a hitman—you can hire them by the truckload these days—but he'll wait until after he cashes in the gold and diamonds."

I wasn't convinced that Hassanein would try to kill me. But I pretended to be so Abdel-Naim would lend me a few of his men to protect me while I tried to find Hassanein before he skipped the country. That was how Hassanein thought: flight before fight. Abdel-Naim arranged to get me a gun, which never left my side since. Then he assigned one of his men to stick to me like a shadow, and he instructed his other men to do as I told them without question.

"That friend of yours—which side does his heart sleep on?"

"Huh?"

Abdel-Naim tapped his nose and winked. "I mean, what's his thing? Is he into dames, drugs, or drink?"

"He used to play poker practically every day," I said. "He raked in a fortune from gambling."

"Bingo!"

The hunt was on. Abdel-Naim set his men on the prowl, starting from Giza Café. That was one of Hassanein's favorite haunts, according to his elderly landlady, who pointed us in that direction. They took only two weeks to find him, out after sniffing into every nook and cranny in Cairo. When Abdel-Naim told me the news over the phone, it was like I'd heard the gospel.

"Your friend's surfaced. He plays poker every other day with a bunch of foreigners in Garden City. They're having a poker party tonight."

After evening prayers, three of Abdel-Naim's men positioned themselves near the gateway to a sprawling apartment building in Garden City. Abdel-Naim's son, Fahim, and another guy sat in a car parked directly in front of the entrance, while Abdel-Naim and I sat in my car on the opposite side of the road. While passing the time, Abdel-Naim related how he'd discovered Hassanein's whereabouts with the help of some of his connections at the Commissariat of Police.

"I told them that Hassanein stole a lot of money from me and went into hiding, but that I wanted to get it back without getting the police involved. I gave them a description and told them about his gambling addiction. Then they used their sources—domestic servants, doormen, and the like—to find him."

Abdel-Naim's connections had facilitated a lot of our business. But to me, this was the coup of a lifetime, as they say.

We waited for five, seemingly endless hours. I was so on edge that I chewed each of my ten fingernails down to the quick. I even drew blood from one of my fingers. At last, exactly five minutes after midnight, a taxi drew up and Hassanein got out. Fahim hit the headlights, flicking them on and off, making Hassanein flinch and squint into the bright light. Abdel-Naim's three men leapt out of the shadows, tackled him, clobbered him on the head, and bundled him into the trunk of Fahim's car. Then we set off in a procession to Abdel-Naim's place in Imbaba.

When Hassanein came to, he found himself attached to a wooden chair, hands bound tightly behind his back. He jerked his head around to take in his unfamiliar surroundings. I began to circle around him, making feints, which made him jump and tremble, though I wasn't actually going to hit him. His bewildered, terrified eyes shifted between me and Abdel-Naim like a cornered rat. I took a step toward him and watched him cower.

"Where is it, Hassanein?"

"I . . . I . . . made a deal, but I didn't get the money yet. You'll get your share. You got to believe me! It's just that I was afraid the police—"

"Where is it, Hassanein?"

I let him go through his feeble excuse a second and a third time. He stuttered and stammered, added bits here, subtracted bits there, piled up the contradictions until he depleted his pack of lies and his story fell apart at the seams.

"I'll give you one week to give me my share," I said. "But right now, I want one gold ingot. As a guarantee of your good faith." I chuckled at that one and gave a wink to Abdel-Naim. He nodded to one of his men who, in a single flowing movement, whipped out a jackknife from his pocket, flicked it open, and sliced off one of Hassanein's earlobes. Hassanein howled as the blood gushed from his ear and drenched his shirt. The terror that made his eyes nearly pop out of his head would certainly loosen his tongue. Abdel-Naim applied some finely ground coffee to stanch the bleeding while the guy with the jackknife stood at the ready to slice off the other earlobe. Before he could do so, Hassanein's head fell to his chest.

A large pail of cold water poured over his head brought him to. He sputtered and shook off the water from his face. Then he saw the jackknife approaching his other ear.

"I'll speak! I swear to God, I'll speak!" he shouted.

He was staying in Giza, he said, chest heaving. He gave us the address and described how he'd hidden the bag in his bedroom, under the floor tiles beneath his bed. We fished the key out of his pocket and sent one of Abdel-Naim's men to the address he'd given us. As we waited, I affixed a makeshift dressing on his ear to stop both the bleeding and the groaning. I drew up a chair and sat down in front of him. Taking my jackknife from my pocket, I flicked it open with a flourish and used it to clean the dirt from under my fingernails while I asked, "Who helps you dispose of the diamonds abroad?"

"Z–Z–Zananiri . . . Jacob Zananiri. I told you about him. He's the only one who can do it. He worked for Cicurel for years."

I had no reason to doubt him this time. His ear must have been throbbing like hell. I brought the telephone over, put my finger on the dial, and told him to give me Zananiri's number. Holding the receiver up to his good ear said, "Tell him you got to travel abroad and might be gone for a while. Then tell him Mr. Abbas will be looking after your business here. put in a good word for me and set me up an appointment." He followed my instructions to the letter, despite his surprise at his trip abroad. How nice and docile he'd become.

A few hours later, though it felt like much longer, Abdel-Naim's guy returned with the canvas bag. I tensed before opening it, but relaxed as soon as I found the contents untouched. Well, apart from the velvet pouch that contained the small stones. About half were missing. He must have sold them already or lost them in gambling. As I fumbled through the bag, my fingers encountered a ferry ticket: Alexandria–Marseille, due to depart in a few days' time. It had his name and passport number on it. So this was probably how he'd invested some of the little diamonds. But I didn't care about them.

I waved the ticket to Marseille in front of his eyes. "Now isn't this nice. What a relief you didn't have to lie to Zananiri after all!" Then I tore the ticket in half and spat in his face.

I turned to Abdel-Naim.

"It's all there," I said, indicating the bag.

At a signal from him, his men closed in on Hassanein.

"You got to believe me, Abbas. I'm not a traitor," he pleaded. "You were going to get your share as soon as I disposed of the stuff abroad. You got to believe me. I was looking out for both of us!"

"You're dead, Hassanein. You should have gone to the gallows with your buddies a long time ago. You just got a reprieve."

"Forgive me, Abbas. I beg you! I'll do whatever you ask for the rest of my life!"

"Your life is over. You gambled on it and you lost."

His begging was pointless. I'd made up my mind the moment we learned his whereabouts. I just wanted to make sure I got the gold and diamonds back first. One of Abdel-Naim's men placed a handkerchief over Hassanein's nose. He passed out without a struggle. They gagged him, carried him outside, and stuffed him back into the trunk of Fahim's car. Then we all drove off to one of our construction sites in Zamalek. I couldn't turn down Abdel-Naim's offer to use it. It was perfect for this purpose.

It was shortly before dawn. We'd just managed to catch the remaining cover of night. I stood next to Abdel-Naim and his men at the edge of a deep ditch into which they'd dumped Hassanein, who they'd bundled, still drugged, gagged, and bound, into a burlap sack. The cement mixer kicked into a rumble, the drum began to rotate, and the truck backed up to the edge of the pit. Then one of the guys pulled a lever to let a thick, mushy stream of concrete slide down the chute onto the burlap sack. As soon as it was completely covered, Abdel-Naim gave the signal to stop before the noise woke up the whole neighborhood.

I flicked my cigarette butt into the pit on top of the moist casting and turned to leave. Just then, I caught sight of a shadow moving inside an upper-story room in a nearby villa directly overlooking our construction site. I froze. The dim light in the room went out and three bright flashes followed one another other in rapid succession.

I turned to Abdel-Naim, who had also seen the shadow followed by the three flashes. He came up to give me a pat me on the shoulder while he silently called over one of his boys and whispered something in his ear. The kid took off at a run. I started to follow, but Abdel-Naim held me back.

"Take it easy. We'll get him, even if he's in his mother's belly."

An eerie silence enveloped us as we waited at the edge of the construction site near the road. Even the intermittent twittering of the birds in their nests seemed nervous. A small cat poked its head out from beneath a large car to make sure it was safe to cross the street, pausing to take stock of us with its incandescent stare.

Abdel-Naim spat in its direction and muttered, "Go back to the grave."

The cat yowled and bolted. At that moment, I wasn't inclined to ask Abdel-Naim about his superstition. At last the kid returned, reappearing from our left. Without so much as a glance in my direction, he sprinted up to his boss, whispered a few words in his ear, waited to be dismissed, then vanished. Abdel-Naim took hold of my elbow, steered me about ten yards to the right, stopped directly in front of a large gateway, and turned to look at me. Over his shoulders I saw the plaque: "Heart of Palm."

Pointing to the upper floor, he said, "Your enemy's that way. Our borders stop here. But if you need us, you know where to find us."

After he and his men left, I felt for my gun for reassurance, while my suspicions swung like a pendulum between the Nubian Bashir and the Greek Helga. Which of them had been up there spying on us, taking photos and God knows what else? I entered the grounds and took a full turn around the villa. It was shrouded in silence. I approached the door to the basement and gave it a gentle shove. It was bolted from the inside. I went back to the street, took up a position next to a lamppost, and lit a cigarette as I stared up at the upper-story windows. A curtain moved. Or did I just imagine it? I took a step forward to make myself more visible. The curtain refused to budge again. Then a strange idea popped into my head. I mulled it over, connecting one dot to the next until I'd consumed a second cigarette. I crushed it underfoot and returned to my apartment without a shadow of a doubt about the conclusion I'd drawn. On my way, I spotted one of Abdel-Naim's men. Abdel-Naim had probably posted him as a lookout. I greeted him with a slight nod. I wasn't about to ask him to leave. His presence there would make her nervous, which gave me comfort.

*

I was sure she'd seen everything from the moment we arrived at the site. Her rigid face, the coldness in her eyes, the way she faked surprise the following morning when I asked why she'd overslept. I found her camera, opened it, and found the film chamber empty. That removed any last doubts that she was the one who'd caught us on film burying Hassanein. She was visibly nervous and taciturn, and didn't even ask me why I was rooting through her belongings. As I searched, I began to relate the story of Hassanein's attempt to double-cross me. She interrupted me before the final episode, which she already knew. And she let me know she knew it.

"May God rest his soul. So, who's it going to be next?" She paused briefly, then said in a cold, flat voice, "May God rest our souls in advance, Abbas. But until then, you and I are going to have to work out a new deal."

"Where's the film, Zeinab? Where the hell did you hide it? Come to your senses or it'll be the end for both of us."

"Go ahead and kill me. Fear died in me long ago. I'm not afraid of you."

I knew where that came from. She thought I killed Sandro. She didn't give a damn about Hassanein and she didn't have an ounce of pity for his wife or child. But how was she to know that that piece of slime called Sandro tried to con me out of my share in our company and the land we built on? I never told her about how I set it up after learning that Sandro had used his palace connections to win a permit to start a franchise of a lucrative international pharmaceutical firm. He was going to open it in Cairo at first. But he leapt at my offer of a partnership when he understood that it came with a plot of land that Abdel-Naim and I owned in Alexandria. Then I discovered he'd started selling shares under the counter to some Jews. I cornered him. I told him I knew of his relationship with Zeinab and that he'd fathered her daughter, and I threatened to kill him. He groveled and swore to do anything I asked. Then he tried to give me the slip. When I learned he'd booked himself passage on a boat to

Italy and made arrangements to sell off the rest of his shares, I had no choice but to act before I lost everything. I turned to the ever-greedy Pouli. I made him my partner, transferred the deeds to the land and the company to his name, and turned myself into a mere salaried CEO. Pouli then used his connections to recuperate the land and all the shares. Apparently, he managed to intervene with the stock market authorities in order to halt the sales. But I didn't care what he did or how he went about it. All that mattered was that Sandro would be left without a fraction of a piaster from the franchise, and would get booted out of Egypt as broke as when he arrived. And that was what happened after he was forced to return all the money he'd made.

Zeinab had begun to trouble me in a way I had never expected. I shook my head to clear it of the uncomfortable thought, but it came back to nag me. For the first time in my life, I'd begun to fear her and I didn't like how the tables were turning—not one bit.

When I'd finished dressing, I turned to contemplate myself in the wardrobe mirror, forcing myself to set those concerns aside and summon my self-confidence. It was time to focus on my upcoming appointment with Jacob Zananiri. I could deal with Zeinab later and let her know who was boss. I picked up the carryall and headed to the door, where I found Zeinab standing with a smirk.

"A double-breasted suit, a hankie in the pocket, white shoes, and even a hat to match. Where are you off to, dressed to kill like that?"

"I'm going to sell the diamonds. We're almost there, Zeinab. We'll have the world at our feet."

"And where, pray tell, do you go to sell a stash like that in broad daylight?"

"Dar al-Maaref. Ever heard of it?"

I returned her smirk. Then I slammed the door behind me, loudly enough to make her think twice before opening it again to ask another question.

Instead of taking my car, I flagged down the first taxi that passed.

"Downtown," I told the driver.

"*Bonsoir,* Monsieur Zananiri," I said as I took a seat in the drawing room of his elegant home in Bab al-Shaariya. He contemplated me with the same startled look that had greeted me the first time I met him.

Two days after concluding the Hassanein ordeal, I phoned Zananiri to confirm the appointment. Then I went to meet him in his office at the headquarters of Dar al-Maaref, a publishing house where he worked as a supervisor in the accounts department. That meeting ended abruptly.

After hearing what I knew about his particular services for Cicurel, he grew tense and stared at my bag in alarm, even though I hadn't opened it. He got up to make sure his office door was closed, then returned to his desk, pressed the button, and instructed his secretary not to let anyone disturb us. When he spoke, he was vague and incoherent. Although I tried to reassure him, he continued to fidget as though trying to wriggle out of an accusation. Suddenly he stood up, handed me a calling card, and escorted me to the door of his office. Before opening it, he whispered, "Meet me tomorrow at seven p.m. at the Margush Hammam."

Cairo's public bathhouses look pretty much alike from inside. So much so that they could have been built by the same person. This was the first time I'd been to the Margush Hammam in Bab al-Shaariya. It was different from the others. Its rooms were more spacious, its ceilings higher. Practically the whole neighborhood was inhabited by Jews. Rarely would you see non-Jews on your way to the bathhouse at the edge of this district. I didn't take my gun with me, but I'd taken other precautions.

After undressing in the changing room and wrapping myself in the large towel I was given, I entered the baths.

Wisps of steam wafted up from the central dipping pool. As I was half an hour late, I found Zananiri already there. I headed toward him, but he pretended not to know me, so I did likewise. Before long, he got up, giving me a meaningful look as he left the room. I saw him pass through the section where bathers sat on stone benches built against the ancient wall in order to breathe some cooler air after the steam bath. In the center was a large stone platform on which you lay for the rubdown. This was performed by the hammam attendant, who scrubbed you with a loofah while applying viscous, pungent lotions. Zananiri passed through another series of changing rooms, looking back in my direction once or twice as he entered a narrow passage, barely two yards wide. I followed him. The passage led to another chamber with wooden benches. We sat with our backs against the moist wall and peered into the invigorating vapors that were as thick as a morning mist. The room had an air of being a part of the establishment reserved for special clients. It probably cost a tidy sum. The bath attendant welcomed me with a broad smile. Zananiri must have already given him a generous tip. I caught sight of Fahim, not far away, who'd arrived much earlier to sniff out possible foul play. He nodded to let me know that no one suspicious was lurking and I was safe. I wasn't worried. Fahim had the gun.

I waited for Zananiri to bring up the subject. Instead, he started to talk about Israel, which had been founded about two years earlier. He was thinking of moving there for his daughter's sake, to ensure her a stable future. He fed me a long story about how his situation in Egypt wasn't secure because the authorities had declined his application for citizenship even though he'd lived here over half his life. He leaned his head back against the wall and sighed.

"I've been here twenty years and I still have to renew my residency permit every six months. My life is here, not in Italy. All my money's in Egypt."

"So why are you buying up tons of real estate if you're thinking of emigrating?"

He ignored the question, but the twitches in his hands and feet betrayed how nervous it made him. He avoided looking in my direction as he returned to the subject of his daughter and how he needed to secure her future.

"Then you should stop your weekly gambling, sir. You should keep Madame Rachel's jewels safe, instead of pawning them. More importantly, you shouldn't go around acquiring the property of merchants who pay you a commission to draw up fake bankruptcy papers, after which you refuse to return their properties."

Zananiri sat bolt upright and jerked his head toward me, causing drops of sweat to flick off his forehead. Every inch of his body was covered with a thick wet sheen, including his widened eyes. He seemed ready to pee on himself. In fact, his legs were pressed so tightly together that he might have already done so already

"You've been spying on me, Monsieur Abbas?" He could barely control his stammer. "Who are you working for? What do you want from me?"

"You have nothing to worry about. As the saying goes, 'Watch your friend well, so you won't have to tell him to go to hell.' Now, listen carefully. We're both in the same boat. Either we both make it to shore or you sink on your own."

I was indebted to Fahim for the lowdown on Zananiri, though the little bit that Hassanein spilled was helpful too. Fortunately, Fahim worked at the Foreign-owned Properties Registrar at the Notary Public Authority, which was where he picked up most of the dirt about Zananiri's business dealings. With that, it was easy to play him. I didn't want to broach the subject of the big diamond directly. I'd work my way around to that eventually. First, I wanted to make him very nervous. I wanted to keep him tossing and turning at night by dropping a bit of my knowledge about his dealings here and a bit about his smuggling activities there. I didn't threaten; I merely made it clear that I could expose him and strip him of everything he owned at the drop of a hat. I may even have given him the impression that I had the power to send him straight to prison. The look in his eyes seemed to suggest as much as he stood to leave, saying, "I'm at your service, Monsieur Abbas. What's important is that we don't draw the attention of the police, the government, and tax department. Please visit me at home so we can discuss this in further detail. But believe me, we're not going to disagree. I swear on my daughter's life."

"You mean your children's lives, don't you, Monsieur Zananiri? According to my source, Madame Rachel is three months pregnant!"

All of which was why I was now in Bab al-Shaariya, in Zananiri's drawing room, seated before his nervous yet curious gaze. It took about half an hour of explaining who I was and what I wanted for him to relax, if only a bit. He remained wary. As I reached into the bag to take out the diamond, I felt the gun. I lifted it up with one hand, revealing its grip, as I reached for the diamond with the other hand, then put the gun back. I was sure he'd seen it. Yet, apart from a slight frown, he remained composed. I held the large diamond just at the edge of the bag to impress him with its size. To my amazement, he didn't bat an eyelid, as though he'd expected to see it.

"Do you know Hassanein al-Masri well?"

The glint in his eye and his hesitation before asking that question told me what he was thinking.

"Of course. And I trust him less than you do. That's why I came here by myself. Incidentally, Hassanein had to leave the country. He might be gone a long time."

He nodded several times. That piece of news seemed to please him, at any rate. He said that Cicurel suspected Hassanein of embezzlement, but his second wife, Paula, insisted on retaining his services. Zananiri leaned forward and said confidentially, "I bet you the two of them had something going on. No smoke without fire."

I responded with a shrug. He dropped the subject and turned to business as a gleam of undisguised cunning appeared in his eyes.

"As you know, of course, Cicurel had an heir, a daughter called Nadia, from his first wife, so naturally, we would have to—"

"As *you* know, of course, Nadia left the country years ago. She never appeared to claim her inheritance then, and there's no reason to expect her to appear now. She knows nothing of the safe. Nobody knows how to reach her, or even if she's still alive. The living are more deserving than the dead, wouldn't you say?"

Zananiri fell silent and lowered his eyelids. Was he embarrassed at being caught out in his little bargaining ruse? Was he thinking about his share of the profits, or about reporting me to the police? Would he tell Paula? At least on that last one I could feel pretty safe: he didn't seem to know her well and he'd just cast aspersions on her honor. He probably hated her. The more I thought about it, the more I was convinced he wouldn't report me to the police either. Anyway, if the idea so much as occurred to him, I'd snuff him out. Our silence was interrupted by a knock on the drawing room door. Zananiri's wife entered, pushing a small trolley carrying some cups, plates, a teapot, and slices of cake. She greeted me with a perfunctory smile. Zananiri introduced us, but she said little. As she started to pour the tea and serve the cakes, a baby began to cry in a distant room. She excused herself and left quickly.

I smiled to myself. Her pregnancy didn't show yet. How on earth had Fahim learned that she was in her third month? That wily bastard. He was worth more than the entire police investigations division.

Zananiri poured me a cup of tea, set a couple of slices of coffee cake on a plate, and handed it to me. He'd selected the largest pieces. He spoke proudly of his daughter, who wasn't even two years old yet. His wife returned, carrying her, cooing softly to hush the crying. She passed the infant to Zananiri, who took hold of her delicately and held her face close to mine.

"This is Batel."

Reading my bafflement, he added, "It's Hebrew, Monsier Abbas. It means 'daughter of God.'"

After his wife left the room with the child, I decided to take advantage of his softened emotions.

"A quarter of the value of this diamond will secure a comfortable future for Batel and her brother or sister who's on the way, if you become my partner and dispose of it using your channels. Then Batel will have the life of a daughter of the Lord."

Zananiri didn't smile at my attempt to humor him. The plate in his hand shook slightly and his breathing grew louder. Still, I had no doubt that he would agree. He must be thinking of the profits in store for him, and only had to hear my offer first.

He lit a cigarette and inhaled half of it in three long puffs without removing it from his mouth. He ground out the remainder in the ashtray, pulled a piece of paper and pen from his jacket pocket, and started to jot down a lot of numbers and notes. I took the diamond out of the bag. Without looking up, he signaled me with his hand to put it back again.

"My good man, I know it like the back of my hand. I bought it for Cicurel a year before he died. It's called the Heart of Palm, after the villa. And I'm the only one who can sell it."

"Why? Do you have some special gift that other diamond merchants don't have? Don't get greedy, man."

"It's not greed, sir. This diamond is famous, both because of its size and because its owner no longer exists. It's got to be cut up and sold under the counter."

"Agreed." I took a large bite of cake, and with my mouth still full, I added, "And we've just broken bread together!"

He laughed for the first time since I'd met him. Then the wily expression returned to his face. Here was an adversary who'd wait to take you by stealth rather than confront you with a sword. He folded the piece of paper, returned his pen to his jacket pocket, and said, "Look, Monsieur Abbas. My fee is fifty thousand pounds, including travel expenses and the cost for having the Heart of Palm cut. Plus I'll take two of the gold ingots and a quarter of the small diamonds. The rest of the stuff is yours. By the way, I'm being generous with you, this being our first transaction. I'll write you an IOU or a check as a guarantee and I'll bring you your money in a week. Or, if you prefer, I can deposit it in a bank of your choice abroad."

Hassanein had said we could make a quarter of a million each just from the big diamond. Even if he'd doubled the estimate in order to con me, I was certain that Zananiri was asking for peanuts. I agreed, though I feigned reluctance. Then, out of curiosity, I asked, "What did Cicurel do each time?"

"Cicurel regularly turned his cash into diamonds and gold. He didn't trust the banks here. Plus, he had problems with his brothers and Paula. I, personally, prefer Egyptian banks. They're safer. The world has just emerged from a major war for the second time. No one can predict what might happen next."

"I need my money in cash. But one more thing, Monsieur Zananiri. Checks or IOUs won't do as a guarantee."

"Well then, tell me what will do, Monsieur Abbas, and I'll do my best to oblige."

"Batel . . . your 'daughter of God.' With her as guarantee, God will bless us all."

12

"I DERIVE MY STRENGTH FROM his existence. Though at times I feel that he's weaker than me, I always seek his protection."
—Nadia

We met at noon on Friday, as was our custom. We were six teenage girls on their bikes, racing down the street that ran alongside the Nile in Zamalek on our way to the Fish Garden, or "The Grotto" as my father called it. We'd take two turns around the park then have lunch inside. My aunt, predictably, was adamantly opposed to these winter outings at first. Contrary to the sedate and sophisticated image she liked to project to others, she was insular, closed-minded, and anxious, especially when it came to me. She still treated me like a child. She was as excessive in her worrying over me as she was in her scoldings. But when my father surprised me with a beautiful white Belgian bicycle for my birthday two years ago, Aunt Zeinab had no choice but to bow, however grudgingly, to a fait accompli. I loved that bike. I decorated the handlebars with different-colored flowers that I'd change every three days. But it steered me down a path I could never have imagined, a path that I pursued to its very end, to my great regret.

I was in the lead as we barreled down the street, staying close to the curb. Suddenly a car screeched to a halt in front of us. It was a large black Fiat, like the government car my father drove, so I thought my aunt must be using it that day.

My father never left the house before midnight on Fridays, his day off. He even avoided speaking to us during the daytime on Fridays.

My handlebars wobbled, but my feet began pedaling quicker, as if instructing my mind to escape forward into danger. I swerved to avoid the car. Just as I began to pass it, its door opened and the driver emerged. Did I fall on top of him, or did he catch me as I fell? It all happened in a blur. The next thing I knew, I was looking up at a ragged circle of alarmed friends fretting over us. The man leapt to his feet with a bright smile and apologized politely. There was something contrived in that apology, but I was struck by his deep, resonant voice and the officer's uniform. I caught sight of one of my friends gawking in admiration at this man in his khaki suit with the stars gleaming on the epaulets. Another, smiling from ear to ear, reached out to shake his hand and thank him. Thank him for what? For knocking me over?

I refused to let him off so easily. I scolded him for driving so recklessly, and for not thinking of the consequences before screeching to a halt on the right side of the road and getting out of the car on the left. He apologized sincerely. I huffed, and slapped the dust and dirt off my clothes. I noticed a large scrape on my knee. The officer—very politely, again—said it had to be cleaned as soon as possible, and invited us to his home so that it could be done right away. He pointed to the stately Lebon building, which overlooks the Nile on one side and the Fish Garden on the other. I refused firmly and he didn't press the matter further. He extracted a calling card from his pocket and presented it to me.

"Captain Murad Kashef, Ministry of Defense."

I hesitated before taking it. Then, before I could, one of my friends snatched it out of his hand and volunteered to introduce us all. When my turn came—and I suspected she deliberately left me to last—she introduced me by my full name and volunteered my address as well. "And this is Nadia

Abbas Mahalawi. She lives in the Heart of Palm villa, right here in Zamalek . . . very close to you!"

Murad's eyes shone as he nodded to me with a smile. He bent down and lifted my bike with one hand; with the other, he picked up the front wheel, which had somehow separated from the frame during my crash. After putting these in the trunk of his car, he drove off, leaving us staring after him with silent admiration. We must have looked like statues of pretty damsels whose knight had just galloped into the sunset on his steed without casting a backward glance.

"I can't possibly approve, Zeinab. There's too big an age difference between them. Twenty years, at least."

My father was adamantly opposed to marrying me to Murad Kashef, the awesome, solemn army officer with a perpetually brooding brow. He had proposed about two weeks after the incident with the bicycle, which he'd returned the following day, along with another that I have never ridden. He had probably devoted that two-week interim to his inquiries into me and my family.

"He's got nothing to show for himself but his rank, Zeinab. Even his apartment belongs to the sequestrations authority, and he won't be there much longer. He's trying to claim squatters' rights under the new rent-control laws. I know his type."

"But he's on his way up. He's got a future ahead of him and he's practically our neighbor here in Zamalek. Look around you, Abbas. Their times have come. Can't you see? The whole country belongs to them now. Look to the future. Anyway, I approve the marriage!"

My father's arguments barely managed to withstand my aunt's onslaught. She persevered as doggedly as she breathed. She swept aside his arguments with her imperious disdain and insisted on setting a date for my engagement as soon as possible. But my father, despite his outward calm, remained unyielding. I was amazed at how tenaciously he supported me for a change. It took over a month to get me to capitulate as the battle for my hand raged around me, with Murad pushing from his front, my father digging in his heels behind his trenches, and my aunt battling relentlessly on all fronts. She tried every tactic: to get at me through my girlfriends, to soften me with kindness, to lure me with Murad's status and influence. "Tomorrow he'll be an ambassador like Amr Pasha next door, and you'll tour the world with him," she said as though she were the foreign minister.

She even tried approaching Mme Maysa, because she knew we were close. Normally, my aunt would rather be struck blind than ask a favor from Maysa. But in this case, she asked her to use her influence to persuade me. Maysa would hear nothing of it. She was dead set against me marrying an officer at least twenty years my senior. She held me by the shoulders and looked into my eyes a long time before the corners of her lips turned down and she said, "He could marry your aunt, dear. But you? Marry Murad? Impossible!"

"But my aunt—"

She shook her head emphatically and exclaimed, "*C'est fou ça!*"

Murad showered us with gifts. He offered to use his influence to cut corners for us, eliminate red tape, facilitate whatever we might need. Some inexplicable undercurrent of animosity between my father and him kept my father from accepting his offers. My aunt, on the other hand, took full advantage. It would be impossible to count the favors she asked for her friends, her acquaintances, and, first and foremost, herself. Murad, of course, was astute and observant. From day one, he turned his sails in my aunt's direction and ignored my father. But there came a point when he shifted tack and began to take advantage of his important and sensitive position to gain leverage over my father. Evidently, he'd learned the limits of my father's influence and connections. So, from courteous and friendly, he turned to cold and aloof, and then to outright impudent, causing my father to nearly have him escorted out of the villa by force one day.

I felt such a heavy weight lift from my shoulders. I cried from relief, hugged my father, and buried my face in his chest to hide from the sparks flying from my aunt's eyes. Sadly, that relief lasted only one night. The following day, dozens of men stormed the house saying they were police, though they were in civilian dress—in short sleeves even, it being summer. They searched the house from top to bottom, apart from my bedroom. They spent a long time on the upper floor and forbade us from watching their search. They took a lot of papers from my father's safe and desk, then held him under guard near the dock. Aunt Zeinab rushed to the phone to call Murad, who'd been in his office expecting that call, as I would learn many years later. Then the minutes ticked by slowly until at last, moved by Murad's invisible strings from afar, the men released my father and sped off in their cars.

Just three days later, Murad called on us again. He asked to see my father alone in his office and strode off in that direction before my father could utter a word. My father followed with heavy steps. Two hours later, my father reemerged, head bowed and physically drained. From that day forward, Murad spoke confidently with my aunt about engagement plans, while my father remained a shadow in the background.

Oddly, I was impressed by Murad's force of personality and his influence over my family that day. His persistence in trying to win my hand encouraged me to see another side of him. More curiously yet, something about him enticed me. But, as I drew closer, I found him like the moon—a waning moon, dark and lifeless. With little enthusiasm and much helplessness, I gave my assent, albeit an equivocal one. This was probably to leave myself a backdoor exit in case Murad failed to impress me again during the engagement period, which I planned to make as long as possible.

Shortly before my fourth year at the university, I chose my gown from Madame Vasso's against my aunt's wishes. She wanted her personal seamstress to make it, even though her own wardrobe was filled with dresses from that atelier. My friends and I agreed that my engagement party should be held at the Heliopolis Hotel. That's where we went, as university students, to see the matinee concerts with the Black Coats and Bob Azzam and dance to "Ana bahibbak ya Mustafa." We loved the place. So we made a collective vow that it was where we would all have our engagement parties. To demonstrate the seriousness of our pact, each of us signed our name in full to a pledge written on a small piece of paper, which I kept. We'd burst out laughing whenever one of us mentioned it. Then one of us would inevitably break out into the refrain, "*Chérie je t'aime, chérie je t'adore, como la salsa de pomodore!*" and we'd laugh harder. I was relieved and delighted that my father didn't object when I told him of this plan. I could tell he wasn't thrilled at it, though, because of the way he nodded with a slight tilt to the left, as though he wanted to pour my words from his ears.

My aunt hit the ceiling before I could finish half a sentence. "Decent people don't hold engagement parties in hotels!"

I told her that our guests knew who we were, and where and how we lived, and that no one would think it a disgrace. She brushed my argument aside, along with the pledge my friends and I had written, which I'd thought eternal. She took that piece of paper and tore it into tiny pieces, most of which missed the wastepaper basket when she flung them in that direction.

"Stop being so silly! Do you want to set people's tongues flapping about how our home's so rundown we had to hold your reception in a hotel?"

I almost made up my mind to use that "backdoor exit" that day. But first I would give Murad a chance to prove the force of his personality and influence on my aunt, just as he'd proven it on my father, with such a debilitating blow. Why couldn't I simply leave Murad? I'm still as puzzled about that as about why I dropped Tarek. I wasn't ready for marriage, and I certainly couldn't picture Murad as my husband. Yet, oddly, something inside me was in favor of this marriage. Was it the desire to be free from Zeinab's law and prison?

Two days later, I had a nightmare. I was in a speeding train with only two carriages. I arrived at my destination ahead of schedule. When I got off, I found myself in a long, dark tunnel. I saw a dim light at the end and started to walk toward it. When I emerged, I saw what I seemed to be a printing press. I couldn't make it out clearly, but it rumbled loudly, the rollers spun rapidly, and it spewed dozens of pieces of paper into the air. People reached up to snatch the papers out of the air and read them eagerly. They began to whisper to each other, but I couldn't make out what they were saying.

I woke up with a start. I had such an ominous feeling. I went over to Maysa's to tell her about the dream. After giving it some thought, she said, "You have to get away from things, dear. Travel, read more, go out with your friends to the movies or theater, listen to music. Why don't you come with us tomorrow for a round of golf at the club? Now *that* will pick up your spirits."

Aunt Zeinab must have had antennae. Not only did she rule out all thought of travel with my friends, she restricted their visits and forbade me from going out with them to the movies or theater. Naturally, she rejected golf with Maysa out of hand without offering a single logical reason. Mme Maysa phoned soon afterward to ask how I was doing. A word or two told her all she needed to know. Adopting a chirpy voice, she said she would give me a puppy as a present. That was just what the doctor ordered to get me out of my depression. "Surely your aunt has grown up by now and isn't scared of dogs like she used to be," she added before hanging up.

I hung up with a smile on my face as I tried to imagine what kind of puppy Maysa would give me. Just as I replaced the receiver, I felt my aunt's hand clamp down on my shoulder.

"That nutty old biddy will be the end of you if you keep listening to her. So she wants to sneak another vile and filthy dog into our home? That's because you snagged yourself a groom, you dummy! It brings out the envy in everyone."

The realization that she'd been listening in on my phone calls aggravated my frustration. I decided to tell her about my nightmare. She nibbled at her lips and said nothing apart from "uh-huh" and "aha," as she would always mutter when absorbed in thought. When I'd finished, she said, "There you have it! The evil eye. It's struck already."

After I had the same dream three more times, my aunt introduced me to a scrawny ancient woman with a very dark complexion, jutting cheekbones, a harelip, and a gold ring in her long, pointed nose. "This here's Fatika. She reads dreams, palms, and coffee grounds," my aunt said. Just looking at Fatika made me more depressed and I was reluctant to take a seat next her. But when she spoke, after I told her my nightmare, she put me at ease. In contrast to her appearance, her voice was sweet and soothing. "Your life's journey will be comfortable and easy," she said. "You'll always get what you want even before you wish it. You'll never lack anything for long." As for the printing press, the pieces of paper, and the people: "God will bless you with abundance and you'll never lose anyone, dear. But a large crow will appear, spread its wings across your skies, and hide the face of the sun from you." She fell silent and frowned. Only when I pressed her did she add, "God is great. Greater than all His creation."

With that, my aunt slaughtered two of the rabbits she raised down by the dock. Then, as per Fatika's instructions, she dipped her hand in the blood and applied her palm prints to the inside and outside of the walls around our villa's grounds. From then on there was no turning back. I resigned myself to the marriage and followed my aunt's directives. "I might as well see what being engaged is like. God works in mysterious ways," I thought.

The date was set for July 15, 1966. That evening I descended the granite stairs of the villa with hesitant steps, as though I might turn and run back inside at any moment. When I reached the bottom, my father took hold of my hand, linked it into his elbow, and escorted me toward Murad, who was seated at the far end of the garden, where they'd built the wedding throne. That was where I used to meet Tarek when we were growing up. Next to Murad was seated a *ma'zoun*, the religious marriage official. He was unmistakable in his brushed cotton caftan, *jibba*, and red fez wrapped in a white turban. Aunt Zeinab stood next to him, dressed as always in basic black, with a large hat of the same color to cover her thinning and graying hair. A sudden chill ran through me. What was that sheikh doing here? This was supposed to be the engagement celebration, not a marriage. That was the agreement—to postpone the marriage until after I finished university.

I turned to my father, hoping for a sign of reassurance, but his face was immobile and conveyed no hint of joy or any emotion. The stiff smile was there solely for the photos being taken by the famous Phillipe, who'd been flown in especially for the occasion. My father relished the attention. I felt his arm urge me forward while his smiling face remained fixed straight ahead. My feet began to falter, then stopped. I drooped to the side like a wilted flower that had been trampled one too many times.

My aunt surged toward us, livid, the feathers in her hat flapping like a peahen torn away from her courtship dance. She shot me a look that made me quiver like I used to when I was a child because it always preceded a slap. If anything, that look had grown crueler over the years, etched into her face as deeply as the furrows that made her look years beyond her age. She addressed my father barely above a whisper, but I heard it, which she probably intended.

"Murad Bey wants to sign the marriage contract tonight, though he'll postpone the consummation celebration. The safest shore is the closest shore. So I agreed and we arranged everything. Talk some sense into the girl. I don't want a scandal. Get to it! You know what I'm capable of!"

In fact, no one actually knew what my aunt was "capable of," because she never had to carry out her threats. She always got her way, mostly after getting my father's approval and sometimes without, but this time I lost my ability to even submit. My head spun, my legs gave way, and a veil of blackness muffled the guests' gasps and screams. After I came to, my friends told me that Zeinab had told everyone that I'd been on a strict diet lately, which made my blood pressure plunge. I'd never been fat and never had to diet. After half an hour or so, I began to relent. But when my aunt insisted I go out there again, I pretended to have another fainting spell. Then the sleeping pill my father had slipped into my hand earlier kicked in.

I didn't get the white dress and veil, the escort of little girls carrying candles, the belly dancers with candelabras on their heads. I wore a black, close-fitting sheath. My aunt had had it altered to bring up the neckline—a lot. Was this a portent? None of the women present ululated, apart from two. One was called Kawthar and the other Afaf. At first, because of the way they were dressed, I thought they were maids my aunt had hired. It turned out that they were relatives of her late husband who lived in some faraway village, and she'd insisted on inviting them. But the only people they spoke with were my father and aunt, which I found strange because Fahim, my aunt's brother-in-law, was there.

After the disastrous night of my fainting spell, I was at the mercy of my aunt's fury, my father's passiveness, and Murad, a bull in a china shop, charging mercilessly toward his goal in field of china and glass. Within a week, I faced the same *ma'zoun*, who'd arranged himself and his registry book in the middle of the reception room. I looked at him once while he conducted the official ceremony: when he recited the previous week's date. As I would soon learn, even before the first go at this ceremony, they'd already recorded all the required information in the registrar next to "15 July, 1966." They were only waiting for me to sign. The same applied now. So, as one pair of eyes glared at me, ready to pounce, another pair looked on in resigned dismay, a third streamed tears, and a fourth pair—Murad's—watched me coldly and smugly above a greasy smile, I took up the pen and slowly signed. A tear trickled down and smeared the ink, blurring my name.

Once we'd performed all the rites and rituals, as arranged by my aunt, the pitiful event ended as quickly as a poorly attended funeral procession. The guests left as soon as they could. There was nothing festive to watch. There was no fussing over the newlyweds. People's tongues began to wag about my ill-fated marriage before they were out the front gate. I caught sight of one of our servants putting a large suitcase of mine in the trunk of Murad's car. I turned to my aunt in disbelief. She bent toward my ear and whispered, "Last week, he'd agreed to the contract alone. But because of your mule-headedness and the scene you made, I had to agree to the consummation as well. Put your faith in God. I've packed everything you'll need in your suitcases. Don't you worry. I still care about you, despite the devilry you get up to."

When I was a child, my aunt used to tell me a story of a little girl in a nightgown, walking barefoot in her sleep, a happy smile on her face, unaware that a monster was lurking in the woods not far away. I was so scared to hear the end that I'd fall asleep before finding out what the little girl did when the monster pounced. Now I was the girl in that story. My smile was bitter because heroines can't change the plot.

Murad stood by the open door to his car with that smug smile still on his face, holding his hand toward me. With a reflex impossible to explain, I took it and let him help me into the car. We drove down the corniche in Zamalek toward the Fish Garden. We would spend the night at his place before setting off the following day for our honeymoon at the Cecil Hotel in Ras al-Bar.

The first time I'd actually been inside the Lebon building was when he proposed. The second time was with my aunt two months ago. I'd seen similarly sprawling and well-appointed apartments in the nearby Labib Gabr and Union buildings, but I was still impressed: the plush antique French furniture, the delicate objets d'arts, the paintings covering the walls—family heirlooms, he told me. Then I caught sight of a small sitting-room suite from Pontremoli's, a recently nationalized department store that now catered to army officers and their wives. That could only have been picked out by my aunt. She had to add her touches, and probably her rabbit-blood palm prints as well.

Murad seemed at least twenty years younger that night. His cheeks were rosy, the veins in his temples bulged, his hair was a remarkable jet black. He left me standing in the middle of the room with my suitcase next to me like a lost traveler as he fetched a large bottle of champagne from the small bar. Then he lifted a cover off a large tray with enough dishes of oysters, clams, and shrimp to feed at least ten people.

He came back to me and embraced me gently from behind, which reassured me a bit. I removed my shoes and my outer garments, and let him lead me to the table. I noticed that most of the plates had the letter "F" engraved on them in gold leaf. I asked him whether that was the initial of someone in his family. He smiled, shook his head in a way that meant that this was not the time for such things, and picked up a piece of food and held it toward my mouth. I parted my lips nervously. But he popped the food into his own mouth and laughed. As he spoke, crumbs of bread flew from his lips. He repeated the silly prank and laughed again. When I refused to play along with it a third time, he frowned. Then he began to attack the food. It was as though he were slowly removing a mask. I barely ate, and any bite I took was merely to swallow my anxiety.

He gulped down the rest of the champagne before I'd touched my second glass, then stood up and whisked the belt from his silk robe with the flair of a magician, exposing himself, totally naked. With a confident smile, he took my hand and pulled me from the chair. He wasn't violent, but he wasn't gentle like before. He led me to the bedroom. I stiffened, gripped with fears of what would happen next. I'd had no experience with men. The little I knew I'd learned from my friend Sophie, who was married, and from another friend who was having an affair with an Italian architect. Apart from that, it was just the disconnected fragments of sensations from stolen kisses with Tarek beneath the tall tree behind our villa.

All of that recoiled in the face of my aunt's blunt and explicit instructions, issued at the last moment like a stern commander sending his troops off to war. In that war, I was to surrender immediately, and lie prostrate and submissive so my adversary, the officer, could take me captive and enjoy my body. That was almost exactly what happened, as though Zeinab had coached Murad instead of me.

In the hallway to the bedroom, my steps slowed as my anxieties fought with my embarrassment and won. At the crack of light at the door, my dread became so real I could touch it, but I didn't have the strength to push it away. I was on a train driven by the force of lust—his lust. It had reached its destination too early, just as in my nightmare. If only I hadn't boarded it.

I lay on the bed half naked, Murad on top of me after shoving my slip up and tearing off my panties. The rest of my clothes were piled up next to the bed like something stillborn. I felt Murad's hot breaths as he licked my ear and neck. He didn't look at my face or utter a word. I closed my eyes. The echoes of my aunt's voice faded, leaving me only with

163

the image of her stern face. Tarek's face as he kissed me also flitted before me at that moment for some strange reason. I felt tears well up and my head seemed about to explode. Before I could answer that question or conjure up more images, Murad pushed my legs apart and thrust himself into me with all his force. His chest muffled my cry of pain, which made his hairy body quiver and his head rise slightly. His hot panting breaths whipped my face. The smell of alcohol mixed with tobacco made me nauseous. A thin red thread trickled down the inside of my thigh. I didn't see it, but I felt its warmth as it emerged from inside me to announce that I'd become a woman.

A triumphant smile appeared on the officer's face. He continued to hold me, almost cling to me, as he caught his breath. Then he rolled off me, jumped out of bed, and trampled on the inert pile of my clothes on his way to the bathroom. I lay in bed shivering from cold and fear, staring at my nightmare fully awake. The next seconds passed slowly, as though to defy time. I heard the water rush from the tap. The volume seemed to swell as the water hit his body, racing to outpace the cascade of tears pouring out my agony on that first of my thousand and one nights with Murad Kashef.

13

"THAT'S LIFE FOR YOU: WHEN it gets sweet it turns sour; when the going gets smooth it turns rough; just as you begin to look up, the shit hits the fan!"—Abbas Mahalawi

"He agreed to leave her with you just like that? He really is a Jew!"

That must have been the third time Zeinab asked me that, her incredulous face expecting a different answer. But I didn't answer. I didn't have to. The proof was right in front of her eyes: Batel, sleeping like a little angel in her crib. Frankly, I too still found it a bit hard to believe. I couldn't imagine what Zananiri told his wife in order to convince her to leave her baby with us as a "marker" until he returned to Egypt with my money. Did my threat scare them that much? It must have, since they had just left Batel with me without a fuss before they boarded their plane. But he also must have felt it worth risking not just his daughter's but his own and his wife's lives for the sake of the fifty thousand pounds, plus the diamonds that he'd earn from our Heart of Palm deal. I'd do it too, if I were in his place.

The baby began to cry. Zeinab picked it up and cradled it. She kissed its angelic face on the mouth and lifted it up and down in the air a few times. When our eyes met, I smiled and said, "Take care not to drop her. Batel's worth her weight in diamonds. Easy goes it, Zeinab!"

She laughed. But I didn't miss the tears at the corners of her eyes. She must have been thinking of Lady. Maybe it was my imagination, but I even thought I heard her whisper that name as she kissed and cuddled the baby. I wasn't going to bring up the subject, but it was she who asked whether it was normal for Jews to abandon their daughters this way. I pointed to Cicurel's daughter, Nadia, who vanished right after his murder and whom nobody had asked after since. Zeinab wasn't convinced. I shrugged and turned my thoughts to a space between heaven and earth: the flight path of the plane the Zananiris had boarded the day before. Surely he must be in Europe by now—maybe already in Belgium, getting the diamond cut.

Zeinab could never let go of a question once she got hold of it. She had to get to the bottom of it and she'd circle around it, fly off, and then strike like a nettled bee.

"And this Nadia, Cicurel's daughter, where do you think she is now?" she asked in a matter-of-fact tone as though talking about the weather. "Suppose she just popped up here one of these days, what would we do with her?"

"Come on, Zeinab! I've told you a thousand times that Paula and Cicurel's brothers inherited the money ages ago. We practically own the villa now, and we got the gold and diamonds. Why should we get ourselves all worked up about this Nadia, who doesn't even live in Egypt anymore? Just drop the subject once and for all. She doesn't even know that her father named her in his will. We have the papers, and the only other person who knew the secret is dead. As for Zananiri, we hold all the cards."

"May the Lord rest your soul, Hassanein. I wonder whose turn it'll be next."

There she went again, her cold flat voice reminding me that she still held the trump card. Although I was certain she'd never play it and put my life on the line, for some reason I couldn't put my finger on, her threat made me feel weak.

"Now you listen here, Abbas. If this business of yours could hurt Batel in any way, I swear by God I won't let you get away with it. You know what I'm capable of!"

The next morning, while Zeinab and I were seated around the breakfast table, the doorbell rang long and persistently. It was Fahim, earlier than usual. He looked grim. Without saying a word, and refusing our invitation to have a seat, he shoved some dishes aside and spread open the *Al-Ahram* newspaper on the table. Zeinab and I stretched our necks over it fearfully, as though approaching the edge of a cliff. I quickly scanned the article, which took up a large space on the front page. Zeinab gasped as her hand flew to her chest. Fahim recited the headlines aloud.

"Deadly tragedy strikes. TWA Flight 902 crashes near Dalangat, Buheira Directorate, killing all fifty-five persons on board. The plane burst into flames thirty-two minutes after takeoff from King Faruq Airport. . . . The movie star Camelia was among the forty-eight passengers. . . . King Faruq expresses his deepest sorrow."

"How awful!"

"Damn Camelia and Faruq! What happened to Zananiri, Fahim?"

I snatched up the newspaper and read the names it reported from the passenger manifest. Jacob Abraham Zananiri and his wife appeared about halfway through the list. Their names jumped out at me as if they'd been written in a larger and bolder font than the others. My large diamond now lay in some field! I shot out of my chair. My heart sank to my feet and my ribs nearly burst. I collapsed back onto the chair. My tongue felt thick and my head feverish. Everything I'd planned and worked so hard to get had just fallen into the government's lap.

"They found all the suitcases open. Everyone's belongings were stolen. The police found nothing valuable. The bastard peasants took everything: money, jewels, watches. They even tore the earrings from the women's ears."

Fahim must have read my thoughts. He was now seated with his legs crossed. I got up again and, like a drowning man grasping for his last breath, I lurched toward him and grabbed his jacket collar. "Are you sure this isn't a pack of lies?" I shouted, as though he were somehow responsible. He merely nodded and patted my hands and my shoulders. Fixing his eyes on mine, he said, "Have Zeinab make us some tea so we can talk."

"What about the baby girl in there, Abbas? What are you going to do with her?"

Neither Fahim nor I responded. Damn that Batel. What good was she now? Not even two years old and already a burden, even an accusation. She was the last thing I needed right now. I couldn't get my head around it. A fortune I'd sweated for and staked everything on for years goes up in smoke in a plane crash in Buheira. Somebody up there must be laughing. Or was it planned? By Pouli, for example? Did Zananiri pull a fast one on me and not board the plane after making sure his name was on the passenger list? The plane was actually headed to Rome and not to Brussels, contrary to what he told me. What else did that sly Jew hide from me? Who robbed all the passengers' suitcases at the same time?

"How can we be sure Zananiri was actually on that flight?" I asked Fahim.

"I already called the airline company. They told me that all the passengers on the manifest had been on board except for one: a young journalist by the name of Anis Mansour. He'd given his ticket to Miss Camelia."

I felt the ground sway beneath me, forcing me to sit and hold my head between my hands. The information Fahim gave me on Zananiri passed before my eyes like film credits: an only child with no siblings, no other living relatives, a wife who conceived their daughter in middle age after a decade of despair at not being able to have children. Zananiri himself was a mystery. Secretive, guarded. In addition to his administrative job at Dar al-Maaref, he secretly traded in portable valuables being shed in large quantities by Egyptian Jews at the time. He amassed a fortune through this trade and acquired a lot of real estate in Cairo and Giza. . . . Wait! Could Fahim be behind this? Could he be in cahoots with Zananiri and have staged some kind of charade?

A brief silence fell until it was interrupted by Batel's cries.

"Where did that bastard Zananiri keep his money, Fahim?"

He jerked his head toward Zeinab, whose eyes were still combing the newspaper as though she might find what we'd lost in between the lines.

"Zeinab, go make us some tea. And while you're at it, check to see why Batel's crying. Maybe she needs to drink or eat something. Hey! Shake a leg!"

Zeinab scuttled out of the room. Half an hour later, she returned carrying cups of tea, her face filled with anxiety. She left and returned again, holding Batel.

"What are you going to do with her?" she asked, shifting her eyes between me and Fahim. "I knew you were up to something fishy when you brought her home, but I've grown attached to her. I can't let her go."

I looked at Fahim, who nodded. He stood up and calmly removed Batel from Zeinab's arms. Zeinab cried out and rushed to block his way to the door. "Tell me what you're going to do with her!" she shouted. "Who else is in on this diamond scheme? How are you going to use her now?"

I lit a cigarette in order to keep my temper under control and keep my voice steady enough to calm her, so Fahim could get out the door with the child.

"There is no scheme, Zeinab! The newspaper's right in front of you. But Batel is evidence, and we've got to get rid of her now and forever. Fahim knows the owner of an orphanage in Rod al-Farag. He's going to take her there. The diamonds and gold and the money we were going to get from them flew out the window with that plane crash. We're left with zilch. Now get some sense into your head and let us deal with this."

Zeinab didn't give in easily. There was a wet sheen to her eyes, which bulged in a way I'd never seen. I began to worry about what she might do. Some tears escaped as she silently reached out to stroke Batel's face, then looked at me pleadingly. I took hold of her shoulders and gently pulled her to my chest.

"We can't have anything more to do with that girl. Nothing good will come from us bringing her up and spending a lot of money her. She's bad news, Zeinab, just like Cicurel's daughter. Remember, just after he wrote his will out to Nadia, he was killed. She's a jinx, like all Jews, just as you always say. She's got to go before things get worse."

After Fahim left, carrying Batel, Zeinab took to her bed with a face streaked with tears. I couldn't get a wink's sleep until dawn, when I dropped off for an hour or two at most. Images of Zananiri's lifeless and probably bloated corpse kept appearing alongside Cicurel's Heart of Palm. That breathtaking jewel had evaporated into thin air or lay incinerated among the debris of the burnt-out airplane. Or maybe it rolled under the feet of some peasant tilling his field near the scene of the crash. Maybe he smashed it with his mattock without knowing it. In the morning, Fahim and I were going to take a little trip up to Buheira to ask around. Fahim has ways to dig up information. Surely if the diamonds were there to be found, we'd find them.

My thoughts were interrupted by a violent coughing fit. I got out of bed and paced until it passed. Suddenly I heard loud and persistent knocks on the door. I found Zeinab there before me, pulling her scarf over her hair as was her habit before opening the door.

"Where's Abbas Mahalawi?"

I approached warily. A police officer stood at the door with three plainclothes men behind him. As soon as he saw me behind Zeinab, he strode across the threshold to the middle of the room and shouted to his men, "Search the place!"

Zeinab screeched, slapped her cheeks and pounded her chest with the palm of her hand. She never could stop these rural habits. Keeping my voice firm and steady, I said, "I'm Abbas Mahalawi. Could you please tell me the purpose of this search?"

"Monsieur Jacob Zananiri filed a complaint against you. He accuses you of abducting his daughter Batel and threatening him."

A bark of laughter escaped my mouth before I could suppress it. I shot Zeinab a look that said "I told you so" as I sat down on the couch, lit a cigarette, and tried to collect my thoughts.

Of course they wouldn't find anything. Fahim had placed her in the orphanage yesterday afternoon. But if I'd waited a day or caved into Zeinab's pleading, we'd be spending the rest of our lives in Tura Leman Prison. My thoughts turned to that son of a bitch Zananiri, who'd reported me to the police before leaving so that he could get his daughter back and rip me off at the same time. He knew I would never be able to report him in connection with the theft of Cicurel's gold and diamonds. But when did he report me? And how? I turned to the officer, who seemed more reasonable now that they couldn't find what they were looking for, and feigning both surprise and annoyance, I asked, "Who is this Jacob Zananiri, officer? And what's this business about his daughter?"

"He's an accounts manager. Actually, it was his neighbor in Bab al-Shaariya who filed the report. Qasr al-Nil police station received instructions to investigate today. As for Zananiri, he and his wife died in the airplane accident yesterday, God rest their souls. Now, if you would come with us, sir."

I accompanied them to the police station to complete the rest of the formalities. Zananiri's neighbor couldn't identify me, of course. In fact, I sensed he was no longer interested in the matter now that Batel's father and mother had died. He spoke at length, but not coherently. Maybe, like me, he feared having to take responsibility for the orphaned daughter. Also, he probably had no proof of any kidnapping or threat. Surely Zananiri wouldn't have divulged anything about our agreement. Before long, Fahim appeared at the station with a lawyer. Zeinab must have phoned him as soon as I'd left with the police. On our way out of the station, he confirmed that he'd left Batel with the orphanage, meaning that the link to me was broken. They would never look for her there. But he also felt it wouldn't be a good idea for me to go up to Buheira right way, as we'd planned.

"Even if they closed the file against you, they could still be watching. They're craftier than the devil and they know how to connect the dots. So you stay put and I'll send some men up to sniff around in Buheira and Damanhur without arousing suspicions; then I'll fill you in on what they come up with."

After three weeks, which seemed like years, Fahim's men returned empty-handed. They couldn't come up with a single thread leading to the whereabouts of my gold and diamonds or a possible thief. So much for the Zananiris, their luggage, and my late fortune. As for Batel, as Fahim learned from his lawyer, the case of her alleged abduction was stamped "unsolved."

About a month later, in one of our last nights in my small apartment near the northern tip of Zamalek, we were awoken again by pounding on the door. Zeinab leapt out of bed, slapping her cheeks in alarm. Before opening the door, she whispered, "If they found Batel, we're done for!"

But the visitor turned out to be a surprise of a different sort. Hassanein's young wife stood at our threshold holding her child, Tarek, clearly at her wits' end and begging us to allow her to spend the night at our place because there were new tenants in her apartment. I hesitated before inviting her in, because the last thing I needed was more disruptions. But Zeinab stepped in front of me, pulled her inside, and set her mind at rest. That was not how Zeinab usually behaved with strangers. Hassanein's wife asked us desperately whether we knew where her husband was.

I surprised myself by how coolly I handled this. "Why, he's in Brazil," I said. "He emigrated there." To my surprise, Zeinab stepped in to back me up. "May he return safe and sound and rich!" Her quick wit never ceased to impress me.

You might have thought I'd punched the poor woman. She burst into tears and wailed. She didn't have a clue as to what or where this "Brazil" was. The following morning, at Zeinab's prodding, I arranged with Abdel-Naim to put her up in a small room in Imbaba for some months until the tenants' lease to Hassanein's apartment expired. Then I discovered that Hassanein had sold his apartment back to the landlord and had taken out a lease on it instead, which meant that his wife and child had to remain in Imbaba. Meanwhile, Zeinab and I became preoccupied with Paula, whose health had taken a serious turn for the worse.

Then one day Fahim interrupted me in the office.

"You have to get married, Abbas."

"This isn't the time for that, Fahim. You know business comes first for me. When things settle down some, then I'll think about marriage."

"Marriage is business, too. You should marry Madame Paula as soon as possible."

"Paula? Have you lost your mind? She's practically at death's door and—"

"Which is why you have to act quickly. You've got to marry her and have a child with her too."

14

"HE DIDN'T REALIZE THAT I'D become a suffix: the 'less' after 'love.'"—Nadia

He admired my composure, loved my submissiveness, relished his power over me, offered a compliment in passing, and was insensitive to my torment. Yet I felt safe with him. Was I starting to love him, or just getting used to him? When I told him I was afraid to be left alone, that's what he did. He left me alone to embrace that fear, and I embraced it so tightly that I grew afraid to let it go.

I'd become a painting in a gilded frame, my luster dulling from being left on the walls of Major Murad's cold feelings. I was there for only three years, but they felt like three centuries. Time added craquelure with a generous hand. My body began to sag from lounging at the club and from the hours spent chatting and gossiping with my friends or at the homes of my aunt's acquaintances.

The age gap between me and Murad hit me as soon as we arrived in Ras al-Bar for our honeymoon. He imagined that every man we passed eyed me with lecherous intent. He had such a boorish way of reacting that he turned my life into hell. He locked me in his cage of jealousy and fed me gifts through the bars: jewelry, some cash to splurge on shopping, a wild night at a disco on the weekends. When he got the urge for sex, he'd climb into my bed and finish in a few minutes. He gave no thought to how I felt, to helping me feel pleasure or giving me time to satisfy my urges. He always switched off the lights, leaving me with no memories to give me some gratification afterward. When he finished, he buried his head between my breasts until he caught his breath.

Murad was a strange, untamable beast. He had an insatiable hunger for everything around him. He was unrelentingly ferocious toward anyone who thought of encroaching on his territory and his money and property, which were growing rapidly. I came somewhere toward the bottom of his priorities.

Five days after we arrived in Ras al-Bar, we received a telegram from my aunt asking how I was doing. That meant: how did my first night go? She also hoped to hear from me soon, which meant: call immediately. It was a long conversation, which she concluded with the news that "they" had "dispensed with the services" of my father. What that meant was that my father had suddenly been fired from the Committee for the Liquidation of Feudalism—the committee formed to document and administer sequestered properties. She didn't have to spell it out. I knew what was expected of me.

Murad was sitting on the veranda of our large wooden cottage that looked directly onto the beach. With tear-filled eyes, I pleaded, "Why do this to my father, Murad? We're married now."

With a smug smile, he said, "Yes, we're married. But not thanks to him. He pretended to agree to the marriage. Then he started to whine like a woman and complain about me. He thought he could scare me off. Instead, I helped him to early retirement."

I was galled by the way he spoke about my father. I kicked the side table where he'd laid his cigarettes and ashtray. The rattle also shook him, a bit. I ran into the house in tears, but as I was about to throw myself onto my bed I sensed him right behind me. I switched direction, raced to the window, and jumped out before he could grab me.

I ran for a bit, then stopped in a lane between some reed beach huts and a row of romantic wooden cottages belonging to the Cecil Hotel. I turned this way and that, wondering which way to go. This was where Egypt's upper crust spent their summers. They formed a powerful barricade against his wrath. Murad's public image was of paramount importance to him. He couldn't bear to see it marred by the tiniest scratch or speck of dirt.

He approached slowly, with a crafty grin on his face. He lit a cigarette, exhaled, and, keeping his voice low, he asked me to come back to the cottage where we could talk about this calmly. He didn't say what "this" was or offer a hint of apology. There was nothing reassuring in the set of his jaws and that rigid smile. I refused to budge. He remained calm but determined, repeating his request in a soft voice. Eventually I caved in to his polite persistence. But the moment I walked through the front door, he pushed me from behind with both hands, and then locked the door and window. At first I thought he was going to hit me. Instead, he took me by force. I was too afraid to resist. With total single-mindedness, he threw me on the bed, forced my legs apart with his thighs, violently tore off my underwear, and buried his head in my neck and between my breasts. When, after a couple of minutes, he'd finished, he climbed out of the bed and went to the bathroom. The sound of the water gushing over his body was as deafening as always. I detested myself.

I knew almost nothing about Murad's work. He rarely spoke about it, and when he did he was always vague. Maybe he did work for an important security agency, as he liked to hint, leaving the rest to my imagination. Or maybe he was a temporary supervisor of the sequestration committees, as I'd read in *Al-Ahram* once. But then, in the few family gatherings he attended, he let it drop that he was on temporary assignment at the office of the Minister of Defense. The "temporary" lasted a long time.

Later that day, in Ras al-Bar, he started to talk about the Committee for the Liquidation of Feudalism for which my father had worked as an agent. From the way he spoke, it was clear that Murad wanted to convey the message that Abbas Mahalawi was a mere civilian employee under Major Kashef's command. We were on the terrace of our cottage, where he like to spend sunsets working his way through the bottles of ice-cold beer nestled amid chunks of ice in a large metal bucket, with me there to keep him company, for which purpose he taught me how to drink beer. He began to relate stories about how, before the revolution, the rich had thrived on plundering Egypt's wealth, which they used to buy gold ingots, diamonds, and jewels, and to build villas and palaces, after which they transferred all their money abroad. I was amazed but, at the same time, on guard in case he was preparing to speak offensively about my family again. But he didn't bring them up at all. He was more intent on vaunting his heroic achievements in the battle to recover all that purloined wealth. The boasting must have soothed him, because all of a sudden, with no prompting on my part, he made a short phone call to his office to tell them to reinstate my father. When he hung up, he smiled at me as though to say "problem solved!"

When we returned to Cairo, I told my aunt how rudely and harshly Murad treated me. I couldn't bring myself to speak about what happened in bed. I parried her persistent questions with an enigmatic smile and feigned coyness.

She looked away and grumbled, "There was a time when you admired him. Or have you forgotten? Praise the Lord that he satisfies you in every way."

Naturally, my aunt blamed me for my marital difficulties. Whenever I complained to her about how he treated me, she called me a nitwit and a failure because I couldn't understand my husband. "You're slower than a lummox pulling an ox," she commented sarcastically one day.

Long before I got married, she used to carp at me: "You got to kill the man inside you." She'd say this at my resistance to spending hours on end window-shopping downtown and wandering up and down department-store aisles. She disapproved of the fact that I was a quick dresser. It would take me less than five minutes to get ready to meet my friends, often skipping the makeup. She would hold me back and make me spend more time in front of the mirror. Standing behind me with a critical eye, she'd impart advice: apply more rouge, don't pin your hair up, let the neckline down a tad, bring the hem up. . . . From her endless storehouse of sayings, she'd add: "A man's brain is in his eyes, dummy," "If you're pretty in his eyes, he'll be putty in your hands," and "The wife who dolls up gets her man home before sundown."

These pieces of wisdom created a barrier between us and shut her ears to all my complaints about Murad during the first year of my marriage. I couldn't bring myself to share my troubles with my father. He'd already suffered enough humiliation when they suddenly dismissed him from work and took away the government car and driver on the same day, and then just as suddenly reinstated him some days later. He must have felt like a puppet on strings that could be cut any moment. He was completely at the mercy of Murad's mood. Should it sour, the curtains would fall, the lights would dim, and my father would be stuck shuttling back and forth between our garden and the Gezira Club day after day, like the white rook in chess: confined to moving horizontally and vertically, and with no game plan other than to pray for the death of the black knight that threatened his survival.

The mysterious nature of his work often compelled Murad to spend as much as a week away from home, and so I began to feel a bigger void than ever. Ironically, despite his absurd jealousy while he was in Cairo, he encouraged me to go out—to the club, for example, or to call on my friends— while he was away on business. When he returned, he'd be eager to hear about everything I did while he was away. Who did I see? What did we do? What did we talk about? What was the latest gossip? He only had to say a word here or there to keep me talking for hours. He did exactly the same with Aunt Zeinab, strangely.

I felt safe with Murad. That was what attracted me to him. Nevertheless, I was uncomfortable with that heavy military guard outside our apartment building. It was impossible to go anywhere without his knowing it, even though I never did anything to merit suspicion. Whenever I left the building, the guards would ask me, very courteously of course, where I was going, and offer to accompany me. I would refuse and even rebuke them. At times I felt their eyes following me, trying to penetrate my brain, which confounded my tongue for no reason. The boom of their greeting to Murad, if he was with me, sent a queasy tremor through my stomach. "Pasha!" they shouted, stiffly saluting with hands held to forehead. He'd respond with a listless half salute, jerking his hand up no higher than his cheek, barely looking in their direction. You might have thought he was whisking away a fly.

My long day began at the club in the afternoon and ended at ten thirty at night at a friend's house or with my aunt. Zeinab continued to treat me like an adolescent instead of a married adult. She refused to allow me to drive, let alone own a car. She forbade me to go to the cinema or the theater, which I loved but which she hated, without my husband. Mme Maysa was out of bounds, if she happened to invite me over. I hated accompanying my aunt on her visits to her friends. Their mindless chatter bored me and made me feel how different they were from me and how like her they were. I was looking for something I lacked. Since I couldn't put my finger on it, I couldn't find it.

I did visit Maysa, of course, but secretly. These were the only social visits dear to my heart. I've always loved that woman. I'd long known my aunt harbored an implacable hatred for her, despite her outward friendship toward her. To me, Maysa was generous, kind, and considerate in word and deed, even if she was strict at school until her retirement. I certainly had more pleasant memories with her than I did with my aunt. When I was young, she would take me for small excursions in her car on Sundays. She'd have her driver take us into the inner quarters of Imbaba or Bulaq. When the streets were too narrow for the car to pass, we'd get out and walk. How warmly she was greeted by the women seated in front of their houses in those cramped alleyways! They'd leap to their feet with joy when they saw her, and invite her into their extremely poor homes. She'd have tea and cookies with them. To me the cookies were dry and tasteless, but she'd smile and say how delicious they were. Then she'd reach into her purse and pull out some white envelopes—some thicker than others, depending on the need—and gently, tactfully, almost pleadingly, she'd encourage the women to accept them.

Once, unable to restrain my curiosity, I asked her who those women were. She smiled and said, "They're good people. They help me get closer to God."

I was so impressed that I had to relate this experience to my aunt. She pursed her lips and said, "She's just like the rest of them. A bunch of thieves. So what if they try to make their money look clean." Then she scolded me and forbade me from going on those Sunday excursions, which forced me to invent ways to do it on the sly.

Maysa's circumstances changed drastically during the years in which I grew from childhood to adulthood. She was forced to cease her charity expeditions and even leave her home. I was in my fourth year at university when they took possession of her villa. Her brother, Amr Pasha, suffered a depression and confined himself to his bedroom. Maysa was forced to virtually beg for a monthly allowance from the Sequestered Properties Department. She tried to sell some of her movable assets on the sly. First it was jewelry and various belongings that the sequestration authorities had overlooked. Then she put her French bed and the rest of her bedroom suite up for sale, followed by paintings and small carpets that the employees at the Committee for the Liquidation of Feudalism thought were valueless. But she couldn't find buyers. According to my aunt, there were people who specialized in buying up the contents of the old villas, and these same people were in cahoots with the Sequestrations Department. They secretly notified the authorities about the contents of the homes they had entered after their owners had died, and while the heirs were trying to sell off the belongings. I later discovered that my father used his connections to keep those people from buying Maysa's furniture so my aunt could get first dibs. Somehow Maysa learned of this and stopped the sale of her bedroom suite. She would rather borrow from friends than sell her bed to my aunt. It took a whole year for my aunt to get her way. As the months went by, Maysa thought my aunt had forgotten about it, but my aunt found someone to buy it on her behalf so, by the end of the year, she was finally able to sleep in that bed.

I pleaded with my father to try to help Maysa out through his influence with the Sequestrations Department. He did nothing. Murad, when I turned to him for the same purpose, forbade me to bring up such matters ever again. My aunt couldn't restrain a malicious glee, but I avoided getting into an argument with her. I never could compete with her rapid-fire tongue and that arsenal of folk expressions that often left me tongue-tied. To my surprise, Maysa had a store of French ripostes that she'd fire off, as though she'd overheard my aunt, which made me laugh.

I couldn't understand why they were doing this to such a refined woman who had nothing to do with politics and whose only crime was that she'd come into a respectable inheritance from her aristocratic father. Could the same thing happen to me if my father died? Or did we fall into the exempted category because of my father's and my husband's influence? My aunt felt certain we did. As she put it: "We're the masters in this country, dimwit." There were dozens, if not hundreds, of families like us who had elegant villas and priceless jewelry and antiques. But no one touched them. However, try as I might, I couldn't get either my aunt or my father to help me understand this mystery.

Eventually, my curiosity drove me to Maysa. She thought for a moment then said sadly, "You'll see for yourself soon enough, when the momentum stops. At that point, the whole of society will be laid bare."

That left me more mystified than before. I pressed her to explain, but she didn't want to speak more on the subject. She only said, "Education, Nadia! That's our downfall!"

As she silently contemplated my face with tear-filled eyes, I wondered whether she was drawing a comparison between my generation and the current generation of students and their teachers. I didn't press her further, out of respect for what she must be going through, but I couldn't help drawing a comparison between her and my aunt. As attached to my roots as I was, something drew me toward Maysa. She reminded me of the mother I had never met, and I felt I belonged more to her than to Zeinab. It was an unsettling feeling.

Maysa, at the time, was unaware that much worse lay ahead for her. Over the next months, as I watched that unfold, I felt we were all sliding down a slippery slope. The sequestration authorities confiscated Maysa's home. She vanished, resurfacing several months later after moving into a small three-room apartment. Amr Pasha had been assigned to an administrative post in the public sector. When he spoke of this experience, he would laugh and mimic a triumphant boast: "I am now Third Warehouse Secretary at the National Bata Shoes Company!" Then he'd add that he'd resigned before even learning the company's address.

Maysa, due to her deteriorating economic circumstances, converted one of the three rooms into a dressmakers' salon, catering to the well-to-do. To my surprise, my aunt brought her many customers. Most were from her new circle of friends and acquaintances among the wives of officers, senior government officials, and even some ministers. Often, she'd insist on personally accompanying these women to Maysa's atelier. She had also begun to act superior to Maysa, sometimes deliberately humiliating her in front of the new customers. She even started to call her merely by her first name, "Maysa," stripped of the "Madame" that my aunt had affixed to her name for as long as I could remember.

As much as possible, Maysa avoided dealing with my aunt in person. She would assign her assistant to tend to us, and confine herself to a nod at her and a kiss on my cheek upon our arrival and departure. She even had her assistant deal with the payments. I was confused by my aunt's contradictory behavior toward Maysa. Why would she practically invent excuses to visit her atelier if she disliked her? When I put the question to her, she denied my suspicions and, of course, upbraided me for my insolence. Her mouth then twisted into a moue, and out of it popped: "When you do what's right, you're met with spite!"

Then came the day when I was trying out a new dress in Maysa's atelier. There were a number of other women in that sparsely but stylishly furnished room. Suddenly one of them gasped and pointed to the pearl necklace that Murad had given me for my birthday.

"*Mon Dieu!* That's Princess Samiha's necklace!"

My cheeks burned and my hand flew to my neck as though I'd just been sentenced to hang. My aunt spun toward the woman and called her "ignorant." The necklace was a family heirloom my husband had inherited from his mother. As the tension thickened, Maysa entered from the adjacent room and, before I knew it, it was war, with Maysa on the accuser's side.

"*Pardon-moi*, Zeinab," Maysa said in a proud and self-assured voice, "but the resemblance is very strong, and what with all the talk these days about the looting of jewelry from families of good standing, well—"

"My name is Madame Zeinab and I'll have nothing more to say to you until you learn how to address persons of good standing!"

We left before I could finish the fitting. My aunt, who had preceded me to the door, sent the driver back in with the payment for my dress. She didn't even put the bills in an envelope, as though the money were a handout. Maysa sent the money back with the driver—inside an elegant envelope—along with the unfinished dress. Afterward, my aunt started circulating a rumor that Maysa's atelier cheated the clients by switching the expensive fabrics they brought her for inferior-quality ones. When Murad came home for the weekend, I wept as I related this incident to him, but he seemed unruffled. He even showed some sympathy for the woman who'd attacked me.

"She's right, you know. A lot of things were stolen by government employees at the time of the sequestrations. To this day, we have a hard time finding the rightful owners because of the poor organization at the time. Why don't you tell me who that woman is? Maybe we can help her."

I truly did try to help that woman who'd caused me such mortification. I phoned Maysa to learn the address. A few days later, a friend of mine told me that the police raided Maysa's apartment and sealed it on the grounds that she was operating a commercial activity in residential premises without a license. The news was splashed on the newspapers' crime pages with her picture and a caption identifying her as the daughter of a former pasha. I then learned that the woman who had remarked on my necklace had also vanished from Zamalek. She would not be seen or heard of again for many years, as would happen to Maysa and her brother Amr.

Soon after that, some of my friends and acquaintances had begun to avoid me at the club. If they were forced to share my company because we were invited to the same function at someone's home, they would remain silent until I left. Meanwhile, my unfinished dress remained hidden in a corner of my closet for years, which pretty much summed up my condition as well.

Murad was punctilious in his weekly invasions of my bed: the same time, the same duration, the same performance, the same rituals, with no emotion whatsoever. Occasionally, I would get a gentle embrace after he'd finished, perhaps as a kind of a pat on the back. This carnal routine brought to mind Tarek's romanticism, which set off a struggle between my mind and my heart: I wanted Murad for the sense of security he gave me and for appearances' sake in society, and I wanted Tarek in private, invisible to all but me. As though I'd conjured whispers beaconing from the distant past, I decided to look him up. I went to his home in Zamalek, but only after taking a circuitous route for fear of being followed. The doorman told me that Tarek's uncle Salem lived there now by himself, and that Tarek had left the country long ago.

"Where did he go?"

"I don't know, ma'am. Some foreign country."

On my way home, I passed by the Heart of Palm. I went straight to the basement, where I knew my father would be working with his secretary, Fahim. After chatting about this and that, so as not to draw his attention to my real source of concern, I asked him whether he'd heard that Tarek had left the country. He turned to fiddle with some files, so he had his back to me when he said, "Tarek went to join his father in Brazil and left the apartment to his uncle Salem. He's chosen his own path, dear. May God grant him success."

Tarek's disappearance preyed on my mind the rest of the day. He'd left the country as suddenly as his father had so many years ago. I'd hoped the Ismail Yassin film that was on TV that evening would distract me, but it didn't make me laugh as his films usually did. Murad had come home earlier than usual that evening. We'd had dinner together and afterward, with the aid of an ink cartridge from a ballpoint pen, he rolled himself a hashish cigarette. He hooted with laughter as though this were the first time he'd watched the film, even though we'd seen it together in the cinema before. Afterward, he settled himself more comfortably on the couch. Then, looking me straight in the eyes, he asked, "Why did you try to call on Tarek al-Masri today?"

15

"To them, a prisoner's mind is the instrument of his crime. So they take possession of it by force."—Tarek al-Masri

I was never able to tell her how I felt about her when we grew up. Whenever the moment arose, I chickened out. And the moments were many, and more favorably arranged for me by fate than I could have ever planned myself. I can't count the times I felt she was ready to receive my declaration of love and to reciprocate it. Her eyes seemed to beckon me to take her into my arms whenever we met. All that couldn't have been an illusion. But then she changed. The extent of the change dawned on me the day my mother died. Suddenly it was show over, lights on, and you find yourself alone in an empty movie theater. It was probably the class difference between us. She was bound to leave me eventually. If I tried to draw near, she'd back away like a sun dipping below the horizon, abandoning me to an eternal night of loneliness, poverty, and want. "Auntie Zeinab" would never accept me, that was for sure. She always looked down on me as her servant's son. Why did my mother submit to that degradation? As for Abbas, I could never dare speak to him about my feelings for Nadia, let alone ask for her hand in marriage.

My foot lashed out against a pebble as I wandered down the street. It flew up and struck the windshield of a nearby car, causing fine cracks like a spiderweb and a big gauzy spot right in the middle. How could an insignificant pebble cause that much damage so quickly? A deep echo inside my head supplied the answer as though someone else were speaking: "Because glass is weak and fragile. If it had been a harder surface, like steel, the stone would have ricocheted and maybe even wounded you."

I continued on my way, fed up with my weakness and lack of resources. The words "Auntie Zeinab" brought a bitter smile to my lips. How she hated it when I called her that. Her face would turn into a nasty scowl. She'd yell some curse and try to poke me in the ribs with her cane. When I was younger, my ears felt the wrath of the flat of her hand, sometimes even after she'd sent my mother after me.

After hours of aimless wandering, I descended the three steps to the front door of our apartment and fumbled to insert the key in the lock because the lightbulb hadn't been replaced. Once inside, I flung my books down on the nearest table and called out to Uncle Salem. He didn't answer. I found a note on the fridge door telling me that he'd gone up to Alexandria for a week's holiday. I crumpled the paper into a ball and kicked it into a far corner. Why would anyone go to a summer resort in mid-April? Uncle Salem was weird, about everything. I went to bed and tossed and turned for a while. Just as I was finally about to drop off to sleep, I heard a pounding at the door. Before I could open it, one of the panels of the double door flew open and fell off its hinges. At least seven men burst into the apartment and spread out like locusts. Two of them cuffed me. As they dragged me outside to the police van, I saw others rifling through my books and papers. There was nothing for them to find there but foreign magazines about foreign music bands. Nadia used to bring them back as gifts for me from her summer holidays abroad with her family.

It wasn't until twenty days later that I learned the reason for my arrest. The first stage in that journey was military prison. The interrogator was in a hurry. He fired one question after another without waiting for an answer or even a nod or shake of my head. The moment a question was out of his mouth a heavy hand thwacked the back of my neck, as though this was one of the rites and rituals of the process. Before I could understand what had happened, the next question was out of his mouth. To my left, someone was taking down my confessions.

A month later I was brought before the Revolutionary Tribunal. I was one of several in the dock. An imposing officer called Gamal Salem presided. I can't recall the two others. In the first session, they introduced the witnesses for the prosecution. For the first defendant, a guy with a PhD in science, four colonels took the stand. Altogether, their testimonies took less than ten minutes. The next defendant was an employee for the Social Insurance Authority who had a BA in commerce. Four captains stepped forward from the second row, performed a military salute, and testified against him. When it was my turn, the judge asked me what my degree was as he shuffled through his papers impatiently, unable to find the answer among them. I told him that I had failed my third year at the university, that I would like to continue my education, and that I'd done nothing wrong. He cursed me, cursed my mother, and reminded me that I'd already confessed to everything during the interrogation. He signaled toward the back of the courtroom. Four conscripts stepped forward to testify that I was a member of the Muslim Brotherhood and was plotting to overthrow the government by force. They swore that (a) they knew me personally, (b) I'd taken part in weapons training exercises, and (c) I'd told them I hated the current government. I wanted to shout, "If they can testify to all that, they must be my accomplices." But I didn't. I lacked the courage. After the fourth witness saluted, clicked his heels, and withdrew, a lawyer I'd never met, who'd been engaged by God knows who, and who spoke so softly I couldn't hear him, stepped forward to defend me. Or, for all I knew, instead of defending me, he might even have told the judges to hand me the maximum penalty.

After three hours on my feet with the others in the defendants' cage, Gamal Salem pronounced his verdicts in a booming voice that shook the walls of the courtroom. Ten years for me. We greeted the end of our first session with relief. Now we'd be able to see the world in a new light. We were to be sent to a graveyard mistakenly called the military prison.

After several weeks in isolation in a room that was as dark in the daytime as it was at night, I was moved to a more spacious cell, though more than ten inmates were crammed in there. Not all of them were Muslim Brothers. What we all had in common was that the officers in charge of the prison thought we were opposed to Nasser and his regime. I didn't have an opinion one way or the other about Nasser. I was sincere when I told the interrogators that I didn't know him. They thought I was pulling their leg.

I don't have to relate the types of torture inflicted on me. I only have to show my back and chest to anyone interested in my life in prison and let their imaginations roam. And that would hardly begin to tell the brutal reality.

The only relief I had during the first weeks in that cell came from a colossal Nubian who had the heart and mind of a child. He told us that he'd been arrested because of a pamphlet that had a picture of someone called Hassan al-Banna. They were handing out this pamphlet after Friday prayers, so he took one and kept it. The police found it when they searched his home and arrested him because of it. He must have told us this story a dozen times, still unable to grasp how it could have happened to him. Did any of us know this Hassan al-Banna, he'd ask with wide eyes. "I swear I don't know him. But maybe if I could just speak with him face to face, he could get me out of here." Then, peering at each of us in turn, he'd ask, "Can you believe what happened to me?" We didn't have the heart to tell him that al-Banna was the founder of the Muslim Brotherhood and was long dead. We'd shake our heads sadly, out of pity for him—and for ourselves as we were in exactly the same position. The Nubian would heave a colossal sigh, saying, "Oh dear Lord!" Then he'd lie down and fall asleep with an innocent smile on his face, as though weary after playing soccer in the street the whole day long.

"Stand still!" commanded the sergeant in the military prison. "Not a move out of any of you!"

We stood in front of our cells in two rows, facing each other, as they decided who to set the dogs on that day. If you listened closely enough, you'd hear the prisoners' silent prayers and recitations of Quranic verses. Even from the communists.

The mere sound of the dogs barking made bodies jump and teeth rattle. Puddles of urine had already formed at the feet of those who'd lost control of their bladders. Now imagine our reactions when they started to parade their dogs in front of us, growling and straining at their leashes, eager to leap on us. I found myself wrestling again with the same thought that had reoccurred at such moments during the past year: what did they do to those dogs to make them hate us so much that they wanted to tear us to shreds, even though we were the ones in cages and they were free? They would come within a hair's breadth of lacerating us with their sharp claws. They were only restrained by their trainers, who calibrated the play in the leashes with the skill of professionals at inflicting fear and pain. The trainers walked with their chests puffed out, filled with the status and prestige that came from being at the other end of the leash. Should a prisoner move back just a little to avoid a dog, the guards would show no mercy. One of them would whip the prisoner with his crop until his back burned.

To keep myself from moving, I closed my eyes and muttered a silent prayer: "Dogs are kinder than humans. May God protect me."

Suddenly a trumpet blared. We looked at each other in surprise at this unexpected interruption. The prison warden rushed toward the door as the eyes of the soldiers and guards followed him with alarm. To us, it was as though the trumpet had sounded from heaven above. We were blessed with a few scarce minutes of comfort, safe from the dogs and beatings, although the guards ordered us to keep still if we shifted in place to ease our feet.

The surprise visitor was Hamza Basyouni, director of the military prison. The trumpet sounded again. We snapped to attention and the guards clicked their heels and raised their guns in a salute. General Basyouni marched between our rows, inspecting us with a steely glare. At his side strutted a mammoth bull-like dog whose pugnacious jaw and drooling chops did not bode well at all. The general, looking even fiercer than his dog, pitched his voice at a boom to issue orders. A step behind him, near the dog's tail, followed a younger and less-senior officer, neck craned to pick up the general's instructions, which, in a nutshell, were: these sons of whores need constant disciplining.

Basyouni walked all the way to the end of the line and returned. We knew what was coming from his previous intermittent inspections. He would pick one of us at random, have him thrown into a nearby cell, and release at least three dogs into the cell after him. The prisoner's agonized screams would echo down the corridor, then quickly subside into fading groans amid the growls and snarls of his attackers. Later in the evening, we'd mourn our late cellmate and enumerate his virtues. The younger officer whispered something in the general's ear. We couldn't make it out, but it apparently pleased his superior because he left with a smile on his face after handing his dog's leash to the officer. As soon as Basyouni left, the officer turned to us with a glare, as though preparing to settle an ancient vendetta. I leaned toward the ear of my cellmate and friend, Adel Ramzi.

"Who's that guy?"

"That's Major Murad Kashef, director of the office of the defense minister. God help us!"

"Why's that?"

"Basyouni's a two-winged angel compared to him."

The major took up a position in the middle, so that he could see us all. As he scanned our lines, he had to tighten his grip on the leash of Basyouni's dog, who had grown excited at the barking of the other dogs and had to prove to them—and to us—his superior ferociousness and supernatural strength.

"Where's Tarek Hassanein al-Masri?" Major Kashef shouted.

"Sir!" I said feebly, raising my hand slightly.

The sergeant whacked me on the back of my neck and pushed me forward.

"You don't raise your hand, bastard. You step forward!"

Murad scrutinized me with a crooked smile. "So you live in Zamalek, you piece of scum?"

I nodded. At a signal from the major, the sergeant pushed me forward, hitting and kicking me until Kashef told him to stop. With that same twisted smile, he spread out his arms like an emcee and said, "This time, we'll use the general's dog!"

Murmurs ran up and down the lines of detainees until a sharp look from Major Kashef silenced them. They had already begun to pray for my departed soul. No one had ever survived Basyouni's dog. That mammoth beast had no mercy for its victims: it went first for the neck, then shredded the legs and eviscerated the rest of him. I'd managed to evade random selection for a whole year. My luck had just run out. I was about to face my last duel with destiny in my life on earth.

"You're a lucky son of a bitch. The dog hasn't been fed for two days. He'll finish you off quickly. Go meet your maker, asshole."

They shoved me into the cell, unleashed the dog after me, and slammed the door. I scrambled to a corner and cowered.

I wet myself. I could hear my heart beating in my ear. That's no exaggeration. I clutched my knees to my chest as hard as I could. Snot blocked my nose and I suddenly got a violent urge to puke. I squeezed my eyes shut. The last thing I saw was that huge dog approaching, teeth bared and emitting a deep, slow growl. Then I passed out.

I swayed back and forth in the prisoner transport van. I was being transferred from the military prison to Abu Zaabel. The soldiers and guards talked of nothing but the miracle that had occurred a few days earlier, when the general's dog abstained from mangling my flesh and bones even though he hadn't eaten for two days. I'll never understand why, but when I came to, after God knows how long—days and nights are the same in prison cells—I found the dog crouched by the door and myself in one piece. He hadn't even touched me. They opened the door and tossed in some food. The dog sniffed at it, so I left it to him. I was starving, but I was scared to touch it. He didn't eat it. He looked at me as though to reassure me he had tested it and it was safe. I ate until I'd had my fill, then fed him the remains. He ate, then went back to sit by the door.

For the next couple of days I was "Sheikh Tarek." All forms of physical abuse had stopped. I was taken to the prison doctor, who treated me for some old wounds. Then, twenty-four hours later, we heard that General Hamza Basyouni had been killed in a traffic accident. The Muslim Brothers rejoiced and praised the Lord. They collected around me as though my blessing would rub off on them. The prison guards' treatment changed 180 degrees. Some asked me to explain certain points of Islamic law. Others asked for fatwas concerning their conjugal relations. Three broke down in tears and begged my forgiveness.

It was all so weird it made my head spin. Yet, even though the owner of the dog had died, I knew that the man who had called me a dog was still alive and kicking, even if he never reappeared at the military prison before my transfer.

The warden called me into his office. He treated me cour-teously and then notified me of the decision handed down from above to have me transferred to Abu Zaabel. At least it's a civil-ian prison, a long way from this hell, I told myself. Adel Ramzi and three others were in the van with me. None of them were Muslim Brothers, which was how they'd classified me.

The van groaned, then jerked to a halt. We'd arrived. Abu Zaabel was totally different, just as Adel had told me. "It revives your spirits," he said.

It was calm and tranquil there. The treatment was extremely humane. The wards were spacious. Ours had some twenty inmates, but there was room for more. There was a high window with enough space between the bars to let in sunlight and a lot of air. Each of us had his own clean bed, and we had enough time to chat and tell stories. They even allowed us to wear wristwatches, which Adel found both strange and amazing. More importantly, there was no physical torture whatsoever.

"It's like they've been saying. You're a holy man!" Adel said, and laughed.

But after only a week in paradise, either he or I must have bitten the forbidden apple. One morning, the loud clang of the cell door jerked us out of our sleep. A new officer entered, surrounded by a train of guards and soldiers. One of them pointed toward me and whispered something in the officer's ear. He pointed toward Adel and whispered something again. I trembled, but Adel was optimistic. He was sure the orders had come for our release.

He was disillusioned in minutes. We were led down a long corridor and put into a dark, and cramped cell. Its ceiling was so low my head touched it, and I was shorter than Adel. There wasn't a single window or even a slit to let in light. I sat in a corner and started to follow the sound of dripping water from a nearby tap, which I was unable to see. The water dripped rhythmically onto what sounded like a metal surface at first.

After a while, the vessel must have filled up some, because the sound changed to hollow plops. After an hour I began to get angry. Two hours later I stood up and turned in place, looking here and there, perplexed. After about five hours, now somewhat accustomed to the darkness, I began to move slowly around the room. I bumped into a metal pail. I moved it aside to stop the sound, but it picked up again from another part of the room. I tried to plug my ears, but my hands and arms grew tired. Somehow I managed to fall asleep. It might have been for half an hour, but was probably less. I was jolted awake when a guard poured a pail of foul-smelling water over me. Guiding myself by the crack of light from the open door, I tried to catch hold of him. But he slipped out and slammed the door before I could reach him. I banged on the door with my fists until I ran out of strength. I collapsed on the floor as the sound resumed, piercing my eardrums like a voracious bird feeding on my brain but never getting its fill.

During more than thirty hours in that cell, I only fell asleep three times at different intervals. I'd look at my watch every five seconds like a madman. I don't think any of those naps lasted more than a quarter of an hour. When it was over, they took me to back to an ordinary cell, though not the same one as before. Only Adel was there. He told me we'd been separated from the others, and went on to explain the new torture system. He'd read about it once. The Nazis had used it. He'd predicted other means and his prediction came true the following day.

"So you're a holy man too!" I said acerbically later that day.

When they led me to that windowless cell for a third time, I desperately tried to figure out what I had to do or say in order to avoid the torture. I told the guard the names of the Muslim Brothers I knew. I invented shortened versions of the confessions I'd given at the military prison. I confessed to other crimes I didn't commit. I couldn't speak fast enough. I was in a race to beat the clock before I got thrown into that room. But the guard was programmed to be deaf and dumb. He didn't look at me or change his stern expression. He didn't slow his pace. When we got there, he pushed me into the room and slammed the door, and I heard his footsteps recede. I sat in the corner waiting for the sound of the dripping water. It never came. After more than two hours, I began to think I heard it in the distance. Sometimes it seemed clear; sometimes it would go away. But in fact there was nothing. I sat in total silence, constantly looking at my watch, waiting for the sound of drips to come at any moment. Then I heard screams. Horrifying screams. Again and again. Those were people on the verge of an excruciating death. Then came the sounds of dogs growling; a child's voice, then a woman's, then a guy whose voice I thought I recognized. Then all the voices jumbled together and began to sound alike. They turned into intermittent groans of pain which then faded and segued into other sounds. Sounds of dogs gnashing their teeth, gnawing on flesh, and howling.

I felt a thin, warm stream of moisture on my inner thigh. It must have been the third time I'd wet myself involuntarily. I couldn't find the metal bucket to pee in. I was too terrified to sleep. I called out for help. I screamed. No one came. Whenever I nodded off, the cries of pain would start up again and then suddenly stop, as though whoever it was had just died under torture. How could they see me in this dark room? How did they know I'd dropped off to sleep? I felt the walls. They were moist, as though water was seeping through them. The voices fell silent for a moment. I shut my eyes to welcome some lost sleep. This time a woman screamed. The piercing scream of a woman whose voice I felt I knew very well. I searched my memory but failed to identify it. I stood up and listened more closely. The sound faded, as though to test my patience; then it suddenly grew deafeningly loud. A woman crying and begging someone not to rape her. She pleaded for mercy. She wept and groaned. Then her voice sounded muffled. Had they tied her up and gagged her? Did they really rape her? They must have, judging by the silence. But then I heard rapid panting breaths and her voice pleading again. She must have escaped the rapist's grip for a few seconds. I thought I heard her call out my name. Now I knew why I recognized the voice: it was my mother's. It was my mother, crying out to me to help her. How had they found her and brought her here?

With a burst of energy, I flung myself at the door and started banging as loud as I could. I collapsed on the floor again. My head began to spin and the floor seemed to shift beneath me. All the contents of my stomach spewed out in one go. The screams began again, this time accompanied by the sound of whips cracking. Agonized groans of pain, followed by screams in rapid succession. Then came a muffled thump, like a body crashing to the ground from a height. At the end, there was an earsplitting siren that made me howl.

Who's doing that? Where? Why don't I hear his voice? Why doesn't he show his face and do what he has to do and get it over with? The questions kept whirling around in my head as I paced in circles in the dark room. On the eighth day, I pounded the walls. I kicked the door. I cried out for my mother, desperately, again and again, until I nearly lost my voice. No one answered. Then a ray of light gently crept into the room and I heard Adel Ramzi's voice next to me. Where had he come from?

"I keep telling you those are tape recorders and amplifiers," he said. "They transmit those noises in order to drive us crazy. It's a new type of torture method. Get a hold of yourself or you'll have a breakdown."

I went over and knelt before him, staring toward where I thought his eyes were. Then I reached up to take his face between my hands, and I shouted, "I heard my mother screaming, Adel!"

"Your mother died before you entered prison, Tarek. Don't you remember?"

I moved away. I didn't believe him. My mind was so messed up. I curled up in the opposite corner. The voice still rang in my ears. It pursued me into the torrent of dreams that invaded the light sleep I had for a few hours. After a month of this, I began to think I was stuck in this place forever. What I found baffling was that they never asked me to confess to anything.

"And they're not going to ask. They want only one thing from you," Adel said, tapping his head. Then he fell asleep again. I wouldn't hear his voice again for a long time, because they transferred me out of his cell. We were physically separated but our souls weren't. I thought about him always. He'd been as wrongfully detained as I had. I'd never met anyone so considerate and kindhearted. We shared a love for music and playing music. We shared the same cell for ages. We'd been neighbors at the wooden whipping post—the "bride" they called it—and we dressed each other's wounds afterward. We slept on the same bedding, nearly touching. He stayed by my side to the end, giving me courage and patience. I saw him again a month or so later in the prison courtyard at recreation time. They'd stopped sending me to the windowless cell by that time. He came up to me and said, "The voices aren't real. Don't believe them, Tarek. It's all amplified sound. Don't let them take your mind away from you, no matter what. Your mother died a long time ago. I swear to God, she's dead."

I was extremely grateful to Adel Ramzi for all he did to try ease my pain, but I couldn't believe him. No machinery in the world could strike such terror into your heart. I'd begun to fear everything. I'd constantly hear voices calling to me in the prison courtyard, but I couldn't figure out where they came from. I knew I was right and that I had to carry out the orders of the voice that was calling me. I was right, and I would take revenge for my mother against all of them.

Yes, Adel Ramzi was merely there to ease my pain and comfort me. Otherwise, why would he have expressed his despair with his fingernails on the walls of the cell we'd shared for so long? With his fingernails, he wrote: "Have you ever tried to wish to die? To look forward to death with all your heart? I did and I succeeded."

You're the one who went crazy, Adel. They were real voices we heard, and they drove you crazy. You just pretended to be sane to keep me from losing my mind too.

The cell door creaked open suddenly. I curled up into a fetal position. Tears streamed down my cheeks. I couldn't bear to be sent back into the dark room again. I wept and begged the guard at the door to leave me alone. I crawled over to him and kissed his feet. He looked down at me with contempt.

"Stop blubbering and groveling like a woman. Your release order came through. For good behavior."

16

"CASES WENT COLD WHEN WITNESSES fell silent, police stopped investigating, and law enforcers let wrongdoers off."—Murad Kashef

I said goodbye to Nadia at our front door with a warm, husbandly hug, after telling her that I had to report to the front in order to inspect the troops with the defense minister. Now I could look forward to a whole week with Nagwa, as promised.

Nagwa was a journalist I'd gotten to know about a year ago. Our department had hired her, on the recommendation of a prominent journalist, to file reports on what women gossiped about as they had their hair done in a well-known beauty salon in Zamalek. We'd noticed her physical potential at first sight and knew her star would rise. She was then tasked with gathering sensitive information from important figures at private parties and functions. My section continued to rely on the reports I submitted on the basis of information I harvested from Nadia and her aunt.

Before her assignment as an informant, Nagwa was subjected to the customary "entrance exam." We fixed her up with an agent of ours who looked like a foreigner, photographed her, then arrested her in flagrante delicto. This was the process with all of our new female agents. It made them less resistant and easier to bargain with. Nagwa caused us no trouble at all. She was soft and pliable from day one, which caught my attention. I also felt that she was sincere in her patriotism and her desire to help us serve the country. Due to the nature of my job, I watched her at work almost every night through hidden cameras. She was unaware of their existence. The following day, when she submitted her report, she was a different woman: meek, bashful. The contrast kindled my interest in getting to know her better. She excited me in a way that neither Nadia nor any other woman had before. But I had to keep a distance, since she was still in our employ.

After a while, her star and her enthusiasm began to wane. I seized the opportunity to write a report stating that she was no longer fit for the secret service. They took my advice and pensioned her off, adding a generous bonus for duties performed in the service of the nation. But she continued to pass by my office in the hope of getting an apartment in one of the buildings in Garden City that now belonged to the National Insurance Company. This was the moment I'd been waiting for. I hadn't wanted to take the first step, so as not to give her a hold over me. I promised I'd do the best I could for her, and our deal was sealed. Of course, I couldn't start a secret affair. I'd have to take her as a second wife. Regulations were clear on that point, even if they were unwritten: if you entered into an extramarital relationship, you lost your job. However, there was a greater obstacle to marrying Nagwa than the trouble of hiding it from Nadia: the need to obtain approval from my superiors. Yes, they required a marriage certificate, but you couldn't marry just any woman, much less a former agent. A coworker in the department suggested I submit a formal request to the defense minister so that he could present it to the commander general. I balked at the idea. But, lowering his voice, he said, "Don't settle for an oral approval. Get a piece of paper and keep it in your pocket. Because, if things turn nasty, everyone will deny they know you, let alone gave you their assent."

I took up a piece of cream stationery with the eagle emblem proudly embossed on the upper left-hand corner and wrote a request for permission to enter into a common-law marriage with Nabawiya Azab al-Dardiri, aka Nagwa. I furnished brief professional and character details, and pledged to divorce her "if, at any point, this marriage is deemed to conflict with the national interests." That last item was at the recommendation of my colleague, who read over the petition and suggested another addition: "You may solicit her services again at any time if deemed necessary." That was where I drew the line, though I added it orally to the minister when I submitted the request.

The approval came through quickly, but with the condition that the marriage remained common-law. Nagwa and I concluded the formalities, obtaining two copies of the contract, one of which I burned; the other I put in my office safe. Nagwa moved in with me in the apartment of her choice in Garden City. I furnished it for her at my expense, though I kept it in my name, of course. It was a great place to spend time with her in a way that was different from the time I spent with conservative, aristocratic Nadia. Nadia was a high-class society lady who was perfect for my public profile. I'd been impressed with her from the moment I first decided to take a wife. There were no other Zamalek girls who suited my purposes at the time. When her father rejected me at first, it was a piece of cake to dig into our files, which dated back to when we first created the secret service archives. I easily found the information I needed: how her father had started out as a pimp who renewed prostitute licenses at the Hod al-Marsoud hospital on the basis of a power of attorney given to him by the most famous brothel keeper in Alexandria: al-Bataa Sayyid Ali. That nugget of intelligence had practically fallen into my lap because, at the time, we happened to be looking for ex-whores to work with us as agents after prostitution was outlawed. It proved very handy when I wanted to marry Nadia. Abbas Mahalawi would never have given his assent so easily if I hadn't broken him by threatening to expose his career as a pimp. Ever since that day in his office, when I showed him what I had on him, he'd averted his eyes whenever he saw me. Not that I would ever expose him, because his daughter was now my wife.

Nagwa compensated for what I lacked with Nadia. Nagwa wasn't as beautiful, but she had a sensational honey-brown complexion, a plumpish body, ample breasts, full lips, and wide eyes. More important, she was great in bed. She was permanently responsive and understood me as a man: she gave me everything I wanted before I had to say it or even think it. Every inch of her excited me, including her voice. Nadia was still shy about removing her clothes and she insisted on keeping the bedroom light on as though we were members of a committee commissioned to make a baby ASAP. The only problem with Nagwa was that I couldn't be seen with her in public because of her history with our agency and what people would think after seeing me with her. So I was forced to keep her hidden within the walls of the Garden City apartment. She accepted these conditions willingly. Her wild passion in bed made me heed the advice of my boss. "Get her perfumes," Badran told me with a crafty smile, without expecting me to respond or ask for an explanation. What mattered was that he visibly approved of this relationship with Nagwa, which encouraged me to continue with it. What mattered more was that I was already married to Nagwa with the written assent of his superiors. In fact, I learned that he had intervened to accelerate that approval to "ensure my psychological stability at work."

As soon as I entered the Garden City apartment, Nagwa told me that Defense Minister Shams Badran's office had phoned three times. I was to report for duty, without delay. Nagwa looked worried. I called the minister's office and learned that he would shortly be heading to General Command to meet with the Field Marshal Abdel-Hakim Amer and other senior military officials. I was to go directly there. I suddenly realized they would have called my home phone first and spoken with

Nadia. I quickly phoned to tell her I was on my way to the office but that I'd been held up by a sudden problem with the car. That should keep her from getting suspicious, I thought. I gave Nagwa a passionate kiss before I left, promising myself a wild fling in bed with her in a few hours' time.

As I exited the elevator on the sixth floor of the General Command building in Madinat Nasr, I found myself face to face with Badran. He had just emerged from a small office and was on his way to the field marshal's office. The reproach in his eyes was unmissable as he shook my hand and lowered his voice.

"This is no time for orgies, Murad. We must remain focused. We don't want some son of a bitch to start bad-mouthing the reputation of our men."

I nodded several times and muttered an apology. Then I asked, "What's going on, sir?"

"Nothing. It looks like they have doubts about our military capacities and want to test us."

We entered the field marshal's office, the minister first. Abdel-Hakim Amer was in the midst of what looked like an important phone call. He was partly turned away from us and speaking in a low voice with the person on the other end. The generals shot to attention and saluted the minister as he entered. He nodded curtly. The door to the situation room next to the office was fully open. I could see dozens of maps and papers strewn pell-mell on the table. It looked like the battle had already begun, from inside that room.

The director of Abdel-Hakim's office pointed to another, ordinary, meeting room, in the opposite direction. He smiled and said, "This is just an informal meeting, gentlemen. It's good to see you after such a long time."

There were endless, boring discussions about the positions of the ground forces. I could barely stifle my yawns. It had been so long since I'd heard this type of talk that it was as though I was hearing it for the first time. I'd obviously become so involved with administrative work, investigations of Muslim Brotherhood cases and the like since my return from Yemen that I'd forgotten battlefield work. For two hours, the men talked about nothing but our armed forces, their levels of preparedness, and the equipment they took with them to Sinai in preparation for an anticipated war with Israel. I caught something about vehicles that were so dilapidated they broke down halfway to the front. Suddenly the door opened. We heard some muffled commotion on the other side, and then President Nasser strode into the room.

I exchanged a furtive glance with Badran. He flashed a cunning smile and signaled me over. I hurried to him and bowed to let him whisper in my ear: "Phone your new bride and tell her you're going to have to spend the night at the office. It looks like we're going to be here till dawn."

Nasser and Abdel-Hakim had a private conversation in the latter's office. It lasted for some time. When they rejoined us, the president seemed calm. He welcomed us and said, "Right now, I see that there's a good chance of war. It could be in two or three days at most, meaning on June 4 or 5. We have to win the battle on the front, like we won our diplomatic battle."

We were like sand statues that shrank as though Nasser had just poured water over us. We exchanged dumbfounded looks until the field marshal hastened to the rescue. Offering the president what was probably his tenth cigarette, he boomed, "And we're ready to march, sir."

"No, I want to say that the first strike shouldn't come from us, or else we'll lose international support. But that doesn't mean that we shouldn't be ready at all times, Hakim."

Air Force Commander Mohamed Sedki stood up, and after requesting permission to speak, reeled off a pat speech about the skills and combat spirit of his pilots. Then he picked up a large folder containing only a few papers and handed it to the president's secretary, who opened it and displayed it for the president to read. After scanning a few lines, Nasser's eyebrows drew into a scowl. The air force commander summarized the contents briefly, probably in order to acquit himself in advance. "We submitted these munitions requests a month ago, Mr. President. We still haven't received the spare parts we ordered from Moscow. As soon as they arrive, we'll—"

Before the commander could say "bombard Israel's fortifications" or "crush our enemies" or whatever, Nasser put up a hand to silence him. He slammed the file down on the table and stormed out of the room with the field marshal and defense minister in his wake.

I posted myself near the field marshal's office to await my orders after the hushed tripartite meeting next to the elevator door came to an end. Before long, the president left and Abdel-Hakim, looking relieved, returned to his office, where he started to make more phone calls. I looked expectantly at Badran.

"Release a press statement from General Command saying the following— take this down, Murad."

I quickly pulled out my notebook and pen from my jacket pocket and prepared for the dictation.

"In a large bold font in red: 'Welcome to the Battles!' Below that another headline: 'How I've missed you, my gun!'—because the president has said that one quite a few times. Now, the first paragraph: 'Our forces are ready to repel any aggression at any time. The military resolve of the armies of the Arab region will compel the enemy to appreciate the consequences of an outbreak of war in the near future. . . .'"

He fell silent for a moment as he stared at the slip of paper in his hand. Frowning, he flipped it over from front to back and back to front. Somebody must have dictated the words to him. He folded the paper and slipped it into his pocket.

"Have our brother journalists complete the news item in the same mode. Get it on the front pages tomorrow with pictures of our soldiers at the front."

"But sir, it's midnight. The printing presses, as you know, sir—"

"Get on the phone to the editors-in-chief. They'll know what to do. That's the banner headline in the first edition of every newspaper tomorrow morning."

I didn't leave my office for two whole days, except to go to the bathroom which was next to the field marshal's office. We spent dozens of hours huddled together, poring over reports and deliberating, but never deciding. Nevertheless, the field marshal and the defense minister seemed relaxed, which helped convince me of their opinion that this was one of Nasser's political ruses. "Thank God we aren't headed for a third war after the Suez war and the civil war in Yemen," I thought as I glanced at my watch and pictured Nagwa.

On the evening before the third day, the atmosphere suddenly changed. I was told to send home for my military uniform. My office manager, whom I'd sent to pick it up, told me my wife had looked at him in surprise and asked him how I could have left to the front a few days ago without it. I slapped my forehead at my blunder. I had a hard time buttoning up the jacket because I'd filled out quite a bit. My belly stretched the gaps between the buttons. But I adhered to the instructions to remain in uniform in preparation for battle, which could occur at any moment.

I woke up at eight a.m. on the morning of the third day, June 5. I'll never forget that date. It wasn't easy getting out of bed because I'd worked late into the evening the previous night. I'd fallen asleep in my uniform, apart from my cap, which I found resting on my chest, slightly tipped toward me because of my growing belly. As I splashed some water on my face, an officer appeared at the bathroom door to tell me to get a move on.

"His Excellency the Minister of Defense is waiting at the elevator."

"What's going on?" I asked as I quickly dried my face. "Where are we going so early in the morning?"

"The field marshal has decided to visit the front in Sinai together with the commanders of the counteroffensive."

"Counteroffensive? What are you talking about? And why are we going to Sinai now? The president said war could break out at any moment!"

My colleague responded with a shrug and left. I tugged the jacket down in front to smooth it out and hastened downstairs, where I caught up with the brass assembled in front of General Command. I had to pause to perform a military salute at least four times to various commanders before I climbed into the car carrying the defense minister, who had decided to ride together with the field marshal. In a few minutes, our convoy arrived at Almaza airport, where we boarded a helicopter bound for Beir Tamada airbase in central Sinai. As we neared our destination and commenced our descent, the air force commander shot out of his seat and headed to the cockpit, feeling for the gun at his side. We exchanged questioning looks as our smiles faded, our banter stopped, and we subsided into a nervous silence. After less than a minute, the door of the cockpit opened to reveal a perfectly etched mask of horror.

Our confusion immediately turned to dread when Mohamed Sedki said slowly, in disbelief, "Israeli fighter planes are bombing the airfield."

"What the hell are you talking about? Have you gone mad?"

"They hit every single one of our planes, sir, right where they were sitting on the runway."

Badran jumped out of his seat. Swaying like a drunkard, eyes dazed, he told the chiefs of staff, "Order the pilot to return to Cairo, now!"

"I've done that, sir. And I've wired orders to the artillery to intercept the enemy aircraft as much as possible."

"No! Not yet, Sedki! Wait until we get out of range first! Get to it, man! Change the orders, now!"

I was sitting in the rear of the helicopter. I was sweating and desperately had to piss. I couldn't see Abdel-Hakim's face clearly. But I could see how he bowed his head and held it between his hands, turning to take a quick look out the window every now and then, before resuming his former position: silent, contemplative, mystified, or maybe just spaced out. It was impossible to say.

As the helicopter swung back, I looked out the window and saw huge pits in the runways. The sound of the bombardment was deafening. We reached Cairo shortly after nine. There was no one to meet us. The convoy of vehicles that had driven us to Almaza was long gone. The airport was empty. We made our way through the VIP arrivals, where we found some civilian staff. None of them dared venture a question as they followed us in silence, as though in the wake of a funeral procession. They didn't know where we were leading them. Nor did I, for that matter.

We stood at the edge of the road until Abdel-Hakim's office director finally managed to flag down an ancient taxi, using his gun. The driver complied. He was an elderly man with terrified eyes behind thick glasses. Even the car jumped and its motor conked out due to the shock.

I'll never forget that scene as long as I live: ten men in military garb—including the field marshal, whose face was familiar to one and all—packed into and onto that decrepit taxi, driven by a man who rivaled it in age and decrepitude. The car repeatedly groaned, coughed, and rasped, threatening to breathe its last on its way to General Command in Heliopolis. The most senior grades of brass, with dozens of medals and stars twinkling on their chests and epaulets, were squeezed in next to and behind the driver, ordering him to go faster, while the old man, fingers trembling on the steering wheel, muttered Quranic supplications. Several of us took up positions on the hood and trunk, gripping the window frames or roof rack. I'd chosen the trunk for fear of slipping off the hood and ending up beneath the wheels.

Back in Abdel-Hakim's office, no one said a word until all the generals had assembled. Then irate discussions erupted at the discrepancy between foreign radio broadcasts announcing our losses and local broadcasts reporting the dozens of Israeli planes we'd downed so far. I'd taken a position to one side, keeping my eyes pinned on my minister for cues as I struggled to grasp what had befallen us just hours after the war began. The only one who had the power to take a decision was at his desk, indifferent to the commotion, making dozens of calls from four different-sized phones. Suddenly a member of the Revolutionary Command Council—I think it was al-Sayyid Abdel-Latif al-Baghdadi (none of us liked him very much)—leapt to his feet, strode up to the field marshal's desk, and shouted, "How many planes have we lost, Hakim?"

"A lot . . . a lot. I don't have any figures. . . . Anyway, this isn't the time for that. There's an alternative plan to defend the troops without air cover."

Being no expert in military tactics, I couldn't understand why al-Baghdadi greeted that with a snort. I looked at Badran, who stared at the ceiling as though the matter had nothing to do with him. A phone rang near to where I was sitting. Noticing the field marshal's hesitation, I picked up the receiver. It was Air Force Commander Sedki. I could hear tears in his voice. I handed the receiver to Hakim. As he listened, he began to hold the receiver away from his ear while his expression grew angrier. Then he exploded, "I told you, I'll manage. I'll manage!"

He slammed down the receiver and turned to his office director, who was busy with another phone call, and told him to put him in touch with General al-Dib at al-Arish airport immediately. Hakim snatched the receiver and asked General al-Dib about the fifty-seven-millimeter anti-tank guns. We exchanged perplexed glances. Why would the commander general bother with such a trifling detail? Badran kept his face blank.

Just then the door flew open, and the room fell silent as we all turned to see who was coming. The aide-de-camp barked, "His Excellency, the President of the Republic." Nasser strode into the room, a bright, contented smile on his face. We raced to our places, but remained standing. He moved around the room, still smiling as he shook hands with each of us, repeating, "How I've missed you, my gun!"

Abdel-Hakim ceded his large chair to Nasser while another chair was brought in and set behind the desk so that Abdel-Hakim could continue to man his phones. The president asked to be brought up to speed on the victorious battle. How was the offensive developing? What were the estimated losses? Hakim kept his answers vague. Nasser asked about the situation at the front. Hakim dodged the question again as he turned to his phones. No sooner did he finish one call than he snatched up another phone to receive another. More than half an hour went by like this. In the few seconds between each call, President Nasser would ask another question, but received no answer. I glanced at the clock on the wall. The hands were moving toward five thirty p.m., but time was standing still. Hakim exchanged a meaningful look with Badran, who signaled me over and instructed me to go fetch the operations progress report. It was on a table in the conference room. We hadn't been near that room for five days. How the hell had the report gotten there? I fetched it and handed it to the defense minister, who quickly leafed through it and then handed it to the president. As soon as Nasser scanned a few lines, his face crumpled into an expression of utter dismay. He bowed his head for a moment, then set the file on the edge of the desk. He swayed, looking like he might collapse at any moment. He turned to the field marshal and said in a voice filled with sorrow and reproach,

"Khan Younis has fallen, Rafah is surrounded, all communications with Gaza have been severed. All that's just on the first day. Is that correct, Hakim?"

The field marshal uttered some reassuring words as he continued to operate the phones. He conducted most of his conversations in a voice too low for us to make out what they were about. Nasser stood up and went into the bedroom adjoining the office. After about half an hour, I grew curious about what the president was doing in there. Making as though I had to go to the bathroom, which was next to the bedroom, I opened the door and saw Nasser lying on the bed, arms locked behind his head, staring at the ceiling. His eyes were moist, as though he was on the verge of tears. When he became aware of my presence, he shot me a stern look that threw me off guard. I pointed to the bathroom and slipped out of his sight. By the time I reemerged, he'd returned to the meeting room. In a low, defeated voice, he told Hakim to broadcast a communique stating, without mentioning any details, that we'd penetrated into enemy territory. No one in the room said a word. He reiterated the request, reformulating the wording of the text. Again, he was greeted with silence.

"Okay. Whatever communique you agree on!"

It sounded almost like a plea. Abdel-Hakim nodded and Badran said something like, "All will be well, God willing." The rest of us stared at our laps with glum faces. Nasser gave the field marshal a look that seemed to plead for just one encouraging word. Hakim snatched up his phones again, speaking to the commanders of each of the branches of the armed forces in turn, in a loud voice that we could all hear clearly this time. The president stood up slowly, using his hand on the edge of the desk to support himself. He seemed to have aged years in those few hours. The operations progress report slid to the floor as he got up. He trod on it as he left the room, saying, without addressing anyone in particular, "I think we should all get some sleep and let Hakim work."

After Nasser left, the defense minister did too, and I headed to my office, preoccupied by everything I'd just seen and heard. Which of the two was commanding the battle? Which commander would take the decision to withdraw? The same one who took the decision to go to war? Or would the president evade responsibility and let the field marshal bear it alone? I didn't want to bring this up with the defense minister before he left. He looked too weary and irritated. But I suspected that this came less from a sense of failing than from resentment at others' interference in our work. No one had ever checked how we were performing our jobs before.

I had just taken my first sip of tea as I prepared to draft the communique per the instructions when my colleague burst into the room.

"Get yourself ready, Murad. Orders from the field marshal. There's going to be an inspection of the troops at the front before dawn!"

17

"WHENEVER I TRIED TO DRAW closer to the ladies of Zamalek, I hit a barrier. I couldn't see it. But I could always feel it."—Zeinab Mahalawi

Nothing could have pulled me out of my depression like she did. The moment I set eyes on her when Abbas first brought her home, crying like any infant would, I grew as attached to her as I'd been to Lady, who'd died four years earlier. I thanked the Lord for this unexpected responsibility and devoted myself heart and soul to raising her. I would only leave her with the servants or nannies when necessary. Some people even thought, at first, that Nadia was my daughter. I'd take her for strolls through Zamalek, pushing her little carriage with her inside it sleeping like a little angel. Whenever I bumped into a friend or acquaintance, I'd boast, "This is Nadia. Nadia Abbas Mahalawi. My brother's daughter."

True, I had to force the last bit out. Still, I had the final say in everything that concerned her. I refused to do all the sowing and let Abbas do all the reaping. It was high time I enjoyed the fruits of what was mine. I couldn't live under his shadow forever. We had both been searching for what we lacked and we both got what we wanted. So I'll let her have your name in public, Abbas. You can be the father. But she'll always belong to me and to me alone.

"There's a phone call for you, Madame Zeinab."

Bashir, my Nubian servant, handed me the receiver with one hand while holding the phone with the other. It was Abbas, telling me to get a photo of me ready so I could bring it to the Gezira Club the next morning in order to receive my membership card. I'd been pestering him about this for months. I didn't care how he went about it, but I wanted to be able to enter the club like any of its regular members. I was every bit their equal. I wanted to erase the memory of my "nanny's" membership carnet and situations I'd rather forget. Surely people there wouldn't even recognize me now. I'd left my job as a telephone operator years ago and my appearance had changed. The times had changed. The whole of Egypt had changed. The aristocratic wives, the titled ladies—all those preserved mummies had to curl up and shrivel inside their homes forever. No one could bear to look at their faces anymore.

After helping me and little Nadia into the spacious back seat of my Cadillac, my driver started the motor and set off for the club. I was proud of that car. Most of Zamalek's residents and shop owners recognized it from afar because of how frequently it was used before and after Paula died. I was determined to keep it, like many other things I'd grown attached to over the past twenty years I'd lived in Zamalek. Perhaps the closest thing to my heart was the Heart of Palm itself, which we'd lived in for two full years after Paula died. But the invisible rapping cane and its ghost, Cicurel's brothers, and the revolution and its men forced us to leave it. Circumstances certainly ganged up against us at the time.

The Cicurel villa in Alexandria was sequestered too. That became the offices of the Arab Maritime Navigation Company. The original Heart of Palm caught the eye of a senior officer, who took it over after it was sequestered. He sold it many years later to the Abu Auf family, but the ghost of the fat man remained and the sound of his footsteps continued to haunt both our place and theirs, in turn. I urged Abbas to sell the new villa and move into another one in Zamalek, but he was afraid a new resident would discover his guilty secret. Hassanein continued to stalk Abbas for years from his cement grave. That fear was like screeching birds overhead pinning him in place, and there was nothing I could do to shoo them away.

The procedures at the club took only a few minutes thanks to Abbas's influence. More importantly, I was exempted from the screening process. Normally, an applicant's name had to be posted for two weeks in the club's entrance hall in case a current member wanted to lodge an objection. That was the procedure I feared most, and my instinct proved right. I later learned from Abbas that Madame Maysa submitted a written petition protesting the club's acceptance of me as a member. It was signed by seventeen other women. He laughed as he handed me the letter of complaint, which he'd obtained in his capacity as a member of the board that had been managing the club for about a year. I set a match to it and watched it burn.

"Now listen, Zeinab. If you hear anything important from those ladies at the club, I want you to come to me on the double and tell me," he said.

"Yes, sir! It's not as if I got anything better to do."

I paid a small fortune that day. Ninety pounds for my membership. But for that club, it was worth it. Nadia was already a member under her father's and mother's names. After they handed me my new card, I couldn't resist the urge—I went to the bathroom, fished out my nail scissors, cut my old red nanny's carnet into tiny pieces, and flushed them down the toilet. I took a deep breath and left the bathroom with my head high. I looked at the women around me and distributed meaningless smiles in all directions, even taking in some women I'd never seen before. I could feel myself imitating Paula's way of walking and her gestures. Maybe it was because of the dress I was wearing. I'd had so many outfits similar to the ones she used to wear. After all, I went to same seamstresses, especially Mme Vasso's famous atelier in the Behler Passage downtown. I once met Umm Kulthum there, as well as other celebrities. I was now like them: one of Egypt's upper-crust ladies. So why did I feel something was missing? I lacked nothing. I just had to eliminate the funny glances from the other women in the club.

I felt Nadia tugging at my skirt and realized I'd been muttering to myself. I took her to have lunch in the upstairs restaurant. Afterward, I left a whole pound as a tip. That would make the waiter remember me, and he'd commended me to his fellow waiters. After lunch I sat for a while on the balcony of the bridge room, watching the club members come and go on the paths below.

Every now and then I'd sneak a glance at a group of women playing cards at a nearby table. I recognized one of them: the lady companion of Mme Ruqiya Afifi, an old friend of Mme Paula's. I caught her eye and smiled. She returned my greeting amicably and invited me to join them. I hesitated because I wasn't good at cards. Most of what I knew was from Abbas's stories about the poker games at Hassanein's apartment in Zamalek. Later, I acquired a bit of expertise from the short rounds of rummy I used to play with Paula. "You're lucky at cards," she once said, and the words stuck in my ears. I had the nanny take Nadia to the children's playground and took a seat at the green baize table. The women introduced themselves and I did the same, introducing myself as the sister of Abbas Mahalawi Bey of the Committee for the Liquidation of Feudalism, giving the proper weight to each syllable. It worked like a charm. The hands dealing the cards froze and the women riveted their eyes on my face. I could see the alarm bells working in their heads, telling them to bend like palm trees before a powerful wind. And did they ever bend and sway! I was ecstatic. Two of the women got up and left on one pretext or another. A third bowed out after the first round. My friend called over others to join us. I wasn't a good player. In fact, I was a lousy one. But I discovered that most of the others weren't much better. They just played the game for the sake of appearances, making like the grand titled dames of the olden days. From that day, my circle of card-playing friends and acquaintances expanded, even if there remained a couple of tables occupied by ladies from the old era who would have nothing to do with us. I lost most of the sets I played with fellow club members from Zamalek and Garden City, but that did nothing to diminish my enthusiasm. The club excited me. It filled me with euphoria and I couldn't get enough of it. But I still felt something missing.

Try as I might, I just couldn't break into the circle of society ladies who had once been Paula's friends. I kept coming up against an impenetrable wall. Sometimes it seemed covered with thick coats of paint. If I managed to scratch away one layer, I'd find another beneath it. At other times it was invisible and elastic. Whenever I encountered it, I'd push into it deeper and deeper, until I plopped into their midst. Before I could pick myself up, it would spring back and eject me.

I couldn't figure it out. A sparkling turquoise sea beckoned me to wade in, only for a wave of types like Maysa to drag me under and toss me back on shore. They just would never accept me. They raked in tons of money from the rummy games I lost, but that made no difference. If circumstances brought us together at the same table in one of the club's restaurants, I'd always insist on paying the bill. Yet, they greeted that with a strange kind of resentment and practically forced their "thank yous" out through clenched teeth.

Abbas sure wasn't pleased with the expenses, since he was the one who ended up paying my bills. That was the agreement we'd struck: to split everything he owned until we died. Or until he killed me. I'd lost my trust in him long ago. But the funny thing was that he was growing softer and more pliable. Maybe that was his way to atone for his sins and crimes against my right. Yes, my right to a life like his. If it hadn't been for me, he would never have become Abbas "Bey"!

I often encountered these high-society ladies at dinner banquets and receptions in Zamalek, Garden City, and, more recently, Heliopolis. Sometimes I'd receive invitations to these functions if I happened to be sitting near the ladies in the Tea Garden, the Pergola Garden, or the Lido. But that transparent barrier was always there. I'd see them behind it and they stayed behind it, casting me looks that forced me to back away despite myself. Their whispers and gestures made me feel they were mocking me, the way I spoke, my slight limp—everything about me. When I brought Hassanein al-Masri's wife, whom I'd made my *femme de compagnie*, with me to the club, I could feel them mocking us both. In fact, I once heard one of them ask another in a whisper that I was sure was meant for me to hear, "Tell me, dear, which of those two are we supposed to address as 'madame'?"

I've hosted dozens of dinner banquets and receptions. I made the last Thursday of every month a fixed date, to ensure my invitations would be reciprocated. Yet my functions were never as well attended as others, and some guests never reciprocated even though I served twice the amount of food and drink. Many would concoct the feeblest excuses in order turn down an invitation, and would add condescending looks. I was sure that if I could just make better sense of it, I'd find a way to overcome it. Apart from the rare occasion, I was always left flummoxed.

Since some of my acquaintances played golf with those society ladies, that's the sport I chose when Abbas told me to try harder to get in with that crowd. He wanted more grist for his reports on the Gezira Club members. "All that walking across those stretches of green turf will give you a great opportunity to shoot the breeze," he said. So I got myself a golfing outfit and gear, hired a caddie to lug around the bag with all the clubs and balls in it, and engaged a trainer.

Golf is such a silly game. I just couldn't get the hang of it. The holes you have to aim for are so tiny and far away. I had the hardest time just hitting the ball at all, let alone hitting it well. Mostly, I just thrashed the air, as happened for the umpteenth time when I caught sight of a woman getting ready to strike a ball. She was a society lady I knew quite well. I observed her closely. She bent over the ball and stayed perfectly still for a moment, focusing. Then, in a flowing movement, she swiveled her upper body and swung. The ball suddenly soared in my direction. "*Ya mama! Ya lahwi!*" I screeched, even though it flew high over my head.

Abbas warned me time and again to stop using expressions like that, but they popped out in spite of myself. Everyone in sight shot me disapproving looks. To top it off, I'd twisted my ankle tripping on a nearby golf hole while dodging the flying ball. No one thought to ask whether I was okay. They just fixed me with their scornful glares. In some cases, I could see their lips move behind the smirks. I couldn't hear what they said, but I knew it was about me and I was sure it was offensive. I flung the golf club at the trainer, who couldn't hide a smirk of his own after exchanging some wisecrack with the caddie. That was the end of golf for me.

"I just can't, Abbas. I don't want to set foot in that goddamn Gezira Club again!"

"You're not the only one. We all feel that way. Anyway, soon there won't be a Gezira Club!"

"What do you mean? Did the government get its back up because of some of those old biddies' gossip I told you about?"

Abbas sighed and shot me a reproachful look for some reason. He then explained that Gamal Abdel-Nasser had decided to turn the whole club into a youth center with no restrictions on membership.

"The world's changing, Zeinab. The good old days are gone. We just made it in time to lick the bottom of the golden plate. From now on, everybody's going to be equal. Imagine going into the club and finding Fahim in his *gallabiya*, lounging by the Lido, sipping tea."

"And all the reports you submitted? What are they going to do about them? Use them as kindling?"

Abbas didn't answer immediately because he was busy arranging some papers in his safe. Then he said, "We did what we could. I told the chairman of the board in our meeting today that we won't be able to write reports about those people when they're at home. Though I must admit, I don't know why the government's so scared of them. They just sit around and shoo away flies. . . . But apparently the army doesn't like the things they say."

I went up to Abbas and put my hand on his shoulder. "I got an idea that will make them happy and even get you a promotion."

He rolled his eyes, but I continued: "Tell them to go fifty-fifty. One half for the ladies and gents, the other half for that youth-center thing they want."

"And what good would that do them? They want to take over the whole grounds in order to—"

"Just listen. Tell them that by keeping a segment for the elites they'll be able to keep their eyes on all of them in the same place, like chickens in a coop. Once they let them run off this way and that, squawking and cackling, they'll never know how to keep track of them again."

Abbas's eyes lit up. He liked the idea. He rushed to phone, dialed a number, and asked the person on the other end to put him in touch with someone called Mohamed Gemiei Bey. He explained my idea, which he called *his* idea as he pitched it to someone of a higher stature. And the person at the other end must have been pretty high up, judging by the amount of "Yes, sirs" and "As you say, sirs" Abbas inserted along the way. After replacing the receiver a few minutes later, his smile broadened. He lit one cigarette after the other as he waited by the phone, which meant that this Gemiei Bey would be calling Abbas back after making some other phone calls. I took a seat on the closest chair and started to smoke too. Half an hour later, the phone rang. After replacing the receiver, Abbas exclaimed, "You did it, Zeinab! They agreed. Tomorrow they're going to announce that they're going to allocate part of the club to the youth center and leave about fifty acres to the club."

He laughed out loud for the first time in years. "Have you ever seen a fifty-acre chicken coop?"

"Congratulations to them. But first things first. Get us a membership in that new center. There's no telling what that government of yours is going to get up to next."

If I weren't afraid that it would put Abbas's job at risk, I'd have shouted at everyone who looked down their noses at me in that club that if it weren't for me their days there would be over, and I'd make every last one of their ladyships and pashas bow down and kiss my feet. Instead, I stopped going there, apart from once or twice a month at most. It no longer held any attraction for me, until after that wall had begun to crumble on its own.

When I did start going back to the club regularly again, it was when I felt, for the first time, that I was a member in my own right. Not because I was the sister of an important member of the National Party Secretariat, but because my friends were my friends because of me and my status. I'd become Madame Zeinab, independently of Abbas's position. The world had truly changed, as Abbas said. But not in the way we feared it would. At long last, the club had begun to let in members who were like me—people I could feel comfortable with and speak with easily. We had so much in common that whatever differences there were between us would melt in a second. I had my own set, who gathered around me whenever I made an appearance. Most of them were younger than me, but their allegiance was to me and me alone. To them, I was an authentic lady. I no longer felt I had to play rummy or golf, or lounge around the pool at the Lido. Eventually my thirst for revenge dwindled. We were all alike now. They'd come down in the world now that their old world had faded and they'd grown poor and were forced to huddle together in remote corners of the club where we barely felt their existence.

One day, I spotted a familiar figure from afar. I'd almost managed to forget her existence. I'd heard she'd emigrated to the States years ago, but apparently not. I felt a knot in the pit of my stomach as some force seemed to lift me out of my coterie of friends, who circled around me like a crescent moon. Their fawning chatter faded and they receded to indistinct dancing shadows, even though they were right next to me. Echoes of her voice from the distant past rang in my ears. I was sure it was her. Time might have changed her, but no one else sat with such poise and composure. No other woman these days was as fastidious about her couture. The next thing I knew, I was walking in her direction with faltering steps, as though beckoned by a mysterious summons. She was sitting with another woman whom I knew quite well. Barely managing to compose myself, I approached. The woman said, "Madame Zizi! Hi! Why don't you join us!"

Maysa swiveled her head to face me with a cold appraising look that stripped me of all my clothes, as though forty years hadn't passed.

My friend introduced me to her, saying, "This is Madame Zeinab Mahalawi."

Maysa's lips curved into an icy smile. "Why, Zeinab, how odd to see you here. I thought you gave up your job at the switchboard ages ago."

18

"WHEN A MAN IS NOT clear in his priorities between me and another woman, it is no great honor if he chooses me."—Nadia

"You haven't answered my question, Nadia."

I don't think I'd ever been so rattled as when Murad asked why I went to visit Tarek. He smiled smugly as he puffed on his cigarette. He boasted of knowing the most intimate details about everything and everyone in Egypt. "Some people think they can get away with anything, but me and my men are always ten steps ahead of them. We can count their breaths for them. Refute their thoughts before they're even out of their mouths, then make them pay hell for it."

After recounting his triumphs, he asked me once again about my visit to Tarek. He was growing impatient. I lied at first: "Since his mother's death, I'd been helping him out with some money, but secretly so as not to wound his pride. His mother used to work for my aunt. She was like a second nanny to me when I was growing up."

Murad didn't believe me. "Anyway, I'm not going to pressure you right now," he said. "You can tell me later in your own time. But if you'd asked me beforehand, I'd have told you that Tarek al-Masri was in prison."

"Tarek's in prison?"

"Yep. He got ten years. He joined the Muslim Brotherhood. They made an underground organization and we found bombs, weapons, and pamphlets at their place. The country's going through rough times, Nadia. We barely get a wink of sleep."

I myself didn't sleep that night. I was tormented by worries for Tarek. After what Murad told me, on top of what I'd read in the press about the Muslim Brothers' conspiracies, I wondered whether Tarek could have changed so much that he would have joined them. He'd always been a nonconformist, but without ever knowing what he wanted. I cried for him and because of him and, as dawn approached, I prayed for him. Only when the morning light streamed through the curtains did I fall asleep from sheer exhaustion.

I woke up in the late afternoon, groggy and weary. I found Murad stretched out on the living room couch, as though he hadn't moved since the night before. But, in contrast to the previous night, he was amiable and solicitous, which somehow made me want to open up to him.

I told him that I'd felt close to Tarek since we were children, and that was what made me pass by his place to see how he was doing. Murad didn't utter a word as I spoke. He seemed to take what I said in stride, almost as though he already he knew it all, including my most distant memories. His hand stroked my hair gently, which encouraged me to ask how Tarek was doing in prison. "They have a better life inside there than out," he said. Then he barked with laughter and held his hands far apart from each other. "They're all as fat as cows from eating so much and sitting around doing nothing!"

I asked Murad to tell Tarek's uncle about this so that he wouldn't go on thinking Tarek was in some other country, like the doorman had told me.

Murad laughed again. "You are so naive! It was his Uncle Salem who informed on him. He told us that Tarek held secret meetings in that apartment in Zamalek. He wanted to take possession of it so he could use it as a gambling den. They're scum, Nadia."

228

I said nothing. I didn't wholly believe Murad. Nor could I deny my feelings for Tarek, even though I was sure he'd changed. My mind churned over questions without answers until a violent headache made my temples throb. I closed my eyes and leaned my head back on the couch, picturing Tarek behind bars in a dark-blue prison uniform, with a dark-blue cap, and significantly fatter than he was before. The loud, persistent ringing of the phone shook me out of my thoughts. Murad stood up and headed to the red phone. That meant it was the office of Field Marshal Abdel-Hakim Amer calling. He picked up the phone and listened, saying nothing but "Yes, sir . . . Yes, sir . . . Yes, sir . . ."

He sat back down and began to pay unusually close attention to the football match between Zamalek and Damietta. Just before the end of the first half—Zamalek was two points behind—the red phone rang again. Murad listened for some moments, then said eagerly, "Understood, sir . . . Yes sir. It's war, of course . . . I'll tell them right away."

He replaced the receiver of the red phone gently in its cradle, then snatched up the receiver of the black phone, his other hand flicking through a small address book for a number. He now spoke with the voice of a commander who expected to be obeyed without question. I'd seen him change this way before, like an actor who could switch instantly from one role to another. He told the person on the other end that Field Marshal Amr wanted war in the second half.

"They want war in that field. Did you get that, or do I have to repeat it?" he shouted.

He slammed down the receiver and returned to the couch.

"Is everything all right, Murad?" I asked, not quite believing my ears. "Is there really going to be a war with Israel, like we keep hearing?"

He laughed so hard that he rolled onto his back. Then he kissed me on the forehead and said, "Didn't I tell you you're naive? If Israel dared lay a finger on us in Sinai, we'd burn them and throw them into the sea. Zamalek's losing against Damietta. His Excellency Abdel-Hakim Amer's a Zamalek fan and he will not accept defeat. So he wants that team to think they're fighting a war they have to win at all costs."

I smiled. I must admit I didn't quite understand what he was talking about, but I felt the force of his authority, which excited me. I tried to focus more closely on the game, if only to alleviate the boredom, although I was also busy applying my red fingernail polish. Murad, his face glued to the TV screen, explained that he'd just phoned the Zamalek team's coach in the changing room at the stadium and told him to give the team a pep talk, telling them that when they got back into the field, they had to play as though they were fighting a decisive battle. That was what he meant when he told the coach that the field marshal ordered "war in the field."

The second half opened with a change in the Zamalek team's lineup, which, according to the sportscaster Mohamed Latif, was "very strange" and "unprecedented." The goal-keeper Shahin had been replaced by Mohamed Harb, the third reserve goalie, who'd never played in a match before, as Latif remarked sarcastically. The game ended with a crushing defeat for Zamalek: six-nil! Only later did it click that the goalie's last name—Harb—literally means "war."

War did break out between us and Israel just six weeks later. It lasted only six days. Murad had been called in and didn't resurface until after the defeat, when Nasser gave his resignation speech. I moved back in with my father for the duration. The army driver who'd been assigned to me drove through the dark and silent streets to the Heart of Palm. A government decree had ordered a blackout in the capital so that Israeli planes couldn't identify and strike strategic targets, as my father had explained over the phone. So all street lighting was banned, meaning not just streetlights but also lighting from shopping windows and electric signs. Dark-blue semitranslucent sheets of paper, like the type we used to use to cover our textbooks at school, were pasted onto the windows of houses and apartments to block rays of interior lighting that might turn them into targets. Some dark paint had been used to dim our headlights and those of the other cars around us. The driver told me it was made out of bluing solution.

Along the way, I noticed a lot of recently constructed red-brick walls in front of apartment-building entrances. They were about a half a yard thick and three yards wide. I also saw a lot of sand-filled burlap bags stacked on top of each other in front of stores and ground-floor windows. "Their purpose is to absorb the shock waves from the explosions of bombs dropped by enemy aircraft," my driver told me in the matter-of-fact voice of a military expert. I felt I was in the middle of a bizarre nightmare.

"Have Israeli airplanes reached Cairo, Mahmoud?"

"May the Lord protect us, and may He be praised what-ever happens."

The vague answer and the resigned way he said it increased my alarm. I feared an Israeli air raid could strike at any moment. We were held up for a while because of protest marches. People carrying pictures of Nasser were calling for him to retract his resignation. The demonstrations weren't large, but they were spontaneous. I felt gloomy and depressed. Suddenly my cheeks burned with shame and humiliation. Then, just as suddenly, I subsided into despair. For the first time in my life I felt that Egypt was lost, that it had truly "lost its momentum," as Maysa once said it would. She was the only one I'd ever heard say that. My father said she'd been infected with the pessimism virus from her ambassador brother.

For days, I barely left my room at the Heart of Palm. Then Murad resurfaced. He was tense, fidgety. All self-confidence had gone out of his voice, which was taut and high-pitched. He looked bedraggled, like he hadn't slept in a week. He said it was all the fault of the field marshal and the air force commanders. He repudiated the defense minister he had worked for, hitched all his wagons to Nasser, and burned his bridges behind him. I'd never seen him so outspoken before. I was surprised at this boldness, and even more surprised when I found myself sympathizing with him. I sensed he was suffering from a crisis deep inside him and it had left its marks on the tired face and hunched shoulders I saw later, when we were alone in my room. He spent the night in my arms.

"The sons of bitches. They made us walk home in the desert in nothing but our underwear, Nadia," he said. His tears choked off his voice and fell on my chest. I held him tighter. He clung to me as he turned his head, like an infant looking for his mother's breast. His body jerked a couple of times, but nothing more. They were more like spasms of fear than desire. He rolled to the side after a moment, then left the bed, head bowed. I didn't hear the sound of water rushing over his body this time. The silence enveloped us in its heavy thickets until morning.

Murad didn't come to my bed again for months. His appearance altered remarkably during that period. He'd aged almost overnight. His hair had grayed after he'd given up dyeing it. He lost a lot of weight. For a while, he refused to leave the house. Most of the time he spent reading the newspapers, watching TV, or speaking for hours on the black phone with his colleagues. The red phone had stopped ringing. His condition worsened after they broke the news, one morning, that Field Marshal Abdel-Hakim Amer had committed suicide. He started to take it out on me, as though I had caused the defeat. At first the abuse was verbal, but it soon turned physical. He got a lot of money from me, but hadn't spent a piaster on our home since his return from Sinai. My father grumbled, but yielded to my aunt's pressures. "The cloud will pass," she'd say. "As soon as he gets back to work, he'll make it up to us."

That period after the war with the ghost of Murad was one of the worst times of my life. He was defeated on the inside and I was the only thing around for him to conquer. He'd climb on top of me, cut off my breath, yet never satisfy himself or me. He'd become impotent, flaccid. He'd threaten to divorce me and leave. I prayed for him to fulfill the threat, but he'd back down at the last moment. He'd say it was for my sake, so I wouldn't have to face these difficult times alone. A volcano was building up inside me and sometimes it would erupt. I'd shout at him to release me, to set me free. But he wouldn't.

There was a woman on the march inside me who refused to stay hidden, and to Tarek she was as exposed as a seaside veranda to a surging sea. I ran into him soon after his release from prison, which was a couple of years after the 1973 war. As I studied his face, I nearly reached out to hold it between my hands, but my mind held me back and quickly erected a wall to hide behind. I waited for him to hop over that wall. He didn't, so I let my shadow peep out to guide him, only to find he had built his own barriers. This distance between us destroyed that initial flush of affection, and our conversation turned arid and devoid of emotion. However, it did not slow the advancing footsteps of the woman inside me.

At first I found it hard to believe it was Tarek al-Masri standing right in front of me. He was pallid and scrawny, completely the opposite of what Murad had led me to believe. He was broken and defeated, haunted by a sense of shame that had become lodged in his face. He told me of his ordeals in prison, the humiliation he'd experienced there for no reason. His eyes glistened with welling tears. Laden with sadness, they overflowed and plunged down his cheeks as though committing suicide in search of a redemption they would never find. Nothing would ease the strains on that haggard face. I didn't have the words to comfort him. He was miles away, even though I could hear his breathing clearly and see his chest trembling from emotion. I moved toward him, on the verge of tears myself, pleading for him to stop.

"You got married, of course."

"Yes . . . about four and half years ago. But now—"

"Some Zamalek dude. From university, huh?"

"No. An officer at the Defense Ministry. His name's Colonel Murad—Murad Kashef. I'm sure you don't know him. He was a neighbor of ours in Zamalek, but—"

Before I had a chance to tell him that Murad and I were divorced, Tarek sprang away from me like he'd been bitten by a scorpion. "I'm not crazy! You're the one who's crazy!"

I stood stunned by the gleam in his bulging eyes that stared straight into mine. They frightened me, but I tried to draw closer to reassure him.

"They stripped me naked and made me perform like women and animals!" he shouted.

I put my hand over his mouth, begging him to calm down and lower his voice. My tears pleaded with him to listen. He shoved my hand away violently and started to talk about how they had tortured his mother and other women. I tried to tell him again that I was divorced. He clamped his hands to his ears, pressed his eyes closed, and shouted, "Stop it! Stop it! It's all because of you! It's your fault!"

I tried to reach out again. He shoved my hand away and turned aside. I stepped back, at a loss. Neither of us had done anything wrong. Both of us had been tortured for wanting something else out of life. We both searched for a missing part of ourselves, only to encounter pain. How could I get through that haze of sorrows to explain this to him? When he told me that his mother had been raped and killed in prison, I feared he was going delirious. I stood transfixed, helpless, my anxiety mounting until my aunt suddenly appeared on her balcony. "Tarek!"

He looked up, gave her a brusque wave, and turned to leave, but he found Bashir in his path, blocking his way.

"Madame Zeinab would like to see you." He made it sound like an order issued from on high. Tarek trudged after him.

I wondered what thoughts were running through his mind as he stole glances at this place or that in the villa's garden. I caught up, quickly wiping away my tears so my aunt wouldn't see them. She had just reached the bottom of the granite staircase in the reception room. She moved slowly and with difficulty now that she'd put on weight, then came to a stop, leaning on her cane, which, for the last two years, had been her constant companion. She welcomed Tarek with feigned affection, then took a seat as she told him to tell her about his plans for the future. Stammering like a student who hadn't done his homework, he supplied short, disjointed answers that only aroused pity. My aunt knitted her eyebrows and adjusted her head covering to hide the relentless assault of gray. With her other hand, she reached beneath her shawl and pulled out a small envelope, obviously containing money. Holding it out to him, she terminated the interview coldly.

"You know the house. If you need anything, just pass by. Your mother did so much for us. We never forget our servants."

It seared my heart to hear her describe his mother that way. I'm sure that was what made him tense up suddenly. But he said nothing. He shook the envelope by a corner as though weighing it. Was he wondering whether to accept it or not? Was it too little? Would he reject it because it wounded his pride? He seemed confused, and his confusion worried us. I trembled at the thought that he might do something reckless. My aunt had stood up and was now resting on her cane, leaning forward as though to willing him to leave. His mouth twisted into a strange smile, out of which came an abrupt laugh as he waved the envelope high in the air for a second, then stuffed it in his pocket and left, shoulders hunched, without saying goodbye. I waited, but he didn't stop at the door to look back at me like he used to when he was a boy and a child before that. I turned to my aunt, but quickly looked away. If

I'd looked at that triumphant glint in her eye any longer, I would have run to my room in tears to fight back old feelings that I shouldn't let resurface. At least not now.

"Well, imagine that! Practically a beggar, but thinks himself such a hotshot. Talk about a mangy cat showing off his coat!"

My aunt didn't expect me to comment. I was saddened by Tarek's sudden reappearance and disappearance, so much so that I lost my appetite and socialized rarely. I'd apply fingernail polish and remove it a few hours later. I had my hair cut whenever it grew an inch. Then I had it cut so short that my aunt quipped that I looked like a woman in a nuthouse. But instead of the upbraiding I'd expected, she seemed pleased at the return of "the man inside me," which she used to nag me about. When I was growing up, I used to deliberately provoke her by combing my long hair with my fingers in front of her. She'd grab my hair and tug it, then say she was just joking. I could tell from the force of that tug and the look in her eye that it was envy. When I used to try on new clothes, walking in front of her slowly like a fashion model, she'd pout, look away, and change the subject. I felt something about me irritated her. Was it because her hair was short and curly? Did it have to do with my friends and the way they mocked her accent, her weird sayings, or that funny way she had of sitting on a couch with one foot tucked beneath her? Or maybe it was because I couldn't bear the chickens and rabbits she raised behind the shed near the dock.

But I do know that, when it came to me, n and o were the first letters that formed in her mind, even before her tongue and mouth shaped the word. Everything I wished for she opposed. And she always had her way: about my hobbies and past times; about my puppy, which she'd poisoned; and about the parrot I'd bought but that she let escape after it said her name in a rude way, even though I'd taken such pains to teach it how to pronounce "Zizi" properly.

She was the one who chose most of my friends and barred others from visiting me and me from visiting them. When Sara, my Jewish friend from my childhood and school-days, returned to Egypt with her father, my aunt forbade me from visiting her. She even refused to allow me to phone her. I found her adamance on that matter so strange. I couldn't go to the theater because it bored her and I couldn't go to the movies unless they were playing a film she liked. Just as she pressed me into a marriage with Murad, she pressed my father into securing my divorce. My aunt's wishes formed the intransgressible boundaries within which I moved. After my divorce, she became even more overbearing. "A divorcee is on everybody's tongues," and only she knew how to keep them from wagging. "I'm looking out for your own good," she'd say.

I kept my problems to myself and kept myself to my room as much as possible until my father returned from abroad. Why did he never take me with him? What was the secret behind those mysterious trips he took to London at this time every year? How did he get Murad to agree to my divorce? He would never answer these questions.

Several days after my father's return from one of those trips to London, Zeinab went on a pilgrimage to Mecca. She took the ferry because of her fear of flying. Airplanes were "the devil's work." It was one of those fears of hers I could never understand, but at last I had some respite. I had at least two weeks to inhale the fragrance of freedom. I asked my father for permission to go up to Agami with some friends for three days. He gave his assent without even asking me who I was going with. Was he trying to atone for old sins? His only condition was that I return to Cairo two days before my aunt was scheduled to return. He gave me a hundred pounds, though I wouldn't need so much money, and off I went, bursting with pressures ready for release.

Agami at the time was still a small, elite resort just west of Alexandria, overlooking the Mediterranean's turquoise waters. It took only two nights there for my life to turn around again. It was there that I met Omar, and that was how long it took me to detect the meaning in the way he looked at me and to hear the voice coming from his heart. I fell prey to his boldness and how he stood out from the others, and I succumbed to his depth and his warmth. I must have come to Agami primed to fall in love, emotions charged, and ready to surrender even before the hunter sharpened his weapons. I was an easy catch for those wide eyes when they laid siege to me and aimed deep inside. I didn't need time to step back, reflect, hesitate, as was the case with Murad, and Tarek before him. After every advance he made, I looked forward to the next. I tried to anticipate it, but he'd still surprise me, which made my affection for him grow.

I didn't wait until it was safe. The woman inside me signaled to the sluices before I knew it. I thought I was hidden behind the dam, but it was transparent, fragile, like crystal, and it fell softly, with a gentle tinkling, at the onrush of this manly wave. I yielded as it surged forward then gently ebbed, etching a furrow where my heart could plant flowers and let them blossom into love. How I longed for that tremor I'd missed for so long. It was as instantaneous as when Tarek, all those years ago, touched my braids in a way that possessed me body and soul. Omar's first look, his first words, his gestures, the way he moved, the way he did everything, his love for life—all these traits enthralled me and turned me into a sleepwalker following in his wake.

On my last morning in Agami, I followed him out to the beach, where he was cleaning the seaweed off a long board. I was already mentally prepared to set sail with him to some remote shore. I had no fear and no intention to return. As I approached, Omar Seif Eddin turned to me with that beguiling smile that set off a turbulence inside me and said, "Want to take a ride with me?"

19

"I FIRMLY BELIEVE THAT WERE it not for two things, my secrets would spread. Those two are my lips."—Abbas Mahalawi

I was all for the idea of marrying Paula once Fahim explained it in full. The same with Zeinab. In fact, she was more enthusiastic than I, as though she'd been praying for it. After the marriage, I moved into the Heart of Palm, while Zeinab spread the news of the marriage and the beautiful baby daughter I had with Paula. She told people that Paula and I got married in secret, so we kept it that way out of respect for her wishes. Then the baby had to be delivered prematurely and incubated. It was such a fraught period, and it delayed our ability to rejoice. With each retelling, she added a detail here, a twist there, like our mother used to do with the stories she told women back in the village. Before long, the news reached every corner of Zamalek. Quite a few people suspected that the child was Zeinab's. Even so, we received numerous congratulations, which Paula would never hear since she'd slipped into a coma and eventually passed away one night two years and a few months after Nadia was born. Eventually, people forgot the subject.

After moving into the Heart of Palm, I left my apartment in north Zamalek to Hassanein's wife and her child, Tarek. Abdel-Naim asked me to let her have it free of charge in view of her helpless condition without a man. I agreed, since I didn't need the apartment, and out of respect for him, although I didn't quite agree with his logic.

Zeinab's and my first order of business was to get the deed to the villa transferred to our names. We delayed the announcement of Paula's death for three days in order to give Fahim enough time to grease the appropriate palms at the Foreign-owned Properties Registrar and other departments at the Notary Public Authority in order to complete the paperwork. Then we buried Paula secretly, at night, in the pauper's cemetery. The next task was to transfer the title of Paula's new Cadillac to Zeinab. That was done at the Cairo traffic department, and quickly, again thanks to Fahim's connections.

The Cicurel brothers didn't know what hit them, but they didn't take it lying down. They refused to believe my marriage to Paula was genuine, despite the official documents I had to prove it, and proving she had borne me a child. They kicked up a hell of a fuss, starting in the courts. They had a lot of weight to pull, through connections that led to right across the threshold of Abdin Palace. I turned to Pouli, but he elected to stay out of this one.

The specter of expulsion loomed. Our lawyer, whom Fahim had hired, told us that we were in a weak position. Paula wasn't the sole owner of the Heart of Palm. She had co-inherited it with Solomon Cicurel's brothers, who let her live there but retained their part-ownership. We hadn't known this. They won the suit against us in the preliminary court, but we didn't give up. We had our lawyer file an appeal on the grounds that we had new evidence to produce: documents confirming the transfer of the title to Nadia Abbas Mahalawi, the daughter I had with Paula, whom I had married several years before her death, as other documents confirmed. According to our new lawyer, our position was now much stronger.

*

"My father wants to see you, Abbas. He's taken a turn for the worse."

I lowered my newspaper and looked up at Fahim Effendi. He looked haggard. About a year or so earlier, Prince Mohamed Ali Tawfiq had won another concession from the palace to develop Zamalek. That was expectable, since he was King Faruq's nephew. The prince engaged three up-and-coming building engineers and excluded Abdel-Naim. Then the palace refused to renew Abdel-Naim's construction license. Pouli refused to help. He got Abdel-Naim a half-year extension so we could complete works in progress, but he would do no more. After that half a year, Abdel-Naim and his work crews were banished from Zamalek. It was heartbreaking to watch their straggly return across the bridge to Imbaba for the last time. The next thing he knew, he had the tax authorities on his back. He had, in fact, evaded some taxes but not all, though he couldn't prove that. They dragged him through the wringers of lawyers' offices and courtrooms, and brought him to the brink of bankruptcy. I didn't abandon him, but I kept my distance. True, I was still his partner. But now that I'd become Pouli's partner in the pharmaceutical industry, that partnership was no longer as important to me as it had been. I didn't get a large percentage of the earnings, even though I owned the factory. But the income was good and the operation enjoyed the protection of the palace. I had to be careful. I couldn't afford to lose that, what with the loss of the diamonds and gold in Zananiri's airplane crash and the looming end of Abdel-Naim's construction company.

Nevertheless, at Zeinab's urging, I made one last appeal to Pouli in the hope that he would agree to some kind to subcontracting arrangement with the new building contractors in order to keep Abdel-Naim's construction firm afloat. Pouli refused out of hand, but it was his attitude more than his refusal itself that bothered me. Not only was he condescending, he threatened to fire me from our pharmaceutical company as though I were his employee. That was true enough on paper, but I still owned the company. I left his office that day defeated, unable to utter a word of protest. He was too powerful.

There was no more I or anyone else could do. The winds had shifted. They now filled the sails of Abdel-Naim's competitors and left his ships marooned. Had Abdel-Naim done something to incur someone's wrath? Had an ill-placed word gotten back to palace ears? Had he bragged to someone about how he'd bribed Pouli? I asked him about this when I went to visit him on his sickbed. He looked away and muttered a stream of curses against everyone, all the way up to the royal throne. That confirmed my suspicions. I had nothing to gain from sticking my head out for him.

"I'm leaving Fahim in your care after I'm gone, Abbas. I can't have him going back to the village with nothing."

I had to bend my ear closer to his parched lips. His once-booming voice had become as frail as the rest of him. His heart had been unable to bear the humiliating exile from the kingdom he'd built over the decades. He'd started out when Zamalek was uninhabited apart from some scattered shacks and hovels. Over the years, he helped turn it into the most elegant quarter of the capital.

Abdel-Naim passed away, heartsick, several weeks later. The younger son, Asran, took his wife and child back to his native village in Upper Egypt. Fahim stayed with me. His father didn't need to bequeath him to me because I couldn't have dispensed with him anyway. As I told Fahim on more than one occasion, I'd need him next to me in my grave to forge my sins into virtues before the angels started reckoning.

I made Fahim my personal secretary at quite a respectable salary. Not that I had any actual work for him or myself at the time. I had an office in a basement where I managed my business affairs, most of which had ended when Abdel-Naim's construction permit was terminated. Apart from that, I had the bank assets I'd inherited from Paula, her shares in the Cicurel stores, and the factory in Alexandria that I owned with Pouli. Apart from that, I lived in a villa in Zamalek overlooking the Nile and I had a driver who opened the car door for me with a bow as I removed my white fedora, climbed into the back seat, and let the car take me to wherever it decided to take me.

Then one day, some months later, while we were on our summer holiday in Alexandria, we awoke to the news on the radio that the army had overthrown King Faruq. The first thing that sprang to mind was my factory in Alexandria. Pouli had taken advantage of the arrangement we made to save the company from Sandro's underhanded dealings in order to take control over it. Later that day, Fahim and I went to visit the factory. We timed it so we'd arrive after the morning shift and just before the curfew. We took a lot of papers with us. Even before we returned to Cairo, they'd forced the king to leave the country.

A few months after our return to Cairo from Alexandria, Zeinab burst into my office. "The lawyer called and told me that we lost our case on appeal. We lost the villa, Abbas! They're going to kick us out of here!"

As they say, disasters come in threes. I called up Fahim to help us find a solution. Three days later, he showed up with a grin from ear to ear and a solution in that diabolical brain of his: the villa next door. That was where we'd buried Hassanein when we were laying its foundations. The owner had died before construction was completed and, there being no heirs, the work had to be halted in the middle of the final stages. Fahim offered to take care of the red tape, as only he knew how to do. Then we completed construction at our own expense. Fortunately, there was very little to do. The villa was already livable. It was the spitting image of the Heart of Palm, inside and out, including the basement. Zeinab was over the moon when I approved of the plan. We took the precaution of putting it in Nadia's name. That would prevent it from being seized during the wave of sequestrations, because she was an Egyptian born of an Egyptian father.

When it came time to move, Zeinab insisted on keeping Solomon Cicurel's large bed, which was still in his bedroom in the west wing. I was mystified by her insistence on that matter. For my part, I had the villa's nameplate removed from the wall next to the front gate and reaffixed next to the gateway to my new villa. There would only be one Heart of Palm in Zamalek. We took a lot of other things as well, leaving the old Heart of Palm as hollow for Cicurel's brothers as the core of a palm tree without its heart of palm. In any case, they didn't get a chance to enjoy it for long. It seems that the July 1952 revolutionaries had it in for the Jews, because some years later they set their sights on their department stores and estates. After Les Grands Magasins Cicurel were nationalized, the brothers tried to transfer the deed of the villa to one of their employees in the hope of being able to sell it. Fahim told me that as soon as he caught wind of their plan he managed to put a wrench in their paperwork at the Foreign-owned Properties Registrar. The following day, I went to the Authority for the Liquidation of Feudalism in my capacity as an ordinary citizen. The government had publicized telephone numbers and addresses members of the public could contact in order to report cases of foreigners trying to sell their assets illegally. I called one of those numbers and made an urgent appointment.

When I arrived, I encountered a young officer whose wooden nameplate on his desk identified him as Murad Kashef. After inspecting me from head to toe, he showed me to into the office of his boss, a brigadier general. I showed him the original contracts of the old villa proving Cicurel's ownership. It was sequestered the following day. Naturally, I'd taken care to conceal all the papers concerning Nadia and Paula in my safe in my new home. Not long afterward, the Cicurel brothers left Egypt altogether, and I began converting all my liquid assets that I'd earned from Pouli and Abdel-Naim into gold bars and small diamonds. These I hid in the basement of the new Heart of Palm for fear the sequestration madness would spread.

That day, after I reported the Cicurels' attempted ruse, I had an idea that I hoped would secure protection for my new villa and other properties. Just as I was about to exit the building that housed the Liquidation of Feudalism, I decided to retrace my steps to the desk of the young, low-ranking officer, Murad Kashef. I told him that I had other information to report that might be of interest to the authorities. It pertained to an eminent individual. I could tell I'd aroused his curiosity, despite the peeved look he gave me for disturbing him again.

"And who might this eminent individual be, Abbas Effendi?" he said with a sneer.

"Antonio Pouli Pasha, sir."

I'd woken up unusually early one day in late September. The autumn breeze was flirting with the fronds of our tall palm tree in the middle of our garden. I was having my morning coffee out back near the dock and scanning the newspaper headlines. When I turned the page, my eye caught a headline announcing that my village in the Mahalla Marhoum district had had its name changed for the second time, along with a lot of other villages. The occasion was the fourth anniversary of the revolution. Or was it the fifth? I'd stopped keeping track. Our village was now called al-Fallaha—the peasant woman. God only knew which peasant woman.

Suddenly I heard a commotion coming from the direction of the front gate. I quickly set down the newspaper and stood up to find out what was going on. I encountered Zeinab coming down the front stairs, looking anxious. A huge moving van was parked out front. The movers were shouting instructions to each other as they carried furniture into the old Cicurel place. The foreman told us that a high-ranking army officer and his family were moving in. The villa had been empty for so long it felt like our new neighbors had popped up out of nowhere. As it turned out, though, I recognized the new owner and we quickly became friends. He was the same brigadier general to whom I had submitted the evidence on the Cicurel brothers' and Pouli's properties. We began to exchange neighborly visits, but he controlled the buttons on this relationship. It was he who decided when I'd call on him and vice versa. To welcome the new neighbors and curry favor with the officer's family, Zeinab sent over dishes of food that she was a whiz at. Before long, she was receiving orders for favorite dishes to be delivered at specified times and in specified quantities.

One Friday afternoon, while we were sitting and chatting about this and that next to the Nile near the dock behind his villa, the brigadier said, "That business about Pouli was a master stroke. Well done, Abbas, my boy! If it hadn't been for you, we would never have found out about that pharmaceutical factory and its franchise, because all the official documents are in the name of some Italian guy called Sandro Vanini."

Just the mention of that name made me clench my jaw so hard I nearly broke a molar. How it pained me to recall how I managed to rescue my Alexandrian company from Sandro, only for it to end up out of my reach forever after it was sequestered as though it were Pouli's. Oh well, at least I'd prevented Pouli from indulging in my wealth, and I'd won the friendship of a high-ranking officer in the bargain. Naturally, I hadn't dared so much as hint that I was the original owner. I didn't want to give off a scent that would send the authorities growling and baring their fangs in my direction, so I let them hold on to the impression that I was some mid-level employee.

The brigadier gave me an affectionate pat on the shoulder, which lightened the fact that he had called me "Abbas, my boy," even though I was older and wealthier than him. He asked me about the properties belonging to certain Jews and

246

other upper-class families in Zamalek. He thought I had more tips to offer because of my partnership with the late Abdel-Naim, who had built so many of the Zamalek villas, and by dint of my marriage with Paula Cicurel, whose estate I'd inherited. I said I was surprised the authorities weren't aware of the facts, since everything was recorded and all the original documents were on file.

"Sadly, many wealthy families used the same trick as the Cicurel brothers but haven't been found out yet," he said. He explained how some property owners arranged nominal sales of some of their homes and assets to their servants, drivers, or other people in order to evade the nationalization measures and sequestrations. "Some of them hadn't even registered their properties to begin with. On top of that, we discovered forgeries in the files at the Foreign-owned Properties Registrar. Even the rubber stamps had been stolen a decade ago and were used to forge original-looking deeds and documents. As you know, the government inherits the estates of foreigners who are heirless. Those people ripped off the government."

"F-F-Forgeries?" I couldn't help the stammer. "What did they forge? Have they arrested the people who stole the stamps?"

"We don't know who they are yet, unfortunately. But we fired two Jews and four Italians from our department because we suspected they might be involved. We also halted the registration of a lot of properties in Giza and Alexandria pending investigations. Anyway, I'm having a young officer who works for me—Murad Kashef—conduct extensive inquiries. Murad's a sharp one. He could tell you where the devil hid his son."

I relaxed and leaned back in my seat, and took the occasion to offer to help by supplying any further information and documents I could come up with. I was eager to secure his confidence in order to keep the authorities from asking me how I got my wealth.

"That would be great, Abbas my boy! As soon as you get the papers ready, pass by my office. We need honest folks like yourself."

"Yes, sir. In a month at the outside, I'll send you all the documents that I—"

"No, I want to see you in my office in two days with what you have."

His tone was haughty and his fingers pointed at me like I was a servant, but I accepted his orders with a wide smile. That evening I phoned Fahim and told him to drop by. He had dozens of ledgers and receipts from the original owners that I could use in order to finish the task quickly. With his help, I prepared a thick dossier on the people who'd had houses built by Abdel-Naim's firm. Zeinab supplied a lot of additional details based on stories she'd heard about the jewels that had once bedecked the ladies of Zamalek and then disappeared into thin air. She told me about a lot of prominent Jewish families, like those of Youssef Cattaoui Pasha, a close friend of King Fuad, and Sir Robert Rolo, a former director of al-Ahli Bank. She had gotten to know them from the times when she'd accompanied Paula to their homes. She practically gave me a full inventory of their contents. Zeinab missed nothing and she had a memory as systematic as an archive. The minutest details were engraved in there and she could retrieve them easily in order to furnish descriptions of everything from jewels and antiques to the smallest piece of furniture in the homes she visited with Paula.

But she certainly could get sidetracked. She would go on and on about some of the idiosyncrasies she would never forget. She had Fahim in stitches when she recalled something about the Menasces, a Jewish family that had been awarded various medals and honors by the Austrian emperor. According to Zeinab, the head of the family, Menasce Pasha, was a snob, and very finicky about whom he shook hands with. He had this fixed notion that Egyptians picked their noses all day long in order to kill time. That was why he always wore gloves. The only time anyone saw his fingers was when he played piano. "He's got a large plantation estate near Qanatir where he hides some of his money in the form of gold bars. His wife doesn't know about it."

The Copts came in for a good share of Zeinab's gossip. She had stories to tell about prominent Coptic families who were major landowners and feudalists: the Wahbas, Khayyats, Ghalis, and Simaikas. Many of them married into British families in Egypt. That became a crucial part of my report, of course. I had her recount the tittle-tattle she'd picked up at the weekend parties at the Wisa family's sprawling hacienda in Asyut and the hunting trips they organized in Fayoum. She also gave me the lowdown on Bobby Khayyat's annual Christmas parties and his legendary wealth. For the cherry on top, I added the curses and insults against the revolution that I overheard with my own ears at the Gezira Club. My memory served me well there. Some of the juiciest came from the mouth of none other than Egypt's star polo player, Victor Simaika, whose expletives against the Free Officers resounded across the club's polo grounds, which was one of my favorite places for basking in the sun during the cooler seasons.

After nearly forty-eight sleepless hours, I reported to the office of my neighbor, the brigadier, at the Liquidation of Feudalism Department. His office director, Murad Kashef, glanced briefly in my direction then turned away. After a moment, he turned around again, inspected me from head to foot, and said coldly, "Aren't you the guy who told us about Pouli's properties?"

"Yes, I am, sir."

"Are you're going to keep popping in here every other week? You could have saved yourself the trouble and spilled it all in your first visit."

"I have an appointment, sir. With the head of the com-mittee for—"

He jerked a finger toward his mouth, ordering me to remain silent, then instructed a sergeant in attendance to show me to the waiting room next door. I swallowed the insult, though it made my blood boil. I was kept waiting for more than two hours. If I fidgeted to make my seat creak or took a conspicuous look at my watch, Kashef shot me a glare that meant, "Don't even think about leaving without permission."

At last I was shown into the brigadier's office. Instead of the welcome I'd expected, he treated me with total disdain. What had made him change 180 degrees from one day to the next? He didn't even invite me to sit down. He kept me standing as he flicked through some papers in a midsize manila folder. Then he looked up.

"Acres and acres of farmland in Mahalla Marhoum. Five thousand pounds in the bank. A Cadillac. A villa in Zamalek. A secret marriage to a foreign widow. How'd you get all that, Abbas? Do you think we're asleep at the wheel, you dolt? Did you think we wouldn't find out you're a screen for the rich?"

"Go on! What happened then?" Zeinab asked breathlessly, sitting at the edge of my bed, one foot tucked under her butt as always.

I sighed and rolled onto my side in order to tell her the rest of the story, though I wanted nothing more than to sleep. Interrogations were followed by more interrogations. Murad Kashef accusing me of serving as a front; the brigadier telling Murad to ease up and showing sympathy—or so I thought until they switched roles. In the end, they believed me. I was not the titular owner of property belonging to foreigners trying to evade confiscation. The property I owned was truly mine. What saved me in the end was the file Fahim prepared containing the payment receipts and check stubs for all the villas he'd built with his father. Were it not for his meticulous record keeping, everything I owned would have been confiscated. I gave them my and Nadia's titles as heirs to Madame

Paula's bank accounts and her Cadillac, which spared these assets from sequestration. It simply hadn't occurred to me that they'd ask others for information about us, just as they asked me for information on others. Everyone was running around ratting on everyone else while the authorities could see everything. Even though I cleared myself, they didn't let me go free of charge. They decreed that my villa was henceforth the property of the sequestration authority, which had the magnanimity to lease it to me for fifty years for a nominal sum.

"Do you want to know what the brigadier said to me before I left?"

Zeinab nodded.

"He said, 'We just did you a favor, Abbas. Now nobody in Zamalek's going to say, 'Why's he an exception?''"

"Fifty years? Let's hope we live so long!" Zeinab said. "Who knows? Maybe Faruq will come back and sack them all. What matters now is that it's all over. You won't have to go back there again."

"Wrong. I'll be working for them starting the first of next month. I've been recruited on the basis of my expertise in the pashas and villas of Zamalek."

"So, what of it? As they say, stick close to the rich and their luck will rub off on you."

In less than a month, the appointment was official. I was decreed a member of the Committee for the Liquidation of Feudalism. Some years later I would become its secretary. On the day the decree was issued, I left the office of the brigadier, bid farewell to the thunderous looks Murad Kashef gave me for no reason, and headed to Garden City to assume my new functions. I drove westward toward the Nile, passing the parliament building and its retinue of elegant villas. Were those villas protecting the parliament or soliciting its protection? I took a left, then swung right, entering Garden City. What a contrast to Zamalek, where the streets are long, wide, and straight, and the villas are comfortably spread out and nestled in spacious gardens. Garden City's narrow, meticulously tree-trimmed streets twist and curve between elegant facades that follow the contours of the roads like a meandering train of palaces.

As I wound my way through those streets, I had a rush of exhilaration I'd never experienced before. It was as if we'd inherited the whole of Egypt overnight. I was filled with excitement, confidence, daring—a sensation unlike any other. Every cloud has a silver lining. It turned out the change I'd feared had benefited me more than I could ever have imagined when I first set foot in Cairo. King Faruq had dreamed of fathering a son to inherit his throne and his kingdom. When he finally succeeded, he found hundreds of heirs apparent, who rose up in rebellion, overthrew him, and inherited everything he owned. I was now one of those heirs. Each of us would get his share of that wealth and of power and influence.

At last I found the address they'd given me: a large residence once owned by an ex-minister who had been one of Egypt's most eminent aristocrats. His estates had been confiscated about two months earlier. One of them was the palace that now housed the Committee for the Liquidation of Feudalism.

Out of the hundreds of estates I'd entered in my new capacity as an agent for this committee, my first remained the most memorable. In the company of a senior ranking officer, a military police detail, and an army of pencil pushers from the Ministry of the Exchequer, I entered the villa of Prince Youssef Kamal in Matariya. At that very moment, Prince Youssef returned from a foxhunting trip in the desert nearby. One might have thought Egypt hadn't had a revolution yet. I was impressed by how fashionably he was turned out that day: supple leather boots up to his knees, a camel-colored moleskin hunting hat, a jacket in British tweed with a pattern of small blue squares shot through with beige threads, and dark khaki hunting trousers tucked into the boots and billowing slightly above them. He saluted us with his leather riding crop, lifted his hat as a gesture of respect to the officer who headed our committee, and took a seat as he asked what our business there was. The officer in charge showed him the sequestration warrant, and asked him to open his safe and to permit our men to take an inventory of the entire contents of his palace. His Excellency agreed, but on the condition that he be given time to change his clothes first. He stood and went upstairs, where he remained for over two hours, giving our staff sufficient time to inventory the ground floor and relieve it of a significant number of portable items.

I smiled to myself as I recalled that night many years ago when our gang of five broke into Cicurel's home and I was casting about for a bauble or two to slip into my pockets. Our officers and employees at the Youssef Kamal villa did exactly the same. They pocketed a silver ashtray here, a small crystal one there. One removed a painting from its wooden frame, folded it carefully and slipped it inside a government-issue manila folder. Apart from such souvenirs, ornamental plates and vases, figurines, and silver picture frames with pictures of the prince and family were lifted from the walls and from tables and laid side by side in a large trunk: the mass grave of the prince's belongings, history, and memories.

The commanding officer, worried by Prince Youssef's prolonged absence, told a nearby soldier, "Go up there and get him even if he's buck naked. We can't let him do something crazy and get us all into trouble!"

Before the soldier was halfway up the stairs, His Excellency the prince reemerged and descended the stairs with a leisurely swagger. He was now even more dapper, in a light-gray suit, holding his trademark short cigar. Rather than fear, I read contempt in his eyes. He slowly surveyed the walls and rooms, and quickly grasped the situation. He smiled derisively and said, "If you would donate the proceeds to a hospital, I would so be grateful."

He called for his private secretary and instructed him to have the servants open all the rooms. Then, indicating some wooden crates, he told our commanding officer that they contained paintings and books. Some he had donated to the School of Fine Arts he had founded in Cairo many years ago. Others were supposed to be shipped to the Egyptian Academy of Arts in Rome.

"Do you mean you planned to smuggle them abroad?"

The prince's eyebrows shot up in surprise. Politely but firmly, he explained that the contents of those crates were his rightful property, acquired from the revenues of his lands. He had disposed of such items in this manner frequently over the years, ever since he'd helped found the academy in Italy. He stared at the officer's face for a second, heaved an exasperated sigh, and excused himself so he could have his coffee on the balcony. Before leaving, he reached for an ashtray that the department employees had overlooked and presented it to our commanding officer. The officer thanked him and was about to put it in our trunk when the prince interrupted him.

"That's to extinguish the cigarette that's in your mouth, sir. That's a Persian carpet you're standing on, not a straw mat."

The officer immediately ordered his men to leave the books. Everything else they were to show him personally, especially the carpets!

Seizing the opportunity of the commotion, I slipped out to the balcony and greeted the prince. He shook my hand in a friendly way, although he was clearly in a foul humor. There was so much I wanted to say in response to his arrogance and contempt, but the thunderous look in his eye drove the words off my tongue as fast as birds taking flight at the crack of a shotgun. I tried to explain to him briefly why the sequestration process was necessary, at least as I understood it. He saw my argument in a different light. He had little patience for socialism. The redistribution of wealth was a goal accomplished through taxation not sequestration, he said. He then turned to the importance of education and appreciation of the arts, every now and then casting a glance beyond me into the interior of his house. He concluded with words that both cut to the quick and provoked me. Lowering his voice, he said, "What I see is not an inventory of my possessions. It's a ransacking. They're nothing but a bunch of thieves. But you, sir—what are you doing with them?"

"What I do is no concern of yours. What matters is that you understand that your home is a museum of riches that belong to the people because it was built on the backs of the poor and the land worked by Egyptian farmers."

He turned away and stared fixedly into the distance. I was so annoyed by that snub that I reported his description of the inventory to our commanding officer, who had been watching me suspiciously from afar. The officer, more indignant than before, told the prince to remove his gold watch and ring. He then sent the clerk with the ledgers to the prince, and had the prince sign below endless columns of inventoried items, followed by a statement vowing the direst penalties for any negligence or dereliction in the fulfillment of his full responsibility for the items of furniture that we had left in his possession in his capacity as a trustee charged by the government with the safekeeping of the public property of the Egyptian people.

Before leaving, I helped myself to a piece of Damascene brocade work. A member of our staff had brought it to the officer from an inner room. As the officer felt the fabric, he asked the others' opinion. When they told him it was made of some cheap material, he used it to wipe off the crumbs of his lunchtime sandwich from his hands and mouth and tossed it aside. I slipped into my pocket. I was well aware of its value. Many years ago, Paula had sold smaller pieces for a couple of hundred pounds each. When I got back home, I showed it to Zeinab. She flipped it over a couple of times, shrugged, and said it would make a good potholder. I snatched it out of her hands. The next day, I wrapped it carefully and presented it to my boss. To spare him the embarrassment of his ignorance, and to spare myself from his wrath, I told him the staff had not recognized its true value. He flipped it over in his hands and looked at me glumly.

I volunteered the answer to the question in his eyes before his mouth had to pronounce it. "The committee overlooked it, sir. Meaning that, technically, it doesn't exist. I suggest making a gift of it to the wife, sir. I'm sure she'll like it."

He gave a satisfied nod, smiled, and stuffed it into his briefcase. It occurred to me that more aristocratic tokens of this sort would keep me in his good graces. I soon discovered that dozens of others in the department had the same idea, and on a grander scale. Most of them would end up stabbed in the back by peers before their stars rose too high.

After the breakup of Egypt's short-lived union with Syria in 1961, the orders came down to nationalize pretty much everything. "It's to keep the big industrialists and entrepreneurs from turning against the regime," the defense minister told us. He said that he had irrefutable intelligence about secret meetings in which they plotted to overthrow the government and eliminate Nasser. No one ventured a question, of course. As the nationalization wave rose, most of us kept our heads down. The heads that rolled belonged to those who imagined they had the wealth and influence to defy the wave.

Since it was unlikely they knew Cicurel like I did, regarding his genius at converting and concealing his wealth, I doubted the authorities suspected what I was doing with mine. But you can never be too careful, I thought in the privacy of my basement at the Heart of Palm. Just that day, my boss had confided, "Everything's changed, Abbas. It's too cutthroat. I'm thinking about taking a very long holiday in London, and not coming back." If he, who was closer to those whose orders he carried out, was afraid of their wrath, how was I supposed to feel? I ventured no comment, so as not to betray my own fear. I'd learned from experience that they smelled fear faster than the Zafer missile. Beneath the dim light in the basement, I secured the last tire around its frame and patted it. About this, at least, I could feel a little safer now. As far as the government knew, all I had to my name was my salary, my inheritance from Paula, and the villa at a nominal rent from the Sequestration Department.

The sequestration process that Prince Youssef experienced took place in many other estates where I helped with the inventories in the service of my country. Most of the acquisitions were sold in public auctions, the revenues accruing to the national treasury. Five years after presenting that gift to my boss, I was promoted to deputy chairman of the committee, which put me within reach of the chairmanship itself. But I lacked the courage to so much as think about reaching for it. There also came a point when I stopped taking part in the sequestration raids and confined myself to desk work. I'd already had my fill of "overlooked" items and feared drawing attention to myself if I overindulged. I was constantly haunted by the specter of being on the receiving end of one of those raids. I'd seen it happen to many others who'd once been close to the higher-ups. Since that time, I would never go to bed without first checking to make sure my gun was below my pillow with a bullet ready to fire and a second in the chamber. The first was for whoever tried to arrest me. The second for myself.

20

"As though his absence were not enough, he coaxed the moon from my skies as well."—Nadia

If love doesn't yank you from one extreme to the other and toss you from the fog of doubt to the bedrock of certainty, then it's like a stagnant pond: it needs a stone. Omar Seif Eddin was that stone. It sent ripples of love through my veins and restored me to life.

Before he asked me to marry him, I learned that Maysa was a close friend of his family. That triggered sharply conflicting feelings. At first I was overjoyed. Armed with my love for Omar and my affection for Maysa, I could march confidently toward my dream for happiness. But then my aunt's incomprehensible hatred for Maysa drove me to despair. It was the nightmare that burst into my sleep, flung my dream aside, and jolted me awake in terror of a force bent on destroying my life with Omar. As usual, my father beat a retreat when my aunt launched her campaign, which was fiercer than ever. She railed, cajoled, threatened. She'd expel me from home, cut off all money, deprive me of any number of rights if I married Omar Seif Eddin.

I couldn't imagine how my aunt had gotten wind of my nascent love so quickly. Was I such an open book that she could scan the news of my heart on my forehead? I denied her suspicions. In any case, my feelings toward him were still vacillating at the time. But she pursed her lips and twitched them back and forth like a mouse, which meant that she didn't believe a word I said. "As your granny said, may God rest her soul, there are three things that can't be hidden: love, a pregnant belly, and a mountain!"

Maybe I didn't have the courage to say I loved Omar, but I'm sure my eyes had a way of laughing that proclaimed my feelings toward him loudly enough for the heavens to hear. He was kind and gentle, a lover with a tender embrace. His family welcomed me when he took me to meet them, but I could sense their aversion to the marriage. At the time, I thought it was because he'd been married twice before and I was a divorcée. I later learned it was because they didn't like my father and my aunt. If their names cropped up in a conversation, Omar's parents' faces turned sour. I felt I was missing some connection between the dots.

What surprised me was Maysa's enthusiasm in favor of the marriage. She tried to win over my father to the idea, but he ceded to his sister's view. "Don't worry, I'll keep trying," Maysa said. "But why don't you pass by the club this afternoon so we can talk."

I wasn't very optimistic when I hung up, but I went to the club anyway, to meet her at the golf course. She was so chic and svelte despite her age, which she was willing to let the silver streaks in her bobbed hair reveal. She refused to dye it, which was quite unusual. After she'd finished with the last of the nine golf balls, she told me she had to get back home for something important but that we could continue our conversation there. We left the club on foot, since she generally preferred to walk, but after about a hundred yards she stopped to complain how difficult it had become for pedestrians because there was no proper sidewalk. After a few more steps, she gave up and we hailed a taxi. It was pointless to continue walking when most of the sidewalk had been eaten up to make way for parking spaces.

In the taxi, she wrinkled her nose as she pointed to the dust on the backs of the seats and the litter on the floor. The driver turned up the volume of the radio so Ahmed Adawiya's grating voice could blare: "It's packed in the city without pity!" Maysa switched to French: "That's not singing, it's braying!" The driver peeked at us through his rearview mirror. I had to clamp my hand over my mouth to keep from laughing. How could I tell Maysa that Adawiya was my aunt's favorite singer? Along the way, she pointed to three shoe stores in a row. Formerly they had been, respectively, a bookstore selling foreign-language books, an antique store, and a flower shop. Before turning off the main road in the direction of her home, we passed by Zamalek Ful and Falafel. She shook her head mournfully. "*Mon Dieu!* Our beautiful island has become synonymous with beans." She gasped. "Look, Nadia!" she said, switching back to Arabic. "They're eating their sandwiches wrapped in newspaper!"

The driver, eyeing us through his mirror, emitted a muffled snort, perhaps from the effort of remaining silent all this time. "Stop fretting, lady. We're all created equal."

Back in her small apartment, Maysa brewed some tea, arranged some slices of coffee cake on a plate, and turned on the record player. With Rimsky-Korsakov's *Scheherazade* softly playing in the background, she tried to reassure me. "You and Omar will have a long and happy marriage. Don't worry about your aunt and father. They'll come around in time, especially if you have children."

She paused for a moment to study my face, as though preparing to impart some disturbing news. "You're not like them at all, believe me. You're educated and well brought up. You should marry the man you love. It's *your* life. You have to choose the partner who suits you. If Paula were alive, none of all this would have happened. They've done enough already."

I was overcome by a strange emotion. I felt as close to Maysa as though she were my real mother, though I was perplexed by that last remark. At first I'd feared that she would oppose my marriage to the son of one of her closest friends and that she'd invent excuses to prevent it. She certainly hated my aunt and distrusted my father enough to do that. She could never forgive them for what they'd done to her and to her brother Amr, who emigrated as soon as he could. That day, though, she dispelled all my misgivings. Before I had the opportunity to respond, Omar did so on my behalf, and in a very practical way. He sent me a letter that I've kept till today. It concluded with the sentence: "So, let us each go our own way: me toward you, and you toward me."

Whether those were actually his words or a line quoted from a poem, that sweet and tender letter settled all my doubts. I married Omar despite the opposition of some members of his family and all the members of mine. I left everything for his sake. I was his third wife, although he was the same age as I. I took a suitcase full of clothes, as I had when I married Murad, and left the Heart of Palm uncertain if I would ever return. My aunt cut me off after sending me away with curses. My father kept in touch with me secretly, but listlessly, as though performing an onerous duty. For my part, I had nothing to lose. At least this time I was at the gambling table of my own volition, not my aunt's. I left Zamalek to live with Omar in his small apartment in Garden City. After less than a year there, he decided to move to Sharm El Sheikh. He wanted to join his friends, who had moved there some months earlier, which was just after Israel restored Sinai to Egypt.

Omar's life was a series of stops on a train journey called adventure. He never stayed in one for long. He'd hop off if his attention was caught by a beautiful scene. He'd spend some time there, until he got bored and left. He vowed that I was his last stop, and I believed him. Maybe I wanted to believe him so I could detach Tarek from my heart and shake Murad's dust off my body and his image from my mind. We lived for a couple of months shy of two years in Sharm El Sheikh, a virgin resort town where everything was beautiful. Omar launched a scuba-diving center and opened a small hotel together with a friend. He invested his whole inheritance in the project. Our days were divided between the surface of the water and the face of the moon. We'd set sail in the morning, dive into the watery depths, and spend our nights beneath the starlight as the moon watched us listen to music, dance, and drink. How we laughed and laughed, as though tasked with conserving Sharm's fun-loving nature.

Omar was mad about life. It was a spring of effervescent waters he drank with eager gulps, insatiably, living every day to the fullest. He never left me for a moment. Near dawn, his eyes would close near my face. He slept in my embrace and awoke to my whispers in his ear. He'd nibble my lips slowly and tenderly, then we'd submerge ourselves in a long kiss, and make love to start a new day. I had never dreamed I could have all this. But then, when you go to sleep at night, you can never know whether your somnial visitor will be a sweet dream or a nightmare. The happiest days of my life were with Omar. When he drew close, the smell of his body permeated my every pore, as though I lay beneath his skin.

The clock stopped for months. Or maybe the hands of the clock were humoring us, performing a coquettish dance to celebrate our joy: moving forward slowly then swinging back in order to prolong our happiness. I rest my head on his shoulder. He wraps his arm around my waist, and with his other hand he strokes my hair. His nearness conjures up images of a waltz. We spin together across a ballroom that we have painted in our minds, never missing a step. I can hear his music. I feel it in me as my feet fall in with it and I draw closer, letting my fingernails brush the tips of his fingers as he turns slowly in place.

I'll never forget how, one night, after a long luxurious kiss, we threw ourselves onto our favorite couch, bodies still clinging together. He grabbed his Walkman's headphones and held one pad over my ear and the other over his, linking our heads as Fairuz's melodic voice called for the flute and song. We were extensions of the same soul, making the moment live longer before it waned and only the lament of the *ney* remained.

At the end of the first verse, he pulled off his earphone and gently removed mine. He picked me up in his arms as though I were his child and started to run. The childish mischief in his eyes gave him away, but I was still ready to be surprised. And my astonished smiles told him he'd succeeded.

What a thrill I felt as he set me gently in my seat in the car, drove us to the dock, and helped me into his small motorboat. It cleaved the placid sea, waking it from its slumber and telling it to make ready for our lovemaking with the prerequisite gentle breezes. The lapping waves bowed to us like maids of honor and the moon peeked out shyly from behind a small passing cloud and glowed. Omar's eyes sparkled and his smile lit his face. He stopped the motor, letting the boat rock in its aquatic cradle and fan our ardor. He pulled off his white T-shirt. His broad bronze chest gleamed in the thread of silver light that streamed down from above like a celestial gift to two lovers joined together at a crucial moment.

"You're crazy!" I whispered, still smiling. "You know it's forbidden to go out on the boat at night."

He responded with a confident smile and didn't give my lips a chance to utter another word.

We awoke one morning to the news that Omar's diving center had been shut down because its license wasn't in order. He did all he could to remedy the problem, but was bounced from one government office to the next, from the municipal to the governorate level. By the time I realized who was behind this, it was too late. I phoned my father. He promised to see what he could do, but he did nothing. When I phoned again, he said he wasn't working for the government anymore. "Once you're out, you're like an orphan. My membership in parliament makes no difference, because I'm just an honorary member. An MP without teeth," he said. I had no choice but to jump from the frying pan into the fire.

Aunt Zeinab's shrill voice assailed me over the phone for the first time in a year, rebuking me as though I'd just seen her the previous day. She didn't even bother to play innocent. She vowed to do worse unless I came back to her. Then she slammed down the receiver and refused to pick up again. Two days later, the governor closed down the hotel Omar had started with his friend. The pretext was complaints about out-of-date food. I could tell he was fed up and was casting about for his next stop. But we couldn't board the next train yet, due an imminent arrival. I was pregnant.

Unfortunately, it wasn't a stable pregnancy. I had to spend the last six months lying down and, for the first time since my marriage, in a cold bed on my own. Meanwhile, Omar continued to chase his first and dearest love: life.

Maysa's phone calls were the only things that picked up my spirits a bit during those lonely six months. She tried to persuade Omar to return to me, but to no avail. He was desperate to team up to start a new venture and move on. That venture would involve a Frenchwoman he had met. He helped her open a hotel through a subcontracting arrangement and she helped him back to life. I made do with an allowance my father sent every month to help me out after Omar fell into the pit my aunt had created.

It took Omar two days to visit me after I gave birth to my baby daughter, Yasmine. "That's a nice name," he said as he held her in his arms and kissed her affectionately. He turned to the doctor to ask how I was doing. Once reassured, he made ready to leave as though he weren't the father of our daughter, or my husband, let alone the hero of a love story that entwined us for a year and a half and lifted us heavenward on a towering wave of happiness and fantasy. That wave was now preparing to break on the shores of reality. Omar, who'd appeared in my life like flicker of light, was about to evaporate like drops of sea spray that drank from each other until they dried up. For Omar it was easy. An ending that fit the beginning with me, as well as his way of life, though I realized this too late.

If I'd married Tarek and had this beautiful child with him, it would have been impossible for him to leave me this way. Why did Tarek have to spring to mind just then? It bothered me that my thoughts turned to him whenever I had a problem with another man. I took hold of Omar's hand and wrapped my pride in a gentle plea. "Why don't you stay with us?" He slowly withdrew his hand from mine, and with it my dignity crumbled and fell at his feet. He had to survive, he said, and survival meant he had to go to France. He had to look out for his future, which he'd almost lost thanks to "Madame Zeinab Mahalawi." Acid dripped from each syllable. Anyway, he said, he was doing this for my sake and the sake of our daughter. It was obvious how he now felt about me, my family, and his decision to marry me. How could his feelings for me have changed so completely? I asked him this question, reminding him of some of the things he used to say. He responded with an enigmatic smile that I couldn't interpret. Then he placed a sum of money next to my ear, planted a distracted kiss on my forehead, and turned to leave. At the door, he paused and said, as though it were an afterthought, "Listen. I don't want to hurt you. I had a great time with you. If you want a divorce, I'm okay with that. . . ."

What could I say to that? When a man isn't clear in his priorities between me and another woman, it is no great honor if he chooses me. So how should I feel when he chooses the other?

For the remaining time he was in Sharm, he was like a body without a soul, at once present and absent. I grew tired of the game of fisherman and fish: the fisherman who plays with his catch by testing its ability to endure deprivation and pain. He dangles it close to the sea to let it dance ecstatically, lowers it until its skin barely touches the water, then yanks it up to watch it flip-flop in convulsions until it nearly utters its last breath; then he dips it back into the water again, and so on. I prayed for him to get it over with, to either be true to my life or true to my death. I couldn't take any more.

When he sprang on me his decision to go to Paris, I insisted on keeping Yasmine. He didn't try to argue or set conditions. It was as though she meant nothing to him. He'd turned over the page of affection so quickly, he destroyed the whole book. I called up Maysa to ask her advice about whether I should get a divorce. I was getting ready to return to Cairo to live in one of the apartments my father owned in Zamalek, since I knew my aunt wouldn't let me set foot again in the Heart of Palm. Omar was a step ahead. He sent me the divorce certificate, left me some money, and paid the bill for the hotel room we'd lived in since coming to Sharm El Sheikh. He paid a full month extra, in order to give me time to collect my things. What magnanimity! He would never understand that it would take me years to gather up the scattered fragments of myself. After Tarek, who took the lion's share; Murad, who devoured my flesh raw; and Omar, who crushed the remaining bones, I had only my daughter left to steer me back to life.

Could it be that Omar's flight was my avenue back to dignity? I'd surrendered my pride in my haste to dedicate my love and devotion to someone who proved unworthy of both. Unless I'd been deceiving myself. Maybe I'd wanted him to love me but didn't want to keep him. What I knew was that sadness had woven a net around my heart and squeezed out what little happiness was left. If only Omar had picked up stakes before this. If only I'd never taken that ride with him to begin with!

I found it odd, as I contemplated my little Yasmine's tiny features, that she resembled me quite a bit, whereas I looked like no one else in my family. I wasn't short, like my aunt, and

I didn't have her light-brown complexion or her fleshy features. But nor did I have my father's complexion, which was as white as the British, and I certainly didn't have his height or eye color. I could see some resemblance between me and my mother, but it was still distant. We shared the same svelteness, wide eyes, and delicate nose, but nothing else. As I placed my mother's picture in my purse, I caught sight of myself in the mirror and spotted a white hair in the parting. I hadn't noticed it before. Had it sprouted overnight to proclaim the advent of old age? Why should I care about old age, when my feelings were already moribund?

I twisted the hair around my finger and tore it out. If only Tarek had Omar's daring and love for life. If only he had some of Murad's confidence and force of character. My eyes welled up. A tear raced down my cheek and landed near my baby's lips. She opened her tiny mouth, thinking it was something to drink. She gurgled softly, either to show she was happy or to comfort me. Her eyes giggled, her hands waved in involuntary jerky movements, she kicked her tiny feet and pressed them into my lap, and smiled. I smiled back. I caught sight of myself in the mirror again and thought, "How much longer will my eyes betray me when I smile?"

The phone shook me out of my gloomy thoughts. I barely had the strength to get up, but I pushed myself to my feet with a grunt and reached for the phone. It was the receptionist. "There's a lady here who's been waiting in the reception area for a while. She wants to see you." I perked up. It must be Maysa who'd come to visit me as she'd promised recently. I threw on some clothes, picked up Yasmine, and left the room. The last time I'd seen Maysa was about a week before I came to Sharm El Sheikh. I bumped into her by accident in front of a well-known record store in Zamalek. She had moved into a new apartment without knowing that my aunt owned the building. I kept that a secret from Maysa because I didn't want her to leave Zamalek and move too far away from me. For the past two years, she'd been complaining about the water cutoffs, the elevator malfunctions, and the poor services in the building in general. I don't know how many times I begged my father to get my aunt to stop playing her childish games, but to no avail.

I skipped down the stairs to the lobby, smiling in anticipation of the hug. As I reached the middle of the lobby, my feet slowed, my smile vanished, and a veil of darkness fell before my eyes. The "lady" was Aunt Zeinab. Her driver called her attention to me. She struggled to her feet using her cane, and tottered slowly toward me, her expression as rigid and stony as always. But when she drew up and scanned my face, her lips parted in an affectionate smile, which was so unusual. With a gentle tone of reproach, almost like a loving mother, she said, "I just saw your face turn inside out. Of course, you thought it was Maysa coming to visit. You'll always be like the tendrils of a pumpkin vine reaching out to others. But if you can't turn to family, you'll have nobody to turn to."

Her Cadillac was waiting for us outside. Amazingly, it had withstood the 350 mile trip after twenty years in service. My aunt smiled proudly, "She's a sturdy one, like everything they made in the old days. But that didn't keep your father from sending along two cars behind us for fear she'd give up on us."

I turned and saw the two Mercedes-Benzes the People's Assembly had assigned to my father. I turned back to my aunt with a questioning look.

She reached out and rested a hand on my arm. "I've forgiven you, my dear. Now, that you're divorced from that Omar character, you should move back in with me in Zamalek. Family's best in times like these."

I didn't resist. There was nothing to keep me in Sharm. After I had packed, I accompanied her out to the car as though under sedation. They put my suitcases in the trunk and I climbed into the back with her. Her critical eye shifted down to my cotton skirt. Pursing her lips, she took the fabric between thumb and forefinger and pulled it away from my thigh.

"It's a tad tight on you, wouldn't you say?"

She wanted me to move to the foldout seat behind the driver, where I used sit when I was a child. Didn't she realize that everything had changed? That the seat of fairytales and dreams had lost its magic? My dreams were now worse than my waking life: one nightmare after another. But at least now I wouldn't face the risk of plummeting from the skies of hopes and expectations. Seeing my reluctance to shift over, she insisted. She said that she wanted to look at my face the whole way home because she'd missed me. As we set off, she pressed the button to raise the glass partition between us and the driver. I stared blankly out the window at the desert expanses and the scattered mountains in the distance as her voice droned on. Suddenly the word "sheikh" yanked me back into the car. Yes, she said, she'd been so worried about my condition that she consulted Sheikh Bahrawi and he gave her the solution. I could feel a weight pressing in from all sides as I waited for her to say it.

"The veil, Nadia." she said excitedly. "Sheikh Bahrawi says you should take the veil and let faith purify your heart."

She said nothing more. Eventually she nodded off, and her rhythmic snoring increased in volume. I was so stunned that I couldn't collect my thoughts. As I began to picture myself in a head covering, a violent headache throbbed at my temples and I too fell asleep.

After what seemed like ages, we arrived home. The moment I stepped inside I was struck by the change. My aunt had had all the Persian carpets removed and a bright-green wall-to-wall carpeting installed. The paintings on the wall had been replaced by Quranic verses about the ills of envy and the virtues of thanksgiving, all in wide ornate gilt frames. I looked at her, eyebrows raised. As she removed her shoes and stroked the pile of the carpet with her feet, she said with almost child-like spontaneity, "It's softer and more comfortable than the rugs, and it reminds me of the fields from long ago."

I put off visiting Maysa for over a week. I wasn't in the mood, not even for her sympathy. I wanted total isolation in my room, away from everything and everyone but my daughter. One day that isolation would become complete. I awoke that morning to find Father, extremely tense, phoning one official after the other. My aunt was on the couch, pitched forward with one foot tucked under her, chain-smoking furiously. Every now and then, she'd come up with a name for my father to call, and would tell him what to say. Fahim stood by his side, with a grimness that added a dark gray to his dark complexion. It was the first time I'd seen him without his tarboosh on his head. I'd never imagined him to be bald. I went up to my aunt and asked her what was going on. She waved me away several times, until my persistence finally made her turn to me with a glare that meant "clear out." So I glued myself to a seat and listened. Then I gasped in horror. One of the apartment blocks my aunt owned in Zamalek—the Taqwa Building—had collapsed at dawn that morning. I rushed to embrace my aunt. She patted me on my shoulder in a way meant to reassure me she was all right and push me away at the same time.

Suddenly I wailed. Maysa's little apartment was in that building. Was Maysa all right? My aunt didn't answer. I looked at my father, but he was too busy with his phone calls. I turned to Fahim. He bowed his head and said, "May God rest her soul. Everyone in the building died."

I ran back to my room. The kind and gentle Maysa, my teacher and my second mother, was gone, and with her went my last support.

The following day, my aunt burst into my room carrying a package that appeared to contain fabrics. Her face was glowing.

"Now, heed my advice and you'll bounce back in no time. Just pray to the Lord to have mercy on her soul. That's the best thing you can do for her. As He said, 'Everyone has his destined time.' You're not going to deny God's truth, are you?"

I wordlessly watched her unwrap the package, pull out a lot of colored head coverings, and place them on the edge of my bed. Then she left, shutting the door behind her with that beatific smile still on her face. When I awoke the following day around noon, the scarves still lay at the edge of my bed where my aunt had left them. They were only a few feet away, but miles away from what I felt inside. After about half an hour, I tentatively reached over and picked one out. The red one. I put it on and stood in front of the mirror looking at myself from within: shackled. I forced my face into a happier expressions, thinking the face muscles might persuade my mind to follow suit and accept that covering on my head. A wisp of hair slipped down over my eye. Then a long strand fell to the right side of my face, followed by another that escaped with a coquettish bounce. Then several others popped out next to my ear, as though they wanted to whisper, "No!" into it. I returned to the pile on the bed and chose another color to match what I was wearing, though it matched neither my femininity nor my soul. I studied my face. It had suddenly aged several years. Now I looked like Aunt Zeinab. I could almost be her daughter.

My mood turned fouler as I heard her footsteps approach behind me. Through my large mirror, I contemplated her in her capacious abaya. *"Allahu akbar!"* she exclaimed approvingly as she drew closer like a black scorpion about to swallow me. She reached up to press down on the top of my head while she shoved my hair more securely beneath the scarf. Then she tugged the ends of the scarf tighter as though afraid my thoughts might escape, and tied a firm knot at the nape of my neck. She stepped back and smiled, satisfied at her work.

"The hijab lights up the face," she said. "Tomorrow you'll appreciate its value when the grooms line up at your doorstep. As they say, a veiled woman is a hidden jewel, like a gooseberry behind its lantern."

I gave her a sharp look out of resentment for her prying into my innermost thoughts and fears. I wore that thing for months and rejected all suitors who tried to approached me via my aunt. They were paraded before me blindfolded, shoved forward by my aunt to present themselves. They were difficult to tell apart. Most of them were recommended by her women friends, with the blessing of that sheikh of hers. They all reduced me to my head covering, to the loose-fitting dress with long sleeves and, above all, to my father's and my aunt's wealth.

As time passed, I realized that my hijab and I were mismatched. Nine months after I first put it on, I took it off for the last time, and I was reborn. At last I could breathe deeply again. As the autumn breezes played with my hair, I rejoiced at rediscovering a dear friend.

Every morning, I was greeted with a barrage of my aunt's rebukes and admonitions, like a sticky spray. "You're going to regret this! You look prettier with the hijab. That's right, stay stubborn until you're too old to marry! No man these days wants to marry an unveiled girl!"

But the words of my dear friend and mentor Maysa, who died beneath the ruins of my aunt's building, still rang in my ear. They have remained as clearly engraved in my mind as the image of her face when she wrote them in my small diary, which I always keep with me.

"My dearest Nadia, be yourself. Don't try to be like anyone else but you. Don't be like those two. You don't belong to them."

Now I resemble myself and no one else. If only Maysa had lived. If only she had remained with us longer.

21

"LIKE A FOX STALKING A bear, only to feed on its leftovers."—
Abbas Mahalawi

I could still hear his howls of laughter from decades ago
when I told him about the pistol I kept beneath my pillow. I
reached under the pillow. It hadn't changed its place in thirty
years. But my grip had changed. I'd grown so weak. I barely
had the strength to rack the slide or squeeze the trigger. Anyway, nobody was likely to come and arrest me. They knew
how much I'd aged.

I laid my head back on the pillow, closed my eyes, and let
the film of my life unreel before my mind's eye. It was the only
form of entertainment I had to help me kill time. I saw myself
sitting beneath the parliamentary dome while the debate over
what would eventually become Law 95 of 1980, aka the Law
of Shame, drifted around me. There was no vote on the agenda
that day, and the chamber was practically empty, as usual. I
needed a place to relax and stay clear of nettlesome political
squabbles, so I decided to hang out in there for a while. I slid
down in my seat to make myself more comfortable. Just as I
was about to nod off, I heard a clearing of a throat and found
the chief of protocol bent toward my ear. His Excellency the
Chairman had arrived and wanted to see me immediately in
the Pharaonic Hall. It would be the first time I had met the
chairman of the ruling National Democratic Party outside

of official ceremonies. He occupied a far corner of the hall. Several rows of seats and benches around him had been left vacant in order to give him privacy and to emphasize his stature. Some of his close associates stood a short distance away, with smiles programmed to broaden whenever he smiled. I ignored them as I went up to him and shook his hand. He invited me to take a seat near him, and studied my face as though this was the first time he'd met me. Then he praised my efforts for mustering the MPs at voting times.

"I've had my eye on you for some time, Abbas," he said, measuring each syllable. "I'm pleased with your performance."

A simple sentence with a nice dose of flattery. Uttered in his well-known stentorian voice, it was more than sufficient to increase my influence and ensure that those around us feared me. We spoke for over an hour, on politics, the state of the country, and the like. He terminated the conversation, saying, "God preserve us. All will be well, God willing."

He signaled to an aide to summon the National Democratic Party secretary. When the official appeared, the chairman said, "Starting tomorrow, I want Abbas in charge of membership affairs, with a focus on youth in the provinces."

My new role was to transmit my years of expertise to young people, induce as many as possible to join the party, and appoint the most promising ones to undertake certain crucial tasks and functions in advance of local and general elections. The party now had a youth base of over twenty thousand. I could proudly claim to be the one who built it up over the course of a decade. It wasn't an easy job. But it wasn't that hard either. The government has loose purse strings when need be, and as long as it's kept under the table. There was tons of money that seemed to have no owner. Our country was sitting on an endless sea of it. So I dipped my cup and sprinkled judicious amounts on young recruits, and they obeyed every signal of my pinkie finger. I'd been given extensive powers. The chairman saw in me talents no one else had seen, including myself.

We met again frequently in his office. Each time, his face was lit with an expression of admiration and satisfaction with me. Each time, he had the party secretary relate some chapter of my life. He was particularly fond of the one set in the aftermath of the 1967 war: how I'd mobilized hundreds in the Socialist Union Party headquarters in the countryside to stage marches in the streets, shouting pro-Nasser chants and calling on him to retract his resignation.

The party secretary inflated my image even more. Why he did that was beyond me. It would no longer be necessary, however, after the NDP's first national convention, when the original core of the party's youth secretariat gave the chairman a standing ovation for ten full minutes. Afterward, he upbraided the party secretary.

"You have this treasure here called Abbas Mahalawi. Why are you letting him go to waste here beneath the dome, even if he is a maestro? This guy here can convince you a bull's made for milking. You got to make him a minister in your next government."

"Yes, Your Excellency. We'll find him a ministry that suits him."

Now I'm on the shelf. Yes, I've resigned from all my posts, and I'm treated as though I'd never held any at all. They forgot I even existed when someone cropped up who they thought was better at doing what I did. How could I tell them otherwise? I had no right to object. I owed them a debt of gratitude for all they had done for me over the years.

I squeezed my eyes shut in my effort to conjure up more memories of my last days in parliament. Life had grown boring now that I'd gotten everything I wanted out of it and more. I felt every morning was my last, and when I went to bed at night I prayed that if Death had to come, it would at least come to me in my sleep. I could fend him off with my mind, but if that went, he'd knock me out with the first punch.

Illness laid me flat in successive rounds, but I was still in the ring. True, I was bound to a wheelchair, but I resisted. I had some health on my side, minimal pain, and a lot of brains.

I pushed myself out of bed and onto my wheelchair, and rolled myself toward my balcony. I watched the Nile in the distance. Small rounded waves in the vanguard raced to peak and break before the others caught up. In some parts, the water was smooth and still. That was what my life was like now. My only interest in life was to make money. I never gave a damn about politics. I had no political ambitions. The only reason I got involved in politics to begin with was to make money. My sole ambition was to become rich, like Cicurel: someone who had everything. That was all I ever wanted.

But had I fulfilled my wish? I wasn't sure.

I had a cushy life in Zamalek. I stuck close to the rich and powerful, and that earned me important positions in the ruling party. After becoming a member of parliament, I kept myself snugly wrapped in its immunity. For twenty years I only had to raise my hand with a "yea" or "nay," in accordance with the instructions handed down to me and those I controlled in the party and the House. I voted in favor of hundreds of bills, resolutions, and agreements that I'd never read in full and knew little about. But I kept close track of which way the wind blew, and if there was trouble brewing my nose could smell it a mile off.

Early on, I began to operate on the belief that the powers that be would do whatever they pleased and, in exchange for not getting in their way, they'd leave the rest of us a nice recreation area where we could play alongside them as long as we stayed in sight and made no noise. I was probably the only one who had grasped how the game worked as soon as the cards were dealt with every round. The rules might change here and there on the surface, and I'd figure them out before it was too late. But if I never suffered a major loss it was because I knew the main ground rule never changed: no matter how low I bowed, they wouldn't hesitate to cut off my head if they had to. Perpetuating power always requires sacrifices.

I was absolutely sure I was right about this. It was why I never wasted energy planning and plotting against those more powerful and influential than I. I was content to live off their crumbs, which Zeinab sucked up like an insatiable tick burrowed in my hide.

Goddamn you, Cicurel! I'd been obsessed since the day I opened your safe, found your treasure, and tried to emulate you. I was never as clever, famous, or successful. But at least now I could die a rich man. I had enough money and property to keep a family of fifty in comfort for the next hundred years at least. Yet no one would remember me. They'd say, Abbas Mahalawi was a good and generous man. That was all. I wouldn't make more of a mark than that.

I was like Cicurel in another way. Now that I'd lost Ibrahim, I'd also been left without a son to carry on my name after I was gone.

Ibrahim, my son, my only child from my flesh and blood, passed away a year ago. I could never have begun to imagine feeling so bereft. I did everything I could think of to save him. But despite the fortunes I spent on his treatment, fate was a step ahead.

Ibrahim Abbas Mahalawi: he was my secret. Not even Zeinab knew about this young man. I didn't have the courage to tell her I'd had a son. Then God stole him from me. Why couldn't He have taken some of my money? Why choose the person I love more than anyone in the world? Why punish me so cruelly in this world when He was going to punish me in the next along with all the others?

I pressed my eyes closed for, what, the third or fourth time? There was nothing left to do but to mull over my memories.

I flashed back to my flights to London at the beginning of June every year. There he is next to his mother in the arrivals hall in Heathrow. When he sees me, he toddles forward unsteadily, arms outstretched. He's just learning how to walk. I crouch to swoop him up and hold him in my arms, his tiny hand gripping my index finger. He grew up so quickly! I step into the arrivals hall and stop. He bounds toward me with long, confident strides. He's in his last year of university. I reach out to shake hands, one man to another. He clasps me in a warm, affectionate hug—his Middle Eastern genes getting the better of him. They're all from me. He looks like me. So much so that I see my younger self in him. He wears the same size clothes I do. To hear his voice and watch his gestures, you'd think he was imitating me. The three of us climb into the car and head to my apartment. On the way there, he tells me about everything he did since my last visit, even though we'd have spoken on the phone once a week without fail. Not that I minded. I could hear it all over and over again. In London, I see his cheeks redden when one of his girlfriends phones him. I worry about his health, about whether he smokes behind my back. When I see his reflection in the mirror as he shaves with care and precision, I see myself. I've revisited these memories again and again. Every detail fills me with joy. Twenty years and nine months passed as fast as a few days, Ibrahim. I couldn't get my fill of you before you left.

How I'd dreamed of a son like him to inherit my wealth and my name. He'd manage factories that produced products bearing my logo, but designed by him. People would remember me whenever they bought them. But that would never happen. I'd emulated Cicurel's cleverness in building up a hidden treasure and his restraint in not tapping it. My fortune entered the Heart of Palm and grew. But now that it could never pass to Ibrahim, I would never let it pass to anyone else. Let them say that Abbas Mahalawi was a thief. Not many would believe them. The country was crawling with thieves, and everyone bowed and scraped to them.

I shook my head sadly. I'd made such careful plans for Ibrahim. He would come to Cairo to live by my side and fulfill my dreams and his. Fahim had already helped me work out a plan for how to reveal his existence so I could openly claim him as my true son and heir, who would carry on the name of the family. But fickle fate claimed him first, in a traffic accident one stormy night. Everyone in the car came out with scratches, except for him. His spine was crushed. He was paralyzed and fell into a coma for two months. I brought in every specialist I could find in London and Paris, but to no avail. They were all as helpless as I.

I stood near the foot of his bed when the machine with all those wires stuck into his motionless body stopped beeping. He seemed the same, lying there on that hospital bed with his eyes closed. I touched his body in disbelief. I kissed his forehead. I soaked his cheeks with my tears. I pleaded with him softly. I called out his name. I begged him. I howled.

They had to drag me out of the room and sedate me. I came to the following day in a neighboring room in the same hospital. I lay there for a week until they discharged me. Illness invaded every corner of my frail body when my only son died, and all my hopes died with him. I only had his picture left to kiss every morning after his scent evaporated and his soul left.

I buried Ibrahim in England, near our home in Brighton. My wife stayed with him there, alone, as bereft and dispirited as I was. I kept his death a secret from everyone. I didn't even tell my personal lawyer there. If anyone asked after him, I'd say he'd gone to a grad school in the US. I hadn't given up yet. I continued to make plans because I wasn't going to die without a fight, even after losing Ibrahim in a wager in which I'd thought all the odds were on my side. I'd forgotten that the player on the other side of the table was fate.

"Al-Khouli's downstairs with the rent for the farm," said my servant, breaking into my reverie. I dismissed him with an impatient flick of the hand. There was no need for me to go downstairs. Fahim would take care of it. I wanted to return to my memories.

How could I have forgotten to recall my land? Didn't it hold the dearest thing I owned: my roots? Had I not watered it, nurtured it, and watched it grow? Had I lost all sense of belonging to it? Who do I think I'm fooling! I bought the land; I didn't farm it. I had a sprawling ranch in Mahalla Marhoum. It was more than eighty acres. But the land was worked by tenant farmers. I rarely went there.

After my mother died, I bought all the land around our house. Our village was now officially called Mahalawi Farms. This time, I was the one who changed the name, after I got into parliament. Its fame soared. Stories about it and me appeared in all the newspapers. Just a few months ago, *al-Wafd* published a long feature story, so long it had to be serialized over several days. Mahalla Marhoum, now Mahalawi Farms, had produced eminent figures since the monarchic era, and the distinguished family of Mahalawi Pasha had forged part of Egyptian history, the newspaper wrote. I was a "self-made entrepreneur and financier" who "championed the peasant" and served as "the voice of the people in parliament." People believed what they read about the famous MP, a member of the general secretariat of the National Democratic Party and the second-oldest parliamentarian in Egypt. According to the article, my father was a Wafdist and I followed in his footsteps. We resisted the British occupation, supported the 1919 Revolution, and put our money at the service of national independence leader Saad Zaghloul, the Wafd Party, and, later, Mustafa al-Nahhas. Although we fell on hard times in the Nasser era, we never complained. Then we pulled ourselves up again while helping the ship of reform reach the shores of safety.

I pictured my drunkard father, teetering in his tattered shoes and threadbare *gallabiya*. I muttered, "You see? I've created a history for you. I erased the taint of prison around you. You are now officially an anti-colonial resistance fighter."

I've lost count of the number of newspaper interviews I've done. The journalists would send me the questions and answers at the same time so that I could check them over before publication. The *Al-Ahram* publishing house produced an important book called *National Figures from the Heart of Rural Egypt*. A whole chapter was dedicated to my family. Thanks to some lazy historians who cited the text without double-checking, the fiction spread far and wide, and was reiterated so often that it became fact. Before the revolution I was "One-Eyed Abbas." After the revolution I evolved into "Abbas Bey" by dint of Abdel-Naim's money, the influence of the Committee for the Liquidation of Feudalism and, above all and before all, Fahim's noble services as a procurer of forged certificates and powers of attorney. Then, after Nasser died and was followed by Sadat, no one called me anything but Abbas Mahalawi Pasha.

Recently, a major publishing house made me a generous offer to publish my memoirs. I was reluctant to accept. In Egypt, if your tongue outpaces your mind, your head flies.

But was this the life I'd wished for? Was this how the journey ended? A rich old man getting sick and dying a slow death. Everyone who least deserved it got a chunk of his wealth, while his son, his true heir, got nothing, for the simple reason that he was dead.

I refused to accept such a conventional ending; I hadn't left the poker table yet. I still had chips to play, and in my pocket I had a last card that no one even suspected. This card would be the game changer and make for an exciting ending. Zeinab I'd cut out of my will completely. I'd leave a bit to Nadia, because at least she was obedient and loved me selflessly. I'd give her ten thousand pounds for every year she lived with us . . . No, make that twenty thousand, plus the apartment in Paris. Nobody knew about that little getaway apart from the senior officials who used it as a garçonnière, and they weren't going to talk. I'd already put the Heart of Palm and the ranch in the village in Nadia's name, in order to keep Zeinab from getting her hands on them. Being an orphan, Nadia was more deserving of charity than others. I'd settled my affairs in the UK with my lawyer there. Some of the proceeds would go to my wife and to Nadia. I'd arranged everything with Fahim. Tonight I'd take the last remaining steps. I'd show him the duplicates of the documents that cut Zeinab out of my will entirely. I'd sent the originals to my overseas banks abroad a couple of weeks ago. The second thing I'd do tonight was put a copy of the map in the safe. That would increase the number of players. Tonight, Nadia and Yasmine would be out of the house for several hours, so I'd take advantage of that. Tomorrow was a new year and a new decade—the 1990s—and a new beginning. Who knew how many more years I had left to live.

I'd already sold most of my properties, and I donated my remaining liquid assets to the home for the elderly that I opened the year before last. I had it built at the insistence of that Sheikh Bahrawi who wormed his way into Zeinab's mind and his hand into my pocket. Zeinab refused to attend the inauguration because it would "bring bad luck." At least the home would immortalize my name and stand as a monument to my achievements.

I smiled when it occurred to me that Fahim might become one of its first patients. He'd been getting more and more absentminded lately. For his part, he imagined I was unaware he'd been ripping me off regularly for some time. Whenever he forged a document I needed, he padded the bill, rewarding himself with a generous commission. But there was nothing I could do about that. I was too old and ailing to start looking around for a new secretary. At least he wouldn't turn against me like Cicurel's driver, Ernesti, turned against him. Also, he was as clueless as everyone else as to where I hid my diamonds—in empty car tires! He, like the others, was going to have a really hard time finding them, if they found them at all. If they only knew what those tires contained. All my money! Converted into diamonds, carefully wrapped and sealed inside small leather tubes, and inserted in the space between the rubber and the rim. Five diamonds per tire, and there were a lot of tires. They were stacked in the basement of my ranch house in Mahalla Marhoum, the last place anybody would imagine I'd hid my wealth. I only went there twice a year. The basement was unguarded so as not to draw attention. Like Cicurel, I made a map. I put one copy in the safe in my bedroom; and the other copy I'd put in the basement safe. My map was more complicated than Cicurel's. I wasn't going to make it easy for some layabouts to wallow in my wealth after I was gone. Anybody who wanted it was going to have to work for it. They were going to have to use their brains and sweat like I did. Only the smartest would win the lion's share of my wealth after solving the riddle I made. Matching wits was the only game I'd ever liked in this world. I didn't think I was very good at any other.

I heaved a contented sigh. I was pleased with the decisions I'd made. I'd rest easy in my grave with a smile on my face while others ferreted for my hidden wealth. I wasn't going to die a nobody. I was certainly not going to die a mere shadow of the old and bloated Zeinab. I was the one who made her. I was the one who pulled her out of the muck and brushed off the village dust and rust, only for the bitch to turn around and sink her talons into me. She was insatiable. She'd sucked up my blood and half my wealth, then tried to shut me out of the picture. I'd become the man in the shadows of the "Lady of Zamalek," as her circle of crones called her. For years she'd basked in the limelight and forgotten where she came from. I was standing in the wings now. But I still had the power to cut the lights and stop the show at any moment.

22

"Egypt's much prettier from high up, if you got something worth seeing once you're up there."—Zeinab Mahalawi

Even though I was the one who insisted on it, Nadia's divorce from Murad was the third blow in my life after the death of Lady and Sandro's flight and then murder at Abbas's hands. I'd wanted Nadia to be with a powerful man like Murad, but he'd grown weak in the last year of their marriage. Not only had I lost hope that he'd be reinstated, he was a step away from prison. Those were dark days for us, when Murad refused to give Nadia a divorce and then fled the country after they charged him with conspiring with the defense minister to overthrow Nasser. To my surprise, when I told Nadia to get a divorce, she said, "I'm not thinking about divorce at this time." She's a stubborn one, so instead of trying to fight, I'd bring her around slowly. I told her Murad's times had come and gone and that his days ended the day the field marshal committed suicide, like Abbas said. I warned her that Murad dragged us down, but that only made her want to stand by him even more.

When I realized it was pointless trying to convince her, I nagged Abbas. That worked. One day he returned from one of those long summer trips he used to take to London, handed me the divorce papers signed by Murad, and said, "Murad's agreed to the divorce and he's going to stay in London. I did my part. Now you go break it to Nadia."

Eventually I got Abbas to explain how he did it. Murad agreed to the divorce in exchange for an exit visa, which Abbas managed to wangle through his connections. Abbas was going to notify the authorities on the day Murad was due to travel in order to get him arrested at customs and thrown into jail. Murad was shrewder. He refused to give Nadia a divorce until after he was safely out of the country. He handed Abbas a check for twenty thousand pounds as a guarantee. When Abbas got to London, he handed the check to some intermediary in exchange for the divorce papers. I couldn't pry more details out of Abbas. Eventually we forgot the matter or, more precisely, we tried to put it out of our minds.

Nadia had a lot of suitors after the divorce. She turned them all down, even though some were very suitable in my opinion. It seemed that the softer I grew as I aged, the more muleheaded she became. After her experience with Murad, I wanted her to have a stable life with a respectable man who appreciated her and her family's worth, but she wanted a man her own age who "loved her like she loved him." I was sure she couldn't understand Murad's needs as a man—why else would he have taken a second wife behind her back? That, too, I learned from Abbas after the divorce. How I'd prayed she'd have a child or two with Murad. Maybe they just needed more time, though Abbas and I had begun to wonder whether Murad was sterile. Whatever the case, after the divorce I had to figure out ways to fill up her day. I wasn't going to let her out of my sight. There was no way I was going to let the fortune I'd built up with Abbas slip out of our hands.

"Monsieur Edmond has been waiting in the hall for an hour, Madame Zeinab."

I nodded and dismissed my servant. Edmond could wait a little longer. More than half an hour later, I had him present himself to me in the back garden next to the Nile, where I was having my morning coffee and reading the papers. He stood politely, hands clasped in front of him, the upper half of his body pitched slightly forward. After leaving him like that long enough to quench my thirst for revenge, I spoke, but without looking at him.

"I want you to give my daughter Nadia piano lessons."

I could hear his hesitation. I slid my reading glasses down my nose a bit, and looked up at him coldly. "Weren't you a music teacher before you opened that school for etiquette in Zamalek? I hope you haven't forgotten how you started out, Edmond."

He nodded and stuttered, "I'm at your service, Madame Zeinab. But that was such a long time ago and I haven't taught—"

"I'll pay you five pounds an hour. We'll make it once—no, twice a week. Surely that's better than hanging around the Gezira Club all day because you're jobless."

Edmond bowed stiffly and left. Actually, he backed out. He only turned around when he was near the end of the lawn. Then my servant called out to him, holding up an envelope. He remained in place, as instructed, forcing Edmond to retrace his steps to collect the envelope, which contained five pounds as an advance. He bowed himself out again, but he couldn't restrain himself. Even before he was out the gate, he opened the envelope, counted the bills, and nearly jumped for joy.

Unfortunately, neither our circumstances nor the conditions in the country were looking up, which added another type of worry. I wasn't the only one who felt that Anwar Sadat was weak and unwelcome. Abbas, who'd worked with Sadat in the National Assembly for three years, put it differently: "He hasn't begun to fill his chair yet." Whatever the case, I put off my projects for five full years until after the October War. Then, almost overnight, everything changed. We entered a new era in which Egypt opened up to a whole wide world from which we'd been cut off for nearly twenty years. Our opinion about the president changed too. Whenever Sadat cropped up in our conversations, Abbas would say, "The guy turned out to be as crafty as a Delta peasant. A wolf with a fox inside him."

My plan was to get into the construction business like Abbas did with Abdel-Naim in the old days. He wasn't happy about the idea, so it took some elbow twisting to bring him around and get him to agree to my conditions. He was showing signs of wanting to settle down and retire, contenting himself with the fortune he'd made. He kept forgetting that the fortune didn't belong to him alone. I was his partner, fifty-fifty at least, and he needed constant reminding of this fact, especially since I was sure he was hiding some of his assets from me because of his annual trips to London. What did he get up to over there?

I'd watched his climb up the career ladder. From the Feudalism Liquidation Committee to the Socialist Union Party secretariat, and from there to the National Assembly's Central Membership Committee. He was a member of the boards of directors of the Nasr Automobile Company and Egypt Insurance Company, but he no longer wanted to invest in real estate. He'd converted all his cash into diamonds. He picked that up from Cicurel—that and selling them in Belgium. Or some of them. He said. From there he flew off to London for a long holiday. He'd tell you it was for R&R, and that was all he'd say on the subject. Afterward, he came back with a sizeable amount of cash. I saw it as yeast, which could rise into skyscrapers if he wanted, but he just hoarded it.

Finally, when I managed to make him see some sense, he opened my eyes to a new method, though it would take guts and a lot of pull. "Forget about the old villas and palaces," he said. "Look at the large spaces in between. What you have to do is buy them up bit by bit, and let Fahim take care of the paperwork." It worked like a charm, thanks to the network of connections Fahim had built up over the years in the Notary Public, the local and foreign-owned property registrars and other government departments. Before long, barely a month went by without some new high-rise lifting its head in the Zamalek skyline.

Business really took off a few years after the 1973 war, when money began to flow again, and we started to call our new apartment blocks "towers," which helped attract Saudis and Gulf Arabs. The ground and first floors we rented out to commercial establishments: big-name restaurants and patisseries or upmarket clothes and shoe stores. Large sections of the area designated for garage space in the official plans were partitioned so they could be converted into smaller commercial spaces. These we rented out as grocery stores and other shops to serve the tenants' day-to-day needs. Fahim's connections with the municipal inspection authorities came in handy here, but it was my money that paid for it all. Or, more precisely, my half of Abbas's money, as per our old agreement, which he always tried to wriggle out of.

The exhilaration I felt when visiting one of my buildings was indescribable. At least ten men rushed out to greet my Cadillac as soon as they saw it coming. They swarmed around it, raising their hands to greet me, and bellowed out good wishes. My driver slowed and pulled to a stop right in front of the main entrance, where they cleared a space large enough to fit three Cadillacs. Out of the back window I caught sight of some of the men racing to catch up so they would be ready to welcome me when the driver opened the rear door. Some bowed and kissed my hand. I was the most famous lady in Zamalek. Everyone knew me by sight. If they saw me in another part of town, they'd whisper and point to me in admiration. I was a hero in the stories they wove. I was one of the first things on their minds; they were one of the last things on mine. They prayed for tokens of approval during my monthly inspection tour with the local real estate agents, who had me to thank for being able to operate in Zamalek. I'd chosen them carefully, based on Fahim's recommendations.

It was the khamsin season and one of its sandstorms struck, blasting our faces with hot, sandy wind. I climbed back into the car, rolled up the window tightly, and waited for it to pass. In no time flat, the storm painted the buildings with a dusty gray film. Then it passed, though I could still see some eddies of whirling dust and dirt particles. I rolled down the sand-covered window and smiled. The first thing that came to view was the shop window of one of the outlets of a chain of stores I'd opened in most of my "towers": Elrimas for hijabs, abayas, and outfits for the fashionably veiled.

But it was not a fully satisfied smile. I still felt something was missing, and that irked me. Why was it that a lump still formed in my throat whenever I bumped into that wall of ladies from a society in which I felt a stranger? They came from a distant past in which I'd stood on the fringes. I'd tried to change that ancient society, but to no avail. They switched to French when I was around. Although I could follow snatches of their conversation, I could never get the French I knew to roll off my tongue like they did. I got nervous for no reason, and my tongue got tied up in knots. They reminisced over the long-gone times of Madame Paula. They sighed wistfully as they recalled her elegance, grace, and poise. I sensed I was the butt of subtle winks and insinuations, but I said nothing. I clenched my jaw so tightly I feared a molar might break, and I heard my heart thumping in my eardrums. After I left them, I returned to the kingdom I'd built. I took heart in the sight of my towers, soaring high enough to block the sun, and I let the admiration and praise of small shop owners work like salve on my wounds. I swore I'd spend every piaster I had, until I owned every last inch of Zamalek, so I could see my adversaries become my followers and grovel at my feet.

Fortune smiled on me when I set out on this project. I was able to demolish more than thirty of the villas that my father-in-law, Abdel-Naim, built with Abbas and before Abbas. My towers now stood in their place. Naturally, I didn't tear down any of the old villas in my neighborhood, so we wouldn't be disturbed by a big influx of residents and the noise and bustle of shops and shoppers. Abbas did his part to keep other real estate entrepreneurs from our part of Zamalek. He also gave me a compliment in his funny way: "They screwed us when Abdel-Naim and I built these villas for them in the 1940s. We got piasters. But your good Lord made it up to us. Praise the Lord!"

My path was not strewn with roses, contrary to what some of my friends imagined. I was forced to "donate" half a plot of land I'd acquired so the government could build a school on it. Then came the time when we found ourselves the object of a smear campaign in the press. Abbas asked me to bend with the wind so he wouldn't lose his new position, so I bent and sacrificed a small villa to the Governorate of Cairo. President Mubarak had just appointed him to the National Democratic Party secretariat. I was sorry to see Sadat go. I missed those days when we could do everything we wanted and felt like we owned the country. Then the guy got himself assassinated right in the middle of his army. I was terrified we were going to lose everything we owned. When I mentioned this to Abbas, he laughed and said, "Nothing's going to change, Zeinab. As your mama, God rest her soul, used to say, 'Those rabbits are all from the same litter, even if one's black, the next one's white, and the one after that is gray.'"

We'd finished our lunch in the revolving restaurant in the Cairo Tower and were now having our coffee. We sat at an inner table because Abbas didn't like heights. Just before sunset, I suggested we go up to the observation deck to admire Cairo's beauty from above. I reached the circular deck before him and leaned against the iron railing, which, like the top of the tower, folded out like lotus leaves. I looked out across Zamalek, at its few remaining villas amid towering apartment blocks. I loved to look down on things from above. I could easily make out ten buildings that I had built recently. I told Abbas to come closer to the railing so he could get a better view, but his fear of heights held him next to the inner wall, where he stood with that ebony cane of his. He only used that cane to make him look dignified. His shadow stretched to his left and grew bigger and bigger until it stopped at my feet.

"Believe me, Cairo's is prettier from up here!"

"It might be even prettier from a different angle," he said with a crafty smile on his face. He returned to our table and I followed, pulled by the force of my curiosity. With that crafty smile still playing on his face, he pulled out a map and spread it out on the table. It was a map of Mohandiseen, a part of town in Giza that had been targeted for development. I didn't know how many times I'd asked him to get me a copy of the urban-planning map after I'd heard it had come off the drawing board. Now he swept his hand over it with a grand gesture and said, "Take your pick, madame."

I stared, mouth agape, unable to believe my eyes.

"Just imagine, Zeinab! All this is just fields, apart from a handful of villas and about fifty apartment blocks."

"You mean they *were* fields. We're going to plant apartment blocks and skyscrapers there!" I laughed and set my finger on a red square.

"That's already taken. We can only choose from the blank ones," he said.

"Who got there first?"

"There are a lot of folks who are bigger than us, Zeinab. There are the officers in the army and the police. Prominent judges and doctors. Accountants and journalists with pull. And before them come ministers, senior officials, and even former officials, but with a reach that extends to the present. Then there are the others like us."

"Plus, there are a lot more people who've got money now. Don't forgot about them. They're going to want their share too."

"Wrong, Zeinab. Those are our customers. They're the ones who are going to buy our units so they can live next door to the bigwigs. That's how the country's been working for the past twenty years. And it's going to go on working that way for the next fifty years at least."

I shook my head. I wasn't convinced.

"Just choose the blank lots or the villas, because it'll be easy to knock them down."

I thought for a moment. Then I set my finger down on a long green strip that almost circled the whole of the residential area like a belt.

"That's for low-income people," he said. "The government's going to build low-cost housing there."

"So, we'll build it for them."

"It wouldn't be worth it for us." He paused for a moment, then said, "It's weird. Each new quarter has got to be surrounded by a belt of slums. It's as though they want to use the poor to frighten the rich. Why would they want to do that?"

"Now that's where you're wrong, Abbas. That's the kind of planning that works in our favor, as you'll see with every square foot we sell."

He raised his eyebrows in surprise.

"All those new residents are going to need servants and workmen. When servants and workmen live nearby, services are more easily accessible and cheaper. Just you leave that part to me and don't worry your head about it."

"But those homes are supposed to be for government employees and others who need a roof over their heads. Not for servants and workmen. It's about politics, Zeinab."

"Let them do the politics and let's us think about what's good for us. No government employee is going to want to live in an apartment the size of a rathole. He'll take advantage of the government offer, then sell it at a profit. So, all you have to do now is cash in one or two of your bonbons so we can get some new buildings built."

Abbas gave the dry laugh he gave whenever I told him to sell one of his "bonbons," meaning his diamonds. He said the price of diamonds was falling and he didn't want to risk the nest egg he'd built up over the years in order to buffer us against hard times. "You never know when somebody's going to stab us in the back," he said. Backstabbing was something he knew about, having done it to so many others.

"Come off it," I said. "Just sell off a couple of the small diamonds."

Then he came up with a brilliant idea for getting money without us having to dig into our own capital: bank loans.

"We'll pass the interest on to our customers. We use the money from the bank to build. Then we pay back the loan with interest after the sale—"

"How's the bank going to guarantee it gets its money back?"

"The villa. We'll use the Heart of Palm as collateral. I got the deed back from the Sequestrations Administration two months ago. The villa's got to be worth at least two million pounds now. That should do it."

Over the next two years, Egyptians living abroad in the Gulf bought up everything we built, even while it was still ink on paper. They paid up front and in full. We earned millions. It was so easy. At first, we came under attack in the press because of the building that collapsed in Zamalek, but we were able to prove that the construction permit was in Fahim's name. He spent a couple of months in jail pending trial, and then was acquitted in the first hearing. As a safety measure, we put all new construction permits in his name, in case more buildings collapsed. I'd always admired the way Abbas's mind worked. I never overestimated him, despite having had to threaten him at times because of the evil side that always got the better of him. For example, I found out that he'd transferred the deed to the villa and everything else that had been in Nadia's name to his. I had to force him to write out a will leaving half of this property to Nadia and the other half to me. He gave me a copy, which I'd hidden in a place he'd never find, and I watched his glum face as he put his copy next to a bunch of small files in his safe. I didn't see any diamonds in there. He was up to something fishy, and whatever it was I swore I'd soon find out.

Abbas seemed to return from some faraway thought, and gave me one of those penetrating looks of his.

"Is it true you don't let Copts live in your buildings?"

"No, I swear!" The question took me completely by surprise. "Most of them left Shubra and went to live in Heliopolis. Anyway, the Gulf Arabs and Saudis have got money to burn, and they don't haggle."

He held that look for a while, then said that complaints had reached the People's Assembly, accusing me of persecuting Christians. Was this a roundabout way of telling me to stop hosting Sheikh Bahrawi's religious sermons in the Heart of Palm? I knew Abbas wasn't thrilled about this, but it was a good way to attract prospective buyers to our apartment buildings and to broaden my influence among the new society women who'd become my friends and customers. Surely I wasn't the first and wouldn't be the last to do this. I knew of a lot of homes that opened their doors to well-known sheikhs who gave their fatwas in exchange for a meal. So many women were taking the veil. It was a fad, and you just had to flow with it.

"Come on, Abbas. Just think that we're doing a good deed that will reward us in the hereafter."

At a signal from my finger, he rolled his eyes and tilted his ear leftward, toward my mouth. Lowering my voice, I said, "It was Sheikh Bahrawi who suggested we build a little mosque on the ground floor of all our buildings so we'd be exempt from real estate taxes." I could tell he was impressed, though he tried to hide it.

"Taking care of mosques is a big responsibility," he said.

I leaned back in my chair, confident that I had him beat on this one. "My doormen take care of them. They fetch their relatives from Upper Egypt to do the work. Anyway, what's it got to do with us? The government sees what's going on and says nothing. If it were wrong or forbidden, surely they would have said something by now. Anyway, if push comes to shove, all our papers are in order, God bless Fahim!"

He fell back on his old maxims: "You have to bow before a strong wind" and "It's a thousand times better to survive in the shadows than to shine at the top and become targets for the worms of the earth." That was when I came up with the idea of a new marketing system. I told Abbas it would end all the fuss about who could or couldn't live in our buildings. "We sell the units unfinished. The customers paint them, tile the bathrooms and kitchens, install the floors, kitchen cabinets, bathroom suites, and the like."

He didn't take to the idea at first. He couldn't see how it was connected to the business about Copts and Muslims. "Don't play games with me, Zeinab," he snapped. "You're going to draw a lot of attention to us."

"Remember how we had to fumigate empty apartments once a year so we could rent them out? Times have changed. Money's flowing now."

But the truth was, I was dodging the question. Ever since I agreed with Sheikh Bahrawi to let him give sermons at home in exchange for him inaugurating my buildings, I'd been blessed with fortune. He was the one who suggested I "shun the Coptic neighbor and the unveiled Muslim." So I did, and my sales soared. I couldn't tell Abbas this, of course. I focused on the larger profit margin and managed to squeeze some funding out of him. Due to their slightly reduced prices, the unfinished units went like hotcakes. That only increased Abbas's anxieties. He came back to me about his fears of all the attention my booming business was attracting in the press.

That could get government regulators sniffing around us and invoking an anticorruption law that would compel him to make a full financial disclosure. Abbas could never disclose the source of his money, of course.

I consulted Sheikh Bahrawi about this and relayed his advice to Abbas immediately. "Make the apartments available to the people in the agencies we fear most, with comfortable installments."

The idea impressed him, but he didn't expect it to succeed. I explained the idea in detail, as the venerable sheikh had explained it to me: "Every government agency has a social club that provides services to its members. What we do is offer them a service: easy installment plans that look so affordable they don't sense their real value. On the one hand, we lose nothing over time; on the other, we earn their eternal protection."

"But do you think they'll go for it?"

"Are you kidding? They won't believe their eyes. Before you know it we won't be able to keep up with the demand. What's important is to choose which of them deserves this service."

Abbas came around to the idea quickly, for a change. He didn't want to get into an argument or a long discussion. I learned why soon enough, and it ruined my sense of satisfaction. When I went upstairs to fetch something, I found his suitcases lined up by his bedroom door. He'd be heading to the airport in a few hours to fly to London, where he'd spend the summer, like every year. He didn't want anyone to disturb him before he left. For the fourth time, I reminded him to have Fahim get the titles to the last five apartment blocks we completed put in my name. Those mysterious trips to London worried me more and more because of the amounts of money he was transferring to his bank there. That was a piece of information I'd picked up recently from the director of our bank during one of Bahrawi's sessions in our house. She'd taken the veil recently. Either he was engaged in some business venture or he'd gotten married. Whatever it was, he was as tight-lipped as ever. When I demanded to know how he spent my money in England, he snapped, "You'll never get enough, will you, Zeinab?"

I knew I'd never pry an answer out of him, but, before he left, I took him down to his office, out of sight of Nadia and out of earshot of the staff. I closed the door and took a slip of paper from my purse. It had four names with file numbers next to them. I handed it to Abbas with a look that said, Do as I say. He snatched the paper, looked it at, and said, "Not again, Zeinab. We've gotten more than enough of your friends' sons into the police academy over the years, not to mention the ones that got hired in—"

"That's what you say every time. But you know as well as I do how these people serve our interests. I choose them very carefully. Or have you forgotten how Fahim got acquitted like a knife through butter? Even those two months in jail were like a holiday in a hotel. Get those four guys enrolled, Abbas. I've given my word."

"It's no use. You'll never get enough."

That silly refrain again. He'd said it so frequently over the past couple of years. I ignored it. I didn't think the way Abbas did. He was too cautious, but I wanted to own every inch of land I set foot on, which meant I had to have solid backing in every government agency. I was afraid of his treachery, but I still had big dreams. My treasure chest of dreams was as full as Abbas's safe.

In the two or three years that followed, he continued that same routine of flying off to London at the beginning of the summer and returning to Egypt at the end. He transferred large sums of money to England and withdrew lots of money from his accounts here, as I learned from the director of our bank.

I was getting more and more worried about my money and about Nadia's rights since her divorce from Omar Seif Eddin. I didn't want Nadia and her daughter to suffer hardship after I was gone. I didn't think she'd marry a third time. Why did I agree to him receiving a full power of attorney from her? Now he was gone, and had put everything in his name and put all of us at his mercy, and at a time when I wondered whether he was entering his second childhood. The old codger had taken to making grabs for our maids' behinds whenever they passed him. At least that was what my new maid told me, and I had no reason to doubt her since I'd hired her myself from Mahalla Marhoum.

Then, all of a sudden, his trips to England stopped. The last time he returned, he looked totally broken and defeated. But would he talk about it? No. For a year and a half, he wouldn't budge from the house except to go up to the farm for a day or two. He wouldn't even take Fahim with him on those trips anymore like he used to. At home, he just stared into space most of the time. It was almost as if he'd given up on life altogether. At Sheikh Bahrawi's advice, I engaged a famous law firm in Britain to have them find out what Abbas got up to over there. The sheikh used that firm himself, and he gave them a good recommendation for me. The recommendation didn't help lower the fees, though. They cost the earth, but they gave me a piece of information that was worth every piaster, even if it hit like a punch in the belly. That was when I decided I had to get rid of him, because otherwise our money would slip through his fingers to some stranger.

Imagine! Pulling such a dirty trick at his age. He goes and marries some nurse and has a child with her. A son, no less! I swear, Abbas, if you think you're going to give him any of our money, you're dreaming. I swear on my mother's grave, I won't let half a piaster get away from us.

If only I could have him declared legally incompetent. My lawyer here in Egypt told me I'd have to prove he was a doddering idiot. I could prove he was a stingy miser, but not an idiot. I turned to Fahim, but that goddamned brother-in-law refused to help, even on the sly. I'd been generous with him, but he remained as loyal as a dog to his master, who fed him more and had been the first to take him in.

So I decided to take Abbas unawares and confront him. I thought I'd throw him off balance and make him quake like I did every time I threatened him. This time his face turned as hard and gray as stone. He gave me that steely look that bored deep into my eyes and made me tremble like I used to forty years ago. He didn't say a word. He didn't even twitch a muscle in his face. He just turned himself around in the wheelchair he sat in most of the time and rolled off, leaving me more afraid than I'd felt in a long time. After standing stunned for a second, I shouted at his receding back, "I'm going take what's mine and Nadia's! Starting tomorrow!"

He didn't look back. Then I realized how violently my knees were shaking.

I had no choice but to put my hope in fate, and I prayed for it to ease the burdens on my heart and end Abbas's time here on earth swiftly Unfortunately, fate decided to go for me instead, after prying into my thoughts. I was so absorbed in them that night that I slipped and fell down the stairs and broke my leg. After some weeks confined to my bed, all the ailments that come with old age began to assail me and restrict my movements. The villa's garden was the farthest I could go. Soon my health declined further, until I found my world confined to the four walls of my bedroom.

Meanwhile, fate conspired with Abbas. It gave him back some health and allowed him to keep all his senses, despite his advanced years. So he could still plan and plot from his wheelchair. But I still had one card up my sleeve: my new maid from the village, who never left my side and did everything I said. There was one last stop on the Abbas train. We'd reach it some weeks from now. Then I'd part ways with him forever.

23

"ALL ISLAMIST GROUPS ARE STRINGS on the same guitar, strumming variations of the same theme."—Tarek al-Masri

After making sure the door was tightly shut, I muttered, "In the name of God the Just and Merciful, there is no might or power but unto God," and switched on the bare lightbulb dangling from the ceiling. I listened to the dogs barking in the distance, the sound of running feet and indistinct curses, and objects being struck by flying stones, the last an empty garbage bin. Some intermittent howls approached, then segued into rhythmic barks. I stood staring at the wooden table in front of me as I waited for the alley to quiet down. After the sounds of the dogs faded, I set to work.

I made a quick inventory of the items I'd asked them to fetch. They were all there. After lighting the small spirit lamp, I crushed twenty aspirin pills in a mortar and pestle and put some of the powder in a glass vial. Then I added a teaspoon of water, swilled the liquid around to mix it, added half a cup of alcohol, set the vial on top of the gas flame, and brought the mixture to a boil while stirring. The heat licked my face. My hand trembled slightly as I carefully added some more aspirin powder, bit by bit. I wiped the sweat off my forehead and cast about right and left until I found the tablespoon, which I used to add the ammonium nitrate. The liquid gradually turned from pale yellow to red. I lowered the heat until the color returned to orange. I glanced at my watch. The blast from a nearby speaker sounding the call to prayer nearly ruptured my eardrums. I could feel pearls of sweat forming on my forehead again. I took the vial off the flame, let the mixture cool, and poured it into another a container, which I'd covered with filter paper. I poured the orange granules that had collected on the paper into a strainer and washed them under cold water. Then I dried them by brushing them with the hot gusts of a hair dryer.

I jumped at the sound of a single knock on the door. The emir walked in, followed by three of his acolytes. His eyes shifted back and forth between the orange grains and my face.

"It's ready," I said. "All I have to do is add the gunpowder and nails, and adjust the timer mechanism."

The sheikh broke into a bright smile. Then his face snapped back to serious. Pushing me aside, he signaled to one of the acolytes to take my place. "Finish it up," he told him. To me he said, "The next time you do this, make sure Hamza here is with you so he can watch and learn. 'The best among you are those who transmit their knowledge to the people.'"

A couple of years ago I would have objected, but not anymore. They're a bunch of semi-educated morons, unable to learn a thing. They'll try to make one on their own, botch it, and come back to me because they needed my expertise. I'm the only one who knows how to manufacture these highly explosive and incendiary pellets. They're called milenite and they're used to make fire bombs. They're one of the favors for which I am indebted to Abu Ayman, who taught me the process. I left the room flicking my prayer beads. One of the acolytes invited me to perform ablutions. I tapped my chest twice, signaling that I'd already done mine.

Our assignment, this time, was to plant the bomb directly in front of the main door of the Cairo Security Directorate, but we knew from our surveillance work that this would be impossible because it was so heavily guarded and because there were dozens of plainclothesmen mingling with pedestrians in the vicinity. When Hamza finished assembling the bomb, I proposed an alternative plan and watched their eyes pop out of their sockets in admiration.

They carried out my suggestion to the letter. We attached the bomb to an old stolen car, after changing its license plates. Hamza drove it to the Islamic Art Museum directly opposite the Security Directorate, parked it, and left. The rest of the plan depended on the Interior Ministry, because they would be the ones who would move the bomb into the interior of the building. From our surveillance work, I'd learned that there was a small garage behind the building. It belonged to the traffic authority. It was where they towed cars for violating parking regulations and where they kept them until the owners paid the required fines. As I'd anticipated, the tow truck came rumbling along after about a quarter of an hour, lifted the front end of the car, and towed it toward the garage. But Thanks to Hamza's ineptness—he'd miscalculated the ratio of gunpowder and nails to the milenite pellets—the explosion didn't cause anywhere near the impact it should have. The radius was relatively small, and instead of hitting the building its force was directed outward, toward the street in front of the garage entrance. So no one was killed, only a few cars were burned, and a few dozen police and security soldiers were injured from glass shards or burns. But to every cloud there's a silver lining: this incident gave me a great inspiration.

Hamza and companions returned with their tails between their legs to receive a dressing down from their emir. "God decreed and so it came to pass," they pleaded. "They strive for nought but to rely on others," I put in, alluding to scripture. The emir was forced to take my side, even though he despised the ground I walked on. Taking advantage of the situation, I insisted that from now on I had to work alone, in the manufacturing process as well as in the reconnaissance work and surveillance of the target. They agreed to the first condition, but not to the second and third. It wasn't that I really minded their presence during stakeouts. I was waiting for the right moment to make my bolt for freedom and turn them in, though I still hadn't worked out exactly how I was going to do that.

"It's Maison Thomas on 26 July Street this week," the emir said as he handed me a white slip of paper with the assignment. I didn't need it. I was very familiar with the address and I had plenty of memories from there. I felt a spasm in my chest as I burnt the paper.

I parked my motorcycle some distance away, crossed 26 July, and went the rest of the way on foot. I was now on my third recon trip, but the first in daytime, just in case they decided to change the time of execution at the last minute, as they often did. I walked past Maison Thomas, on the opposite side of the street, then turned around making as though I'd forgotten something, and passed it again. I stopped at a nearby newspaper kiosk and examined the used books as though searching for a particular title. Then I bought an *Al-Ahram* newspaper and stood scanning its pages casually while keeping my eyes on the storefront. I watched the comings and goings, the activities around the customers' sections, the staff performing their various tasks behind the granite counter. I switched positions, choosing another newsstand across the street, in order to observe the place from a different angle. Suddenly I heard a voice behind me.

"Tarek? Tarek al-Masri? I can't believe it!"

I didn't flinch. I'd learned how to check my reactions long ago. I now went by the nickname "Abu Ayman," owner of a small perfume and herb store in Bulaq al-Dakrur. On my national ID card I was Amgad Radi. Who the hell here knew my real name?

I continued to examine the titles of used books, but all my senses were on the alert and I instinctively felt for the bayonet

I had hidden beneath my *gallabiya*. Then it hit me, because this was a voice I could never forget or mistake for another. Her footsteps approached lightly from my left. Her face rounded the corner of my eye and then appeared in full in front of me, inspecting my face with wide eyes.

"Tarek? What are you doing here? What are these clothes you're wearing?"

It was so hard not to soften even a little in front of Nadia's exquisite face. It was impossible to keep my heart from beating louder, my breathing from growing more rapid, and my tongue from knotting up. As I stared at her, I caught myself wondering whether I could penetrate that mysterious gaze, "pierce it like a hymen," before admonishing my errant mind. I cautioned myself not to yield to bodily lusts and mouthed "God keep me from Satan" three times, plus a short prayer to steady my nerves. Then I gave her a calm smile. She extended her hand to shake mine. Almost automatically, I avoided the flesh of her palm and took hold of her elbow. I shifted her to my right and steered her away from Maison Thomas. I felt a twinge of anger at myself for not shaking her hand.

"This is where we used to meet when we were young," she said. "Do you remember?"

I nodded. As we walked, her eyes remained fixed on my beard and my *gallabiya* as though she were observing some alien being. Before she could pepper me with the usual questions I got from people after my return to Egypt, I told her that my financial circumstances were awkward these days. I went on about how fate had turned its back on me, how I'd lost my job and now made do with some administrative work at the Islamic Sciences Society in Imbaba.

"But why are you dressed like some imam in a mosque?"

I barely managed to keep myself from laughing out loud. She was always a tenacious one. As we turned right, onto Hassan Sabri Street, I leaned toward her ear and lowered my voice. "The police are after me, so I had to take on a disguise.

Anyway, this is proper religious attire, according to the Sunna of the Prophet—"

"May peace be upon him," she muttered, but I could tell she wasn't satisfied. Her pace slowed as she took hold of my arm. "Let's go someplace where we can sit down for a bit, have a cup of tea, and talk."

"I can't," I said lowering my voice again. "I'm being watched."

Her eyes widened in alarm, which suddenly aroused a sexual urge in me. I nearly wished she would reject my excuse, but after a moment of wavering, I asked her why she hadn't taken the veil. I was sure that would put her off. Instead, she caught me off guard. "I'm glad you haven't given up on the violin despite your circumstances."

"Violin? No. No. That was a long time—"

"Why are you doing this, Tarek? I see the bow beneath your clothes."

I was struck dumb. I instinctively readjusted the bayonet tied to my thigh, as I gave her a silly smile and I took a couple of steps back. I had to end this meeting, which had needlessly dredged up so many memories from the past. I could tell something in her mind clicked, but that didn't keep her from asking with great concern why the police were after me. I concocted some story about debts I owed and sentences passed against me for paying with bad checks. Then, for no reason at all, I repeated the bit about how I was forced to disguise myself. For a moment I thought her mind had wandered and that she wasn't listening to a word I said. It turned out she'd been listening to my innermost thoughts.

She smiled, making her face appear more radiant and youthful than her forty years, and said, "I'm divorced again, for the second time. Such is life!"

I said nothing, though my face must have lit up brighter than it had in years. Since I would never have the chance to sign my name next to hers on her third marriage certificate,

I barricaded myself behind silence. I always felt inferior in her presence. Once, many years ago, I'd confessed my love to her. Her silence had been enough for me to realize she didn't feel the same toward me, so I chose the safest path. Then she left me and married my executioner. How could I ever forgive that? Now she told me she'd gotten a second divorce from him, meaning that she had returned to him even after knowing how he treated me—surely he would have bragged about it. It was funny how I desired her now, despite this sudden surge of hatred toward her. She was always was so proud and arrogant. Now, after losing everything, she wanted me. She thought that her smile could erase her sins and make me forget everything that happened to me because of her. That'd be the day.

She pulled out a piece of paper and pen from her purse, wrote down a number, and handed it to me.

"This is the number of my private phone. In my room. No one answers it but me. Give me a call when you can. I'd love to hear from you, Tarek. And if you need anything at all. . . ."

I hesitated for a moment. Then I took the piece of paper between thumb and forefinger and plucked a phone number out of my head to give to her. I waved goodbye as I hailed the first taxi that swung around the corner. "Cairo University." I told the driver in a loud voice as I climbed in, so as not to give her a clue where I lived. As we drove off, I swung around in my seat to watch her through the rear window. She was standing at the corner, writing down the number I'd given her in a small red notebook. She still had that puzzled look on her face.

"Who was that veilless woman who made you abandon your post?"

My emir sounded nothing like the "brother in Islam" they jabbered about 24/7, and much like an interrogator in State Security. I ignored the question as I focused on the food I was preparing in the room I shared with two other guys from our cell. They'd accompanied me on the stakeouts of Maison

Thomas, which the organization had targeted because it sold booze and pork. The emir stepped closer and repeated the question, but in a less aggressive tone.

"Her name's Nadia. She was a classmate at the university. Now she gives private piano lessons."

As long as they were spying on me, I thought, it would be better to give them something befitting Nadia as they would see her. So I made her a graduate of the Classical Music Conservatoire. With no prompting from me, they pegged her as an upper-class lady from Zamalek. When you looked at Nadia, twenty-two years after university, what else could she be other than the Nadia they thought they saw today?

"She handed you a piece of paper. What was on it?"

"Her phone number."

"Give it to me. And give me her full name and address."

"I tossed the piece of paper out the window and didn't commit it to memory. And I don't know her full name or where she lives. That was a phase in my life I don't want to remember, master."

"A Copt, huh?"

"No. Muslim." Preempting further questions, I said, "I'm fed up with your tailing me. I don't have to work with you. I came to you of my own free will when you needed me. I don't want to talk about this anymore."

The emir continued to eye me skeptically as the four of us sat down for a meal. As I ate, my mind wandered back to my meeting with her today. What did she feel when she saw me? Did she hate me? Had she missed me? Why couldn't I take a single step toward her when I met her? Why did I always back off, or, at best, remain rooted in place? What had I become? Such a heavy question. I'd always tried to avoid it. I was over forty, and what had I achieved? Nothing.

The answer was heavier than the question. It was horrifying and deeply depressing. I looked up and my eyes met the emir's. I could tell he hadn't lifted his eyes from me from the moment we sat down to eat. I took the offensive to parry the suspicion that oozed from those shiny eyeballs.

"Why don't you trust me? Why don't you give me a gun like the others? The bayonet almost slipped off today. I could have been—"

He held up his hand to silence me. He emitted a loud belch as he scanned the faces of the others, who never uttered a peep in his presence.

"You still have a ways to go till you reach the point where you can carry firearms. Dedication and obedience are the keys to earning trust. You haven't given us anything to make us trust you like the others. You're still being tested."

I left the table angrily. They still treated me like an outsider. Their suspicions were like the floodlights in the prison court-yard that hold every speck of dust in their glare. There was no safe escape. God damn them all! I never liked them and I never trusted them. Now all I wanted was to protect myself from them. That had become my sole ambition. How sad.

The emir sounded the call to prayer. We fell in behind one of his favorites who led it. When we finished, the emir said, "Remain among the 'restrainers of anger,' Abu Ayman. 'Allah sides with the patient ones.' If you want to leave us, you're free to do so, but only after the Maison Thomas oper-ation, God willing."

Apart from an exasperated sigh, I remained silent. After my release from prison in the mid-seventies, my economic circumstances went from bad to worse. I couldn't get a pub-lic-sector job because of my record as a political criminal. So I took whatever jobs I could find, but they never lasted long. Each time I thought the worst was over, I found the world closing in on me more and more, until I felt I was about to suffocate. After leaving the Muslim Brothers, I joined the Nas-serists in the hope this would land me a decent job and give me some upward mobility. It was the same reason I'd joined the Muslim Brothers to begin with, though that had only landed me in prison. The types of torture I suffered inside convinced me that even if I were damned to Hell for killing an innocent soul, my punishers down there would be more merciful than my torturers up here on earth.

The leftists welcomed me with open arms. They painted a beautiful picture of their utopia and of themselves as a noble vanguard in a society floundering between the wall of illiteracy and the bliss of ignorance. Sadat didn't put up with them for long. A few months after I joined them, he set the police on us. In order to shield myself from prison, I turned informant and tipped off the police to the identities of the Nasserists I knew and their meeting places.

I returned to the Muslim Brothers when it became clear that the government had not only accepted but embraced them. I was scared at first, but the Brothers welcomed me back to the fold as if I were a prodigal son come to his senses. They assigned me to the "guidance and steering" branch. That was where I acquired my formal introduction to their recruiting methods and realized they'd performed the same routine on me when I was a student. It was more intricate than I'd imagined at first. It began with a scout on campus. He'd be on the lookout for introverted, dejected types, short of money and short of friends. Such traits were like recommendation letters. They would accelerate a candidate's recruitment. Then came the screener. His task was to develop a closer familiarity with the candidates in order to select the most suitable. He was on the lookout for the qualities of obedience and loyalty, above all. Those who passed this sifting process were taken to the "educator," the "master," the "family officer," and so on in the endless chain.

I recoiled into my shell when Nadia's friends at university mocked me. One of them dubbed me "the crooner" when he learned that I loved music and played an instrument. A guy my age with a friendly face came up to me one day on campus while I was alone and brooding. He said he knew me from somewhere. I swallowed the bait easily. Bit by bit, he drew me out as we roamed the streets near Cairo University until he really did know me. By late afternoon, we'd reached the Bein al-Sarayat area. The call to prayer sounded, so we prayed together in a nearby mosque. Afterward, I realized that I didn't even know his name.

We met again a couple of days later. He introduced me to friends of his who were students in the Faculty of Engineering. We spent a lot of time together over the following days, taking walks, sitting in coffeehouses, just hanging out and talking. They'd bring up some subject, put some questions to me, and tell me how awesome my ideas were. Little did I know that I was a lamb being fattened for the slaughter. They let me loose to frolic in the pastures of praise and attention, and the next thing I knew I had one hand on the Quran and the other on a gun as I swore eternal allegiance to our Supreme Guide.

Most radical groups are interchangeable once you look beyond their names. Except for the lefties. What most pisses me off about them is that wide fake smile of theirs when they speak to you. True, they say we Muslim Brothers have a greasy smile when we speak, but leftists are still different. They're fussy. They won't associate with just anyone. You have to support culture and freedom of opinion. These are the passports into their society, after which everything is negotiable. At least they don't have the Muslim Brothers' lethal flaw: the Brotherhood sticks its nose into every aspect of your life. Every day, it takes a broom into the nooks and crannies of your brain to sweep out the dust of ideas that belong to others.

I struggled for years against a relentless world. My financial situation grew worse and worse. I became like a stray dog: finding a meal in a garbage can one day, being pelted with stones by pedestrians the next just for getting too close to them on the pavement. The government at the time was encouraging young men to fly off to Afghanistan and Pakistan to fight the jihad against the Soviet Union. It selected some, then looked the other way as they slipped across the borders to those destinations. Abbas Mahalawi came to mind as someone who could assist me. His picture was in all the papers. He was the "strongman" in the National Democratic Party. Surely he could help me in some way—maybe give me a favorable mention in the quarters that counted. I was reluctant at first, but as every other alternative evaporated I felt I had no other choice. By some miracle, I managed to convince them to allow me into the NDP building on the corniche next to the Hilton. They wouldn't allow me to use the elevator so I had to climb seven floors on foot. Sweating and gasping for breath, I told his office manager I wanted to see "Abbas Pasha." The guy stared down a nose wrinkled in disgust. Pointing to the door, he said, "Go to the end of the hall. Health and social services are on the right."

I told him that I wasn't ill and didn't need health services. I was there to meet Abbas Pasha. He ignored me for over an hour, occupying himself with this and that. When boredom nearly drove me over the edge, I wrote down my name in full on a slip of paper, went up to the office manager's desk, lowered my voice, and said, "Tell the pasha that Tarek, the nephew of his brother Hassanein, is here."

I returned to my place and sat down again, confidently placing one leg over the other. The plan worked. Holding the slip of paper I'd given him, the office manager entered Abbas's office and stayed in there a long time. Finally, he reappeared with a bright smile on his face. I stood up, ready to be taken into the office of Abbas Mahalawi. Instead, the office manager took hold of my elbow and escorted me to the door. He stuffed an envelope into my pocket and said, "The pasha says take this hundred pounds to see you through and never show your face here again."

So back I went to the Muslim Brotherhood and resumed my routine in "Guidance and Steering." My sole wish now was to go to Pakistan. And why not? There were so many stories going around about young men who went off to fight the jihad and earned tons of money without dying. That dream seemed within reach: flying off to wage some jihad. I'd fight in the ranks of those crazies for as long as I could bear it; then I'd grab my pay and fly to Europe, where I'd open a restaurant, with musicians entertaining diners every night.

I confided my dream to an official in my branch. He gave me the standard sticky smile and referred me to the next higher up, who told me my idea was the work of the devil, who had blinded me until the whole world turned black before my eyes. Within a few weeks, thanks to their help, I was on a plane to the Arabian Peninsula. I found work as a salesman and an accountant in an herb and spice shop. There was no music here. It was probably taboo, which made no difference, because sorrow and pain had drummed that special part of me out of my mind.

While in Riyadh, the Brothers introduced me to a guy called Abu Ayman, whose nom de guerre I'd eventually adopt. He was the one who persuaded me to join his organization, al-Gamaa al-Islamiya. What did I have to lose? Unlike all the others, he promised me houris and rivers of gold and silver in this world, not just in the hereafter. So I stuck with him. After a few months, we left the arid paradise of Riyadh for a wretched Yemeni hell, where I was assigned to the Gamaa's training camp in the desert. Compared to that torment, the lapping flames of the Muslim Brotherhood back home were like balsam on both body and mind. I tried to get out of it, but that was not an option. The threat in their voice was palpable. I knew without being told that no one left there without their permission, except in a coffin. I took extra care to watch my back.

Eventually I grew accustomed to the routine in the Qadisiya camp. It was round-the-clock military and moral training. The latter involved memorizing the Quran, studying prescribed interpretations of Prophetic Hadith, and listening to countless histories of the Companions of the Prophet and the deeds they performed to spread the power and glory of Islam. Every other day, we received a lecture on how to strengthen resolve and build fortitude.

I saw myself staring into space on that endless expanse of sand. To my right, an elderly camel with half-closed eyes munched on some wild grasses as though intent on sucking every last bit of juice out of them. He was so meek and patient. If I had his patience, I'd be riding him around the desert for the next twenty years, while the rest of the world sped toward the twenty-first century. I heaved a sigh. I hated the desert and everything to do with it. I spent three lean years there. My beard grew down to my belly button; my face withered beyond recognition. I'd become a stranger to myself.

Once again, that heavy question assailed me: what have you achieved, Tarek? I couldn't bring myself to admit that the sum total was a big fat zero, like the rear end of the emir who had his back turned to me now while talking on the phone in a low voice. All I wanted was to return to myself. But I couldn't. Time and change had followed me down my circuitous path, erasing the traces that would guide me back. Every group I joined believed it was the most righteous, the most worthy of allegiance, the rightful heir to the caliphate. I no longer cared how right or wrong they were. I just wanted money. I wanted enough to cushion me against misfortune. I wanted to be able to live in peace, but these people were not the sort who simply wave goodbye and let you move on. They'd kill me if they even suspected me of planning to take the exit ramp. Al-Gamaa al-Islamiya gave me a place to live and some money after I lost all my savings during an American strike against our camp. Everything was burnt to a crisp: money, arms, munitions, people. Abu Ayman died in a huge explosion. My tutor in the manufacture of firebombs, time bombs that you set using washing machine timers, nail bombs, and other IEDs was blown to bits, like he'd done to others dozens of times. I managed to survive, carrying with me the expertise I'd acquired from him. I was picked up by another member of the organization, who came across me roaming the streets of Sanaa. Instead of sending me to a safe house, he invited me to stay in his home for a while. When he learned of the knowledge I'd stored in my head, his eyes lit up as though he'd just struck gold. He sent me back to Cairo to meet the emir of al-Gamaa al-Islamiya in Giza and I became his follower, even though he was at least two years younger than me.

"You're never satisfied," the emir said, interrupting my thoughts. Giving me a haughty look, he repeated it again to make sure all his acolytes were paying close attention. He listed the many favors he had performed for me and the gifts of money I'd received from him and the group.

I responded in the same arrogant tone. "I am the best bomb maker in the country. I have a right to—"

"You have no rights!" he shouted. "You are a part of a group. You have the same rights and duties as everyone else. If you don't fall in line, you're out. You have one day to come to your senses. After that, you'll have no one to blame but yourself!"

After the emir left, the others went to sleep early as usual. Like a dog with its tail between its legs, I crept into a corner and lay down on my side, placing one hand beneath my cheek, leaving the other free to pick my nose and wipe the snot on my *gallabiya*. My thoughts returned again to that question that haunted me like my shadow. My whole life and all my ambitions had been reduced to my meals and mattress in this suffocating room. I'd become like an animal in a pen that only thought of two things: food and sleep. I didn't even have Uncle Salem to return to. He was the one who'd reported me to the police in order to keep them from finding out about his gambling den. According to my mother, he was just like my father. The Muslim Brothers said he'd erred and should be guided back to the right path. Al-Gamaa al-Islamiya said he was a heretic and should be killed. I simply hated him and wished him dead, along with many others. But they didn't die. If I killed the people who persecuted and oppressed me, society would damn me as a terrorist. If those tyrants continued to rule us, hundreds of terrorists would rise around us with every passing day.

I should have stayed with the leftists. If only I hadn't betrayed them. At least they were peace loving. I could probably have found some administrative job with a cultural newspaper or with one of their political parties and stayed below the government's radar. Here, with the champions of "Islam is the solution," I couldn't even find a solution to my simplest problems. I took out my wallet and extracted the slip of paper Nadia had given me. I spread it open and read the number a few times to commit it to memory. Then I burned the paper and smiled in the light of the small flame. The smile remained incomplete.

24

"PEOPLE IN THE SHADOWS WALLOWING in their ill-gotten gains: they're the perfect customers for a man like me whose wealth is others' secrets."—Murad Kashef

I relaxed in my seat while the host described my political and military career to TV audiences, as she did every week. I kept a restrained, dignified, yet confident smile on my face. Most of her account was fiction, but people believed and liked it, even though my true story was more powerful. People love those who deceive them. Even the "major general" she used to address me was an exaggeration. I was a brigadier general when I left the service. So many other faces had resurfaced from the past and now peered at people through their television screens. Why shouldn't I stake a place for myself in that window so that people could see me too? After my return to Egypt, I learned not only how to play by the rules of the game, but how to bend them in my favor. True, I wasn't an independent player and I didn't make the decisions anymore, but I raked in money from the game that involved excavations into ancient files and ledgers. And there were so, so many of them.

I reiterated my fictions in my interviews. I departed from the script sometimes, but they liked my delivery. I'd written legends in the CVs I gave to show hosts, and I'd had journalists write lengthy articles about me in exchange for generous fees willingly covered by my current bosses. They appreciated the value of manufacturing a solid past to back me up if I was to serve as a bogeyman or make my weekly television appearances as security expert-cum-strategic analyst-cum-veteran politician, as they chose to remake me when I returned to life in Egypt. I was controlled by others now. I didn't have the right to choose my own path, or else I'd lose everything they gave me in the blink of an eye. Yet I was lucky. If they hadn't taken me in, I'd have been living the rest of my days alone in my apartment, begging for handouts. On the other hand, if I'd thought of striking out on my own, outside their umbrella, I'd have met my maker in a freak traffic accident or by involuntary suicide.

Thanks to their intervention, I received a full pardon from the sentence that had been handed down against me in absentia. Now I was the deputy chairman of a political party. True, it was a political party that few had heard of and whose members could be counted on a single hand. It was still official, and it was my passport to appearing on Channel One and writing a daily column for *al-Jumhuriya* newspaper called "Mr. Citizen."

I hailed a taxi. "Zamalek," I told the driver as I settled into the seat.

I gave him directions to my new address at the end of Abul-Feda Street at the northern tip of the island, where I'd rented a tiny ground-floor apartment. To think that I'd once lived in the Lebon, the grandest residence in the whole of Zamalek. Oh, to be middle-aged and over the hill! Visions from the past flashed before me unbidden, just to make me more depressed. As we passed the Revolutionary Command building near the Gezira Club, I recalled the military tribunal I was brought before shortly before I fled the country. Every detail was as clear as though it had happened yesterday: the suit worn by the former chief of intelligence, General Salah Nasr. The somber tie he never changed. His insistence on polishing his shoes to a gleam so they'd shine behind the brass rail of the defendant's box. The rail was low enough for the presiding judge to see our faces clearly even when we were seated. My ears still buzzed with the whispered pleas of Salah Nasr and his aide Brigadier Hassan to retract my confessions. "It's just a storm in a teacup," they said. I almost laughed out loud right there in the courtroom. They didn't have a clue that they were the biggest sacrificial sheep in history since the one slaughtered by the Prophet Ibrahim. I also lost my temper with them once: "Yes, the field marshal's dead. But life goes on even if it's sick, broken, and beaten."

As we swung through the roundabout, the faces of my former supervisors flickered before my eyes. I paused at the image of Shams Badran and recalled his last words to me before I fled to London. Some days after my arrest he sent me a lawyer with the message, conveyed orally: "Confess a little and you'll gain a lot. Only Salah's head is going to fly."

I did confess, thinking they now saw me as a witness for the state, but then the former defense minister sent me a second message—typewritten this time—saying, "When you see its teeth, don't think the wolf is smiling. Be careful! Sincerely, Shams."

To my surprise, it was Abbas Mahalawi who offered to get me a travel permit. I'd asked Badran to arrange to take me with him, but he left me in the lurch. I have no idea how Abbas got the permit, but he smiled when he handed it to me together with a special passport. I soon understood why. I was to divorce Nadia. I signed a twenty-thousand-pound check, handed it to him with one hand, and took the exit papers with the other. Once in England, I handed him the divorce papers and took the check back. It was a win-win battle. The only loser was Nagwa. I divorced her a month after Abdel-Hakim's suicide. I was afraid of the scandal if news of that marriage came out, and was worried that it would be used against me after everybody turned against us. It was a pity, because at the time she was pregnant with my only son. At least I'd done right by him. I managed to get him enrolled in the Military Academy. He was going to graduate in a couple of years. I was living my youth again through him. It was beautiful to see history repeat itself after fifty years.

I met my former boss, the ex-defense minister, in London. In fact, I lived with him for several months. That was as long as we could stand each other. When I reproached him for abandoning me in Egypt, he invented some feeble excuses. He continued to treat me like I was his underling even though, at the time, I was his partner in a small grocery story we opened on the outskirts of London. I'd learned that he had managed to smuggle out a lot of important documents and records on some senior officials. After weeks of snooping around the house, I discovered the hiding place. I stole them before parting ways with him for good. I knew he'd never report me. Thieves don't go to the police when their stolen goods are stolen. Anyway, he'd lost all his teeth and claws. He was now a tame old goat whose only concern was to have a pasture to eat and sleep in every day.

I don't like talking about my life in exile. After my return from London in the mid-1980s, empty-handed, my savings nearly depleted, I did the rounds of old-time friends and acquaintances: former officials, pensioned-off generals, and the like. I wasn't entirely without resources. I had a weapon that was hard to argue or haggle with: ancient records and documents revealing those people's origins and how they made their wealth. One day, I received a phone call. That led to a meeting with an important official who told me that certain people were keen to meet me. They'd been keeping tabs on Badran and found out I'd stolen the documents he'd smuggled out. The official's functions reminded me of the powers I used to have in the sixties. Titles had changed, but that was all. And why should I care? What mattered to me now was money and getting my old life back.

A couple of days later, a large black car drew up below my balcony, which was close enough to the ground that I could make out the men inside. I went out, climbed into the back seat, and off we set off toward eastern Cairo. We arrived at the building I remembered so well. It always seemed deserted when you entered it, but if you pushed open any of the closed doors, you'd find a hive of activity on the other side. Behind one of those doors, I was given a friendly welcome that conveyed an undercurrent of menace. I detected it easily, having packaged messages that way myself in my day. I'd actually expected a worse reception. I'd also already decided to agree to whatever conditions they set. So, after hearing their generous offer, I accepted it immediately.

They had not forgotten my services to the country, and now it was time to put the past behind us, they said. The presidential pardon, revoking the prison sentence that had been handed down to me in absentia, was a down payment on the great bond of trust established between us that day. My instructions were clear: keep a safe distance from those still in the seats of power. Don't mess with them. At least not until their turn came, which was not for me to decide. It did not have to be spelled out that, if I made a wrong move, my employers could silence me instantaneously and bury me alive, together with my secret documents and tapes.

When asked to explain my "technique" with personalities who were no longer in the public eye and who now wallowed in their illicit fortunes, I said that such people were perfect customers for a man such as myself, whose wealth was secrets. I would wangle an introduction to a target, work my way closer to him, then whisper a well-chosen word or two in his ear to terrify him out of his wits. Some time later, I would send him an envelope containing some of the dirt I had on him. It could be all the information I had, but he would have no way of knowing that. He'd always suspect that I had more. I made a mint this way. Sometimes I'd even partner up with a former target to use the same technique against others who threatened him or stood in his way. Everything in Egypt had a price.

My new bosses gave me the green light to continue my game. What did they want in return? I asked.

"Nothing. Except from now on we're the ones who are going to choose your customers."

That was fine by me. Under the new rules of the game, I was merely the cat's-paw in their games with others. What did I care, as long as I could make money? That was my right after the long years of drought, jobless and on the run in London from a ten-year prison sentence in connection with a case of "the deviation of duty within the intelligence agency." In those days, the vile Abbas Mahalawi was on his way up again, this time in the NDP. It was probably his third ascent in his sparkling career. On his way up, the bastard acquired a reach long enough to get to me in London and keep me out of work and housebound. I'd thought we'd settled our scores when I divorced Nadia, but he obviously wanted me out of the way for good. But now I was back. His wings needed some trimming first: his turn had come in my game of secrets excavated from a buried past.

As much as I enjoyed this scheme that I was now pursuing for others, I never forgot Abbas Mahalawi. I'd been keeping tabs on him for the past four years. Recently, I'd learned that they had dispensed with his services, along with other members of the NDP's old guard. Obviously they were clearing the way for the party's new secretary-general and his younger coterie. But some of those old-timers had roots that had sprawled widely and deeply into the Egyptian soil over the last couple of decades. They'd amassed untold fortunes, making them the de facto rulers of Egypt. However, the winds had clearly shifted. I asked my new employers if I could have Abbas Mahalawi as a "customer" now that he'd been promoted into the shadows. They greeted my request with indifference mixed with an element of surprise, as though shocked at my desire to flagellate a dead man. How could they know I'd been waiting for this moment for ages? I knew for certain that the Mahalawis' combined worth was in the hundreds of millions. I wasn't going to let them wallow in it alone. I was going to get my share, and I didn't have the slightest doubt I could. I could probably get it all with the documents I had. Nadia would be my key. She would hate herself if she knew the truth about her family, while Abbas and Zeinab would lay their fortunes at my feet to keep that truth from passing beyond my lips.

"Where to in Zamalek, sir?"

The taxi driver's question pulled me out of my reverie. I looked out of the window to get my bearings and said, "Take the next right and drop me off at the Heart of Palm."

25

"I HADN'T LOST MY MIND yet, even as I stood, devil-may-care, at the brink of madness."—Tarek al-Masri

We finished Friday prayers at Amr Ibn al-Aas in Old Cairo. Exiting the mosque among a crowd as thick as the congregation on the Day of Judgment, I pushed ahead of the others in my organization as though I had nothing to do with them. As I bent over to tie my shoes, the emir leaned to my ear while putting on his own shoes. "Get rid of your beard. Keep your mustache and keep your hair long."

I gave an imperceptible nod. He left in the direction of the Citadel with his acolytes in tow. I hoofed it toward Giza, crossing Abbas Bridge into the hubbub of pedestrians and itinerant vendors of Giza Square. Adel Ramzi, my cellmate from prison all those years ago, suddenly leapt to mind. I could almost hear him making a racket like that on his own, belting out some lyrics while strumming an electric guitar. He got out a year before I did. I'd bumped into him three times since my release, in different circumstances each time, and he never lost that special spark of his. Shortly before I left to Saudi Arabia, he had found a job with a band at a nightclub on Pyramids Road. I hadn't seen him since my return.

I switched direction and headed over to his place in Zamalek. He lived in a ground-floor apartment at the northern end of Bahgat Ali Street, close to my father's apartment, which my uncle Salem had taken over. What made me want to visit Adel now? Was it really because his father was a barber or was it so I could pass by Nadia's house? Did my mind need to concoct some lame excuse to reassure my feet, which were driven by Nadia's sudden appearance in front of Maison Thomas? Maybe memories come back to us the way disasters hit us: when it rains it pours.

I got off the microbus at the beginning of 26 July Street, cut through a couple of back streets to Mohamed Mazhar, then turned left so I could pass in front of the Heart of Palm and check it out surreptitiously. This was actually the third time I'd cased the place, and each time I was torn by contradictory feelings I'd always avoided. I could feel them building up inside like a seething volcano about to burst through my ribs, especially when I thought of Murad Kashef going in and out of there every day. I hated that place and everyone inside—except for her. The longing made me slow my steps in front of her house, though I was sure she'd lied to me. She wasn't divorced. Or maybe they'd separated but he was still living in there, with her. I looked up toward her window hoping to catch sight of her, but all the windows were locked. The place looked deserted, lost in a deep slumber like the remains of an ancient city. I noticed that some boards were missing from the side of the small sentry box, which stood to the right of the gateway. That too appeared to have been unused for a long time. There was a barrel inside it pierced with random holes, betraying the rust that was corroding it from the inside. My steps grew leaden. My mind urged my feet forward, but my heart held them back.

As I neared Adel's place, I caught sight of him hailing a taxi. I recognized him instantly, despite the toll age had taken. Some part of me commanded my frozen feet to move. I ducked into the nearest building entrance and cowered in the shadow, heart racing. Suddenly, in that darkness, my blood ran cold and I had a violent urge to pee. Maybe I even wet myself a bit. Murad Kashef was watching me.

I crouched down and recited a stream of supplications and incantations to calm myself. It took me half an hour to summon the courage to venture out again. My knees still trembled as I walked the rest of the way to Adel's place. I was totally drained by the time I got there. His father's barbershop occupied the left side of the ground floor of the building. It had a new sign: a large pair of scissors, a black silhouette of a man's head, and the words "Ramzi's Salon for Men." I crossed the street toward the shop, then switched directions in order to enter the building itself. I rang the doorbell. I could hear slow, shuffling footsteps. Behind the panel of frosted glass in the door, I saw the fuzzy shape of a tall, skinny man with disheveled hair. The panel opened first; then the door swung open to a beaming face and a satirical "If it isn't Sheikh Tarek, the fiddler. It's been ages, comrade!"

I smiled from my heart for the first time since my return to Egypt. That surprised me. I'd thought my smile had died and that I only used my lips to curse and pray for the demise of those who set me on the path that I was now so desperate to leave behind.

Adel's spirit hadn't changed, but his body had. He was skeletal. In the three hours that we spent together in his "kif corner," as he called it, I could see why. After swallowing a few colored pills, he carefully freed a brown lump from a yellow piece of cellophane and set it to one side. A tiny dune of white powder had been given pride of place in the middle of the low table. He used the edge of a book of matches to carefully divide the powder and arrange it in thin lines. Then he unfolded the matchbook, rolled it into narrow tube, stuck one end in his nose, and inhaled the lines one by one. He closed his eyes and leaned his head back for a moment. Opening his eyes, he gave me a goofy smile. Then he turned his attention to rolling joints. These he chain-smoked until the room filled with a heavy cloud that clung to the air and alternately descended around us like a shroud or hovered overhead as though eavesdropping. Adel never opened the windows. He hadn't even left his house for about a year, he said. His musical instruments were distributed around the room. You could tell from the position of some of them or the way they gleamed, that they were the ones he played most often. Probably his old musician friends called in on him from time to time to relive the past and jam. Adel was a brilliant guitarist. He was also a mad composer of a new wave of music. However, the nightclub customers didn't like it, so he'd lost his job a year ago, he said.

"So, tell me, why are you running around like a dervish on the Mulid of Hussein? Have you gone back to your Muslim Brothers?" he asked, eyeing me from head to toe as though vetting me for a job. He reached for his rolling papers and started to roll himself another joint as eagerly as though it were his first.

I chuckled, but didn't answer. I was grooving to "Hotel California," which he'd just put on his record player. I closed my eyes and listened to the lyrics, patting my thigh to the rhythm, especially during the guitar riffs. When I opened my eyes, I found Adel watching me with a smile.

"Believe me, man, nature beats nurture," he said. "Leave those religious crazies and come hang out with us here. Take a couple of tokes. Listen to some decent music." He sucked on the joint, held his breath, and released a thick cloud. "Come on, man. You never fit in with those guys and they never liked or respected you. Soon we'll perform again for audiences who appreciate our music. I'm sure of it. This fad for the crap people listen to these days can't last. We can't go on like this much longer."

"And you? How can you go on like this?" I said, gesturing around me.

"And what made me pop into your head all of a sudden? It's been a decade since I last saw you."

I smiled and stroked my beard. "I was in Saudi Arabia, man. When I got back, I thought I'd drop in on your dad and get me a shave."

Adel roared with laughter and lit another cigarette. Then he stretched his hand toward a mini fridge that was just within reach, pulled out a bottle of beer, and opened it with his teeth.

"I don't have anything to offer you to drink here except cold water. Or, if you want, you can get up and make yourself a cup of tea with milk."

I didn't want. What I really liked about Adel was that, despite everything he'd been through, he held on to his "fuck you, world" attitude. Even in prison, he more than anyone else inside knew how to make himself at home between those four walls. Adel ended up in jail for a crime he didn't commit—like most of us. He probably wasn't very political at first, even if he leaned toward leftist views, but would have been able to cite communist dogma line and verse after all the time he spent with them inside. The difference between us and him was that he was never brought to trial and was never interrogated, not by intelligence or the prosecutor's office or even by military prison authorities.

For him, it was straight from home to hell. He was a prisoner without papers, alive but nonexistent. Pretty much like what he was now. His real crime was that he fell in love with a girl at the same time another guy did. Adel got engaged to her first, but the other guy had enough pull to end the engagement prematurely. He had Adel arrested and thrown into the clink, where he was forgotten for years. It was not until some Eid feast, or whatever season it was for a presidential amnesty, that someone remembered his name and he was released along with a bunch of ex-cons for "good conduct and behavior"— which was how he'd entered prison to begin with.

Ironically, the powerful man who had Adel disappeared soon grew bored with Adel's ex-fiancée and divorced her. When Adel asked her to marry him, she rebuffed him angrily, as though he'd dumped her instead of the other way around. Then she married someone else. Adel had told me this story before. At the time, he'd seemed stoic enough to grin and bear it, but now, as I looked at him, he seemed defeated. A boxer who'd been knocked flat one too many times, sprawled on the canvas, looking pleadingly at the referee to have mercy and sound the bell. He sat with his back propped against the wall, emaciated legs stretched out on the floor, shirtsleeves rolled halfway up his arms, revealing bluish veins zigzagging just below his skin like small garter snakes.

He opened an eye to a squint, like a wounded fox, weary of battle but determined to fight to the end. "You don't look right to me today," he said. "You have this mutinous look in your eye. Like you got the devil on your back."

I shrugged and yawned. My attention was caught by a large picture of a veiled woman hanging on the wall. "That's my mother. May the Lord have mercy on her soul," he said.

"Your mother? In a veil? You got to be putting me on. All of us in prison thought you were a Copt."

Adel laughed so hard his eyes watered. "You mean just because I never prayed together with you guys you were going to kick me out of my faith, you bunch of heathens?" He downed half a bottle of beer in one go and continued, "Okay, now that you know I'm Muslim, put in a good word for me with that organization of yours, man. Give me guidance, ye of the 'Islam is the solution' set. I can't believe the crap you've been scribbling all over the walls of the schools in Zamalek. You've totally messed with the kids' minds. Turning them off art and music. I mean, everything's a sin in your book."

I put up with a few more minutes of his sarcasm. When I'd had enough, I said, "You tell me this, Adel. How can you live like this?"

"Who said we're living? We're the living dead. We were slaughtered long ago and we've been running around without a head ever since. We're just pretending to be alive until we really do give up the ghost. The first one did this to us, the second one made us do this and that, and the third one is doing more than that. And we're never going to stop letting this and that happen to us."

"What the hell are you talking about?"

"You know, but you're playing dumb. It's your Muslim Brotherhood friends who called our current president the Wise One and the one before that the Faithful, because he wanted to win your friends over. The one before that we all hailed as the Leader, adored by millions. We're a religious people by nature. We love the Lord deeply—when we need Him. But we worship the Leader, the Faithful, and even the Wise One, and we'll never bring them to account for a thing they've done."

"Okay, you're right. We like to create idols. When we get fed up with them, we break them and make new ones. But I have nothing to do with all that."

"Hah! So you've struck out on your own now? Or are you playing dumb again?"

I wasn't going to let his sarcasm egg me on again. I stood up, swayed, and nearly fell over. Adel burst out laughing. "You got a secondhand high, man! That's proof of the high quality of my stuff."

I giggled for no reason. I went over to where his instruments were lying. A strange tingling inside me cast me back ages ago to when I used to meet Nadia in the back garden of the Heart of Palm. My hand reached out to touch an old oud, gently, as though it were her hand. I picked it up and ran my fingers along the strings as though stroking her hair. I strummed the opening bars then began to play Umm Kulthum's "Who can I turn to?" Adel started to hum along.

I stopped after the first refrain and set the oud aside. I looked at Adel, taking in his glassy eyes, then I went to the window, opened it and pulled over a chair, so as to be as far as possible from his smoke.

"Stop talking politics, and tell me why you're living this way without hope," I said. "Why are you fucking yourself up like this? You're better off than me and so many others. At least you've got your music and you can do what you want, or you can try to, and your father supports you, and he's doing okay. So what's with you?"

"Dig this, man, and don't be an ass. My father, you, me, everyone out there in the street . . . we're not living. We're just acting the part, like extras with a couple of lines to deliver. Very cheap extras, like the ones in rent-a-crowds. As for the ones who don't know how to act, their job is to pull up a chair, play spectator, and clap. Me, I'm a musical extra. I'm there to complete the set. But I say what's inside me. There's nothing wrong with that. I mean, sometimes people deviate from the script." He fell silent for a while. Then he exclaimed, as though answering a question no one had asked, "Yes! And we're all sick!"

"Sick?"

"Have you ever been to Qasr al-Aini Hospital?"

"Once, a long time ago, when I—"

"We're living in the Arab Republic of Qasr al-Aini!" he announced dramatically, then downed the rest of his beer. "Every now and then this guy in a white coat comes up to you and says, 'I know exactly what's ailing you and I'm going to treat you using my method.' So you get to be his guinea pig. He tests a bunch of the wrong medications on you and you get sicker, the pain grows worse, and you die. Others thank him and applaud. Until their turn comes. Every doctor is surrounded by a huge army of nurses, assistants, herbalists, charlatans, and snake charmers. Then there are the officials with all the rubber stamps to complete the picture and make you feel like you're a real hospital. But we die anyway. Do you know why this happens?" Before I could answer, he said, "Because the guy's not a doctor and he knows fuck all about medicine."

Not only did Adel and I fall silent, so too did the noises from outside. Maybe it was like Adel said: everyone was watching us, like statues, after learning their allotted role in life. But no one applauded for Adel Ramzi after he spoke. They would only applaud the self-acclaimed doctor. I had nothing to add. Like Adel, I'd chosen my role. I might depart from the script as well.

Adel strayed into a world of his own. He stared with leaden eyes at an oil painting of a young woman in her twenties, with wide eyes and a shy smile. His eyes seemed to water. Was that his ex-fiancée? Oddly, for a second there, she resembled Nadia. The cheekbones. The hair. A look in her eye that seemed to reproach me. I grew uneasy, then tense. I looked back at Adel to find him rolling another joint. His fifth? Seventh? I'd lost count. You couldn't miss the trembling in his fingers as they slowly worked to mix the tobacco with the crumbled hash. I moved over and sat down on the floor next to him.

"You should have killed her and freed yourself of the suffering she caused you. She doesn't deserve to live."

Adel turned to me, his eyes filled with a deep melancholy. "And who'll ease my suffering once she's dead and gone?" For the first time since I set foot into his apartment, he seemed totally lucid. His voice softened. "I fall asleep staring at her picture every night. I look at those eyes, at that pretty smile. . . . Do you want me to leave all that beauty and survive on her guilt? Shame on you, Sheikh Tarek. You don't kill a rose just because you got pricked by its thorn."

I thought of Nadia, the flower of my life, which had nearly wilted. I grew restless, feeling my frustration build up inside me, pounding at my ribcage, but I kept it penned in. I stood up to leave. I avoided shaking Adel's hand for fear I'd burst out crying, and headed to the door.

"Hey, where are you going, fiddler?" His voice sounded frail and desperate. "Don't tell me it's going to be another decade before I get to see you again. We've only got so many decades left."

"I told you already. I'm going to your dad to get my beard shaved. It's my only solution."

I raised my hand and waved it high in the air to say goodbye. I couldn't look back. It was already hard enough keeping the tears from spilling down my cheeks. After shutting the door behind me, I was drawn more and more to the idea of deviating from the script.

We left our place on two motorcycles. I rode one and they followed some distance behind me on the other. I'd been haunted by a sense of foreboding since the previous day. I was almost positive they were going to betray me in some way. Maybe the emir ordered them to eliminate me. Why else did the two of them keep whispering furtively and giving me nervous looks? But how? I was the one carrying the bombs and they were unarmed. I tried to focus on the road ahead to avoid crashing into a swerving car or a spaced-out jaywalker and giving the game away. I'd made up my mind to inform on them after the Maison Thomas job. The government would help me. I wouldn't be the first or the last to do this. A lot of others had snitched on their organizations and were rewarded with a cushy life and a new identity. There was this police officer who'd called me in for questioning once but couldn't find anything to pin on me. He gave me his phone number. I could give him a call and tell him everything I knew about these guys. Which wasn't much. I probably didn't even know their real names, but at least I'd clear myself. Then he'd get a promotion and I'd be reborn. I was plagued by second thoughts. If they were caught, they'd be tortured and spill everything to the police. They'd surely confess my role in the bungled Security Directorate bombing, after which the police would show me no mercy. The Interior Ministry was the target of that operation, after all. In such cases, when it has to do with the police's rights, a whole different set of rules comes into play. They would never let me go, even if the Prophet himself descended from heaven to plead my case.

As we approached our target, I set aside the dream of escape and rebellion. It was time to get to work. My two escorts stopped right in front of Maison Thomas. I parked my motorcycle a short distance away. According to the plan, one of them would make as if to leave, but would take up a post nearby in order to keep watch. After setting the bomb, the other guy and I would make our getaway on his motorcycle. The stolen motorcycle I'd just parked would be left behind to mislead the police.

I tightened my grip on my briefcase as I passed my colleagues, then crouched low to keep out of view of the customers inside. It was almost two a.m. The street was nearly empty and there were only about ten customers inside the restaurant, plus the four employees. I clicked open the briefcase. It contained three small time bombs that I'd made myself using a new method I'd just invented. I took one of them, which contained only a small amount of explosive substance, set the timer to detonate in fifteen seconds, and placed it right below the front window. I quickly crept away and readied myself to hop on the back of the motorcycle. As I drew near my colleague, his hand reached into his jacket and pulled out a gun. He gave me no time to do anything but gape. He fired at me twice and sped off. I howled from the pain. A bullet had struck my shoulder. The other missed. Some people in Maison Thomas were about to rush outside. I took to my heels and ducked down a side street. Before I reached the end I heard the explosion. I turned left and slowed to a walk, keeping one hand pressed on my shoulder to stanch the bleeding, which fortunately wasn't severe. No one was following me. I must have managed to turn the corner without being seen. I picked up the pace again and headed in the direction of the Heart of Palm, which was close by. I stopped at the kiosk nearest to it and dialed her number. The vendor took stock of my shoulder, where the bloodstain had spread a little, and his eyes bored into my face, scrutinizing every feature as if about to paint my portrait. After innumerable rings, Nadia finally answered. She sounded groggy. When I told her who I was, she was fully awake. I just had a minor motorcycle accident,

I said, raising my voice slightly in order to peel the salesman's prying eyes off me. I told her I was bleeding and, lowering my voice as I went around to the side of the kiosk, I added that I couldn't go to a hospital. I told her where I was. The light in her bedroom flicked on. I made out her silhouette behind the thin curtains. A few seconds later, she appeared at the gate, signaling for me to come inside. I returned to the front of the kiosk to replace the receiver. The vendor's expression had softened and he wished me a speedy recovery. I hurried along the pavement, sticking to the shadows of the thick hedges, and slipped through the gate. She took me straight to the cellar, and within a few minutes she had the bleeding under control.

Over the next three days, I felt drawn back to a point in the remote past, when Nadia was in her teens. After all, she hadn't changed that much. She had filled out a bit and her skin had lost some of its luster, but her spirit was the same as always. I felt as though I could alter the course of fate, marry her, and regain my father's right to the villa and its riches. Before she died, my mother told me that Abbas had cheated my father and forced him to flee the country forever. Not a word had been heard from him since. Did Abbas frighten my father that much? Maybe he laid a trap for him—got him implicated in a crime, for example. Would that have kept my father from asking after us, even from afar?

I shook my head to clear the question from my mind. I had to stop letting it nag me since I'd never find an answer. I could never get one from my mother, who died young. All she ever said was, "I put my faith in God. He'll deal with Abbas, the traitor."

Despite the way Nadia had treated me in the past, I had an overwhelming desire to make love to her right there in the basement. I wanted to do things with her body and imagine Murad Kashef watching me in bed with his wife. But she blocked my advances even if there were moments when I felt she was encouraging me. How I wished I could succeed with her, then make her feel the loss and defeat I'd felt when she left me. If only I could get her to make love to me just once before I left this villa, because after I left I'd never be able to be near Nadia again. I wouldn't even be able to set foot in Zamalek again.

26

"I WAS IN THE BACKGROUND of a blurry picture, unnoticed by all."—Nadia

I concentrated on the sound as closely as possible. Those heavy footsteps and that rapping cane were gradually receding. Or so it seemed from where I stood in the cellar. Tarek was now sitting on the edge of the large gilt-framed bed, his eyes beckoning to me while the expanse of the mattress behind him spoke of what would happen if I approached. A diabolic gleam in his eyes told me he was ready to pounce. I didn't wait to make sure. Nimbly as a ballerina, I took several long, light strides toward the basement door. My knees almost gave out me when I discovered I'd left it ajar. I peeked around it. Suddenly I heard the cane thumping again. My heart leapt to my throat even though the sound was remote. I stole upstairs to my bedroom and struggled to collect my wits. The phantom with the cane couldn't have been my father. I also ruled out my aunt, because she couldn't have gotten out of bed and made her way downstairs on her own, even using her cane. All the household staff were asleep, I was sure, and our neighbors in the old Cicurel villa never got up this early. The whole of Zamalek was probably asleep right now. As for Fahim, he never arrived before noon, if he came at all.

Despite the logic of my deductions, I tiptoed to my aunt's room just to make sure. I stealthily opened the door and peeked in. Her half-open eyes gave me a jolt, but I relaxed immediately because that was how she always slept: like the sleep of the dead. Her cane was propped on the edge of her bed, leaning toward her slightly as though to keep vigil over her and to intimidate others at the same time.

I returned to my room and locked the door, even though the sound had faded. Had the ghost returned after all these years? It had been so long since the last of his weekly appearances that I'd nearly forgotten about it. The stories my father used to tell me about it when I was a child scared me so much I'd be afraid to close my eyes and go to sleep. I glanced at my watch. It was six in the morning. I had snuck enough food and drink down to Tarek to last him till the following day. I also cleaned his wound and changed the bandages for what must have been the fourth time. Why did he clutch that briefcase so tightly to his chest that you would think it was part of his body?

I still had the whole day ahead of me before the New Year's Eve gala. Murad would be coming over before that. That visit frightened me—it reeked of impending black-mail—but I was dying of curiosity. What more could he have to tell me than what he'd revealed a few days ago?

I took out my red diary, added a new entry, and recorded the date: December 31, 1989. I used my pen to comb some strands of hair from my forehead and scratch my scalp, then I set the tip on my lower lip as I contemplated what I'd just written. Maybe I'd over-philosophized a bit, but it still seemed a powerful ending to the story of my life, even though my life wasn't over yet. I'd decided to write this diary some time ago so that Yasmine could read it one day and avoid repeat-ing my mistakes. It was also a way to release the emotional pressures that had gnawed at me during the past year. Tarek's sudden reappearance turned my life topsy-turvy. There was a wall between us, lined with pride. He was as introverted as ever and probably needed a hand to pull him out of his abyss. When I started to reach out, I drew back. That glint in his eyes and that strange tone in his voice frightened me. It was as though fate wanted me to relive some opening scenes in my life, but from a new perspective. A nightmarish one. Now that disaster called Murad had resurfaced too. Apparently, both of them still saw me as their bridge to safe shores, but forgot that I was not the same person I'd been twenty or more years ago. Had fate also forgotten that people change?

The whir of the wheelchair shook me out of my thoughts. I could hear it approaching in the corridor. I sat up in bed and smiled despite myself. He never could give up that horrid habit of spying on us—all of us: me, Yasmine, the household staff, even my aunt. I set my diary down on its open pages, and slipped out of bed as lithely as a cat on the scent of food, and stealthily opened the door. He was directly in front of me. A flash in his good eye betrayed a momentary alarm, followed by annoyance at being caught in the act. He returned my smile with a stiff smile of his own, but there was no hiding that mixture of cunning and embarrassment in his face. He turned his chair in the opposite direction and headed to his room. I hastened to catch up, took hold of the handles of the wheelchair, and pushed it gently. Bowing his head, he surrendered to my care and rested his hands on his lap. I bent forward and planted a kiss on his cheek. He reached up with a slender hand, the veins visible beneath the aging skin, and patted me on the cheek. When we reached his bedside, I helped him up. There was a meekness in the eyes of this elderly man awaiting the final world from a fate that had so far granted him eighty years minus a few months. Still, there was no serious sign of the end to his long journey. His mind was as alert as ever to everything around him. His arms still moved freely and smoothly. He had such a powerful will to live, although some months ago he seemed to deflate and close in on himself for no apparent reason.

"Are you sure you don't want to tell me something, Papa?"

His grip tightened on my arm. I leaned my head closer to him while tightening my embrace to keep him from falling.

My long hair slid over his face, hiding his eyes. When I flicked it back, I found him staring at me in a strange way, almost as though bidding me farewell. I also thought I detected a glimmer of remorse in his eyes, as though he wanted to apologize for something. His recent stroke made him difficult to understand. He took hold of the tires of his wheelchair, and tapped them several times with his forefingers, giving me a meaningful look. He pointed to his chest, then spread his hands wide apart and signaled with one hand to indicate someplace far away. He took hold of my hand and set it on the wheelchair tire. I couldn't make out what he was trying to say. I fetched a piece of paper and a pencil from his desk and handed them to him. Shoving my hand away, he tapped his head several times. He stared at me for a moment, then bowed his head in frustration and exhaustion. I didn't press him further.

Once again I was overcome by the suspicion that had been haunting me for a while and that Murad had confirmed. Abbas was hiding something from us. Many things, in fact. He couldn't get up by himself. That much I knew for certain, but how could the strong, tense grip of that large hand I had just felt on my arm possibly belong to this half-paralyzed man who now stared blankly at his feet? And what of that voice that sounded so much like his and that I sometimes heard in the distance in the middle of the night or shortly before dawn? Surely all those sounds and feelings couldn't be figments of my imagination. He must be able to speak and move. Could he be that phantom night visitor who haunted us so many years ago?

I shook my head to clear it. I may not have lost my mind yet, but I was on the way.

"General Murad is waiting in the small reception room, Madame Nadia."

I brusquely signaled the maid to leave and glanced down at my watch again. There were still ten hours to go until the

New Year's Eve gala. I couldn't think of an excuse not to go without upsetting Yasmine. After I helped my father lie down in bed, I stood next to the bed, arms folded, contemplating the whites of his eyes as his gaze seemed to latch onto the ceiling. Then he snapped his eyes closed as though to hide from my anxious scrutiny. Maybe he was afraid I'd read the truth in his one good eye, which had sunk deeply into its bony socket. The other had long since surrendered to the drooping lid. I left the room to let him sleep and headed downstairs, with the image of Murad Kashef, the source of my current nightmare, fixed in my mind. I'd recorded every scene in my red diary since he began to plague our house again, threatening to expose me if I didn't give him what he wanted. Murad would never have dared to confront me like this before my father fell ill and lost his position and most of his influence. Now, he acted like he'd been given a green light to torment us.

He'd unveiled parts of the truth in his last visits. He did it in a dramatic way that was meant to stun me and make me cry, which I did. Copiously. I had to reach for the nearest chair for support, and then I sank into it. My blood seethed like molten lava as I listened.

When I recall that evening, I see myself in a small, darkened theater. The curtain opens. No one bows or greets the audience. I am the audience. Murad steps onto the stage, a grim, confident, inscrutable, grim mask. The light focuses on him and him alone. I sit in the darkness on my own, girding myself. Murad removes his beret, which ruffles his graying hair. His eyeballs are nestled deeply in the sockets of his thin, haggard face, but they give off a frightful gleam. His gestures hold me at the edge of my seat in the back row, curious but dreading the revelations that are about to pass through those lips. I have no intention of applauding. My hands tremble. He embarks on a long soliloquy about my family. He speaks in a taut, high-pitched voice with a sneer in it, but his delivery is smooth and eloquent, as though he is reading from cue cards containing excerpts from my life's story. He pauses dramatically, then resumes. "It is now time that you learn the truth about yourself. Then think about my offer, don't reject it out of hand."

I shift in my seat, trying to appear relaxed. I try to return that smug smile with a smugger smile, but my lips tremble too much and I fail. I can't even control my stammer when I make a last attempt at denial: "You're lying, as usual. I was—"

He puts a finger to his lips to silence me. I obey, almost automatically.

The real performance was grimmer. He fixed his steely gaze on me and advanced slowly toward me as he spoke. The words lacerated my flesh and opened wounds I thought had healed since I'd seen him the previous week, sapping more of the pride I had managed to cling to over the years. I fought as hard as I could not to believe him. The rest of my life, which had lasted forty years so far, was still uncharted, but I wanted it to be as normal and balanced as possible. Despite this, I felt myself weakening. Perhaps it was my curiosity to hear the end that undermined my attempt to dent his confidence. Then suddenly I tumbled from the superior height I'd assumed and lay stunned and broken at his feet. I looked up at him towering over me, huge and powerful, and I felt small and insignificant, which was how he had always made me feel.

"Should I go on calling you Nadia or do you want to know your real name?"

That was how he opened his "presentation." He stood, feet planted apart, arms folded across his chest, eyeing me with a mixture of censure and contempt.

"What do you mean, my real name?"

He didn't answer. Obviously, his intent was to provoke me by suggesting I had a different origin. Or was this his way of introducing an element of intrigue so I'd pay closer attention? I feigned indifference, and for nearly two hours I took pleasure in my ability to conceal my interest. During much of that time, he spoke about my father. A web of fabrications, I was sure. The hatred he felt for Abbas gave him sufficient motive to invent a lot of fictions about the humble beginnings of the Mahalawis and the shady deals my father had made on his way up the ladder. For some weeks now, Murad had been trying to get a rise out of me this way, but failed.

"I refuse to agree to anything you—"

"You'll agree once you hear me out."

Even if there was an element of truth in what he said, we were not as evil as he made out in his sick imagination. I said nothing and preserved my composed facade because I knew that infuriated him.

"You've always been so naive. They're all a bunch of greedy bastards who've conned you your whole life long."

I reared up like a snake and struck.

"Shut up! You know very well whose daughter I am. Don't you ever speak like that about my mother or my father, or even my Aunt Zeinab!"

Murad laughed. "May God rest their souls," he said sarcastically and laughed again.

"Now you've begun to go senile. Do you think me and my family have already died?"

He took a seat, crossed his legs and lit a cigarette, assuming that air of inscrutability that he'd cultivated during his years in Intelligence. He always liked to boast that from that position he could "see our underwear" for the past thirty years. I continued to feign indifference, but I was shaken, and as he continued to speak I finished half a pack of cigarettes. Then he said something that shook me to the core.

"Abbas has a Jewish son called Abraham Edersheim. He uses his mother's maiden name. He lives in London."

I felt my head spin. My father bore a son in London? When? How old was he? Who's the mother? Edersheim? What kind of a name was that? The questions rushed at me like a stinging *khamsin* wind that obscures your vision and muddles your mind. I withered in my seat, barely able to feel my limbs. Murad disappeared for a moment. When he reappeared and resumed strutting back and forth, he gestured at me with our nutcracker, which he must have fetched from the nearby study. He spoke without pause, as though being fed lines from a prompt box and as if bent on driving me mad.

He had seen my father in London four years after our divorce. The 1973 October War had ended about nine months earlier. It being summer, there were so many Arabs in London you might have thought it an Arab capital or a seasonal pilgrimage destination. Murad droned on, interrupted only by the crunch of the nutcracker as he consumed one walnut after another, relishing in flesh he extracted from the inner folds and crevices of the shell.

He dwelt on numerous details about what Abbas "got up to" in London, from gambling at the Playboy Club to arms trafficking in league with our former neighbor, an ex-brigadier who left the service and emigrated to Britain not long after I married Murad. Murad said that he had tried to strike up a friendship with them over there, but my father rebuffed him and the brigadier treated him with contempt. The ex-officer hadn't forgotten how Murad had turned against him when he hitched his wagon to the defense minister and stranded him on the shores of compulsory retirement. Unable to return to Cairo, Murad remained in London, but he kept his distance from my father and the brigadier. His voice was thick with rancor as he accused them of fighting him at every turn and getting him fired from every job he got, no matter how menial. Every once in a while, he'd bump into Abbas or hear some news about him, until one day the brigadier met a sudden death. He fell from the balcony of his apartment. It was chalked up to suicide. His stash of cash and jewels had vanished. Abbas, too, had disappeared for many months until he resurfaced one day in the company of his little son and British wife."

"Would you please get to the point?"

He paused and stared down at me coldly, his greasy smile slowly broadening. He cut the story short, saying, "The kid's grown up now. The last I heard he left London to go study in the States and his mother left with him." Murad took a deep puff on his cigarette. "I'm still not sure where in the States, but I'll find out."

"Please, Murad, tell me more."

"Oh, I forgot to tell you, Abbas bought a house in Brighton twenty years ago. That's where he spent his summers every year. He lavished money on his wife and son, Abraham. As I said, the kid uses his mother's family name. He also converted to his mother's faith. He's a Jew now, like her. Oh, and did I tell you that the brigadier who committed suicide was an arms dealer and Abbas made a fortune through him? Afterward, he—"

"Tell me about my Jewish brother. How old is he?" A slight croak had crept into my voice. That was what I was eager to learn more about.

"He'll turn twenty-one next year, but here's the strange thing. Your father had drawn up a will naming him as his heir. Then, about a year ago, he revoked the will completely. He'd engaged a British law firm. They have that old will on file, with his signature on it and the stamps of the notary public. I managed to get a copy of that and some other documents. I lived a long time in London and I still have connections, you know. But time is running out, Nadia. You've got to pressure Abbas and Zeinab—threaten them if you have to—so that we can get our rightful due. Or would you rather I dealt with them in my way?"

He paused to let the threat hover in the air. Then he continued: "What you have to do is to tell them that you want to protect your family's name from scandal. Only the threat of scandal will frighten Abbas into hearing you out and even giving you all his money. His record of fraud and swindling in collusion with Fahim, a son in England and a Jew no less, not to mention the arms trafficking and the possibility he gave the brigadier a shove off—"

I held up my hand to silence him. I was no longer interested in how my father spent his time in London. By cutting to the end, Murad had spoiled the earlier chapters. I was completely drained, but mustered the strength to say, "I don't believe a word you said. You've always been a spiteful liar. Nothing you've told me can hold an ounce of water."

"You'll believe me soon enough. In a week at the outside you'll have photocopies of all the documents. I'll fax them to you. But forget about all that because it's not important. There's something more important than Abbas's shenanigans in London. It's the main reason I'm here. It's about you, personally, and you need to know it before making any decision."

I lit a cigarette with a trembling hand, inhaled deeply, and exhaled a long stream of smoke. Then, in a sad and weary voice, I asked, "What on earth could be more important than all these calamities you just told me about?"

"Abbas Mahalawi is not your father, Nadia. And Paula Cirucel is not your mother."

27

"THE OLD LION DOESN'T GO out to hunt. But he'll still devour anyone who comes into his lair."—Murad Kashef

Fate had paved the way nicely. Abbas fell ill after being booted out of the National Democratic Party and stripped of all his old weapons. Before that, I would never have dared to approach him, let alone threaten him. I needed Nadia as my key into the old lion's lair, but this required a strategy attuned to her particular mentality and emotional makeup. If I just came right out and threatened to expose the truth about herself and her family, she'd probably defy me out of sheer muleheadedness and call my bluff, regardless of the consequences to herself. Or, worse, she could go to the other extreme and commit suicide. In either case I'd come out empty-handed. So I had to play her carefully. I had to prick her flesh and make her bleed before going in for the kill. It had to be done in stages, each time stanching the bleeding at the last moment by dangling a lifeline before her. That lifeline consisted of her only route back to safety: her vanity and self-esteem as the aristocratic Nadia, the elegant lady of Zamalek who had lived in the lap of ease for forty years.

I'd planned well, but she certainly didn't make it easy for me. She managed to give me the slip a few times, until I paid an uninvited visit to her home. I repeated the visits until they became a weekly routine, then notched them up to a daily routine so she wouldn't have room to even think about evading me. Yet she still had the power to throw me off guard. She had a way of looking at me at times that made my forehead break out in sweat. She was like a mirror that showed me the parts of myself I didn't like to see. Maybe that was what made me up the pressure. She broke down in tears at first. Then she rallied and feigned indifference and called me a liar. She succumbed in the end, however, when I told her that I had all the official documents, both the forged ones and the real ones. That and just enough of the truth broke down her resistance.

I compiled a large file containing all the information I had. For the documentation I lacked, I relied on my memory. I still had many of the old recordings from the bugs I'd planted in the villa years ago, and I transcribed them on reams of paper. I'd revealed bits and pieces of their contents with each visit, but I hadn't given her a single paper yet. If I showed all my cards, she'd be able to bargain from a position of strength. I had to squeeze whatever I could out of her first. She, her father, and her aunt were all scum. Like so many others, they stole and plundered in the shadows. If I didn't have something to put the fear of the devil in them, they'd have me tossed into prison and no one I knew would lift a finger. Everyone would shrug and avoid getting involved in "family disputes."

After softening her with that first revelation about her father's son, I threw the other bomb in her face. I whipped out her original birth certificate and shoved it beneath her nose to prove that Abbas Mahalawi and Paula Cicurel were not her real parents. I read out her full name, emphasizing each syllable and watching her expression as she read the words. She was good, but I caught the twitch in her left cheek. She was the only daughter of a mere railway worker, and had been orphaned as an infant. Her real father's family put her in an orphanage when she was around two years old. Her mother had died in childbirth and her father died soon afterward. The relatives couldn't afford her or just didn't want the hassle of bringing her up. Then along came Zeinab and Abbas, who chose her to become a Cicurel heiress. As to why they chose her in particular, maybe it was because her age at the time suited their plans. Who knows what really went through heads at the time. In any case, the orphanage agreed to let them adopt her, on the condition they kept her real name. Which they didn't. With the help of Fahim, they forged a new birth certificate making her out to be Abbas's and Paula's daughter, Nadia, and heir to the Heart of Palm and the Cicurel fortune. I also managed to get hold of the forged birth certificate. They had taken pains to give it a foreign twist by adding another middle name—Elvira—to make it appear as though Paula, a foreigner, had chosen the name. That happened to be the full name of Cicurel's real daughter as it appeared on her birth certificate, according to people in Zamalek. According to the gossip around that time, the Cicurels had an aunt by that name from Thessaloniki.

"They just bought and sold you, believe me. Everything had a price. Even our marriage cost them an arm and a leg."

"What do you mean?"

"I had to blackmail Abbas using some information I'd dug up about him. It was easy. He cares about his reputation. Your Auntie Zeinab was different. She's a cunning bitch who didn't turn a hair when I threatened her. But she agreed to the marriage instead of the engagement after I helped her smuggle her money to Beirut."

"Beirut?"

"Yep. Things were tough back then. It was practically impossible to get money out of the country. The nationalizations and the confiscations created quite a panic. So I used my connections to help them get fifty thousand pounds out of the country and have it deposited in a bank account in Zeinab's name in Lebanon."

I could see her mind working, connecting dots from the distant past.

"You're the one who had Madame Maysa's atelier sealed and forced her and her brother Amr into penury?" Her voice broke as she said that.

"That's right. Zeinab asked me do that as a favor because of some funny argument they had. I don't know what it was about. I wasn't party to their disputes."

Tears began to stream from Nadia's eyes as she asked, "Did Maysa know the truth about me?"

"I don't know. But at the time I asked your father for your hand, half of Zamalek had their suspicions about your origins. That's what made me do my research. Nobody believed you were Abbas's daughter because Paula at the time was old and suffering from a heart condition. There were a lot of rumors going around at the time. Some said you were Cicurel's daughter. Others that you were Zeinab's illegitimate daughter. So I dug deeper in order to find the truth before I married you. I couldn't find anything solid at the time, but it didn't matter anymore. I'd grown fond of you. I really did love you, Nadia. You are the only love of my life. Believe me."

My little speech failed to calm her. The tics in her face multiplied and her jaw muscles were working overtime. Her hands trembled so much she couldn't light her cigarette. I helped her light it. Her hands were as cold as a corpse's. I resumed my account of the Mahalawi clan. They had registered the villa in her name in order to block the Cicurel's brothers' claims on it. That was what kept the villa from being sequestrated under the nationalization laws. On paper, Nadia was an Egyptian Muslim. Then, some years ago, Abbas managed to reacquire his title to the villa, which he used as collateral in order to obtain some loans. I told her what I had learned from tracking Fahim's movements. Recently, he'd had all of Abbas's property made out in his name in order to deprive Zeinab of everything. They used the same scam they pulled to take possession of the Cicurel villa forty years ago, but now Zeinab

354

was the victim. The papers she had were forgeries. Abbas had the authentic originals signed by himself.

I watched her face as she absorbed this information, and I prepared for my next step. It was my turn to inherit my piece of the Mahalawi pie, not by using threats or blackmail, but through an agreement with Nadia. This was her right and mine. It was our "end of service" settlement.

"We have no time to waste, believe me. This is our best opportunity to twist their arms because of their particular circumstances at this time. Remember, he's put a lot of his assets in your name. So just do as I say and don't be stubborn."

She sat there as still as a stone. But that was enough for one day. I'd broken down her defenses, and on my next visit I'd be able to strip away the remaining layers of skepticism. I could almost feel my share of the Mahalawi wealth within reach. I left the villa at about six p.m., then rang her up from my place about an hour later. I didn't want to give her the opportunity to think calmly. When she tried to give me the cool-and-indifferent routine, I made her snap to attention. I laid out my conditions and followed them with a thinly veiled threat as to what I would happen if she failed to do as I asked. I thought I'd couched it in sufficient sympathy and understanding, but apparently not.

"Are you threatening me, you bastard?" she shouted. "You're telling me you're going to tell the police about something that happened forty years ago? Do you think they're going to punish them, or even prosecute them at that age? As for my Jewish brother, you haven't shown me one piece of proof yet. I don't believe a word you say. Even that so-called birth certificate is probably a fake. You're trying to destroy me. But I won't let you. I'll ruin you first. I'm going to report you, Murad. I'll make sure you go to straight to hell!"

"Calm down, Nadia," I said, struggling to keep my voice calm. "I'm right here in Zamalek. I'll be back over in a minute. These things shouldn't be talked about over the phone."

I returned to the villa as quickly as I could. I chose Abbas's office for our interview this time. I made myself comfortable, crossing my legs, while Nadia remained standing, her nerves frayed.

"Where did you get the idea I wanted to send Abbas and Zeinab to prison? However, if the police got wind of what he did, the government would confiscate this villa and everything in it. He got it all through forgery. God knows how he got the rest of his money. But tell me this: when you report me to the police, what are you going to tell them? And that's not to mention the scandal, Nadia. Or should I call you by your real name?"

Before she could answer, I stood up, went over to the window overlooking the Nile, and opened it all the way. In the distance, a fisherman was approaching slowly on a small felucca. I watched him for a while as he cast his net and waited. I too waited until after I lit my fourth cigarette. Then, without turning toward Nadia, who I knew was still confused and tense, I said, "Now, be sensible and think clearly, because otherwise you'll find yourself in the street even if the police don't touch you. I have a lot of proof—more than you can possibly imagine. I have a whole bagful."

I waited for her to answer, but none came. The room was so silent that I thought she must have left, but when I turned around, there she was, as still as a wax statue. After watching her for some moments like that, I wondered whether I'd driven her over the edge. At last she spoke, though in a barely audible voice. "Frankly, I still don't believe you. So far, it's just words. Nothing but words. I have to see the documents for myself. I want to see them all. Fax them to me and send the tapes you have. Send me copies and keep the originals, if it makes you feel better. Afterward, we'll meet again to discuss things. If it's as you say, I'll agree to your conditions and give you the money you want."

This time, I was the one who remained silent. I guess we took turns with that. I turned back to the window and filled my lungs with the fresh air. I caught sight of the fisherman again. He was smiling. His son at the other end of the felucca came over to help him. The net was full of little fish.

28

"EVERYBODY LAID THEIR PLANS WHEN they started out. Fate kept the surprises for the end."—Nadia

Yasmine and I had left home for the New Year's Eve gala at ten p.m. I was exhausted with worry and not in the mood at all, but it was the only way to escape the strange ideas that were pursuing me like furies. If only I could kill Murad and get him out of my life forever. I was shocked at myself for even thinking that. I had never felt that way about anyone before, but the thought had been whirling around in my head for hours. I would tell Tarek about Murad's threats and ask him to end that nightmare. I was sure he would do that for me.

A gentle nudge from Yasmine brought me back to my whereabouts. Indicating the violinist, she said it that was her favorite instrument. She was only nine, but precocious. Amazingly, the violinist resembled Tarek quite a bit. He was absorbed in a solo piece. He finished to an enthusiastic round of applause and I joined in, even though I had barely listened to it. Yasmine, still applauding excitedly, looked at me and asked whether I was tired. I nodded. The audience fell silent as the orchestra struck up the next piece. I stole glances at her beautiful face as she became rapt in a raucous Japanese composition that was unfamiliar to most of us. But my mind was not on the music. The hammering drums of anger drowned it out. Murad couldn't be telling the truth. Yet he said he had the documents to prove him right. Could it be true that I was not Abbas's daughter, but the daughter of Cicurel or, instead, of a simple railway worker whose family put me in an orphanage? Why had Abbas kept this from me? Why had he given me his name? Why did his sister Zeinab have to meddle in my life so much that she had ruined it? Who were those two people to me really? What put them in my path and let them set its course?

My thoughts turned to my supposed brother Ibrahim—or "Abraham," as Murad called him. I pictured him with long, curly sidelocks and a little black cap on the back of his head. I mentally clucked my tongue at myself. How ridiculous could I get? My mind was such a muddle. Then my supposed "real" name popped to mind. I was on the verge of tears. I focused on Yasmine's serene, dreamy face in the hope it would pull me out of this vortex, but suddenly my fear welled up again. In a matter of days, Yasmine, along with the whole of Zamalek, would know the truth if Murad went through with his threat. It would kill her. I prayed it was all lies, but I had to protect her. How? I was at the end of my tether. My nerves were sputtering out like the candle commemorating my birthday, most of which was ruined by Murad. I left my seat at least three times, pretending I felt nauseous. I shed torrents of tears in the bathroom. As I contemplated my bloodshot eyes in the mirror, I felt a powerful urge to commit suicide. The knocking on the bathroom door shook me to my senses. I returned to my seat in the concert hall, planting a slight smile on my face to allay Yasmine's concerns for me for the remainder of the concert.

Afterward, the audience, elated by the music and the celebratory atmosphere, went outside to watch the fireworks. I jumped at every boom and flash. Later, there was a traffic jam at the exit as people in cars and on foot waited for the president's convoy to pass. He too had attended the performance at the Opera House. Normally it would take only a few minutes for us to reach the corner of our street by taxi.

Tonight it took over half an hour. There was a barricade at the end of our street, so Yasmine and I got out and went the rest of the way on foot.

I was transfixed by flames rising from the roof of the Heart of Palm as we quickly wove our way through the backed-up cars and crowd of pedestrians. The flames didn't seem large, but the powerful jets of water made them leap and dance. As we came closer, I could see that parts of the walls were blackened. Our tall palm tree had fallen. Its crown was charred. It had crushed two cars on its way to earth: our black Cadillac and our neighbors' car. The flames had scorched the Cicurel villa next door, and a portion of the wall between it and our grounds had collapsed. There was a hole in the wall of the basement. The ground next to it was carpeted with pieces of brick and shards of glass. Many cars parked in the vicinity had been pelted by flying debris. Dozens of firemen were struggling to control the fire, which, I learned, had broken out about an hour earlier. The lights on top of the police cars and ambulances flashed across the faces of the hundreds of onlookers who were craning their necks, even from afar, to watch the disaster. I pushed my way through the crowd, supporting myself on Yasmine's shoulders. An officer approached and introduced himself as an official from State Security Investigations Service, the SSI.

"I'm sorry for your loss, ma'am. My condolences."

I burst into tears, though he hadn't yet told me who had died. Suddenly I saw my aunt being carried to an ambulance on a stretcher. I rushed toward her. She had a narrow escape, one of the firemen told me. The fire hadn't reached her bedroom, but it took the firemen a long time to find her because she was hiding behind a large column on the second floor. She must have rolled herself off the bed and dragged herself on her arms to get there. Her eyes bulged in abject terror. Her hands clasped her jewelry box like a lifeline. She stared at me in alarm and confusion, but said nothing. According to one of the rescue workers, she had lost the ability to speak. That must have been why she hadn't called out from her hiding place. I pried the jewelry box from her grip with great difficulty. Her body jerked and she vomited violently. As they quickly slid her stretcher into the ambulance, the attendant physician attempted to reassure me: "It's from the severe shock. But the good Lord has granted her a new life."

For more than half an hour, I remained outside, until the fire was extinguished. I recalled trying to get into the basement several times, but they held me back. Apart from that, my recollection of everything else during that period was vague, until the SSI officer reappeared in front of me. What was a state security investigator doing here? The officer told me that the two bodies were still in the basement, and that the medical examiners and forensic technicians were examining the crime scene.

"Was there somebody living in your basement?"

The ground beneath me began to spin again. The officer took hold of my arm to keep me from falling as they brought a chair to where we stood near the villa gateway. Yasmine took my other hand and stood next to me silently, tears streaming down her face. We couldn't sit inside the villa. They wouldn't allow us in, but it wasn't clear whether this was because of the damage the fire had caused. I caught sight of our staff in the garden, in tears. They were huddled together in a row, some with rumpled hair, others barefoot. There was soot on their clothes. Two soldiers were guarding them. The officer told me that they were under suspicion and would have to be detained. I turned to the villa. There were large cracks in the front wall, a portion of the stairs to the front door had collapsed, and half the first-floor balcony no longer existed—perhaps the heat of the fire was too much for it and it had ruptured into the bits of brick and stone strewn across the front garden. There were two corpses in there, the officer had said. So Tarek must have died, along with my father. Had they met? Spoken with each other? How could my father have made his way down to the basement in his half-paralyzed condition? Someone must have helped him. But who? Not Fahim. He never came over at night. Tarek? I looked up at the officer, wiping away my tears so I could see him more clearly. I shook my head to indicate that no one had been living in the basement. Then I asked him what caused the fire.

He studied my face for a moment, then said, "An incendiary bomb."

The answer thundered between the walls of my skull. At that moment, the rescue workers emerged from the basement carrying the two bodies on stretchers, both covered with white sheets. I stood up, asking the officer if I could take a last look. He nodded. A rescue worker lifted the sheet off my father's face. The sight was unbearable: his face was an atrocious grimace. The contents of my stomach spurted out of my mouth as I staggered back. The officer took my arm to lead me away, but I insisted on seeing the other corpse. I wanted to say good-bye to Tarek too. I struggled to steady myself as they lifted the sheet from the face. It was Fahim.

Today, I learned who I really am. I'm Batel Jacob Zananiri, the daughter of a Jewish diamond merchant. He and my real mother died in a plane accident after he had left me with Abbas Mahalawi as a security deposit for a diamond.

I am a bird with wings clipped by adversity. It wants to fly but it can't even keep its head up as it walks. I had no tears left to cry. I grappled for a sense of direction with no one to help point the way. When I searched through old trunks filled with memories, my wounds reopened. Hundreds of old photos lay scattered before me. None showed my real mother and father. There were pictures of me as an infant and a child, pictures of Zeinab and Abbas with Paula, and even some of Fahim Effendi. I came across photos of my wedding with Murad and photos of some of my childhood friends in the backyard near the dock. I stared at a photo of the Heart of Palm bedecked in festive holiday lights. Now, a month after the incident, it stood dark, charred, and gloomy, on the brink of collapse. I feared it would be condemned by the municipal authorities.

I was a fractured reflection on the surface of a stagnant pool, someone torn from her roots her entire life, with only her remaining years to piece together her origins. I sifted through the pictures and papers for a third, fourth, fifth time. Every time, the train into the past screeched to a halt with a loud whistle at Zeinab's ugly face and Abbas's laconic smile peering out at me from ancient photos, telling me in unison: "You have no roots but us. Accept your fate and don't be ungrateful. We erased your history."

I reread, for the third time, the letter Zeinab had given to me after her release from hospital. I could barely believe my eyes. She and her brother did to me exactly what the government did to the Egyptian Jews when it expelled them: confiscated their property and erased their history.

I was like Sara, my childhood friend, who lost her mother and then had to emigrate and leave everything behind her. The same thing had happened to all the other Jewish families who had been our neighbors in Zamalek. I would have been one of them, going to temple on Saturdays, carrying my little velvet bag with my prayer shawl and Torah. Afterward, I'd come out holding a green sprig like the one the rabbi used to give Sara, who kept hers until the fragrance faded. How could I bring myself to hate Abbas's son when I was a Jew like him? We might not be able to choose our faith but we can choose our humanity.

The truth about me cut deep. Faces flashed before me of people who'd had to leave, never to return. For me, there was nothing left but fog, the whistling wind, and the deafening ticks of a pendulum drawing me forty years back to the day my father and mother died in the plane crash. I too would have died if they hadn't left me behind, a hostage to their greed. Could they have had some premonition of impending

danger? Did a voice whisper to them to spare my life by consigning me to Abbas and Zeinab, thereby abandoning me to
this slow death I was enduring today?

I do know they abandoned me for the sake of money.
Perhaps my mother felt she had no choice and succumbed to
my father's pressures. Maybe it wasn't greed that drove him.
Maybe he was poor and needed money so he could give me
the dignified life he felt I deserved as his only child for whom
he had waited so long. No. No, he couldn't have been poor.
Otherwise he couldn't have left behind all that property for
Abbas and Zeinab to plunder. No, my father was as avaricious
as Abbas. I didn't deserve to be related to him.

I broke into in tears again. It was futile to search for
answers. My poor brain threw in the towel.

I moved into one of Abbas's small apartments in Zamalek
with Yasmine and Zeinab. During the month after the incident, I was summoned at least four times for questioning. In
the last session, I was given yet another shock—or, more accu-
rately, cause for bereavement. Most of the questions revolved
around some Christian man called Amgad Munir Radi,
whose ID card they found in our basement. It had Tarek's
picture on it. To compound my surprise, he was known to
the police as an active member of a terrorist cell. They recognized his photo and found a match with fingerprints from
our basement. They told me he was the one responsible for
the Maison Thomas bombing.

Tarek must have discovered Abbas's large safe while he was
down in the basement. He must have decided to help himself
to its contents when he saw Abbas and Fahim down there. But
why in the world were they there to begin with? Abbas hadn't
been down there for about a year, and it had been several
weeks since Fahim had last been to the villa. Tarek would have
seen them open the safe. Then he probably overheard them
say something that made him show himself and force them to

speak. Why else would he have tied them up and beaten them, as the police told me he had? He then planted one of the time bombs of the sort he used in the Maison Thomas attack. He'd had them in that briefcase of his all along. No wonder he'd kept it clutched in his arms as he slept and refused to show me its contents. He brought the house down on the people I'd once thought of as my family. I'd told him that Yasmine and I were going out that night. So he took advantage of our absence to avenge himself against Abbas and Zeinab. As well as against Fahim, who had the ill fortune to cross Tarek's path that night, because surely he meant nothing to Tarek.

The investigators let me know another curious detail. They said that Tarek could have blown up the villa and everything around it sky high, but instead he used a relatively small amount of the explosive substance and oriented the bomb in a way to minimize its impact. Why would he do that? My heart told me it was to spare me.

Tarek might have grabbed what he believed was Abbas's fortune, then killed him, set off the bomb, and fled. Yet he only got crumbs. That little safe, which was spared from the flames because of its steel casing inside a recess in the wall, couldn't have contained much money. It probably contained only documents. What documents? Documents about me and my true identity? The memoirs of Abbas Mahalawi? Did Tarek take them? Why? They found him hiding out near Abbas's farm in Mahalla Marhoum. What on earth drove him there? He'd burned everything he had on him before he died. He was killed in a shootout with the village guards, who thought he was a thief. Now he was dead and I'd never be able to learn the rest of the story from him.

The basement safe lay empty. All of Abbas's papers were in the safe in his bedroom. There was nothing special about these documents except for one. It was a design of some sort, like an intricate crochet pattern. I could only make out what seemed to be a palm tree with a lot of tiny circles around it.

"What does this paper mean, Madame Nadia?" the investigator asked.

"I have no idea. I've never seen it before."

"Whose handwriting is this?"

I lit another cigarette as I shook my head to indicate I was as mystified as he was.

Had Tarek found out about the real me that Murad mentioned? If only he had known. If only he could have told me he did it for my sake. Why did he come to the villa that night? Had he planned a robbery from the outset?

I could hear echoes of his voice. They called to my soul like a melancholy reed flute, but they made my mind sound the war drums against everyone and everything.

The investigations were still in progress. Many of the same questions must be nagging at the investigators, but I wasn't going to risk telling them why Tarek was in our house. There was no point dragging my wounded pride through a maze of red tape. I had more than enough to deal with thanks to what I'd learned about Tarek and learned from Murad and Zeinab.

I was under suspicion. That was obvious from the questions they asked me and the many times I was called in. It was equally obvious that they were stymied. I was the only link they could find between Tarek and Abbas and Fahim. They couldn't figure out the nature of that link and I would never lead them to its source. I would not let them into the chambers of my heart. They would never understand that I had loved only once in my life and that I'd received so many shocks that I'd lost all sense of being alive. I moved like an automaton, purely for Yasmine's sake. The only one who knew the truth was Murad, and he was blackmailing me and draining the last of my will.

"We would appreciate a convincing answer this time." The investigator's voice interrupted my thoughts. I stared at my lap in silence. He asked me again how I was related to the individual on the forged ID they found in the basement.

This time, though, he used Tarek's name. "We know that his mother used to work for your aunt," he said, as though expecting this piece of information to jolt me into a confession.

I injected a tone of great surprise in my voice, which I hoped sounded convincing: "The poor woman died twenty-five years ago. I haven't seen Tarek since. That picture on the ID—it's so strange. It doesn't look like Tarek at all."

I almost felt sorry for the inspector, whose furrowed brow betrayed his helplessness and frustration at my silence and my persistent denials. He breathed a long, exasperated sigh, then extracted a small file from beneath some others and gave it to me to read. My nerves were so frayed by this time that they couldn't tolerate more surprises, but since this latest one was so absurd, I was able to approach it with a welcome sense of detachment. I raised my eyebrows as I read the autopsy report on Abbas Mahalawi. The medical examiner had found that he had been administered small but regular doses of a toxic substance. His last dose on New Year's Eve may have caused his death before the explosion, but that had not been confirmed yet.

"God rest his soul. Abbas must have had a lot of enemies," I said. "I knew nothing about his work or his acquaintances. If you find out who was behind this, please let me know."

I wasn't particularly interested in who killed Abbas. To me, he died the day Murad revealed who he really was. Then Zeinab mutilated his corpse when she revealed that I was Batel, daughter of the Jewish diamond merchant Jacob Zananiri.

During the three months since Abbas died, Murad pestered me nearly daily. He threatened to expose me to the police, to my daughter, and to the whole of society if I didn't accept his terms. Poor Yasmine! She was at her wits' end from the tension at home due to my strained nerves. She couldn't stand Murad and even less his boorish son, a student in the military academy who visited us with his father once.

"Do you think that Omar Seif Eddin would take custody of Yasmine if he learned of your real identity?"

That wasn't a question. It was blatant threat. I had no shadow of a doubt that this would be Murad's next move, but even if he managed to contact my ex-husband, I could already venture a guess as to how he'd react. Omar had lived in Paris since our divorce. He called up Yasmine every few months to see how she was doing. He'd seen his daughter three times in all since he moved to France, and that was when we went to Europe. The communications between us were sparse, but I knew he'd left his French lady friend and that he was in financial straits. At least he had no desire to come back to Egypt and would never think of taking my daughter from me. He couldn't afford to support her and he didn't want the responsibility. Yet the very thought of losing Yasmine struck me with mental paralysis. I gave Murad some deeds to some of Abbas's properties in the UK and asked him to go to London to help me sell them. My aim was to shut him up with a gesture to reassure him he would get what he wanted. I would never let a soul take my daughter away from me.

Yasmine begged me to arrange a holiday for us together so that I could take a break. I'd practically have a nervous breakdown after every visit from Murad, but I couldn't leave Zeinab alone at home. Although she was released from hospital ten days after the incident, she never regained her ability to speak and she'd lost the will to live. It was clear from her feeble signals and gestures that she was waiting for death; indeed, willing it to come. Strangely, they found in her stomach traces of a very small dose of the same poison they'd found in Abbas's body.

Had Zeinab tried to commit suicide or had someone slipped poison into her food as well? But who? The doctors couldn't answer and, of course, Zeinab wouldn't. She refused to even hear of the subject. My suspicions went immediately to Tarek al-Masri, but that line of thought only drew me back into a labyrinth.

I still had an hour before the appointment with my shrink, whom I'd recently begun to visit regularly. I didn't feel much better, but I'd begun to accept reality. I hadn't told Murad that I was Batel. Something told me it would be wiser to keep him in the dark about the real beginnings of my story. If writing is therapeutic, Murad was the complete opposite. He had a knack for turning me into a nervous wreck. He and that sleazy son of his with the smarmy smile, wraparound sunglasses, and lewd innuendos.

I swallowed my third tranquilizer, opened my red diary, and picked up my pen.

Nadia was never my real name, but no one would tell me the truth. I've picked up stories here and there, and arranged them so I can see them clearly. But there is still a piece of the picture missing. All of us float on a sea of fictions. Some of us get dragged down by an undertow and drown. Others cling to the life raft of penance in the hopes of reaching the shores of truth, even if spent and emaciated. Because, perhaps, they will still have a chance for redemption and a new beginning.

I reread the passage carefully. It seemed logical and it expressed my current condition now that Murad had showed me the documents. He gave me copies, and these, together with Zeinab's last letter, formed the naked, horrifying, grievous truth. Were someone else in this position to ask my advice, I'd tell them that sometimes ignorance is a blessing.

At any rate, it was now my turn to play my last card. Then the picture would be complete and we'd see who came out the winner, though unfortunately, in this game, I feared we would all end up losers.

I reopened the jewelry box that Zeinab was clutching when they rescued her from the fire. In addition to some jewels, it contained a paper on which Abbas had signed some properties over to her. For the first time, I noticed that a portion of the wooden lining had been chipped away. I could make out the edge of a photograph beneath it. Unable to pry it out with my fingers, I fetched a pair of tweezers. After some difficulty, I extricated three small, ancient photos. They all showed the same subject: a lot of men in a construction site, standing next to a hole with a large sack at the bottom. One picture showed a truck that seemed to be dumping sand into the hole. The photos were grainy and the light was poor, but I could make out Abbas among the men. When I showed the photos to Zeinab, the color drained from her face, but I was unable to pry information out of her. Apparently, she'd decided to say no more than what she had written in her last confession. If she thought that cleansed her, she was wrong. I had not forgiven her yet. I returned the jewelry box to her. Then I held out a piece of paper and pen, and asked her again to answer my question. She looked away. Then she took the pictures and carefully reinserted them in the box.

As I lay on the couch, I contemplated the large painting of Abbas Mahalawi that the servant had fetched from the basement of the burnt-out villa in Zamalek. He stood tall and proud in a hunting costume made of British tweed and an elegant camel-hair cap. He cradled a large hunting rifle in one arm. I'd never seen him with it. In fact, I never knew he went on hunting expeditions at all. It was unclear when the painting was made and, as I searched my memory, I doubted I'd ever seen it before. Judging by Abbas's features, it was probably painted in the sixties. My hand, as though under its own volition, snatched up the crystal cigarette lighter and hurled it at the painting, creating a long slash down the middle. I got up, strode up to the painting, and tore his face into tiny pieces, leaving a headless body in hunting suit. I lit my fourth cigarette and turned my thoughts to Murad's proposal: his silence in exchange for half my wealth. Obviously, he wanted to secure his and his son's future using Abbas's money. Soon I'd have all of it, since Zeinab Mahalawi already had one foot in the grave, according to what the doctors told me.

"Aren't we going to Europe like you promised, Mommy?"

I exhaled the cigarette smoke upward and gave Yasmine a big hug, kissed her on the forehead, and forced myself to smile. Then I reached for the phone, dialed, and waited. The person at the other end greeted me effusively after I identified myself. I told him I wanted to reserve a suite and supplied all the necessary details.

"Will this be a short-term stay, ma'am? We can make it renewable if you wish. . . ."

"No. Make it a year . . . Yes, a year at least, please."

I replaced the receiver and contemplated the photo on my ID card. I felt the muscles in my face contract. Into a smile or a grimace? I couldn't tell. But at least I didn't cry.

29

"My sorrow stretches from my heart to my throat. Whenever I touch my neck, my chest hurts."—Zeinab Mahalawi

I folded the newspaper and set it on my lap with the photo of Abbas facing up. His funeral took up half the front page of *Al-Ahram*. A large banner headline blazoned his name, preceded by a Quranic verse. Below, in a smaller font, it read: "Abbas Mahalawi Bey has passed on to the mercy of the Lord."

He was always obsessed about his last rites. He even wrote his own obituary many years ago when he left parliament and the National Democratic Party. Long ago, he taught me that paying condolences and commiserating with people in times of hardship was a shortcut to their hearts. I befriended dozens of ladies using this simple method: a telegram and a condolence visit, which afforded an opportunity to mingle with the bereaved's acquaintances. It worked like a charm, especially with the ladies of Zamalek, who had once snubbed me but who later became close friends and tried to keep in my good graces because they would eventually need apartments for their children. Abbas must have used this method countless times in order to win personal favors and advance those secret business dealings of his. He certainly didn't have any close friends.

I looked at his photo again. His white fedora, that half smile, the drooping right eyelid. My tear glands had turned to stone. I couldn't cry for him yet. There was a malicious glee in those eyes. They said, I stripped you of everything you had, apart from your anger, which you can take to your grave. I passed a fingertip over his face, then pressed down on his eyes, hard enough to punch through the paper and leave a hole where his face had been. Using my fingernail, I tore downward toward his throat. Then I took hold of the front page, crumpled it into a ball, and threw it away—but not far enough. It perched at the foot of the bed. A breeze blew in from the balcony and lifted the rest of the pages, and they flitted around the room until they fell to the floor and hid beneath the bed. But the crumpled page with his photo didn't budge from its place near my feet.

You met a horrid ending, Abbas, but you had it coming. I wish I could have killed you with my own hands. Fate beat me to it. It's always been kinder to you than to me. So now you won, and you're laughing at us from beyond the grave. You left all your diamonds, gold, and cash to your British son and had your lawyer make sure your assets in Egypt didn't end up in our hands. You left me and Nadia nothing but the villa and the farm in Mahalla Marhoum—the scraps—even though we were your life partners. You would never have gotten where you were if it hadn't been for us. God curse you to eternity and back.

Naturally, Nadia couldn't make heads or tails of the map Abbas had left in his bedroom safe. Nor could I at first, when she showed it to me. What were all those silly circles about, when the safe in the basement was empty? I knew he hid his money somewhere like Cicurel did. The problem was where. The guy who destroyed our villa must have cracked the safe downstairs and emptied it out before skedaddling, but Abbas wasn't stupid enough to leave his diamonds down there. He would have hidden them somewhere else—maybe someplace connected with his annual trips to London. As for the thief, now there's a mystery for you. Why didn't Nadia want to talk about that? Could she know who it was? She'd been hiding the newspapers from me, apart from the one with Abbas's obituary.

Abbas must have had a really nasty falling out with some-body to make him want to kill us in such a brutal way. But who? Would he strike again or had my brother's death quenched his thirst for revenge? So many questions left unanswered.

I fumbled inside the jewelry box next to my bed and pulled out the old photos. They brought a bitter smile to my face. If Abbas had found them, I wouldn't be in Zamalek at this moment. I'd probably be lying down there next to Hassanein or, at best, banished back to Mahalla Marhoum decades ago. I looked at the photos of Abbas and those other men dumping the sack containing Hassanein into the pit and then watching as the truck poured cement over him. I devel-oped the film and printed the photos myself. I lost count of the times I had to use them against him. He searched everywhere. But I hid them somewhere he never thought of looking: Paula's jewelry box. He never suspected how scared I was, despite the weapon I held over his head. If I ever had to act on my threat, Abbas would have gone to the gallows and I would have gone to prison. I needed to remain free and I needed him by my side to help me. If only I hadn't threatened you, Abbas.

So here I was. I'd lost my brother, I'd lost my voice, and I'd lost a chunk of my memory. I felt tired all the time, and since the fire I'd kept getting woozy. Or had the woozy spells started some weeks before that? Nadia had started to treat me differently. She'd grown remote. She eyed me with suspicion, and also with an unmistakable degree of disdain. I knew the look. I myself had directed it against a lot of women. Now it had boomeranged, and from the person dearest to my heart. Could I be wrong about that?

I was tired of my mind going around in circles, like the Tilt-A-Whirls I used to ride in the Mulid of Sayyid al-Badawi when I was a child. It was Abbas who kept an eye on me and my sisters while my parents watched from a distance. He was the one who made sure I didn't fall off as I soared high in the air on the swing boat while my mother shot me warning glares when the hem of my *gallabiya* flew up and revealed my leg.

I removed the covers from my legs and hitched up my nightgown to inspect the burn scars. They were still large and ugly. Why didn't Nadia have the doctors do some plastic surgery at the time? Why make me feel humiliated when my friends or neighbors visited? I'd have to tell her off about that.

Where was I? I looked around in confusion until I recognized my surroundings. Since my release from hospital, I kept getting memory lapses. Not only that: my parents and my sister Kawthar kept appearing before me. Kawthar was buried in Mahalla Marhoum. Abbas and I didn't go to her funeral. In fact, Abbas forbade her husband from arranging a large funeral ceremony and publishing an obituary in the newspaper. My brother didn't want news of our dirt-poor rural roots going around. I agreed with him. We were still at the foot of the ladder at the time, and a lot of nasty people wished us ill. On the other hand, when my mother died, he arranged a three-day ceremony in Cairo, in Mahalla Marhoum, and in the NDP headquarters. The sheikh reciting the Quran had to pause every five minutes to let in the hundreds of people who'd lined up outside the funerary tents to pay respects.

My own end might be near, but I was at peace with myself. At least I wasn't a murderer like Abbas. And I did more for Nadia than her family ever would have. Speaking of them, I'd have to tell her that I tried to stop Abbas from accepting her as a pledge for the diamond, but he refused to listen. Then her parents died in that plane crash. Abbas's accomplice all along was Fahim Effendi, who met his maker alongside his master. Loyal to the end, weren't you Fahim, you son of a bitch? You couldn't even bear to outlive your master.

I shifted my position in bed. I hadn't lost everything yet. At least I still had Nadia. She'd pray for me after I died. And if Yasmine had a daughter one day, maybe she'd name her after me. The bastard Abbas left me with a pile of forged deeds and documents. Even if he had conned me out of his will like he'd conned me all his life, the people in Zamalek would remember me, not him. I was the one who was there when they needed a helping hand; I was the one who opened the doors of the Heart of Palm to them for holidays and celebrations. Come to think of it, I'd bequeath enough in my will for Nadia to carry on the tradition of a Ramadan table big enough to feed five hundred poor people. It would be called the Lady Zeinab table. Yes, the table of the Lady of Zamalek. In fact, starting from next Ramadan, I'd make it big enough to feed a thousand.

I opened my eyes to find my maid holding a glass toward my face.

"Your medicine, Madame Zeinab."

I drank half the contents of the glass and pushed it away from my mouth. It was bitter. She tried to make me drink more, but I pushed her hand away again and glared at her. She had no choice but to obey. I'd lost the will to live. There was nothing left for me to live for. I closed my eyes so I could conjure up the image of my mother. I didn't see her during her last illness before she died. My hands trembled as I clutched my pillow. When did my hands start trembling this way? Why couldn't I remember anything clearly except for my family? Yesterday I heard my father's voice scolding me for staying in bed till noon. "Hold on! I'm coming!" I shouted. Then I woke up and found myself in my room. I called for Nadia, then remembered I'd lost my voice.

I clutched the pillow as tightly as I could. Despite how hard my mother was on me, I missed her embrace. I felt so alone. I had such confusing feelings for Abbas. We'd grown so far apart years before he passed away, to the point that I wanted to kill him. Now I missed him. I signaled to the maid to fetch me his picture from the dressing table on the other side of the room. I smiled as I planted a kiss on his forehead. I put my finger on the top of his head and stroked his hair. I hugged the picture tightly to my chest and cried silently. How I wished I could regain the power of speech just once and then be struck dumb again forever. I wished Nadia could hear me tell her that I felt her pushing me away despite how close I'd felt to her my whole life. I was afraid she was going to leave me soon.

I tried to shoo away my maid, who stood looking down on me anxiously. She pulled up a chair and started to recite the Quran in my ears while she stroked the top of my head and held my hand. Good Lord! I hadn't gone off my rocker yet. I just wanted to be able to speak so I could persuade Nadia to forgive me. I broke into tears again. The maid wiped them away using my silk handkerchief, which had my name embroidered on it in gold thread. It was my Mother's Day gift from Nadia and Yasmine last year. I took it, folded it, and placed it inside my nightgown next to my heart. I didn't wrong you, Nadia. I was as much Abbas's victim as you were. Were we wrong to hide the truth from you? What would you have done had you known? You might have hated us and left.

She said nothing after I told her that she was Jacob Zananiri's daughter, Batel. It was impossible to read what went through her mind when I told her that Abbas had accepted her as a pledge for the large Cicurel diamond that Zananiri was going to dispose of in Europe. Of course, I wouldn't dare tell her the whole truth. I didn't tell her that Fahim had forged a power of attorney authorizing us to make financial transactions in Zananiri's name. Using this and other forged documents, we acquired all of Zananiri's properties in Cairo. Fahim was a pro at forging deeds to estates belonging to deceased foreigners who had no heirs in Egypt, in order to keep the government from inheriting them. Zananiri's assets were the yeast we started out with. As they grew, they compensated us for the loss of Cicurel's gold and diamonds. They were actually Nadia's inheritance, being the Zananiris' only heir, but Abbas cut ahead of her in line, using the forgeries, and had Fahim put Nadia in an orphanage—under a false name, of course—in order to cover up their tracks. That was when she stopped being Batel Zananiri, who'd been reported kidnapped. Some months later, I managed to convince Abbas to adopt her. By that time, Abbas had been cleared of suspicion of kidnapping and the case had gone cold. So, for a short time, Batel became the daughter of a simple railway worker whom Fahim had known. Then, after taking her out of the orphanage and bringing her to live with us as his daughter from Paula, Abbas gave her his name. That was the key to the scheme to inherit the villa, and the key to a social profile acceptable to the people of Zamalek, who had never really accepted us. What suspicions they had when Paula died and Nadia appeared. But with time they forgot, or at least pretended to forget.

What made me grow so attached to Nadia the moment I laid eyes on her? Maybe I felt God had decided to compensate me for losing Lady. Maybe I felt the guilt of Mrs. Zananiri, who was forced to leave behind her daughter as a pledge for a diamond her husband planned to sell in Europe. Abbas never really loved Nadia. He played the role of father and grew into the part, but not to the point where the role took root in his heart. It was always a pretense. He made Murad divorce her because I pressured him. He agreed to her marriage to Omar Seif Eddin simply to spite me. He was always ready to sacrifice her if it served his purpose. He was even ready to return her to the orphanage after he got his hands on Zananiri's property and after we left the old Cicurel villa. By that time, he had already renamed her Nadia after Cicurel's daughter. He even gave her an extra foreign middle name, like Cicurel's daughter had. It was only on her birth certificate. It was a weird name—Elwira, or something like that. I didn't even know how to pronounce it. He was obsessed with Cicurel. He tried to model himself on him in every way, but I also suspected that, at least somewhere in the back of his mind, he wanted to throw the neighbors into confusion and let them think she was Cicurel's daughter. It certainly wasn't easy for us after Nadia came into our lives. No one believed that Abbas fathered her with Paula before she died. I'd never forget what he said about her: "She brought us bad luck: we lost the villa and a revolution broke out." Were it not for me, Fahim would have put her back in the orphanage when Abbas told him to.

Surely it wasn't right for Nadia to learn all of these ugly details. No. In fact, it was *not* her right. We were the ones who'd made Nadia. We did her a favor. Abbas showed her affection and he spoiled her. He'd give her things that I'd expressly forbidden in order to spite me. She wouldn't know that, but still it would be so ungrateful of her if she thought ill of us.

It suddenly occurred to me that if she got hold of Abbas's papers and learned the truth from them, she'd hate me and probably kick me out of the house. Abbas would never tell the whole truth. He'd make himself out to be the angel and me the devil. I decided to tell her everything before my memory faded for good. I had to make sure she understood, accepted the truth, and forgave me, even if it wasn't really her right to know it all. I signaled to the maid to get me a pen and paper. I wrote everything I could recall. Then I broke down in tears.

The best years of my life took flight as autumn crept in and laid siege. Now the winter storms were turning the rest of my life to hell. All I had left were stories that had grown as old as my body and as flimsy as my memory. So many details had gone missing, fluttering away into oblivion like withered leaves. In a short time, no one would be left to remember them at all. They would hurt Nadia even more. She could turn against me, but she'd understand. She'd appreciate the position I was in and how I took care of her all these years. My stock of hope had nearly run out and my stocks of dreams and ambitions were depleted. My greatest desire now was to die in my sleep so as not to suffer more. The most beautiful things came and left in their allotted time. It was hard to have nothing left to do but lie here beneath my blanket, waiting for death to come knocking on my door some cold winter night. At least she'd know the whole truth before I was taken unawares by that cruel visitor who came only once in a lifetime.

Just as I folded the four sheets of paper on which I'd written my account in a large script, the door flew open and Nadia burst in like a sandstorm. She had a dark scowl on her face and she was too agitated to stand still. She gave some kind of signal with her eyes to the maid, who nodded and scuttled out the door. What were the two of them plotting? To kill me? Had the maid gone off to fetch a rope to tie me up before Nadia smothered me with my pillow? I trembled as I shrank into the mattress, pulling the blanket up to my chin as though it would protect me. A spasm seared through my chest and I felt short of breath. I hid the pillow behind my back and tucked the photos beneath them. If Abbas had been there, Nadia would never have dared to treat me this way. I gave her a loving look and struggled to smile. My lips felt stitched together with a thick thread. What was this? She'd turned to the closet and started to gather up my clothes.

I clapped in order to get her attention. With a gesture of my hand, I asked her what she was doing. She didn't answer. I held out the folded sheets of paper. She snatched them from my hands, read a few lines, and gave me a strange look I'd never seen before. It only lasted a second. Then she started to read again as she moved away. She had confirmed my fears that the end was near. I would never tell her that the paper Abbas left her was a map to where he'd hidden the diamonds and gold: in our home in Mahalla Marhoum. I was pretty sure I'd figured out exactly where, but I wouldn't even give her a hint about that until I made sure I'd won her back to my side.

30

"So many things inside me have broken without making a sound. I can't glue them together again or make up for their loss."—Nadia

"Unfortunately, Nadia, you have no other options. You have to do more to help yourself."

That was my psychiatrist's refrain in my last five sessions. In his opinion, I had to bring myself to accept my current situation. I should remain Nadia Abbas Mahalawi, upper-class socialite from Zamalek, daughter of a wealthy established family. He also advised me not to turn down Murad's offer out of hand. I should play along and try to silence him, even if I had to bow to his demand for a quarter of my inheritance. The risks were too great. I could never tolerate the impact of the scandal. The toll it would take was incalculable.

"No amount of money could compensate for your loss. There's no medicine that can repair the damage," he said. "Anyway, why do you refuse to be Nadia? Abbas and Zeinab gave you the best education money can buy. They lavished money on you. Even if they were crooks or forgers, they're through. Abbas is dead. Zeinab can't speak or move. Tarek was a terrorist and psychologically disturbed. He was an opportunist who took advantage of you and died. He's not worth even thinking about. The whole problem now boils down to General Murad Kashef, your brother Abraham, and your daughter, Yasmine. These are the people who define the new reality you have to deal with."

I wasn't sure how to respond to my shrink's advice. In previous sessions he spoke of divine retribution: "God alone has the power to exact revenge from immoral criminals whose advantageous circumstances enabled them to evade justice on earth. Divine justice does not recognize crimes marked 'unsolved.'" Nice-sounding words, but they had nothing to do with my reality. Murad and Abraham weren't the problem; neither was Yasmine. The problem was inside me. I was living the life of another woman. She was not the real me and her life wasn't really mine. It belonged to Nadia Abbas Mahalawi, not to Batel Jacob Zananiri. I was battling so many conflicting feelings. I really was trying to adjust to my new reality, but it was so hard when everyone still saw me as Nadia. New reality? It wasn't new at all. It was old as I was. What was new was what would come next. I'd always been a puppet manipulated by others. Some used it. Others were amused by it. Few truly wanted it. My shrink didn't understand that not every painting had to be in color. We needed to step back from the easel and contemplate our work carefully. Perhaps its perfection could be attained in charcoal.

I leaned back on the couch, set my feet on the coffee table, and stared blankly at the walls. As I reached for a cigarette, my fingers encountered a small picture frame. It was another old photo that I'd come across in the basement when I went down there some months after the fire. I took it with me, along with some other things. It was taken by Abbas in the early winter of 1939, according to what was written on the back. It showed Zeinab, not even thirty yet, a crafty smile on her face, in the black Cadillac with the elegant Mme Paula, who stared haughtily at the camera. I felt an acrid taste in my mouth. I picked up the picture and looked at it more closely. It seemed to encapsulate an important phase in my history: the prelude to my arrival into their world. Fifty or more years of lies and deception were summed up in that photo.

The phone rang, rousing me from my dismal thoughts. The caller reminded me of an appointment and asked me whether I wanted to keep it or whether I preferred to change the date. I told him I'd be there at the agreed-upon time. I was fairly comfortable with what I'd arranged for Zeinab. I hadn't told Yasmine yet and I wasn't sure how I would explain it to her. Still, she would handle it better than me. I downed a couple of sleeping pills, despite my doctor's objections to the amount of sedatives I was taking, and went to bed. As I nodded off, I muttered, "Yes, I admit I'm stubborn, as Zeinab always said. If I fall into the sea, I'll either swim to safety or I'll choose to drown. That's how I am."

The following morning, after dressing, I went to Zeinab's room. Her maid was with her, as usual. Zeinab had grown attached to her to some years ago, though none of the rest of them could stand her because she was so unctuous and was always spying on us. Zeinab brought her down from the farm at Mahalla Marhoum. After she fell and broke her leg, she wanted someone to help her change her clothes and keep her entertained. The maid was administering Zeinab's medicine when I burst into the room. I signaled for her to fetch the other large suitcase and started to remove some of Zeinab's clothes from the closet. Zeinab's eyes shot back and forth between the two of us and, with a hand gesture, she asked me what was going on. I didn't answer. She signaled that she wanted a pen and paper, but I refused. I didn't want to hear another word from her. I didn't want to learn more truths. She could take them with her to the grave.

I shut the door and went up to her, close enough to feel her weak breath on my nose. "Who was it who tried to poison Abbas?" I asked. I received the same response: a shake of her head, after which she looked down and closed her eyes. Then she opened them and raised them slowly toward me.

They were filled with fear. Abject fear. She asked for a pen and paper again, and again I refused. I couldn't stand her and I couldn't believe her or those tears that had frozen at the rims of her tiny eyes. Her silence served as the answer to all my questions. I lifted her off the bed and set her in her wheelchair. I removed the blue diamond ring she'd worn for years and placed it in my pocket, then pushed her toward the door. When I opened it I found the maid. She had been eavesdropping. She immediately understood the look I gave her. I'd be dealing with her soon.

The fight seemed to drain out of Zeinab as we made our way to the car. The maid helped without saying a word, as I'd instructed. I planned to fire her when I returned from my errand. As I was about to open the car door, she stepped forward with her head bowed and handed me a small medicine bottle.

"It's the medicine for the madame and the late Mr. Abbas," she said in a barely audible voice.

I turned the bottle over in my hand. It had no label or anything to indicate its contents. I showed it to Zeinab. She jerked her head back in surprise, shot the maid a furious stare, then turned back to me with eyes widened in alarm. After I settled Zeinab in the rear seat, I took the maid by the arm and led her away from the car.

"What is this?"

Tears poured down her cheeks as if she'd been exposed for complicity in a crime. "Madame Zeinab told me to put a drop of this into Mr. Abbas's orange juice every morning. She said it would pick him up and make him better. Then, about a week before the fire, she got really mad at Mr. Abbas and her blood pressure shot up. So I put a little bit in her juice as well. I swear by God, Madame Nadia, I thought I was doing the right thing."

Ha—if the worst disasters don't pack a laugh! I gripped the bottle nearly tightly enough to smash it. I told the maid to get into the car next to Zeinab and never to speak of this matter again. I couldn't tell the police that Zeinab had been trying to murder Abbas by slow poisoning. After putting the wheelchair in the trunk, I climbed into the driver's seat and switched the motor on. Along the way, the radio broadcast a Quranic recitation. We listened in silence, as though in a funeral procession, until we arrived at the home for the elderly in Maadi.

Zeinab's jaw dropped on seeing the sign at the entrance. It bore Abbas Mahalawi's name. She turned to me with such a meek and resigned look that I could practically hear the questions she was unable to utter: "What kind of place is this? Why is his picture on the wall? Why are you doing this to me?"

I had a volcano of rage inside me, and it would be better for everyone if it remained dormant. I said nothing, though I felt like shouting at those pleading eyes brimming with crocodile tears that this was exactly what you deserve for having taken me from the orphanage and changed my name twice, and thinking you'd grant me a new life for your own selfish sake after plundering my father's and mother's property. Now I was going to return the favor. I was consigning you to an old-age home founded by your brother who you wanted to poison to death. They'd look after you and make sure you lived out the rest of your days in dignity. Maybe that would make you atone for your sins. At least they'd take good care of you in your capacity as the sister of the founder. My conscience was at rest. Wasn't this how the sad story started, Zeinab? I was giving you an ending that matched the beginning.

Her baffled eyes took in her surroundings while her teary-eyed maid rolled her chair down the path that cut through the garden to the administration building. She caught sight of a bust of Abbas on a pedestal in the middle of a flowerbed. Her lips moved, mouthing something incomprehensible like a mad woman. I walked alongside, silently. She grabbed my hand and squeezed it tightly. I felt myself recoil. She had probably given my tiny hand a squeeze when I was an infant in the orphanage. She'd selected me like a piece of new furniture for the house, to decorate her life and make up for what she lacked. Again I was seized by the desire to shout: Why did you and Abbas lie to me all these years? Why did you rob my father and mother and force them give me to you as a pledge? Why did you make me reject Tarek, force me to marry Murad, and deprive me of Omar? Zeinab's muteness held me back.

Maybe it was a form of divine mercy. Her muteness spared me the torrent of lies she would spout if she could speak. She would probably think up dozens of excuses and invent dozens of fictions in order to cast the whole blame on the late Abbas, but she'd been silenced forever. Now she could repent of her sins. I could feel myself weakening before her pleading eyes and the hand begging my forgiveness, which I would never give. I wrenched my hand free. I was struggling to keep control of myself because nothing she could do would help her. Some things just came too late, like the kiss of an apology on the forehead of a corpse. A couple of tears trickled slowly down my cheeks. I took a few steps ahead so she couldn't see my face. I knew I never wanted to see her again.

"You've had more than enough time to think it over, Nadia. I am not going to fly to London alone . . . Nadia?"

Every muscle in me tensed just from hearing that name. It belonged to another woman, from a different life. Nevertheless, I nodded. I turned to Murad, a sour smile on my face, as I arranged the words in my head. I couldn't afford to lose control over my nerves as I did so often with him. I made a wry comment about his son: "He doesn't look like you at all. But surely he couldn't have gotten that oily smile from his mother?" The purpose of this type of chatter was to annoy him so I could regain my composure. When I felt more in control, I said I would follow him to London soon after he left. He was going to find prospective buyers for Abbas's properties in the UK. "Once we sell them off, I'll give you your share," I said.

"Okay. But I still need guarantees. I know you've been selling off Abbas's assets here, but I haven't said anything. I'm flying to London the day after tomorrow. I'll be expecting you there. I'll give you a month, max, to arrange things."

I picked up the phone and booked a flight while he looked on and followed my conversation closely. When I hung up, he seemed mollified, and even more so when I agreed to show him Abbas's safe. I opened it in front of him and held the door open. It was just as I'd found it the day of the fire—totally empty. I also showed him the map Abbas had left me. He was as puzzled as I was. He gave me an address and the telephone numbers of the British law firm he dealt with to facilitate my dealings there, especially as concerned my brother Abraham. Then he had the nerve to spring a marriage proposal on me. "We need each other more than ever," he said, and spoke of how deeply he felt for me. He was such a ham. I told him to stop the nonsense. He stood up, approached, and tried to take me in his arms and kiss me. I pushed him away, but not before he managed to plant a kiss on my forehead. He turned to leave. Then, just before reaching the door, he turned and extracted a small device from his pocket.

"Forgive me, Nadia," he said. "I recorded our whole conversation today. It's not the first time, I can assure you. You just can't trust anyone these days. If I don't see you in London within a month, I'll come back and expose you to Omar and to the police."

I spat after him as he left. I stretched out on the couch again, settling into it as though it had become my new home. I used to love lying on it when I was young, but my aunt always scolded me. That was why I was so determined to salvage it from the Heart of Palm and bring it here to this apartment. I lit another cigarette and exhaled a large cloud of smoke. I contemplated the cloud as it metamorphosed into strange shapes. Some seemed to resemble me. Others

I thought looked like Murad or Tarek. I watched them expand, rise into the air, and evaporate.

I fell asleep right there on the couch. Early the following morning, I dressed quickly and left the apartment carrying my passport, which had Yasmine registered on it as well. I applied for a visa at the consulate and received it later that day, around noon. Then I went to the airline, where I met the director, who had known us for years. After the usual pleasantries, I told him I was there to book tickets to Europe for myself and Yasmine.

"To London, of course, as you told me on the phone, Madame Nadia?"

"No, no. Cancel the London flight, please. Make it Paris."

No one else knew of Abbas's little getaway in the French capital. I had the only key. It was still in my name, unlike other things that were once in my name until his greed got the better of him. Who knew? Abbas might have other properties scattered around the globe that no one knew about. If so, their secret was buried with him and Fahim.

Once in Paris, I wasted no time. Two days after I arrived, I went to the bank to ascertain that my transfer had arrived into my account. I made that transfer exactly a day before I left Egypt, after having sold off everything I owned in Egypt over the preceding months. I'd used a prominent lawyer for this purpose, to ensure that Murad wouldn't learn of the transactions. It was easy. Abbas hadn't left us that much and I didn't touch Zeinab's share of the inheritance. I received payment for the properties in cash—Egyptians keep more money under their mattresses than they do in banks. True, I probably got only half of the real value for the estates because I was in such a hurry, but that was better than leaving the table empty-handed. I sold off everything without the slightest qualms, except the Heart of Palm. I wavered three times before signing the contract. I felt as though I were selling off my whole life: my memories, my childhood—everything for better or for worse. They all lived there with me. They all passed through this place. I wish I could have kept it, but my fear of Murad and my haste to leave made me sell it, complete with its furniture and all the junk in the basement, as though the place might collapse any second.

I can still see the surprise on the face of the man who was acting on behalf of a major bank, which bought not only the Heart of Palm but also the farm in Mahalla Marhoum. How he gaped at those dozens upon dozens of old tires stacked on top of each other in the basement like a wall. God knows why Abbas kept all those old tires. He certainly wasn't a miser.

"Did Mr. Abbas Pasha trade in rubber in the past, Madame?" the agent asked with a mixture of surprise and concern. "The barn is filled with old tires!"

I shook my head in a way that meant neither yes or no, while my frown said, "Why are you asking me about a pile of junk?" The man must have feared that his silly question about old dust-covered tires might make me change my mind about selling the farm at such a steal. So he accepted my silence as assent, and avoided annoying me further.

After I signed, his curiosity got the better of him again. On our way back to Cairo, he asked, "So, should we just dispose of them as junk, ma'am? Or do you need them for something?"

"Do whatever you want with them. Burn them, if you like. As I said, I don't need anything here."

On my third day in Paris, I turned to my next and most important step before the deadline Murad had given me ran out. I phoned the publishers in Beirut with whom I'd signed a contract several months earlier. The manager told me that they had they'd received my final revisions and that the book was now at the printers. The first copy fresh off the press would be on his desk in a few days. He confirmed that he would send it to me and not release the book to distributors until he had received written authority from me, as per our agreement.

When I hung up, I turned to Yasmine and asked her to make herself free for me today so we could take a long walk and discuss something important. I struggled to stay composed before her innocent surprise and added, "There's a story I have to tell you in connection with a new book I'm having published and that will appear soon. It's called *My Name Was Never Nadia*."

The last night of December 1990 marked a new birthday for me. I'd shed all my fears and conquered my weakness. I received the package containing the advance copy my publisher sent me by express mail. My heart raced as I slowly opened it. I glanced at the picture of me on the cover. It showed just half of my face, as though I were truly half a person. My hand trembled a little as I flicked through the pages, until I came to the last and most important section: "Documents." It was an appendix, but it took up almost a third of the book. It contained all the letters written in the hand of the eminent security and strategic expert Major General Murad Kashef, some containing his account of his heroic deeds, such as planting bugs in the homes of many prominent families, including mine. It also contained all the documents he'd faxed me, photocopies of the documents he showed as proof he was telling the truth about the nefarious deeds of Abbas and Zeinab Mahalawi; some photos I had of them; photos of my forged birth certificate; my ID card as Nadia Mahalawi that had been forged by Fahim; my authentic birth certificate, faxed to me by the first orphanage I was placed in; the transcripts of the tapes in Murad's handwriting; the birth certificate of Abbas's son Abraham, and a picture of him with his mother in London; Abbas's will naming Abraham as heir, which Murad had managed to get from Abbas's law firm in London; an old birth certificate belonging to Cicurel's daughter, Nadia Solomon, which I'd found in Abbas's papers and which had somehow ended up in Murad's hands; and photocopies of many papers on which Abbas had jotted down notes and reminders.

My heart pounded violently. I downed a couple of tran-
quilizers without water, then went to the window to watch the
light white streaks of snow make a modest attempt to cover
the street. It floated down like tiny curls of cotton. The particles stuck to the ground but melted within moments. They
didn't have the strength to last long enough to spread a white
blanket on that black asphalt road that stretched to infinity.
My heart gave a leap as the fireworks lit up the sky around and
above the Eiffel Tower. They were far from where I stood but
I could see them clearly. When they stopped, the darkness set
in for endless seconds. Then they began again, to the accom-
paniment of loud reports and fizzles.

Thirty minutes passed at a crawl as I thought about what
I would write. I took a deep breath to settle my nerves, then
picked up my pen, opened the book to the first blank page,
and wrote a dedication:

To Mr. "Brigadier" Murad Kashef,
I am going to tell you a secret with the first edition
of my book, *My Name Was Never Nadia: The Memoirs of
a Lady of Zamalek*. Read it carefully. Hopefully it will
entertain you in your final days.

I signed it. I couldn't bring myself to write my real name,
Batel. However, for the first time in my life I used a name that
I myself had chosen. It was one of the three names I'd been
given, but it was the one that I decided I would keep for the
rest of my life. I tightened my grip on the pen to keep my hand
from shaking and wrote "Ilham Mohamed Hussein." It wasn't
as smooth as I'd hoped, but it was clear. A tear escaped despite
myself. I sighed, picked up the pen, and signed again, this time
in a minuscule script barely large enough to read: "Nadia."

SELECTED HOOPOE TITLES

The Girl with Braided Hair
by Rasha Adly, translated by Sarah Enany

The Magnificent Conman of Cairo
by Adel Kamel, translated by Waleed Almusharaf

The Critical Case of a Man Called K
by Aziz Mohammed, translated by Humphrey Davies

✳

hoopoe is an imprint for engaged, open-minded readers hungry for outstanding fiction that challenges headlines, re-imagines histories, and celebrates original storytelling. Through elegant paperback and digital editions, **hoopoe** champions bold, contemporary writers from across the Middle East alongside some of the finest, groundbreaking authors of earlier generations.

At hoopoefiction.com, curious and adventurous readers from around the world will find new writing, interviews, and criticism from our authors, translators, and editors.